The Love Garden

DAVID BLACKBURN

ISBN: 1988263042
ISBN-13: 978-1-988263-04-5

DEDICATION

To all who have suffered at the hands of others.

Advance Praise for The Love Garden

"Just a fair warning . . . when starting this book make sure you don't have anywhere you need to be or anything you need to do because you won't want to stop reading until you've finished it all!"

-Eliza Brown

"The Love Garden", by David Blackburn is hands-down one of the most original and well-crafted novels I have read in a long time!

-Jhonni Parker

"I thought this was an excellent novel that captured my attention from the beginning and never once let it go"

-Darla Ortz

"For once it seemed like the characters were anything but the stock, ordinary typical hero/heroine but instead all the demons, motivations, secrets, and I don't want to focus too much on it, but the psychological/mentally traumatized angle had me really intrigued"!

-Laura Clark

"The author, David Blackburn, sets the scene and characterizations in a skillful way that not only pulls us in, but creates great visualizations and elicits genuine emotional investments in the characters".

-Sherrie Warner

CONTENTS

ACKNOWLEDGMENTS

Karen Anderson
Sister – Early typing

Hayley Watts
Daughter – Typing, changes, formatting,
Emailing, publishing, website, Facebook.

Kelly Lamb
Editor (Kellyaelamb@rogers.com)

Jill Veitch
Webb publishing – Editor (Jill@webbpublishing.ca)

Eric Blais
Cover art (Ericblaisart@shaw.ca)

Shauna Paynter
Editor – Publisher - Red Apple Publishing

PROLOGUE

The young teen heard the sounds she had been dreading: the shuffling footsteps, the creaking door, the drunken breathing; she knew what was coming. In the half-light, she could see him approaching as he had done on too many other nights. She closed her eyes and willed herself away from the coming intrusion, away from this house where she was trapped in the one place in the whole world she should have been safe – her own bedroom.

Later, after he had left the room, Carly could still hear his conniving words. Words that didn't seem to make sense when connected to the vile acts he forced on her. "I love you. You're so sweet. You're beautiful." These were all phrases that were supposed to express real feelings and happy thoughts. What crap! What a liar! She eased her eyes open and stared upwards, toward the ceiling. She should be crying, but there were no more tears. Crying was done, replaced by hate and thoughts of retribution. One day she would even the score. Oh, how she would get even.

Why didn't she notify the proper authorities? She thought of doing that but doubted anyone would believe her, especially her mother. She also didn't think any punishments meted out by the courts were sufficient to make up for the crimes committed against her. The punishment she had in mind would be worth the few years of pain she was willing to endure until she could serve justice her way. She would wait until she was old enough to drive a car. That would give her freedom and escape. If she could suffer through this agonizing nightmare until then, she knew she could control the rest of her life on her terms. She would tough it out.

One thing she was learning from this terrible ordeal was the power of control. One day, she would have control over her destiny, control over other people and control over the evil person who would get everything he deserved and then some. One day.

Carly's father died when she was a young child. This untimely loss hit Carly's mother extremely hard, and she eventually succumbed to the mind-numbing lure of the bottle. Drunk or near drunk most of the time, she didn't want to hear or didn't really care what her new husband, a fellow drunk she had met in a bar, was doing to her beautiful daughter. Too young to understand what her mother was going through, Carly tried many times to describe the dreadful deeds her stepfather was forcing her to endure, but her mother always dismissed these pleas as unfounded cries for attention or outright lies.

Crushed by the constant rejections, Carly withdrew completely into a beautiful fantasyland where she was safe from all the pain. She dreamed of traveling to faraway places; shimmering lakes, soaring mountains, pristine beaches and sunshine, lots of sunshine. Warm sun on her shoulders gave Carly a lift, even on her most depressing days; so it was ever constant in her make believe journeys. Whenever she felt the need, and it was often, Carly willed herself away to her sun-filled happy place, always feeling better when she returned to her real world. And deep inside, she clung to the knowledge that her dreams would one day come true. This thought gave her strength to patiently wait for the day she would be free. Free to control her life, free to pursue her dreams and free to avenge the wicked acts of an evil tyrant. Revenge, as they say, will be sweet.

Through sheer willpower Carly managed to make it through

the next couple of years and finished high school with a very good grade average. Shortly after graduation she left home to start a new life.

Carly found it difficult to settle down as the need for revenge haunted her while her active imagination pulled her in a more tranquil direction. The damage done during her important formative years was too great and vengeful thoughts dominated Carly's every move. This led the beautiful, intelligent young lady on an unbelievable and heartbreaking journey.

CHAPTER ONE

S yd eased his precious Vette into one of the visitor parking spaces beside a very luxurious apartment building. He sat and stared at the impressive structure for a couple of seconds then lifted his athletic frame from the comfortable leather seat. The early evening breeze tussling his wavy hair felt good, adding to his upbeat mood as he strode confidently up to the giant glass door.

"Wow!" he muttered. "What a fancy place!" He scanned the intercom directory, found the name he was looking for, and dialed the associated code. A moment later a soft voice answered. "Hello, who is it?"

"It's Syd, Georgia." Syd replied.

"Hello Syd. I'm almost ready. If you don't mind waiting in the lobby for a few minutes, I'll be right down"

Georgia buzzed the door latch. Syd thanked her and pushed the heavy glass door open. As he stepped into the elegant lobby, a plush leather couch on the far side of the room beckoned to him. Unable to resist the urge to find out if it was as comfortable as it looked, he strode across the soft oriental carpet and lowered himself into the embracing upholstery. It was heavenly. His eyes closed, and his mind wandered, stolen away by the soft lighting in the high ceiling and the super soft leather against his body.

Minutes later, a tiny voice broke the spell.

"Good evening, Syd."

Syd sprung awake. His eyes focused on Georgia, expensively dressed, elegant, sexy and smiling ear to ear, reinforcing his move to ask her out when they met at a party a couple of weeks before. His heart jumped as he struggled to his feet. Still groggy from the short nap, he felt guilty for not greeting her in a more respectful manner when she entered the room. He reached for words.

"Uh, sorry, Georgia. I didn't hear the elevator. You look fabulous. How are you?"

"I'm great, thank you. Sorry to sneak up on you like that. The elevators here are designed to not make any noise, and the carpet allowed me to sneak right up on you. You looked so relaxed, I didn't want to disturb you because I knew exactly why you drifted away. You see, I spent almost an entire night in the same spot you just vacated. One night, I came home late, sat down on this couch to take my boots off and promptly fell asleep. I didn't wake up until morning. So funny! Anyway, enough about this great couch, shall we proceed to our destination? You do have a place picked out, don't you?"

"Yes, I do. I made reservations at the Station House. Is that okay with you?"

Georgia lifted her arms high above her head with an enthusiastic reply.

"Woohoo! That's more than okay. Thank you."

Syd had figured Georgia would appreciate the fine dining venue he had purposely chosen. He was counting on the sumptuous food, ambient atmosphere and his amorous skills to put Georgia in the mood for some loving later in the evening. Georgia's enthusiastic response refocused his mind on that goal.

"I take it that is a yes." He laughed and pulled the front door open. Georgia nodded politely and stepped out into the evening air. Syd followed close behind.

The drive across town was filled with laughter and light

banter, signaling to Syd that the evening was off to a great start. The fun teasing eased as Syd parked his fancy car in the Station House parking lot. A few short steps took them to the front entrance where, after they had passed through the giant door, they were greeted by the most stunning woman Syd had ever seen. He stared. Georgia noticed. She was not impressed. The hostess, Carly, started to pay far too much attention to Syd than her job required. Syd, forgetting Georgia for the moment, bought into Carly's flattering overtures and exchanged compliments in a steady stream. Georgia steamed. Carly knew what she was doing, but it appeared Syd did not.

Carly struck Syd's name from her reservation book and then showed the couple to a quiet corner table. She led the way. Syd's eyes followed her gracious moves. Georgia's glare followed Syd.

Syd had seen and dated many gorgeous women before, but none had oozed the sensual sexuality as Carly. He was captivated by the skimpy white dress and ample amounts of silky smooth skin that glowed under the artistic house lights. He loved how her shiny black mane accentuated her high cheek bones and gleaming white teeth. Her fine sculpted features competed for attention with beautiful tanned legs, a taut round ass and gravity-defying breasts. The same half-exposed breasts Syd had brushed against as he helped Carly find his name on the reservation book at the entrance podium.

Carly knew how she affected men and used her good looks to full advantage, playing tricks and flirting just for kicks. But as had happened with other men in her life, Syd struck a certain cord. He was tall, handsome and, judging by his clothes, very successful. He might fit into her plans. She was interested.

Carly seated the couple, wished them a pleasant evening and turned toward Syd. Making sure Georgia did not notice she winked at Syd, smiled, and quickly left them alone to sort out the evening, not caring one way or the other how it turned out. She was on a quest; her dirty work had just begun.

Georgia's icy glare kept Syd's eyes from following Carly's graceful retreat to her duty station. Instead, he stared into Georgia's squinting eyes and braced for the dressing down he was about to receive. The words came spitting across the table, stabbing Syd's ears into painful acceptance. His chauvinistic, sexist behavior was laid bare and shredded by the razor-sharp epithet, causing him to squirm in discomfort.

At the end of the tirade he admitted his indiscretions and, unaccustomed to enduring this kind of upbraiding, offered a rambling apology. Georgia didn't completely accept this apology but did agree to a type of truce. The meal was enjoyed as well as could be expected. When it was finished, Georgia excused herself to visit the ladies' room.

Immediately after Georgia had left the table, Carly magically appeared next to Syd with a small piece of paper and a pen, which she placed in front of him.

"Syd, would you please write down your phone number for me?"

Taken by surprise, Syd asked, "What?"

Carly changed her tone. "Look Syd, just give me your fucking number. I'm going to call you."

Heeding the authoritative voice, Syd quickly scribbled his phone number on the small piece of paper and handed it back to Carly. She looked at the paper and smiled.

"Thank you Syd! I'll be in touch, but I want to warn you. Don't try to reach me here and don't show up here. Just wait for my call. I'll talk to you then. Bye."

She turned and walked quickly away, leaving Syd to wonder what just happened.

Georgia returned to the table and noticed the faraway look on Syd's face. She questioned him. He dismissed his thoughts as work related. None the wiser, she did not give the matter any further notice. She thanked Syd for a great meal. Syd apologized for spoiling the evening and kicked himself for not staying the course for what may have been a great night. A quick flashback to the phone number episode tempered that thought.

The restaurant bill was settled, and Syd drove Georgia to her door in silence. With Georgia safely home, he faced the drive across town to his apartment, wide awake and stirred up, thanks to Carly. His mind raced, full of questions. Why did she take his phone number? Why? Such a beautiful woman. He couldn't believe she was interested in him. Thinking of her didn't end with the question of why, he had an erection. Pity! No one to share it with.

He finally arrived home but, as he had feared, did not get any sleep. Visions of beautiful Carly danced in his head.

The next few weeks were frustrating for Syd. He waited for the gorgeous girl in the restaurant to call, but the call never came. He tried to forget her, to no avail. Finally, just when he had almost given up, Carly called. It was a very short call explaining to Syd that she had to leave town for a while and promising to call him for sure when she returned. The call was terminated and Syd, not doubting Carly's sincerity, prepared to wait for her next call. He hoped the conversation would be longer than this, much too short, first call.

CHAPTER TWO

Carly traveled east, then after changing highways, she journeyed south. Her destination was somewhere between three and a half and four hours away, depending on road conditions. She settled in for the drive, not concentrating on anything much except the distant retreat she so desperately yearned for. It had been more than a year since her last visit and now, as the road hummed below her, she wondered if she should have given warning of her pending arrival. She had never called ahead on her previous sojourns but, then again, she had never gone more than six or seven months between visits. Had things changed? Would she still be welcome? Would the good feelings return? And why was she so concerned? The long stretch of time without any contact bothered her, but she crossed her fingers and hoped for the same warm reception she had received on all of her previous visits. She skirted past several large cities with endless bedroom communities until the familiar exit sign came into view. The next off-ramp led to a meandering tree-lined country road. For some reason, modern development had not yet reached this little piece of heaven. Carly was very happy with that. Remnants of the past could still be found; a rough barn, the remains of a log house and half-buried fences, each with a story to tell. As these interesting structures came into sight, Carly tried to picture the pioneers who traveled this same storybook trail many years before automobiles were even thought of.

Carly always welcomed the transition from busy freeway traffic to a relaxing drive through beautiful countryside. The change put her in a happy mood, setting the tone for an emotional reunion that was quickly approaching. As she got closer to her cherished sanctuary, the pretty scenery took a backseat to her mental preparation for the always tear-filled occasion.

It wasn't much longer before she passed the rusty old village welcome sign and turned right at the next intersection. A quarter mile down this sparsely inhabited lane lay the refuge she could no longer stay away from. Two minutes later, the sight of the little house surrounded by multi-colored flowers brought tears to her eyes. She parked in the driveway next to an old Chevy and sat quietly for several minutes; gathering her thoughts. One thing was certain; she was where she wanted to be, where she had to be. The realization jolted her into action, inspiring her to leap from the car and boldly stride up to the front door of the foliage covered haven. Her heart pounded as she pushed the doorbell button. A slightly older woman pulled the door open a few seconds later and gasped.

"Dianne, Dianne...what the?" she exclaimed. "Come in. Please Come in."

"No, it's not...it's, yes, it's me, Dianne. It's good to see you, Sadie."

Carly caught herself. She had forgotten that to this lady she was Dianne Thorpe, a name she had chosen from a phone directory years earlier.

Sadie led Carly into the front hall, closed the door and stepped back.

"Let me look at you. You look so good. What a delightful surprise!"

Sadie pulled Carly closer in a warm embrace. Carly shuddered as familiar feelings raced through her body. She wrapped her arms around Sadie and closed her eyes. Sadie felt the same rush of emotions as Carly. A ray of sunshine had reappeared in her life. They held each other tight for several minutes, afraid to let go. As pent up tensions drained from their souls, they slowly relaxed and gently separated. Carly looked a little sheepish, guilty for staying away so long, however upon seeing the radiant smile on Sadie's face she knew that nothing they had ever shared had changed.

She whispered, "I'm so sorry for dropping in on you again, Sadie. I hope I'm not intruding, am I?" Carly blurted out even though she knew the answer before Sadie had a chance to speak. But out of respect for Sadie, she had to ask.

"Oh, Dianne, of course you're welcome here. You know that. Why do you always ask? Now come right in and stay as long as you want. Oh, you look so good." Sadie clutched Carly's hand and pulled her closer as they ambled into the living room. Carly made herself at home on the brightly colored couch while Sadie went to the kitchen to prepare tea. She returned to the living room, placed tea and homemade cookies on the coffee table and then sat on an old chair across from Carly.

Sadie was delighted with her surprise visitor as she listened to Carly updating details of her life since she had last dropped in. Sadie in turn told of her quiet life tending to her fantastic garden, her volunteer work and how much she missed Carly and thought of her often. Carly apologized for causing such concern, stressing that it wasn't intentional. Sadie knew that. She smiled. Carly was relieved that Sadie had not brought up the subject of Carly's troubled childhood. Sadie was very concerned for Carly and constantly sought more information in her efforts to support her beloved friend. But today she wisely stayed away from the topic leaving it for a more appropriate time.

The two very different souls had been acquainted for more than eight years. They had met in a public library shortly after Carly had finished high school and hit it off immediately. Soon, they became very close. Over time, Sadie learned of the troubling emotional problems that Carly was trying to overcome. She lost many night's sleep thinking of ways to help her cherished friend. The few times Carly had given her a glimpse into her troubled past gave Sadie a starting point for what promised to be a long road to recovery. She constantly looked for any opportunity to continue the healing process. Their close and progressively intimate relationship depended on Carly freeing herself from the emotional poison that, if not addressed properly, could destroy her. It could destroy what they had built together. Sadie was smart enough not to force the issue, but their slow advancement was frustrating for her. The next few days and weeks may provide an opening for a continuation of serious talks when the time seemed right. She suspected there could be tears and angry words. Given the tension of the subject and their developing intimacy, Sadie longed to engage in further explorations of mind and body. She was open to support Carly without exception.

Sadie's offer for Carly to stay as long as she wanted was genuine. Sadie needed Carly as much as Carly needed her, maybe more. Settling into Sadie's garden paradise reminded Carly of her childhood escape fantasies. The beautiful flowers and soothing encouragement Sadie provided, created the perfect setting for the help Carly had been avoiding for too long. After a few weeks of watching Sadie work in the garden, sharing hearty meals together and slogging through deep conversations, she felt much better than she had before arriving at Sadie's welcoming door.

The weeks turned into months and in this time Sadie unselfishly provided a receptive ear whenever Carly agreed to discuss the delicate details of her angst filled childhood. Carly was beginning to trust that Sadie was truly a soft place to land. Very little new insight was gained from the few talks they had however and after five months, Carly's restless spirit told her it was time to leave Sadie's peaceful world and return home. Sadie begged her to stay but it was no use. Carly had to leave and that was that. Early one morning she packed her car. After a tearful farewell, Carly drove away from a very sad looking Sadie, who was left standing in the driveway next to the old Chevy.

Sadie watched Carly's car disappear down the tree lined country road. After a few minutes she turned and shuffled her weary body back to the house. The few steps leading up to the front door seemed much steeper than usual. She managed the climb, pushed the front door open and entered the quiet abode. Sadie had very seldom slammed a door closed in anger in her life but her present state of sadness and frustration caused her to lash out with a mighty shove. The door met the frame so hard the resulting shock wave caused a picture to fall from the living room wall. Sadie ignored it as she headed for the kitchen to fetch a well needed glass of water. She filled a jug with water and ice cubes, grabbed a glass and carried them outside to the patio table. She sat very quickly. Her wobbly knees would go no further. She filled the glass with water and took a thirst quenching gulp. The soothing liquid was heavenly. A painful thought grabbed her attention. How many more times is this going to happen? "DIANNE, DIANNE... WHY, WHY DIANNE?" she shouted. Then silence. Her eyes closed as scenes and conversations with Carly took her back in time.

The first meeting with Carly in a public library was ever present in Sadie's memories. That fateful encounter always appeared as though it happened yesterday. The scene vividly came into focus. A gorgeous young lady, not long out of high school, noticed Sadie reading a child psychology text book and asked if she could sit next to her. Sadie, normally shy, was immediately attracted to Carly and said she would love to have some company. Carly sat and introduced herself as Dianne, her made up name. Sadie offered her hand in a friendly greeting. They felt at ease immediately as the easy flowing conversation took them in many directions. It wasn't long before Sadie was impressed with Carly's intelligent, inquisitive mind. After more than two hours of talking they were startled when the library lights dimmed signaling closing time. Before they stepped out into the cool evening air, phone numbers were exchanged and they agreed to meet again. A great friendship had begun.

Over the next year they met many times, forming a very close bond. Sadie, who had been single all of her life, felt especially close to Carly. Very soon secrets were shared. Sadie was shocked when Carly revealed details of her troubled childhood. From that moment on, she vowed to help her dear friend heal from all the hurt she had suffered as a child. Sadie's academic training in psychology and teaching background was put to good use. However, she found the slow pace of progress very frustrating. More than a few conversations ended in arguments or silence which caused Sadie to have many sleepless nights. Adding to her turmoil was the realization that her feelings toward Carly were much deeper than friendship.

One day Sadie mentioned she had the chance to purchase a little house many miles away. Carly's enthusiastic response to "take the offer" disappointed her. She started to cry. After some discussion, a deal was made when Carly promised to visit while also hinting she may not see Sadie at all if she didn't buy the property.

Sadie made the purchase and moved to the quiet country town many miles away.

She missed Carly immensely. Carly kept her promise and did visit, but only when she felt like it. Sadie's heartfelt efforts to help her were greatly appreciated. Carly also knew that Sadie was a large part of her life. The comforting garden and Sadie's soothing manner were a lifeline she could not pull away from. Visiting Sadie was very enjoyable but there was always a point where she felt refreshed enough to return home. Every parting tore Sadie's heart out. Each time she begged Carly to stay, to no avail. For Sadie, the pain grew worse with every goodbye.

As her mind traveled back through the many good times and also the painful moments with Carly, a chill engulfed her. The next few weeks would be unbearable.

The soothing country road did not impress Carly now. She had to get home. Once she reached the highway her thoughts focused on the work awaiting her at the end of the long drive. Before leaving to visit Sadie she had vacated a small house she had been renting and placed all of her belongings in storage. She had also put down a deposit on another rental home that the landlord was fixing up and was now ready for Carly to move into. Her first stop was the landlord's house where she paid the first month's rent and obtained the keys to her new home. Next, she paid a visit to her storage unit to retrieve some personal items. She then drove the short distance to her new residence; the main floor of a delightful old mansion. She parked next to the front entrance and entered her suite to view the landlord's finished product. After inspecting the enhancing colors and workmanship, she set about planning her furniture arrangement. The next week kept her busy as her furniture and clothing were delivered and situated in the one bedroom and den layout. Toward the end of the week, she placed a promised phone call. A man answered.

"Hello."

"Hello. Is this Syd?" Carly asked softly.

"Yes, this is Syd speaking." Came a confident voice.

"Syd, it's Carly. How are you?"

"I'm fine, thank you. How was your trip?"

"Very good, Syd. Thanks for asking. What have you been up to lately?"

"Not very much outside of work and a few nights out with some friends. I wondered when I would hear from you. It's been close to six months now, hasn't it?"

"Close to that, Syd. Anyway, I'm back, and soon we will be free to get together. Is that okay with you?"

Syd jumped at the question, unable to mask his excitement in response.

"Tell me when and where, Carly, and I'll be there." Carly cut him off.

"Not so fast. I still have a few things to settle, but I'll call again soon. Bye."

Carly hung up and went back to her work.

CHAPTER THREE

About two weeks later Carly called again, as promised. This time she was ready to give more than a salutation. It was late in the evening when Syd heard the phone. He picked up the receiver and answered in a sleepy voice.

"Hello."

"Hello, Syd. It's Carly."

The sweet voice grabbed Syd's attention.

"Carly, how are you?" he answered, now very wide-awake.

"I'm fine, very good in fact, and you?"

The mesmerizing sultry voice continued.

"I'm doing well, thank you. I'm happy you called."

Carly, in a more talkative mood than she was in her two earlier calls, started the conversation.

"I'm glad to hear that, Syd. I have been working all day on my computer and finally took a break. You were on my mind so I decided to call."

Syd, who's only reference to Carly's work was the night he met her in the restaurant, was surprised to hear this. He asked.

"Your computer? What are you working on?"

Carly, pleased that Syd had expressed an interest in her mind-absorbing pastime, gladly explained.

"Most of today, I spent researching British history, just one of the many subjects I am interested in. Those English kings really had fun, building castles and beating up the Scots and the French, not to mention beheading their wives. Makes our benign city existence seem tame in comparison, doesn't it?"

Syd chimed in. "Sure does."

Carly laughed.

"Why are you doing all this studying?"

Syd asked, his curiosity piqued by this surprising revelation that Carly was not only stunning to look at but was also intelligent. He hung onto her every word.

"No special reason, Syd. I just have to keep my mind busy, kind of like therapy. In my spare time, I dive into whatever topic strikes my whim at the moment, to the point where sometimes nothing can distract me."

Syd was intrigued. He wanted to hear more. "Very interesting. What are some of the other subjects you are learning about?"

Carly eagerly answered, pleased to acknowledge his interest.

"Thank you for asking. This may come as a bit of a surprise, but I like to learn about engineering, chemistry, biology, history, medicine, agriculture, space travel and many other subjects that make me think a little deeper. My curiosity leads me down many paths, and it must be satiated or I feel deprived. Is this a little daunting for you to digest?"

She asked in a mocking tone.

Syd let his mouth disengage from his brain.

"But you work in a restaurant," he foolishly replied.

Carly had anticipated this reaction from Syd. She used the opportunity to commence the early steps for her need to be in control. She scolded Syd.

"What are you saying? Are you demeaning my line of work? Do you think that greeting customers in a restaurant is below me? Come on, I'm waiting. Let's hear it before I hang up on you."

Syd had meant nothing of the kind and, not realizing Carly was intentionally calling him out, tried to set her straight.

"I'm sorry, Carly. I'm really thinking that with your great inquisitive mind a more stimulating work environment would keep your interest. That's all. I'm sorry if I offended you."

Carly could have easily prolonged her ruse to gain and keep control but chose not to. Instead, she pretended to accept Syd's apology and explained how she felt about her current employment.

"My job is for subsistence, Syd. It allows me to survive and gives me the time to do the things I enjoy, such as research. Plus, the knowledge I gain from my studies gives me some great comebacks when I meet someone who thinks they are smarter than me. You should see the looks I get when I use my brain power to put a smartass customer in his or her place."

"I can imagine," Syd remarked. "Are you trying to reach some sort of goal through all of this studying?"

"Not at all." Carly answered. "I just enjoy learning. It's recreation to me, but that's not to say I don't enjoy other activities. I'm pretty well-rounded, a little different than the average girl out there, that's all."

"I wouldn't say you're much at all like the average girl." Syd agreed with Carly's self-assessment. "You seem pretty amazing to me. Please fill me in on some of the activities you enjoy."

Without going into detail, Carly complied with Syd's request.

"Thank you for asking. I love many of the same things most people do; dinners, dancing, travel and really great sex."

Syd's groin tightened. "Now you have my full attention."

Carly knew she was getting a rise out of Syd, but she wasn't lying, she really did enjoy taking a large bite out of anything that caught her fancy.

"I'm not trying to tease you. I like to do it all." She explained. Syd couldn't contain himself.

"Count me in." He exclaimed, unable to mute his enthusiasm.

"Not so fast." Carly cautioned. "Now is not a good time. We must practice discretion for the next while, if that's okay with you?"

Syd's smarts kicked in. He knew Carly meant what she said. He paid heed to her warning.

"No problem. I am curious, but it's not my place to pry into your affairs. I'm sure if there was something I should know you would tell me, so discretion it is."

"Thank you, Syd. I see it's getting late. I'll call you next Wednesday, and you can fill me in on your favorite pastimes. Talk to you then. Bye."

Carly hung up abruptly without waiting for Syd's "good bye" or agreement for the Wednesday phone call. Syd stared at the phone for a few seconds then broke into a dance.

"Wow! Boobs and brains," he shouted as he skipped around the room. "Boobs and brains and adventure and sex. My kind of girl."

CHAPTER FOUR

The week went by surprisingly fast for Syd. As he drove home from work, the following Wednesday evening, he wondered what would hold Carly's interest when she called. He knew he had better be careful and not over embellish anything. She was far too smart to be fooled by any fabricated stories, no matter how mild the tale. He made a decision to be very diplomatic and hold her attention with his charms. He'd better be vigilant tonight, he thought, as he opened up the apartment door. Less than fifteen minutes later, he snatched up the phone after one short ring.

"Hello." He spoke up confidently.

His greeting was answered by a sweet voice.

"Hi, Syd. Carly here."

"Carly? This time, you're early."

"Yes I am. What are your plans for this evening?"

"Nothing much. I'm sitting here with the newspaper and waiting for a special telephone call."

"You don't have to wait any longer. Can I change your plans?"

"I'm all ears, Carly. What do you have in mind?"

"I would really like to meet you for a bite to eat and a glass of wine. Feel up to it?"

"This is a pleasant surprise. I'd love to meet up with you. Do you have a special place picked out?"

"Yes I do. If you know your way around, there is a small café on Central just west of Boulevard. Do you know where I mean?"

"Carly, that's the industrial district. Couldn't we choose something more upbeat?"

"Think discrete, Syd. That part of town is virtually dead at this time of night. The only other customers will be shift workers on their breaks. We'll be left alone to have fun without a waiter poking his nose in every five minutes."

"Good point. What's the name of the place?"

"The Boiler Room. You can't miss it."

"Sounds quaint."

"Oh, you'll see it's not so bad. Besides, we'll be focused on getting to know each other."

"You're so right. It's a date. What time?"

"How about eight thirty? I'll be in the rear, past the counter."

"Eight thirty it is. In the back of The Boiler Room."

"See you then. Bye." They both hung up.

Syd glanced at the clock and saw that he had a couple of hours before he would have to leave. He wondered what clothes to wear for The Boiler Room. He chuckled out loud. Maybe coveralls and steel-toed boots. Surely Carly wouldn't wear anything too flashy with her insistence to use discretion. As he prepared himself for this most welcome surprise date, he realized that Carly was a spur of the moment person. His juices were flowing in anticipation of a delightful evening, The Boiler Room notwithstanding.

Syd, a confident, good-looking man, stood six feet tall with a muscular build. That always impressed the girls, who seemed to migrate toward him without much effort on his part. Now that Carly had made the first move, he felt very sure of himself, unaware that her brash, controlling manner was unlike anything he had ever encountered.

He hummed while he showered. After drying, he shaved with

extra care. His wavy brown hair required some attention but behaved after a few choice strokes from Syd's favorite hair brush.

Selecting the appropriate clothes proved challenging, but after searching through his closet, Syd settled on upscale casual and not too dressy. New slim jeans and a striped cotton shirt made the cut along with shiny black boots. He dressed and took a long appraising look in the mirror before donning his trusty well-worn leather jacket. After locking the apartment door, he rode the elevator to the parking garage, skipped to his Vette and hopped in. He carefully guided his pride and joy out to the street and headed for the industrial area on the other side of town.

The digital clock on the dashboard told Syd he would arrive at The Boiler Room on time. He had no need to rush. The twin mufflers growled in unison as he worked through the gears. He tried to give his throttle foot a break and slow down, so he could visualize the rest of the evening. How would the date play out? He was floating on air and very curious.

After negotiating the light evening traffic, he found the street he was looking for and soon spotted The Boiler Room Café sign. Stationary transport trucks lined both sides of the road, forcing Syd to park three blocks away. He didn't mind this little inconvenience seeing as he would have run all the way from home for this date if he had to. He walked briskly to the open door of the tiny eatery and stepped inside. He made his way past the counter as Carly had instructed and scanned the few tables in the rear, unprepared for the emotional rush awaiting him when his eyes zeroed in on the dark-haired beauty perched on a wooden chair in a corner of the room.

'Wow, she's stunning!' He thought. His throat suddenly felt very dry, and his breathing changed cadence. Carly sat with her legs crossed and her tight, black velvet pants showed every muscle and graceful curve of her long legs. A matching sweater with a dangerously lowered zipper, tried valiantly to contain her braless breasts with little left to the imagination.

As Carly turned to greet him, Syd couldn't help but wonder how those delicious mounds stayed in place. He made a note to keep an eye on them.

Gesturing, with a well-manicured hand for Syd to sit beside her, Carly presented an inviting smile.

"Nice to see you again, Syd. You look good."

Syd dropped into the chair next to Carly.

"Thank you, and you look ravishing, Carly."

"Thank you." She answered. Her arresting eyes stared straight into Syd's.

He sat, mesmerized by her beauty for a few seconds then glanced around the room. He leaned closer to Carly and spoke in a soft voice.

"Carly, if the food matches the surroundings we are in big trouble."

Carly laughed. "Not exactly up to our standards, is it? I see the truckers eat here, and you know what they say about eating where the truckers eat…it must be good."

"You have a point. I hope you're right."

Carly picked up a bottle of wine from the table. "I ordered white wine, Syd. Was I being presumptuous?"

"That's a six-cylinder word, Carly. White wine is great. Thank you."

Carly filled two wine glasses, handed one to Syd and raised her glass in a toast.

"Here's to new friends."

Syd touched his glass to Carly's.

"Here's to new friends." He repeated then added. "And new adventures."

They sipped the wine slowly and studied each other intently. Carly broke the silence.

"I'm surprised. This wine is good. Who would have thought?"

Syd nodded in agreement.

"Must be those truckers again," he joked.

Carly laughed and leaned closer to Syd. She whispered in his ear.

"The Duck a l'Orange is not on the menu, but I have it on good authority that the fish and chips is excellent."

She giggled. Syd joined in with a hearty laugh. He was happy to discover a sense of humor. Carly reached for two menus that were lying on one side of the table. She handed one to Syd and flipped the other one open with a mock look of aversion on her face. She continued with her humorous banter.

"Syd," she cautioned. "Before we choose, is your medical insurance in good standing?"

The wisecrack caught Syd by surprise, causing him to laugh just as he had a mouthful of wine. His running nose and tear-filled eyes added to the light-hearted joshing, as Carly reached over with a napkin to help Syd clean his face.

Snickering and chuckling interfered with the menu reading. After a few minutes of unflattering remarks aimed at the choices, they both settled on burgers. Double cheese for Syd and extra mushrooms for Carly, both orders complete with greasy pan-fried potatoes. Noticing that the owner/manager/cook/server was busy behind the counter, Carly left the table and glided over to place their order. As she leaned over the counter, Syd, following her every move, paid particular attention to her delectable firm ass.

"Holy fuck, could I have fun there," he mused, unable to ignore the tingling sensation in his groin. Carly pranced back to the table, her breasts bouncing to a beat all their own. Syd stared.

Carly noticed.

"Ah ha! Caught you." She giggled and plopped down in her chair.

"I was, ah, just, ah, kind of looking."

Syd stumbled over his words in a feeble attempt to mitigate his impudent behavior. Carly laughed. "Just kidding! They are all mine, completely natural, and I'm very proud of them along with the rest of my body. I have good genes. I don't mind you looking just don't hurt yourself and don't drool."

Again she laughed, and then changed the subject.

"Last time we talked you learned a little about me and what I do in my spare time. Now I would like to find out about you; your likes and dislikes and what dreams you have for the future. Tell me if there is more to this man than a pretty face and a cute ass. I don't even know what kind of work you do. The way you present yourself I suspect you are quite successful."

Syd was very pleased with the direction the conversation was taking. For Carly to enquire about his life was an indication that she was interested. He sat up straight and thought for a couple of minutes before answering.

"Thank you for asking. I'll start with my work. I'm employed by Metro Insurance in the fraud investigation department."

Carly interrupted. "You follow people around?"

"No, we hire investigators to do the legwork for us. My job is to gather enough evidence to make a strong case for prosecution and recoup some of our losses. I help to keep premium prices down and ensure that deserving customers can receive compensation when they need it."

Carly nodded knowingly. "I'll bet you see some real scammers."

"I certainly do," Syd enthusiastically agreed. "It's amazing what some people think they can get away with and they are so stupid about it. They don't realize we've seen all the tricks. 'Sir, you say all of your family photographs and important papers were in your car when your house burned down? Wasn't that fortunate?'"

Carly choked on a laugh. "Oh, that's so stupid. Did that really happen?"

Syd laughed and answered. "Yes, and it's not uncommon. One guy bought a can of gasoline and a lighter on his credit card an hour before his garage burned."

Carly doubled over. "Oh, Syd! So funny! Ha, ha, ha, unbelievable."

"Straighten up, Carly. Here's our food."

The owner/manager/cook/server was now standing next to the table. He plunked the food-laden plates down, spun on his heels and walked away without so much as a smile.

"And a nice day to you too." Syd snarled. Carly equally unimpressed with the service added her thoughts.

"Guess we're not his kind of people. At least the food looks edible. Try not to make me laugh until we've finished eating. Enjoy!"

The conversation stopped as they tucked into the ample feast. When they were nearly finished, Carly resumed the dialogue.

"Tell me what you like to do in your spare time."

Syd perked up. Carly's interest in his work and now asking about his leisure activities appeared genuine. He eagerly answered.

"When I'm away from the office I like to keep myself busy both mentally and physically. I enjoy a good party, although I don't attend as many as I used to. During the week, after work, I check the stock markets and watch the evening news. I also try to catch a few football and baseball games on TV when I can."

"Yearn to travel?" Carly asked.

Syd liked that question. His enthusiastic reply burst from his lips.

"You bet! About every two years I have to get away in the winter to some place hot. Kind of recharge my batteries and beat the seasonal blues. I love that sun and sand."

Carly closed her eyes. "I can hear the surf now. How about romantic getaways?"

"With the right person, I too can 'romantic getaway' as well as anyone," Syd gushed.

Carly pulled away, as Syd reached over to touch her hand.

"Uh, uh, no touching," she admonished, barely interrupting the easy-flowing conversation.

Syd was confused. Up to this point, Carly had been flashing her eyes and pressing her leg against his in a very seductive manner. In his mind, her behavior gave him permission to get friendly. Carly's rejection of his innocent touch didn't make sense. Not wishing to rock the boat and complain, he pretended to ignore the incident, but his confidence had taken a hit. He did not realize that Carly's confusing behavior was part of her plan to gain control. Another half hour of delightful chitchat flew past, and they agreed to meet again. Carly made the first move to leave the little restaurant, insisting on paying the bill. Syd objected. Carly noted that it was her invitation. She pointed out he would have plenty of opportunity to pay in the future.

Carly paid the bill and asked Syd where he had parked. He told her it was about three blocks away. Carly pointed to her car just outside the restaurant and offered to drive him to his. He readily accepted, excited to be able to spend a few extra minutes next to Carly. He slid into the passenger seat and pointed down the street to his car. She drove toward the spot Syd had indicated but instead of stopping to let him out she accelerated telling Syd to stay quiet. Syd was mystified. What was this woman up to?

Carly turned into a dark alley a few blocks down the road and turned off the engine and lights. Syd, thinking he had the right signals, leaned over to embrace her.

Carly pulled away. "No kissing, Syd. It will only lead to emotional difficulties for us."

"Then why are we here?" Syd asked.

"I just want you to completely relax with me," Carly purred. "Put your head back against the headrest and push that button on the door."

Syd pushed the button and felt the back of the seat recline.

"That's it, all the way back," Carly commanded. "Take a deep breath, close your eyes and relax."

Syd's confusion gave way to thoughts of pleasure as he realized Carly was unzipping his jeans. After Syd's zipper was undone Carly undid his belt buckle and fly button. Then she released Syd's erect penis from the confining clothing.

"Oh, that's beautiful, Syd, so big and hard."

She caressed Syd's penis and testicles gently for a couple of minutes then lowered her head to finish what she had started. Carly knew what she was doing. Syd couldn't hold back. Waves of ecstasy engulfed him as a powerful orgasm floated him away. As he returned from the consuming sexual high, he opened his eyes and studied the back of Carly's lovely hair while she milked him dry. As Syd's erection started to fade, Carly gave it a kiss and tucked it back into Syd's pants, then she pulled herself over to her seat. Syd sat motionless, staring skyward. He was still confused but very happy. He searched for appropriate words and spoke softly.

"That was so good. Thank you. Thank you so much."

"My pleasure." Carly purred.

"No, I think it was my pleasure. Yes that was so, so good. You go to the HEAD of the class."

Carly laughed. "Ha, ha, Syd, always the joker. Don't ever stop. I love it."

Syd changed his tone. "I can always joke around, but I still don't know what is going on here. We haven't kissed. I haven't touched you. What gives?"

"We can kiss later, right now it's too soon. As far as touching me, here, play with these." Carly unzipped her sweater and Syd, needing no more encouragement, let his hands and face explore every inch of the nicest breasts he had ever touched. As he licked and teased Carly's nipples, he slid his hand between her legs. Carly pushed it away.

"Not down there tonight, Syd, just keep playing with my tits. It feels good." After a while she eased Syd away and re-zipped her sweater.

"Don't you want some pleasure?" Syd asked.

"Not tonight. I'm all right, but I see you're ready again. Better take that home and do the next one yourself."

"I'll probably do that."

"I know you will…just think of me."

Carly wasted no time getting Syd back to his car. Leaving him standing in the middle of the road, she called out.

"Talk to you next week. Bye."

Syd watched her speed away, then found a darkened doorway and masturbated.

CHAPTER FIVE

T he next morning, the drive to Metro Insurance took on a new dimension, as the events of the night before played through Syd's mind in vivid detail. Although he had relived the evening many times during the sleepless night, here he was reviewing the date from start to finish one more time, looking for answers to his main question: Why? What were Carly's motives? And why did he feel so powerless in her presence? Of course he was delighted that she had chosen him for her little tryst but he couldn't shake an underlying suspicion that he was being used in some sinister way he couldn't understand. His biggest fear was the realization that he could not tear himself away. He was hooked and he knew it.

As he entered his office cubicle a familiar voice caught his attention.

"No sleep again? You busy guy," the intruding voice asked.

"You nailed it Marty. No sleep again and I'm tired, very tired," Syd gruffly answered.

Marty yearned for more. "Details, Syd. Details."

Syd spun around to face Marty, who was peering over the cubicle divider. "Sorry Marty. I would love to tell you all about the interesting time I had last night. Even I am having trouble believing it really happened. My wildest dream came true but it has left me with many questions to deal with. I can't tell you any more than that. You'll have to wait until I get things sorted out."

"You're confusing me, Syd."

"You and me both, Marty. For now, let's just say I am having fun and at the appropriate time, I will satisfy your curious mind."

Marty had no choice but to accept the explanation. "Fair enough. Try to get some sleep tonight. You look awful. Say! How about those Hawks last night?"

"Didn't catch the game. Anyway, I have work to do."

Syd turned back to his desk, leaving Marty scratching his head, wondering what kind of tangled web Syd was caught up in now. Marty's quiet life didn't compare with Syd's "man about town" escapades and he looked forward to any lurid tales offered up from the neighboring cubicle. Most of the stories were made up by Syd for the fun of watching Marty's reaction. This was Syd's morning recreation and now, for once, he had Marty waiting for the fleshy details of a true story. If all goes well, Syd would have a good story to tell. The next few days were painful for Syd. The way his loins ached made him wonder if the brief fling with Carly was worth the pain he was in. Normally for Syd, any sexual encounter was taken at face value. If it led to something more, fine, if not, he would move on. This time, however, he felt himself being pulled toward uncharted territory. The promise of great rewards pushed aside the feeling that he was flirting with danger. Along with his strong fascination with Carly's unique appeal lurked another less obvious emotion. He was feeling an unfamiliar closeness. The challenge now was to find any weakness in her hard-headed independence. From past experience, he knew there must be some tiny vulnerability he could exploit to his advantage, if not sufficient enough to give him control, then perhaps enough to keep him on an equal footing.

Finally, Wednesday evening arrived. Syd, sitting in front of his TV set with the daily newspaper in his hand, was unable to concentrate on either the basketball game or the items in the paper.

His mind focused on formulating some plan or strategy to use when Carly called. He was still grappling with how to restore his confidence when the phone interrupted his thoughts. A wave of anxiety swept over him as he picked up the receiver.

"Hello," he quietly answered.

"Hi, Syd! Carly here. How are you?"

"Carly, I recognize your voice. I'm fine, thank you. And how are you?"

"Very well, thank you. What have you been up to this week?"

"Not much, just chasing down scammers and con artists."

"People trying to screw Metro?"

"You bet. It's job security for me, though. So how about yourself? More research?"

"Nothing too deep, Syd. Just some home construction studies. I was passing by a row of large houses last week, and I noticed that each one had a different roof line. So, I was curious to see just what was holding each roof up."

"And I'm guessing that you found out."

"Yes, I did. There are many different ways to support a roof in a wood framed house. Some of the factors that determine the type of support system required are the angle of the roof, the clear span below the roof and the snow load in a particular geographic location. For instance, on a flat roof, the span and load are calculated, then the type of support can be determined. Most short spans can utilize a simple engineered joist structure. Sloped roofs, the simplest being a gable roof, can be supported by a rafter system, usually fastened to a ridge board at the highest point of the roof and anchored to the top plate of the outside wall of the house. Rafters in older homes are most likely to have an intermediate support or a dwarf wall in the attic while newer homes rely on manufactured trusses, either a fink truss, which uses a "W" support or a Howe truss, which uses a vertical support in the center."

"Whoa! Carly, enough about trusses. How will I ever keep up with you?"

"Oh! You don't have to keep up with me, Syd. I'm sure there are lots of subjects in which you are far more knowledgeable than I am."

"Perhaps, but all of that can wait. I'd like to see you again. When can we get together?"

"I'm sorry to say it won't be soon. I'm still trying to deal with some personal matters. I'd like to see you too. Please try to understand."

"I certainly don't want to crowd you, but I'm finding the wait very difficult."

"Suffering are you?"

"To put it mildly, yes."

"Anything I can do for you?"

"Yes, there is. You can come over here and sit on this."

"I'd love to, but I can't right now. I think you'd better do it yourself until we can get together."

"That only helps for a short time, I'd much rather be with you."

"That's nice to hear. I'm not trying to tease you. I feel the same way. I'll get some of my problems sorted out, and then we can get together. Let's change the subject before we get too excited."

"It's too late for that, Carly."

"Oh! Oh! Ready to play are you? Let's see. What can we do about that? How about a little phone sex? Are you into that?"

"That will do it. I'm so ready."

Carly began to moan into the phone. Syd had already started to masturbate a few minutes earlier. He tried to describe his feelings as he fantasized making love to Carly.

"Oh! Carly I wish you were here. I want you so much."

Carly hushed him up.

"Concentrate on the job in hand, Syd. I'll help you get there."

Carly moaned louder and urged Syd on.

"Yes! Yes! Syd. Oh yes. I can feel you now. So good. Oh! Oh!"

Syd joined her.

"Yes! Carly. Yes! Mmm. Mmm. Oh, Carly, I'm coming. Oh! Oh!"

Syd went quiet except for a couple of deep breaths. Carly spoke softly to him.

"Sounds like you came."

"Yes, I did. Thank you. I wish I could have shared that with you."

"What makes you think I didn't participate?"

"What? You didn't."

"Yes, I was with you all the way. I guess we were both horny."

"Yes, you might say that, but wouldn't it be much better if we were together?"

"Of course it would. Don't worry, we will."

"Then let's get together."

"As I keep saying, Syd, not so fast. I'm not in any position to go there right now."

"I'm sorry. I'm trying to understand. I would really like to spend quality time with you...perhaps dining or live theater. A chance for us to get to know each other. Is this some kind of problem for you?"

Carly bristled at the question. Her angry response pounded Syd's ears.

"Listen hard, Syd. Here's a warning for you. If we start seeing each other, we will still have to be very discreet whenever we get together. There is something I must put behind me, and I'm sorry I can't share it with you. I'm dealing with my problem as best as I can. When I feel comfortable enough to see you, I will, but if you keep on about it, I won't see you at all. Is that clear?"

Syd suddenly felt very weak. He offered up another groveling apology through his now scratchy, dry throat.

"Sorry! I don't mean to be pushy. I promise to back off."

Carly, proud of her intimidating lecture, ended the conversation.

"Good! Have a great weekend. I'll call you next Wednesday. Bye."

The line went dead. Syd slumped against the wall, staring at the phone in his hand. He soon recovered enough to shuffle to a kitchen chair and sit down. With his chin resting in his hands, he tried to sort out his feelings. One thing was certain, Carly was walking all over him and he was powerless to stop her. Women were usually putty in his hands, and if they weren't, he moved on. Now he felt beaten at his own game, unable to accept the role reversal.

He spent the rest of the evening sipping beer while trying to think of some way to put himself back in charge. Walking away from Carly was not an option, as much as he would like to. Instead, he focused on how to win back the self-confidence Carly had so skillfully taken away. The evening dragged on without any sign of relief to his dilemma, eventually forcing him to bed where his tormented mind did not allow him any sleep.

The next morning at Metro Insurance, Marty, who had noticed Syd's obvious lack of sleep, leaned over the office cubicle hoping to hear a juicy tale. Syd, without looking up from his desk, let out a very loud "FUCK OFF, MARTY."

Marty, who was wondering what Syd had been up to all night, before the vulgar outburst, was now even more intrigued, but he was smart enough to heed the harsh warning.

He went back to his desk, and for the rest of the day, kept an ear out for any sign that Syd may be open for conversation.

Syd wanted to enjoy his nasty jab at Marty, but the unfinished Carly business, left over from the long sleepless night, pushed all else from his mind. He could not figure out why Carly and her mysterious ways were causing him so much grief. It didn't occur to him that, by not taking his own advice to flee from a situation in which he had no control, perpetuated the turmoil. Realizing he would not get much work done if he allowed his personal life to interfere, he pushed Carly aside during the work day and used his chores to keep his mind from wandering into that confusing territory. Nights were a different story with Carly dominating Syd's thoughts, even during exciting sports broadcasts.

The work week finished and Syd endured a painfully slow weekend where, no matter how hard he tried, he could not come up with any solid plan that would give him the upper hand in his dealings with Carly.

Panic flooded over him Monday morning, when, as he slumped in his office chair, he realized that Wednesday evening, and the hoped for phone call, was approaching and he hadn't the faintest idea of how to salvage his self-assurance. Unlike the week before, Syd now allowed thoughts of Carly to compete with his work. Slowly, from Monday morning until Wednesday afternoon, those thoughts gained ground until they pushed all other topics from Syd's mind. As he drove home from work that evening, still with no clue how he would stand up to Carly, he decided to act nonchalant and hope for the best. Without any other plan, he had no choice.

Once home, he fixed a sandwich for dinner and quaffed it down with a bottle of beer. For the next few hours he scanned through the evening newspaper, watched some sports on TV and generally tried to keep busy. Every now and then he found himself glancing at the telephone that sat silently on a small corner table. Time slowed to a crawl and he wondered if Carly had decided not to call. He waited a while longer.

At ten forty-five he called it a night and headed for bed just as the phone rang. He leaped to answer.

"Hello."

"Hello, Syd. Carly calling."

"Hi, Carly. Kind of late, aren't you?"

He tried to sound confident.

"I know. Would you rather I didn't call?"

"No, it's just that I'm a little slow at this hour, that's all."

"I know, Syd, some of us need our sleep. How about a little wake up activity? Feel up to it?"

"I don't understand. What are you getting at?"

"Want some company, asshole?"

"Right now?"

Syd asked, not quite comprehending Carly's suggestion.

"Of course, right now. Are you dense?"

Carly replied, annoyed at Syd's slow reaction to her offer.

"Uh, uh, yes, of course." Syd stammered nervously.

"That's better." Carly teased. "I need your address."

Syd, finally getting with the program, slowly recited his address.

"I live at 1604 Park, apartment 302. I'll be waiting for you."

"Thank you, Syd. I'll see you in a few minutes. Bye."

Syd replaced the receiver and took a deep breath. He could hardly believe Carly was on her way up to his apartment. Carly was on her way over to see him, which must mean she wants him. It didn't bother Syd that the visit was planned by Carly on her terms, he could live with that. She was coming to his apartment, and that's all that mattered. His excitement grew as he waited for the front door intercom to buzz. He did not have to wait long. The intercom beckoned, and Syd leaped to answer.

"Hi, Carly."

"Hi, Syd, I'm on my way up."

Carly sang cheerfully into the intercom.

A few minutes later, she glided through the apartment door that Syd had left partly open. The sight of Carly rendered him almost speechless.

"Wow!" Was all he could say.

"Thank you!" Carly acknowledged his joyful appraisal. She wasted no time. Stepping closer to Syd, she placed one arm around his shoulders and cupped his genitals with the other.

"Where's your bedroom?" she whispered.

"My bedroom?" Syd asked.

"Yes, take me there. We're going to bed."

Syd pointed down the hall.

"It's down here. Follow me."

He turned and walked toward his bedroom, Carly followed.

Once in the bedroom, Syd started to straighten up the messy bed and nearly had a heart attack at the sight of Carly a few feet away…completely naked.

"Oh, wow! Carly, wow!" He gasped.

Carly stood absolutely still, her smooth skin shimmering in the dim light cast by a small lamp on the bedside table.

"Come here, Syd," she purred.

Syd stepped closer. Carly, starting with Syd's shirt, undressed him, and then gave him the softest, most sensuous kiss he had ever received. Syd pulled Carly tightly against his erect penis. Carly moaned.

"Oh, Syd, You're so ready. Let's get into that bed."

They scrambled into bed, cuddled and played for a few minutes, then Carly instructed Syd to lie on his back. She then worked her way down Syd's stomach with her tongue. When she reached his penis, she licked and played with it and his testicles before expertly bringing him to the verge of ejaculation, then she stopped and stood beside the bed.

"Didn't want me to stop, did you?"

She said as she smiled down at Syd who was ready for a repeat of the pleasure he had enjoyed on his first date with Carly.

"No, I didn't. You had me there. I almost finished. Come here, I'd like to give you some pleasure."

"That would be nice, but before we do that I have a big surprise for you. Close your eyes and stay just like that until I tell you to open them."

Syd closed his eyes and listened as Carly shuffled around at the foot of the bed.

She whispered and tip-toed to the bedroom door.

"Don't open your eyes yet. I have to get something from my purse in the living room."

Syd waited an agonizing few minutes, then he eased one eye

open. His heart skipped a beat when he looked down at the empty spot on the carpet where Carly's clothes had lain. He flew from the bed, ran through the apartment and made it to the living room window just in time to see Carly's car pull away from the curb.

"SHIT, CARLY! SHIT, SHIT, SHIT!"

Syd screamed as he staggered into the kitchen with his penis still erect ready for action. To ease his let down feeling, he spit on his hand and masturbated, soiling the kitchen floor.

During the long, sleepless night he relived every contact and phone call he had with Carly since the first meeting in the restaurant, trying to figure out if he had missed something. He had never been involved with anyone like her and couldn't get her out of his head. He was stuck and not happy with his inability to handle the situation. How did Carly take control of his thoughts and emotions? That question was driving him nuts.

Morning arrived and Syd dragged himself into work in very rough shape. Marty, who had not dared to venture anywhere near Syd since being told where to go a week earlier, sat in his cubicle staring at his computer screen. He had noticed the sad appearance of his friend and was dying to know the story behind it, but self-preservation kept him at his desk. Then he heard Syd's voice.

"Hey, Marty. Get over here."

Marty leaped from his chair and slammed into the cubicle divider, almost knocking it over.

"Syd, how are you?" he breathlessly asked.

"I'm not as good as I'd like to be, Marty."

"I can see that. What's been happening to you?"

"I can't tell you much, but I have a question for you."

"Shoot, Syd." Marty was all ears.

"Have you ever jerked off in the kitchen, Marty?"

"WHAT?"

"Have you ever masturbated in the kitchen?"

"That's absurd, Syd. The answer is no."

"You should try it some time. It's fun. Now you can fuck off again."

Marty, caught completely off guard by Syd, scooted back to his chair. Syd turned to his desk and buried his head in his hands, on the verge of tears.

The rest of the day dragged by. Syd left early. When he arrived home, he drank a quick beer and lay down on the couch where a short nap turned into a much needed all night slumber. When he woke in the morning, he felt well rested for a very short while until images of Carly rudely interrupted his thoughts.

Every day for the next week was hell for Syd as he cursed Carly up and down for the cruel, humiliating trick she pulled on him. He had no idea what her motives were for such behavior and he was toying with the notion to throw in the towel and give up on her. He knew if he gave her an ultimatum she would call his bluff and say, "it's been nice knowing you!"

Could he live with that? Would he suffer? Did he have the balls to carry through with it? He was reaching the end of his rope as the unsettling days and agonizing nights took their toll. To relieve his agony, he might give it a try.

It was Wednesday evening again, and Syd almost wished for the phone not to ring. He had not prepared any kind of speech or strategy to use if Carly called. He was certain he would vent. He had to. Carly needed an ear full, and Syd knew once he got started, she should watch out.

Shortly after Syd settled down on the couch to watch a game on TV, the phone rang. Syd let it ring a few times before answering.

"Hello," he growled.

"Syd?"

"Yes it is." Syd answered in a very unpleasant tone.

"Syd, how are you? It's Carly."

"Very pissed off. That's how I am!"

"Oh! My! My! Temper." Carly mocked Syd's mood.

That cheeky statement pushed Syd over the top, he let all of his pent-up venom loose. "What kind of fucking game are you playing Carly? Come on. Let's hear it."

Carly had engineered this verbal exchange through years of practice. It was going exactly as she had planned. Her answer flew from her lips.

"I am not playing any kind of game, Syd. I am very serious. What happened last week was a warning shot across your bow. It will serve as a constant reminder as to who is boss in this relationship. I do not take shit from anyone, and nobody tells me what to do. I live my life on my terms. I am not trying to remove your balls, and I still want you as a man. Also, for your comfort, I don't want to run your life. If you can live with my terms then we will get along. If you can not then I have nothing for you. What do you say?"

Syd, with the wind taken out of his sails, had an immediate attitude change. Carly's words stung and he crumpled like a wet paper bag. He struggled to find the right words needed to keep the field level.

"Carly, Carly...Ah, not so fast. Give me a second here. That's a lot to digest."

Carly interrupted Syd's muddled reply.

"Yes, it is. I make no apologies. Take your time. I'm not going to hang up on you. I need a sincere answer."

Syd took a few moments to compose himself, then continued.

"That's so heavy, Carly. I have no desire to take away your independence. In fact, I find it attractive, kind of sexy. So if that's your main concern, we will not have any problems getting to know each other."

Carly cut in again.

"Syd, getting to know each other and getting together are two different things. As you are aware, I am coping with personal problems that I cannot share with you and may never be able to. The operative word for the next while, and maybe longer, is discrete. You must take that to heart and not push me for answers.

Is that clear?"

Syd, beginning to understand what Carly wanted to hear, replied.

"I hear you loud and clear, Carly. Loud and clear. I want to respect your need for privacy and will do everything I can to earn your trust. Whatever is bothering you must be very serious. I hope I can be of some help to you."

"You may, Syd. Someday, but not for a while…maybe never. Let's drop it for now, shall we?"

Syd, fearing that staying on the touchy subject was unwise, agreed with Carly's suggestion.

"Good idea. But I still want you to know the way you made your point was a little harsh. Don't you think?"

Carly laughed.

"You mean last Wednesday? Syd, I learned a long time ago that in order to get a man's attention, a good place to start is his cock. I probably went overboard a bit. The point I was trying to make was for you to realize how important it is to respect my privacy. Without that tough-love lesson you might not have paid heed to my message. I do want to see you again because I really like you. Think about my needs and prove I can trust you. It's in your hands. I'll call next Wednesday. Have a good week. Bye!"

Syd stared at the silent phone then slammed the receiver down.

"Fuck! Power hungry bitch!"

He stomped around the living room, waving his arms in the air and talking to himself.

"Fuck! Fuck! Syd, how did you ever get yourself into this spot? I know! Staring at a pair of tits. That's how.

The self-deprecating rant carried on through the evening with breaks for snacks and beer. Syd questioned himself and answered the same questions over and over with no resolution in sight. Should he stay the course and hope for the best, or is Carly too much for him to handle? He went to bed without any idea where his emotions were taking him, and surprisingly he fell fast asleep until morning. When he awoke feeling refreshed, he made a decision. Knowing he could not forget Carly, he vowed to not let her grind him down. He would treat her kindly, keep his manhood and smooth out any problems as they arrived. This vow calmed him down as he dove into work he had been neglecting. The week seemed to fly by as Syd completed several important work projects helped by his re-born confidence. Seated on his couch, Wednesday evening, he looked forward to Carly's call, anticipating a more pleasant conversation than the drubbing he took last week. He did not have to wait long.

"Hello."

"Hi, Syd, It's me, Carly."

"I know your voice, Carly. How are you?"

"I'm fine, thank you. Are you alone?"

"Yes, I am," Syd answered, surprised at the question. "Why do you ask?"

"I'm coming up to see you. Be there soon. Bye!"

Syd replaced the receiver. "Now that's confidence," he mumbled. "Give me shit last week, invite yourself over tonight. Carly, if you had balls, you could use them for bowling. I wonder what stunt she has in mind for tonight."

The intercom buzzed, Syd answered.

"Hi, Carly, that was fast."

"Yes, Syd. I wasn't very far away."

"Come on in."

Syd pressed the door release and opened his apartment door. A few minutes later, Carly pranced through the open doorway into Syd's waiting arms.

"Syd, this is for you."

Any doubts Syd had about the outcome of the evening were erased by Carly's soft lips pressing against his. Instantly, the two became one and any conflicts hovering over them were lost in the moment. At the end of the long kiss, Carly buried her face in Syd's shoulder and cried. Syd held her tight.

"Thank you, Syd. Thank you."

Carly sobbed.

"I've been thinking about you and couldn't stay away any longer. My demons are trying to keep us apart, but my body is telling me something else. Tonight my body is winning. The evening is ours to enjoy, no bad thoughts, no stupid questions, no stupid answers, just fun. I'm staying the night, so let's enjoy each other."

Carly danced into the living room, Syd closed the apartment door, and then turned to follow her well dressed, statuesque figure. His mind was racing, his heart was pounding, and his loins were on fire. From her large sequin studded purse, Carly produced a bottle of white wine.

"Syd, would you be a sweetheart and open this for us, please?" She asked.

Syd recognized the bottle.

"Holy cow, Carly. That is good stuff."

"Only seventy-five bucks, Syd."

Syd took the bottle from Carly and carried it gingerly into the kitchen. As he applied the cork screw to the bottle, he couldn't help joking under his breath.

"Only seventy-five bucks, Syd."

Carly waited on the living room couch. Syd entered the room with two glasses of wine, handed one to Carly and eased himself onto the couch next to her. Carly raised her glass.

"Here's to a wonderful night together."

Syd touched his glass to Carly's

"Yes! I couldn't have said it better. Here's to a wonderful night together."

Carly took a large sip from her glass and then placed it on the end table next to the couch. Syd watched in awe as Carly tugged off her sweater and there was no bra underneath.

"What are you staring at?" Carly asked, as she dipped her

fingers into her wine glass and spread the sweet nectar over her nipples.

"Let's get started. Go for it, Syd."

Syd needed no further encouragement as he bent down to suck on Carly's raspberry red, wine-soaked nipples. He was thinking, seventy-five dollar wine on million dollar tits! Wow! Syd enjoyed the feel of Carly's breasts. Carly loved the motion of Syd's tongue. When the action stopped for another toast to a great night, Carly motioned to the bedroom, where they soon ended up. They undressed each other and slid into the large comfy bed. Many minutes were spent cuddling, caressing and sipping wine, until sexual needs could no longer wait. Carly rolled Syd onto his back and treated him to some very satisfying oral sex, stopping before there was no return for Syd. She then rolled onto her back next to Syd and spread her legs.

"Oh, Syd. I need some of that."

Syd couldn't wait to return the pleasure. He licked and sucked the sweetest pussy he had ever tasted. Carly went wild.

"Oh, Syd. So good. Oh, Syd, Syd."

Syd lifted his head, moved his body over Carly and started to enter her. She gently pushed him away.

"Could I be on top the first time?" she asked.

Syd nodded and rolled onto his back. Carly slowly mounted him, feeling his penis slide deeper inside, then she started a steady up and down motion, pausing just long enough after each stroke to increase the pleasure. Feeling Carly's inner muscles work, Syd matched her rhythm. The tempo built until the sweet moment arrived in a frenzied orgasm for both of them, then they lay together, touching and kissing, before falling asleep. Several hours later Syd rolled over and helped himself to the lovely Carly who readily accepted him and together they reached another climax, then they slept a while longer. About four o'clock in the morning, Carly whispered to Syd.

"Syd, I am going home now. I want to sleep in and you have

to go to work. I don't want to distract you. Your loving is wonderful. We'll get together again soon."

Syd sat up. "I'm going to miss you. Thank you for a breathtaking night. I'll be waiting for your call."

Carly left the bed. Before dressing she bent down and kissed Syd gently on the forehead.

"Yes, it was an exceptional night, wasn't it?" she whispered softly. "I enjoyed every minute. I'll miss you too, so you can count on that phone call. Try to get some sleep. I'll let myself out."

Carly dressed and left the apartment. Syd rolled over and tried to get to sleep but he was too worked up for that to happen. He wanted Carly again. Not only was he horny, but his mind couldn't stop reliving the night and trying to figure out Carly and her unorthodox behavior. Syd knew that if this was a one night stand, he would suffer. He crossed his fingers.

The alarm clock beside Syd's bed told him to get up and get ready for work. He did not want to face the day. He was happy that his sexual tensions had been taken care of but nagging doubts lingered concerning his future, thanks to Carly's earlier shenanigans. There was nothing he could do about it now, so he got out of bed and prepared for work.

When he walked into his office cubicle, he called out.

"Hey Marty, get over here."

Marty had been waiting for such a call, and scooted over to Syd's office, grinning ear to ear.

Syd offered him a chair. Marty sat.

"Marty, I owe you an apology. I've been so irritable lately. I'm sorry. Things have changed, and I'm much more settled now and I am happy."

Marty waited for a story to emerge. He waited in vain. Syd went quiet, waiting for Marty to press him for information. Marty remained silent. Syd broke the suspense.

"What are you waiting for? Details? Sorry, I can't help you. I have to get to work now so you can fuck off again."

They both grinned. Marty returned to his desk feeling manipulated and confused. Syd dove into his work load confident that he may have a future with Carly in spite of an ever present premonition warning him to be very cautious.

CHAPTER SIX

Now that Syd knew his sex life with Carly would be as good as he had hoped for, he tried to imagine what other aspects of a relationship with her would be like. There was no doubt about her intelligence, far above average. Perhaps too smart. Good stimulating conversation, as a bonus to good sex, intrigued Syd. In the past, he had many good sex partners whom he eventually walked away from in frustration at trying to maintain an interesting friendship. Here now was someone he may be a little more compatible with. Several questions still nagged him as he tried to justify his feelings. What was she up to and how did she gain so much control over him in such a short period of time? The fact that she was a little coarse at times didn't seem to matter as much as the two main questions because he could be just as crude.

Since that night with Carly he was horny all the time and masturbation only eased the tension temporarily. Why didn't she call more often, especially since he knew she enjoyed him as much as he enjoyed her? He thought of phoning some previous girl friends who would readily accept his invitation for a sexual romp, but resisted the temptation, figuring, rightly, they would not fill the void left by Carly. However painful, he decided to just wait for her call.

Another question nagged at him. What was she hiding? Why

so secretive? Did she have a troubled past? Old boyfriends? Lured by her beauty and trapped by her sexuality, he was unwilling to heed the warnings that appeared interwoven with the good thoughts and unanswered questions. He hoped for the best and waited, impatiently.

Wednesday night again and Carly phoned. Syd answered right away.

"Hello." He was hardly able to contain his excitement.

"Hi, Syd. How are you?"

"Horny, Carly. Very horny."

"Me too. Isn't that amazing? One little romp."

"Must be chemistry, some sort of gift."

"It is like a gift, isn't it?"

"Yes and I look forward to more."

"I do too."

"So when are you available?"

"Unfortunately, not right away Syd. I have things I must do. For one thing, I'm still getting settled in my new apartment."

"Perhaps I can help you. I'm big and strong."

"Thank you, but the moving part is all taken care of."

"Then what have you left to do?"

"Oh, things like changing accounts, changing addresses, notifying friends, and I just want some time alone to get settled, try to make it feel like home, if you can understand."

"That makes sense, but it doesn't help me miss you any less."

"I know! When I'm comfortable, we can get together and have our fun. I'll call next week. Bye."

The line went dead.

"Shit! Carly, not again. Look what I have for you."

Slumped against the wall, Syd wondered if he would ever get used to the sudden goodbyes. Longing for Carly, he again tossed around the idea of calling on some old girlfriends but quickly reconsidered and dragged himself to bed for a fitful sleep. The next few days dragged by, including the weekend. He had been lulled into thinking the painful days were over after that last erotic night with Carly. Not being able to see her for a second week was pure agony. He anxiously waited for Wednesday and the expected phone call.

Wednesday finally arrived with Carly's call.

Syd, hovering by the phone, answered. "Hello, Syd here."

"Syd, sweetie. How are you?"

"So so, Carly. You sound happy."

"I am. I've finally managed to clean up some loose ends."

"Good for you."

"I have something to tell you."

"What's that?"

"I'd rather tell you in person. Can I come over?"

"Do you have to ask? Of course you can."

"I'll see you shortly. Bye."

Now Syd was torn between the pleasing thought of seeing Carly and the possibility of her telling him something he wouldn't like. He didn't have to wait long. The intercom buzzed. He quickly answered and let Carly in the main door. Then he opened his door and waited until a few minutes later Carly skipped down the hall. Syd was again struck by her mesmerizing beauty.

"You sure look good, plain old Carly," he complimented.

"Thank you, and so do you. Come here."

Syd stepped forward into Carly's arms and a good long kiss. Pausing, he asked, "What do you have to tell me? I'm curious."

"It can wait. Let's go to bed."

"Awe do we have to?"

"No. We can forget it if you like."

"Like hell. Let's go." Syd raced Carly to the bedroom.

After some wonderful lovemaking, they lay intertwined for a while. Syd asked, "Can you tell me now?"

"I can! I'm staying the whole night. So we can get used to each other." Carly answered.

Syd gulped. "That's wonderful! Carly, fantastic!"

Carly laughed. "I thought you would like that idea." She gave Syd a great big kiss.

They didn't get much sleep that night, so Syd decided to take the day off from work. At noon, over freshly brewed coffee, Carly told Syd she had a great night and looked forward to another. Maybe Saturday, after she finished work. Mid-afternoon, she slipped out the door while Syd went back to bed to get some sleep. He slept right through the evening, then left the bed to have a bite to eat and catch up on some sports news. Then he went back to bed and slept soundly until morning. He awoke well rested and very happy.

A leisurely snack of toast and coffee prepared him for a good day at the office.

When he arrived at work, the spring in his step and grin on his face told Marty there must be an interesting story here somewhere. As Syd reached his desk, Marty popped his head over the cubicle wall.

"Hey! Happy boy, what have you been up to?"

"Oh! Marty. Wouldn't you like to know?"

"Yes, I would. You look so deliriously happy. What HAVE you been up to?"

"If you must know, Marty, it has to do with a new girlfriend."

"I could have guessed that. By the way you're glowing, she must be something."

"Yes! She is something all right. She is something and much more. Even I may have trouble handling this one. I'm hoping for the best."

"Very interesting. Tell me more."

"Not much to tell, but if something really interesting happens I'll be sure to let you know. Now if you'll excuse me, I have to check my messages. I'll talk to you later."

"Okay. Good luck!"

Marty returned to his desk very curious about Syd's latest adventure. Syd checked his messages and then put in a very good day's work, humming happily to himself all the while. Marty noticed and wished he could see inside Syd's head. It was torture for him not to share Syd's secrets. Syd knew this and hummed just loud enough for Marty to hear. He glanced over at Marty every now and then and chuckled to himself, a slightly evil chuckle. At quitting time, he glided home, had a quick dinner, watched some TV and then went to bed early. He slept soundly until morning. Upon awaking he wondered what he was going to do all day. Then the phone rang.

He answered, in a sleepy voice.

"Hello."

"Hi, lover boy!"

"Carly, Carly, How are you?"

"I'm great, Syd. Great!"

"Why the call so early, love?"

"I wanted to catch you in case you went out. Remember I said maybe I could come over after work tonight?"

"Yes, I remember. I think that's a good idea. What have you decided?"

"I didn't have to decide Syd. I can't wait to see you. So is it okay if I come over around two in the morning?"

"Of course, it's okay. More than okay. Give me a call when you get close, and I'll let you in."

"I'll do that. Talk to you then. Bye."

"Bye, Carly. See you tonight."

When Syd hung up the phone, he knew whatever he did all day wouldn't involve his mind. His thoughts would be on Carly and her late night visit. He passed the day by snacking, straightening his apartment, running a few errands and generally puttering until it was time for bed. He showered and shaved and hopped into bed where he lay awake until the phone rang. Carly was at the lobby door. Syd talked to her on the phone while she pushed the intercom and he let her in. Within a minute, she was in the apartment and in Syd's arms. They were in heat. Stumbling down the hall, they managed to make it into bed where the lovemaking took on new meaning. Nothing else mattered as waves of pleasure engulfed them. They were swept into unfamiliar territory. A mind-numbing, euphoric, engulfing togetherness that neither one had experienced before. Syd had hoped for something like this to happen, although nothing could have given him any idea it would feel this wonderful. Carly, however, was completely taken by surprise at how enslaved she felt. Losing control didn't matter as she floated away into a new dimension. After the tender lovemaking slowly subsided, the exhausted couple drifted off to sleep well into late morning.

Waking before Syd, Carly studied his even breathing, planning his future as he innocently slept in her arms. Pressing her lips to his ear, she kissed him until he responded by pulling her closer.

"Morning, Syd."

Syd's eyes flickered. "Oh! Oh! So nice!" He kissed her softly. "So nice, Carly."

"Yes, isn't it so nice?"

He rolled over, covering her upper body, his mouth lightly chewing at her neck. "Oh! That tickles. Oh! Ha! Ha!" She laughed.

"Good morning. Good morning. Good morning." Syd worked his tongue and lips around Carly's exquisite soft neck, "Good morning."

"Oh, Syd. What a beautiful way to wake up."

Syd's hand slid down to initiate sexual activity but it was gently intercepted by Carly, "Let's have a day of anticipation. Later today, we can re-explore each other. What do you think?" She asked.

"I can go along with that, although I have a feeling it will be a long day. Now that you're here, what should we do today?"

"I would love to spend the day with you, but I haven't been home yet. I want to relax, take a long bath, you know, those kinds of things. Last night, with you, was wonderful and tonight I will be ready for you. I promise."

"I'll look forward to it." Syd smiled, kissed her cheek and then leaped out of bed.

"Will you have coffee with me?" he asked.

"Yes, please and some toast?"

"Coming up...coffee and toast for two."

Syd walked into the kitchen and turned the coffee machine on. He then washed up in the bathroom and returned to the bedroom. The sight of Carly exercising naked on the floor, caught him off guard.

"Oh sure! Point that at me and then make me wait all day. Thanks!" he moaned. Carly looked up and laughed.

"Keep this picture, besides, how do you think I stay this way? We all need a little help and look at you standing there in all your glory. I have eyes too."

Syd bent down, and kissed Carly on the stomach, which caused her to snicker, starting a chain reaction with them rolling around on the floor, laughing. A quick embrace and a soft kiss then Carly went into the bathroom while Syd dressed before going back to the kitchen to prepare some toast. Teeth sparkling, hair shining, and clothing accentuating her assets, Carly bounced in to join Syd, kissing him on the cheek as she brushed by.

"Here's your toast, and your coffee is on the table." Syd announced. Carly carried her plate to the table, Syd followed.

While they ate and sipped coffee, Carly started the conversation, prodded on by Syd asking her to step out with him one evening.

"I know it's hard for you to understand, but I'm taking a bit of a chance just coming here to see you. It's part of my past problems I've been telling you about and not likely to go away any time soon, so we can't just step out as you would like. We will get together and be very discreet about it or you won't see me at all. Perhaps you will know why, sometime in the future, but for now we must keep our affair secret. Is that clear?"

"Okay, okay! Calm down. I'm sorry. It's just that I thought that since you went away, you cleared things up, but I guess you haven't."

"My going away is just one small part of my situation, Syd. Absolutely, no one must know we are seeing each other. Give me your word."

"Absolutely, no one Carly. No one."

"Good, because if anyone finds out, I'm out of here and I won't be back, ever."

"Somehow, I really believe you. You have my word. I will keep our secret."

"Thank you. For the next while, when we meet, it will probably be here. After I am comfortable in my new place, we will meet there, where I will feel safer. Another thing, we will not be able to go out together in public, at least for a while."

"That will be a little frustrating, won't it?"

"Not really. We don't have to go out in public to have fun. Your pattern is to fuck any girl willing to accept a couple of drinks from you. Why should it be any different when the roles are reversed? I paid for the first dinner, remember?"

"You mean you only want me for sex? Carly, you make me feel so cheap."

Carly glared. "Fuck off! We both like to fuck so let's make the most of it."

"You make it sound so predatory," Syd snarled.

"I'm only telling it like it is. All I want from you is good sex. I don't need anything else. I know you are intelligent, and we will have a great time with your sense of humor, but as far as any emotional commitment, I can't promise anything. So, you're either in or out. If you're out, I'll be on my way so as not to waste any more of your time. Clear?" Syd was upset but did not want to lose her "Ouch! Carly. Heavy! I'm confused, but I'm in. You can count on me. I'm in." Cradling him in her arms, Carly gave him a long gentle kiss, "It's not as bad as it seems, Syd. I just need privacy, and for your peace of mind, there isn't anyone else."

"That's good to know."

"Thanks for the coffee. I must get going. I'll see you tonight, not too early and get some rest. You'll need it."

"I'll be ready. See you tonight."

As the door closed behind Carly's limber figure, Syd slumped onto the couch trying to digest the last half hour. He wondered if Carly was normal.

He spent the rest of the day anticipating another night with Carly, not accomplishing anything much and not hungry enough to eat a large dinner. Carly showed up mid evening with a shrimp ring and a nice bottle of wine. Sprawled on the living room floor, they toyed with the snack and drank the wine, slowly undressing each other until they made love on the carpet where they fell asleep. Sometime during the night, they made their way to bed and slept soundly until morning. Syd woke first and without waking Carly, went to the kitchen. Returning to the bedroom, he whispered, "Carly, oh Carly."

Carly stirred. "Syd. What? Oh you sweetheart. What is all this?"

"Breakfast, love. Eggs, muffins, strawberries, melon and coffee."

"Oh! Here, I'll hold the tray. Come on back to bed and help me eat."

The next half hour was spent eating and kissing, the food on the tray between them dwindling. When the food was gone, Carly placed the tray on the floor and turned to Syd. "Now, let's have dessert." She giggled.

They enjoyed each other again, finishing the morning with a shower together. After dressing, Carly embraced Syd. "That was a wonderful night and morning. And thank you for the surprise breakfast. I could get used to this."

"I hope you do. I could find time with you habit forming."

Carly agreed, "I feel the same way, but I must go now. I'll call real soon and see you sometime this week. I know I won't be able to stay away too long."

"Music to my ears, Carly. If you miss me as much as I miss you then I know we'll be together again before long. I'll be waiting."

Syd watched Carly leave, feeling more at ease in spite of the faint underlying suspicion that something was not quite right. A couple of days later, Carly was true to her word, staying with Syd two nights that week and all the following weekend. The pattern continued for the next two weeks when, before leaving on a Sunday afternoon, Carly felt secure enough to offer Syd her cell phone number. The week before, they had a loud argument when Syd, frustrated at not feeling included in some form in Carly's life, wondered aloud why they couldn't be seen in public, why she wouldn't meet his friends and why he didn't have the right to call her. Carly called his bluff, and he folded like a deck of cards.

Now, a week after that confrontation, Syd got the coveted phone number, promising not to be a phone pest and also reassuring Carly that her desire for privacy would be respected. Carly believed him.

Syd called midweek and Carly had another pleasant surprise for him. She gave him her address, inviting him over with instructions to not write the address anywhere, park down the street from her house and to use the back door. Syd promised to comply with her wishes, arriving at her back door forty five minutes later, "Carly. How are you? What a charming old house!" he exclaimed, as Carly opened the ornate back door. "How did you ever find this? What a gem!"

"I'm fine, and you're right it is a gem. Just luck. I actually found it two months before I was ready to move, but knowing how difficult it is to find these places, I grabbed it immediately. That was one of the things I was busy with when we met."

"You were smart. Show me around."

"All right, follow me. You can see what a cozy bright kitchen this is, and just down the hall is a nice newly updated bathroom. Here take a look."

"Yes, very nice. And a soaker tub. We can make good use of that."

"Yes, a nice addition, isn't it? The next room is supposed to be a spare bedroom, but you can see it's my den and off limits to everyone. Most of my mornings are spent there, and I don't like to be disturbed."

"Holy Christ! How many books are here? A hundred, two hundred? Are you starting a library?"

"Those are my reference books. To keep my mind occupied."

"Wow! Quite a computer system. I would never have guessed."

"Surprised? A good-looking, horny girl...smart?"

"After that lecture on roof trusses, I kind of surmised but never in all my days would I have thought..."

"Yes, kind of surprising I suppose. If you look, you will probably find a book on almost any subject you can think of, and don't forget, I can reach an unlimited source of information on my keyboard."

"Oh! Carly. My mind is boggled."

"Mind boggling...you nut. This next room is the bedroom, which is not off limits."

"Oh! Thank the Lord for that. Nice and cozy. Very nice...very nice."

"And this room is the bright colorful living room where you are welcome to watch your sports, when I'm not keeping you occupied."

"Thanks for the consideration. I'm very appreciative."

"Shall we christen my bedroom?"

"Do you have to ask?"

After making soft sensual love, Syd fell asleep next to Carly, happy to finally gain her acceptance. In the morning, he woke early to prepare for work. To his pleasant surprise, Carly bounced out of bed to prepare a pot of coffee.

"Don't expect this to happen often, Syd. I just thought I'd like to have a coffee with you before you leave for work. We fell asleep early last night, and now I'm wide awake. So! No use wasting time in bed."

"I'll have a coffee with you, then I'm off to work, in a wonderful mood, thanks to you."

"I'm glowing too. Oh! It feels so special, so stimulating, so...so invigorating." Syd crossed his fingers, hoping the feeling would last. "Yes, all of that, and more. You're right, it is invigorating." He finished his coffee, then got up to leave for work. "Thanks for the coffee and the loving. Talk to you later. Bye."

"Bye, Syd."

They kissed and Syd skipped out the door. Watching him leave, Carly whispered to herself, "Syd, you will be just perfect. Yes, just perfect. Please don't screw up my plans." She crossed her fingers and looked up to the sky. "You sent me this beautiful man, didn't you? Thank you so much. I will take good care of him. I give you my word."

During the next few weeks, Syd spent a lot of time at Carly's house. Unable to fill his friends in on the details, he satisfied their curiosity by making sure they knew how happy he was. They all waited for the day when their hero would tell the tale of his latest adventure, sure that it would prove to be a worthy story.

Sitting at Carly's kitchen table one evening, he seemed preoccupied.

"Something wrong?" Carly asked.

"Nothing really wrong, just that I'm a little stuck, that's all."

"Stuck? Like what do you mean?"

"The lease is up for my apartment, and it looks like the rent is going to increase significantly"

"Maybe you could find a cheaper apartment."

"I may have to, but I don't like the idea of moving."

"This is a long shot, but do you like it here?"

"What are you saying? Of course, I like it here."

"You spend a lot of time here, so why not just move in?"

"Just move in? I suppose I could. You wouldn't mind?"

"Not at all, just don't crowd me and obey the rules."

"Oh! Those rules. I promise. Any new ones?"

"Of course, there are. You already know not to go in my den, not to disturb me in the morning, not to call me at work, not to tell anyone about us. If you move in, you will get your mail at the post office, always park down the street, always use the back door, don't talk to the neighbors, especially the ones living upstairs, they use the front door anyway, so you shouldn't see them, and don't tell anyone where you live. Okay?"

"Should I wear a disguise?"

"Don't get smart. Can you live by those rules? This is important to me."

"It all seems so unorthodox, but yes I can. We'll make it work. I don't know what you're hiding or hiding from, but I want to be with you."

"And I want you with me. Let's make it work."

"That's a good choice of words. Let's make it work."

A few days after Carly invited Syd to move in with her, he got news that Ed, one of his best friends, was being transferred to a distant city by his employer. A farewell party was planned for a Saturday evening at the Anchor, a local pub.

Syd could not persuade Carly to accompany him to his good friend's send-off. Unable to get time off from work was the excuse she used, but Syd knew this to be a lame argument. Several noisy disagreements ensued, and in the end Syd joined the happy gathering by himself. During the evening, he was constantly fielding questions as to why his girlfriend was not with him. "She had to work" was the easiest answer, so he stuck with it. He wished she was by his side in all her radiant beauty, but it was not to be, so after wishing Ed every success in his new location, Syd slipped away early and headed to Carly's house. Carly was still at work so he let himself in and went straight to bed. Soon the sounds of Carly entering the house and getting ready for bed shattered the stillness. When Syd heard the tiny footsteps approaching the bed, he knew his frustrating evening was over. The warmth of Carly's smooth skin pushing against his waiting body as she slid in beside him felt wonderful. Syd pulled her closer.

"So! How was the party?" Carly asked.

"Great, but I wished you were there."

"Sorry, no can do."

"I know. It's just that all the guys keep asking about you."

"Not by name I hope."

"Oh no! Just...where's your girl?"

"And you said?"

"She's working. You'll see her someday."

"We don't know when that will be. Better just leave it alone."

"It won't be long. Will it?"

Carly's tone suddenly turned icy. "You're not listening are you? You know we went through this before. If you keep on about it maybe you'd better not move in with me." She turned her back to Syd, leaving him sorry he had breached the touchy subject again.

Slowly he inched closer, easing his arm around the curve of her waist. "You can hold me, but keep that cock out of my back. Good night." Carly hissed.

"Night, night." Syd kissed her neck. She slept, he didn't. In the morning, Carly awoke to see Syd lying awake, looking at her.

"You look tired."

"I am."

"So what will it be? Follow the rules and move in, or don't move in and find someone else?"

"Not much of a choice there. I want to be with you. I just wish there were some way I could help you with your problems so that we can lead a normal life. If you would only confide in me a little, maybe it would help."

"I'm sorry, but nobody can help me right now. I have to deal with my situation in my own way, on my own terms. So, if you can try to understand and try to be patient, everything will turn out fine. You'll see."

"I hope you're right. I'll try."

"Thank you. Here I'll help you get back to sleep." She crawled under the blankets.

"Oh! Carly. Oh...Oh...es. Oh! Yes. Mmmm."

"There, now you can go back to sleep. I'm up for the day. Talk to you later."

"Carly. Oh Carly. I owe you one."

"I'll collect later. Have a good sleep." Carly left the bedroom and went to the kitchen where she made a pot of coffee. Then she freshened up in the bathroom, before quietly reentering the bedroom. Syd slept peacefully.

She whispered, "Oh! Syd, you beautiful boy. You are so perfect for me. If you don't screw things up, you will be a part of my life forever. Forever, Syd, forever." She kissed Syd's cheek, dressed, then after closing the bedroom door behind her, she entered her den where she spent the morning and part of the afternoon. Satisfied with her day's work, she closed up the den and headed for the bedroom. By the bed, she stripped off her clothes and crawled in next to Syd.

"Come here, Big Boy, I've come to collect."

Syd stirred slightly.

"Hey, I've come to collect. Come on, get with it."

"What? Wha...Oh! Carly."

"Yes. It's Carly, and I hope you're all rested, cause I've come to collect."

"Collect? Oh! Yes, I remember. It's your turn."

"Hey, now you're talking. Come on, get going."

Syd snapped awake. They kissed and played and Carly collected the IOU from the morning. "Oh, Syd. We're so good together. What a gift, just getting better and better."

"I know, love, so much magic. May it never end."

"Everything ends sometime, but for now let's pretend that this will somehow last. Perhaps forever."

"How can anything like this not last?"

"Hard to imagine, but circumstances, things, people and just plain shit seem to fuck up many relationships. Let's keep our fingers crossed and just have fun."

"I'm all for that but I'd still prefer to know a little more about you. If I may, maybe I can help clear up some of your troubles?"

"Don't go there, just relax, don't go there." Carly scolded.

"Okay. Let's just relax."

They kissed and drifted into a light sleep for an hour. When they woke, the afternoon sun had faded into half-light.

"Before you go I'll make some dinner. All right with you?" Carly asked.

"That would be great. Thank you. I missed the whole day, and I'm starving. How about you? Have you eaten today?"

"No, I haven't, but now that I think about it, I'm starving too. You clean up. I'll crack some wine and start the food."

Carly laid out some cold cuts of meat, a small salad, shrimp, sliced cheese, crackers and dip and a bottle of wine, before Syd entered the kitchen. From the doorway, he remarked on the spread, "Spoil me, spoil me. Thank you! I think I'm going to like it here."

"It's a two-way street, Syd. We can spoil and pamper each other, you know."

"And that's how it will be. I need a kiss before we eat." They kissed passionately.

"That's not a before eating kiss, Syd. That's a before bed kiss. Get your kisses straight. Will you?"

"Sorry. I guess I got carried away."

"No problem. You want me on the table or on the floor?"

"You serious?"

Carly broke into a wide grin. "Gotcha!"

"Shit! You bugger. Let's eat." They laughed and giggled until the food and wine had disappeared.

A week later, Syd met up with his landlord, paid his rent, and gave his last months' notice. Carly had given him instructions to sell off or get rid of everything that was not absolutely essential to him. When he moved into her place, he was only to bring his clothes and personal papers with him and any toys he may need. Anything else he wished to keep was to be put in storage. Carly stressed strongly to not use her address for any purpose at all. Syd promised to heed her warning. Whatever she was hiding, she was dead serious about, and he was not about to cross that line. The next couple of weeks kept him busy selling off furniture, disposing of old clothes, organizing his papers and securing a small storage facility for the assorted items not welcome at Carly's house. Finally, when the day arrived to move in with Carly, he was surprised to find one carload, with room to spare, was all it took. Carly was pleased with that, thinking it was nice to have a man in the house but without all the junk they seemed to accumulate. Someone had very thoughtfully built two clothes closets in Carly's bedroom. She emptied one for Syd's clothes and file box. His CD collection, in a cabinet, was placed in the living room, next to Carly's entertainment center. His stereo system was in the storage area with all the other items he wanted to hang onto.

He moved in on a Sunday, two days before the end of the month, giving them a full day to get used to the new arrangement. There wasn't much to get used to, seeing as Syd had spent much of the last two weeks there anyway, but Sunday was chosen as the most convenient day. That afternoon, Carly decided to celebrate by filling the apartment with the aroma of roast beef and baked potatoes. Syd relaxed with the Sunday paper, feeling very much at home, remarking from time to time, how the great smells from the kitchen were tempting his appetite. Before Carly called him for dinner, he put the paper away and set the table, complete with candles,

"Thank you so much. You've just earned a whole lot of points.

I'll put them on the plus side of your ledger."

"I don't need any more points, do I, love?" Syd asked.

Carly looked up and answered gruffly, "You need as many as you can get. With your mouth and my volatility you can go into the red instantly."

"Oh yes, I forgot, quick count them up. Look, I'm wiping the table." They hugged and laughed.

"What I started to say, is that it's the little things we do that go a long way to create an enjoyable atmosphere. If one of us starts to slacken a little, let's vow that the other one has the right to prod a little."

"Maybe we won't have to."

"It's still very early, and as you may guess, anything can happen. I'm just saying that we should be vigilant and remember this conversation."

"Good idea! You have my permission to kick my ass when required. Changing the subject, how's dinner coming?"

"Ready when you are, my sweet, if you don't mind carving."

"Let me at it." Syd carved the roast while Carly laid out the rest of the meal and opened the wine. With smiles and caresses they enjoyed the sumptuous feast, then at the end of the meal, Syd raised his wineglass.

"Thanks for the great meal. Let's drink to our future happiness."

Carly raised her glass, "To our future. May it all work out."

"We'll make it work. We have to."

"Time will tell. Let's be wary and not get our hopes up too high."

Something in the way Carly said that disturbed Syd, but he decided to let it slide, "Come on love, I'll help you with the cleanup."

"Thank you. What a sweetie."

After the dishes were sorted and placed in the dishwasher, they cuddled on the couch, catching the end of an old film on TV.

When the credits were rolling, Carly mumbled, "That meal has made me sleepy. Can we go to bed early?"

Syd agreed, "My sentiments also. Let's go."

Before getting into bed, Carly embraced Syd, telling him he did not have to try being quiet in the morning, "If I wake, I will be able to look at your cute little ass as you get ready for work, and if I don't wake I will dream about it, so I win all around."

"Oh, Carly, you just want my body. You're such a sex fiend."

Carly laughed. "I know, and you're not." She shot back.

"I could be talked into it," Syd responded. They kissed and climbed into bed expecting to make love but instead went happily to sleep curled up together.

CHAPTER SEVEN

Syd showered early Monday morning. After his shower, he reentered the bedroom and heard Carly's sweet voice.

"Nice ass, mister!" She giggled.

"Oh! Good morning. I didn't mean to wake you." He apologized.

"That's all right. Come here."

Syd walked to the bed and kissed Carly softly.

"Have a good day!" she whispered.

"Thank you. I will," Syd answered, in an equally soft voice. Carly rolled over and Syd got himself ready for work. He drank a cup of coffee that Carly had thoughtfully prepared the night before and then drove happily through the morning traffic to Metro Insurance. In the office, Marty came over to Syd's desk, as he had been doing every workday morning for the past couple of months, hoping to learn the reason for Syd's contentment, only to get sports talk and a silly smirk from Syd. The pattern of their morning talks had not changed in the past ten weeks and that was driving Marty crazy. Try as he might, he could not get Syd to divulge the tiniest morsel about his private life. In the past, Syd had enthralled him with tales of conquests and carousing, but now nothing except that silly grin. Marty returned to his desk, wondering what Syd was up to, assuming, by the way Syd laughed and sang all day, that it had to be good.

That evening, after catching himself almost driving to his old residence, Syd danced through his new door, and called, "Honey, I'm home."

"Hi! Sweetie! Have a good day?" Carly cheerfully called back.

"Yes I did, love. Thank you. And did you have a good day?"

"Yes I did, and look here, spaghetti and wine, all ready for us! Come and sit up."

"Oh! Princess. What a pleasant surprise to come home to. Thank you."

"My pleasure. I enjoy a little domestic activity, but don't ever think it comes automatically with the territory. You fuck up in any little way, and you'll see just how fast the pleasure stops."

"Don't turn me into a wimp Carly."

"I'm not. You're still a man but in this house, I'm the boss and that won't change. Sorry to push your buttons but that's the way it is. Let's eat."

Carly smiled and blew a kiss to Syd. With the short lecture hovering in his mind, he studied Carly carefully wondering what to say next. Finally, he decided to play it safe and not say anything at all before digging into the delicious pasta. Part way through the meal, Carly's little tirade forgotten, they launched into a light banter on their respective day's activities. Carly talked about her latest research, and Syd about some insurance scams. When the meal was over, Carly stared straight at Syd.

"I suppose you want to watch the game now." She spoke in an icy tone.

"Uh, I was kind of hoping to, but it's not that important."

Carly broke into a grin. "Gotcha! You go right ahead and watch it. I'll join you shortly."

"Shit, Shit! You rat. I'll never figure you out."

"You're not supposed to. Now go on out and watch the game. I don't need any help in here. Go on now."

"You don't have to tell me again. I'm gone, but first . . . ." Syd embraced Carly and kissed her lightly on the lips. Before leaving the kitchen, he called back. "You're some woman Carly."

"I know," she answered, and then continued in a whisper not intended for Syd's ears. "You haven't seen anything yet."

After cleaning the kitchen, she joined Syd on the couch, snuggling up to him, not paying attention to the game as it played itself out.

"Good game!" Syd exclaimed.

"I'll take your word for it."

"Let me replay it for you."

"Would you rather do that than make love? You have a choice."

"What game?"

"Good choice."

They romped on the couch for a while before retiring to the bedroom where they enjoyed a very satisfying love session. The next two days passed very pleasantly for the happy couple. When they went to bed Wednesday night, Carly reminded Syd that she would be working the following three evenings.

In the morning, she woke at the same time as Syd. "Good morning, Honey," she cooed.

"Morning, love." Syd smiled.

They shared a light kiss.

"You're on your own tonight. Are you going to be all right?" Carly asked.

"Of course. Are you forgetting I've been on my own for years?"

"Just checking. I really meant, will you be able to prepare dinner okay?"

"I'll be just fine, love. You just go and have a good evening at work. Don't worry about me"

"Okay, I won't. You have a nice day. I'll try to be quiet when I get home."

"That won't be necessary. Just crawl in next to me, and I'll be happy."

"Me too. See you then."

Carly rolled over. Syd kissed the back of her neck, then slipped out of bed to start his day.

That evening, the first time Syd had been alone in Carly's home, he missed her. Not just her good looks or the affection they shared, but the way he enjoyed her company. Carly was able to add something to almost any subject being discussed and also shared in Syd's bizarre sense of humor. Yes, he really missed her that evening.

For dinner, Syd fixed a steak and eggs and a bottle of beer. Half watching the news on TV, he wondered why he missed Carly's company when she was only just at work. It wasn't as though she had left him or anything like that. Still, he missed her and it bothered him a little. He wondered if this could be the start of something special.

After eating, he flipped through the television channels, looking for some interesting sports. Finding a couple of college games settled him for a while, but they didn't hold him and he turned the TV off to put some CDs in the player. Casting a curious eye toward Carly's study room and knowing it was out of bounds, he decided a quick look around wouldn't hurt. The sight that greeted him as he entered her office stopped him cold. Although he had managed to catch a glimpse into her private refuge a couple of times, he was still taken by surprise at the total volume of text books and computer equipment crammed into the tiny room. Carly had two computer screens, two keyboards, a printer, and a fax machine, side by side on a console, with shelving above holding software texts and computer discs. All other available wall space was taken up with floor to ceiling shelves filled with textbooks. On the floor were several cartons of books waiting for shelf space. As Syd scanned the shelves he saw that some were marked as to the category of books it held. He noticed labels on the shelves such as botany, chemistry, art, etc. and saw that the labeled shelves contained the proper texts. Then one label caught his eye: SEX.

"A little studying couldn't hurt you, Syd," he muttered to himself while reaching for the first book on that shelf.

This volume, taken from the left side of the shelf, was a text written by the associates of a leading medical school in New York City explaining the complete male and female reproductive systems in humans. Thumbing through it, Syd saw that it was highly technical, containing charts and diagrams aimed at medical students. The next five books were similar. As he opened the sixth book, geared more toward consumers than medical people, Syd was able to understand the text a little better. This work covered much of the same information as the medical texts but in terms the average layman could understand. Syd quickly replaced it. The next five books covered the topic of sexual diseases, from transmission through prevention to cures. After scanning these books, Syd found one that more closely resembled his idea of sex, a text on human sexuality. Settling into Carly's chair, he took his time reading this selection, paying attention to chapters covering the topics; why people are compelled to have sexual activity, what happens to the human body during sexual activity and emotional feelings before, during and after sexual activity. The next couple of books were similar.

Then Syd found a very interesting book, *The Illustrated Book of Sexual Massage*, complete with colored photographs of sensuous, curvaceous models. He looked at every page. As he worked his way to the right of the shelf, the books became more graphic, from massage to sexual problems and sexual techniques, finally to what could only be called pornography. All of these volumes were illustrated with large photographs of models and married couples in every possible sexual position imaginable.

Syd spent the next two hours "studying," finally crawling into to bed at one in the morning, very horny. He fell asleep, but shortly after, woke up to Carly's shrill screaming.

"Wake up, you bastard, wake up."

"What? Oh Carly! What's happening?"

"I'll tell you what's happening, you bastard. You're leaving."

"What? What's the problem?"

"You've been in my study room. That's the problem."

"Carly. I didn't..."

"Yes, you did and don't try to deny it. You know not to go in there. I left powder on the floor. Your foot prints are all over. I knew I couldn't trust you. What were you doing in there? GET UP!"

"Carly, Carly. Calm down. I was only looking. I was bored."

"I don't want you poking around in my stuff. What were you looking at?"

"Just the type of books you have, especially the SEX section."

"Found the sex section did you?"

"I certainly did."

"Read any?"

"Yes."

"Make you horny?"

"Yes."

"Good! You'll have to do it yourself. Want me to leave the room or watch?"

She pulled the drawer from her night table, spewing the contents across the room, "Here's some slippery lube."

She threw a tube at Syd, then stomped from the room, slamming the door behind her. Sex was now the farthest thing from Syd's mind as he lay on his back contemplating the turn of events. He eventually rolled from the bed, replaced the items in the drawer and returned it to the night table. Easing the door open, he saw Carly dozing on the couch. Fighting the urge to touch her, he closed the door, dreading the long wait for morning.

He tossed and turned all night, until it was time to get up. As he prepared for work, he was very careful not to wake Carly. He was not willing to find out if she still carried the rage from the night before and quickly left the apartment, unaware of Carly's hateful glare at his back. Before stepping outside, he pinned a note to the door, which read, "Sorry! Love Syd."

In the office, Marty was once again told to "Fuck Off," and quickly retreated. The day dragged by for Syd. At quitting time, he wondered whether to just go directly to the Anchor pub or go home. At least in the bar he would be with friends who didn't turn his emotions to mush, and he could drown his problems. Squaring his shoulders, he vowed to head straight for home to face any surprise Carly had waiting for him. As he entered the apartment, his heart stopped at the sight of his suitcase in the hall with a note attached. He snatched at the paper and read, "Start packing. Don't call. Have a nice life. Carly."

"Fucking overkill, Carly. Fucking overkill," he screamed, before kicking the suitcase down the hall. Instead of packing, he started to pour himself a liquid backbone, in preparation for a confrontation with Carly when she got home. Luckily or unluckily, he hadn't decided which, the fridge was well stocked with beer, enough to carry him late into the night. Sometime after midnight, his cell phone rang. He knew who it was.

"Hello," he snarled.

"Syd, where are you?" A shrill female voice asked.

"At home," Syd answered

"At MY house?"

"Yes."

"Why are you still there?"

"Carly, we must..."

"Why, are you still there? I left a note. Can't you read?"

"Carly, we have to..."

"Just leave, Syd. I don't want you there when I get home."

"Carly, listen to me. We must talk."

"There's nothing to talk about, besides you've been drinking, haven't you?"

"Yes, but..."

"Listen. I'm coming home in a while, and I'm bringing someone home with me, so I don't think you should be there when we arrive. Get the picture?"

"WHAT?"

"You heard me. I'm bringing someone home. GET OUT!"

"Carly, Carly. All I did was look at a few of your books. I'm sorry."

"Trust is trust, Syd, and now I can't trust you."

"And you're using my little indiscretion to see someone else. That doesn't make sense, Carly."

"Relax. I'm not bringing anyone home. I'll go to his house."

"What?"

"There isn't anyone else, Syd, but now you realize how easily there could be. I'll be home soon. You get the couch tonight. We'll talk in the morning. Good night."

Carly hung up. Later, as he lay wide awake on the couch, Syd heard her come in. Without turning on any lights, she made her way to the bedroom and slept well. Syd tossed all night. About ten a.m., he heard Carly call.

"Syd, come here."

Not knowing what to expect, he crept into Carly's room and stopped dead at the sight that greeted him: Carly spread out on the bed, naked.

"Don't just stand there with your tongue hanging out. Put it to work, and do a good job. You might get to stay."

Syd obliged, giving Carly a prolonged orgasm, after which she returned the favor, figuring Syd had suffered enough. She watched him fall asleep then left the bed to shower. After her shower, she dressed, went to her den and immersed herself in studies for a few hours. Later in the day, she prepared a large meal, brought it to Syd and nudged him awake.

"Carly, Carly, Oh! What's this?"

"Your last meal. Before you leave."

"What? I don't think I'm hungry now."

"Just kidding! But you know I'm still angry. Here, give me a kiss." They kissed tenderly.

"Eat up, and then we'll talk."

"Should I hire a food taster?" Syd asked.

"The food is safe. I'm not that angry."

Syd picked at the food while trying to analyze the past twenty four hours, studying Carly as he ate. Carly toyed with him, staying aloof and neutral, knowing Syd was becoming more agitated as she paced the room. When he had finished the meal, he was reluctant to start the conversation, fearing the worst.

Carly watched him agonize, then plunked herself down on the end of the bed.

"So, you fucked up."

"I'm sorry, Carly!"

"Don't bother apologizing, Syd. It won't do you any good."

"But I only..."

"Shut up! You know my rules, and you broke them. When you moved in here you agreed to follow those rules, but no, you chose to completely ignore my feelings. Frankly, Syd, I'm disappointed in you. I really wanted us to have a special life together, and now...I don't think I can trust you. It's so sad; I really like you."

Carly played Syd like a windup toy, switching from lecture to silence with a piercing stare. Her true feelings were not revealed as she seduced Syd with her carefully laid out plan, letting him suffer a while longer, before breaking her silence. Whatever Syd was about to say was not important to Carly, she wouldn't listen anyway. Her agenda was pre-set.

She spit out one questioning word. "Well?"

Syd sputtered, "Does it have to be this way, Carly?"

Playing dumb, Carly pretended to not understand. "What way, Syd?"

"Over," Syd squeaked.

"What do you think?"

"I'm so confused. I don't think I did anything that bad."

"You don't think you did anything that bad?" Laying it on, Carly raised her voice, "You broke one of my rules. That's what you did."

"But I only..."

"Never mind the 'but I only.' You broke a rule. All of my rules have equal value. Whether you sleep with someone else, or snoop in my office; you suffer the same consequences. You fucked up."

Lapsing into silence again, Carly let Syd stew, raising her hand when he tried to speak.

"I don't want to hear it. You've caused enough grief for us. Let's just drop it for now, and see what we can work out. Okay?"

"Thank you!" Syd whimpered.

His relief was visible. Carly, unable to contain her true feelings, ran from the bedroom. Pulling the door closed behind her she smiled and danced. "Yes! Yes!" the words escaped from her lips, in spite of her attempt to muffle them with her hands.

Thankful for the reprieve, Syd stared at the ceiling, muttering to himself, "You're some woman, Carly, some woman. What have you got yourself into, Syd?"

CHAPTER EIGHT

One evening, early the next week, Carly sat curled up with her latest book, a volume chronicling the destruction and deforestation of the Amazon Basin Jungle. Syd sat across from her reading the newspaper. Carly was mesmerized by the fact that the World Bank had unwittingly helped in this destruction by bank-rolling noble but misguided attempts by various Brazilian Governments to relocate settlers to the huge Amazon area. The murder of Chico Mendes, a world-recognized union organizer and leader in the fight to save the jungle, finally awakened the rest of the world to the plight of this magnificent country. The jungle itself helped in the deforestation by not having a soil base sufficient to support most kinds of agricultural activity. The eco-system of the jungle survived by feeding on decaying vegetation and air and water borne nutrients. Carly sat spellbound by these facts. Syd noticed.

"What are you reading, love? You seem to be far away."

Without looking up, Carly answered, "A wonderful book about the wanton destruction of the Amazon Jungle. Those poor Indians and rubber-tappers suffered years of persecution at the hands of greedy ranchers, large mining companies and crooked government agencies."

"How is that?" Syd asked.

Carly recited what she had learned, "The Brazilian Government tried to relocate many thousands of settlers from the south of Brazil to the Amazon area."

Syd was puzzled. He asked, "Tried? Didn't it work?"

Carly filled him in. "No. You see the plots allocated to each settler proved unable to support agriculture once the vegetation was burned off. Greedy ranchers and large corporations forced many of these settlers from the land, in order to expand their holdings which required vast tracts to be profitable."

Syd wanted to know more. "How did they do that?" he asked.

Carly answered his question in very few words. "Intimidation and outright murder. Not pretty."

"Wow, interesting. That reminds me of a story about a couple of settlers right here in America."

"Oh! Oh! Where are we going with this one? I'm listening," Carly groaned.

Syd started his tale. "Years ago, a couple traveled out west to settle and start a ranch. They found a picturesque valley and managed to get the ranch operating. One day, the husband said to the wife, who was in the primitive kitchen baking bread. 'I think we need a name for our ranch, don't you?' The wife paused for a moment and answered. 'That would be nice. What did you have in mind?' the husband replied. 'Maybe the name of a wild animal. We see them every day.' The wife suggested. 'Something like Grizzly Bear Ranch or Lone Stag?' The husband nodded. 'That's close, but I'm thinking of a more exotic name. Perhaps if I went outside and looked around I'll come up with something.' So the rancher went outside, hoping to see something interesting that would help him name the ranch. A while later he ran back into the house. 'I have it! I have it!' 'What will our ranch be called, dear?' his wife asked. The husband answered, 'How about, Two Dogs Fucking Ranch?'"

"Ha, ha. Oh, Syd. Ha, ha, ha. I might have known. You're so incorrigible."

"A true story." He winked.

"Sure, Syd, sure."

They went back to their reading. Syd broke the silence, "Oh look here. The company that makes 'Poly-Filla' is getting into the cosmetic business. They want to manufacture a makeup product for older women."

"Let me see that."

"Just kidding."

"Asshole."

The pattern Carly and Syd had set, in their first week of living together, was followed closely for the next six weeks. Sunday to Wednesday evenings were spent together with Carly either reading or studying and Syd with his head buried in the newspaper or watching TV. Weekend evenings, when Carly worked, Syd would go to the Anchor to socialize with his friends and endure the pressure for him to produce his beautiful girlfriend for their approval. The kidding seemed never ending.

At home, whenever Syd brought up the idea to venture away from the house together, Carly brought him to his knees with threats and anger. Finally, even Carly grew tired of staying home and agreed to a compromise with Syd, a weekend away from the city, where Carly would feel more at ease to be seen in public with Syd.

The very next weekend, Carly's employer let her take Friday and Saturday off. On the Friday, Syd left work early to head straight home, where Carly had two suitcases packed. With Carly next to him and the suitcases in the car trunk, he smiled to himself as he followed the Friday afternoon commuters on their way out of town. Carly had suggested a resort some three hours away and Syd had agreed enthusiastically. Once the city limits were behind them, Carly reclined her seat slightly, reached over to caress Syd's hair, and whispered, "Can you dance?"

Syd whispered back in response, "If I have to."

Carly pulled away. "Wrong answer, jerk."

Syd quickly recovered, "But with you I can do anything, sweetie."

"Nice bail-out, but you're still a jerk." Carly winked.

The talk continued with Syd trying to explain, "Men were not meant to dance."

"Oh! What were they meant to do?"

"Fix the car. Fix the taps. Mow the lawn. Watch TV. You know, men things."

"This weekend, you're going to dance."

"I know, love. I was just kidding."

"I know you were. I'm starting to catch on. That's scary."

The traffic thinned out along with the buildings as the turn off to the two-lane road, that would take them to the resort, appeared. Syd turned the car from the four lane highway onto a beautiful country road.

"Two hours to go. Hey wake up!" he shouted.

Carly jumped. "Oh! Oh! What?"

"You dozed off."

"Guess I did, didn't I?"

"Think you'll need the rest for later on, sweetie?" Syd asked.

"You'll need a rest." Carly giggled.

"I like that talk, love."

"Truthfully, I'm just so relaxed, the fresh air, the rhythm of the car, very soothing."

Syd pointed ahead. "Look over there, sweetie."

Carly followed his gaze, "What a clear vibrant sunset." she was visibly moved, "Why can't we have these in the city?"

Syd answered her question, "The buildings and lights. The sun is still there but those buildings and lights."

"Damn buildings and lights." Carly giggled again.

"Shall we pull over here and watch for a while?" Syd asked.

"Yes. Good idea." Carly agreed.

Syd parked in a widening of the road, Carly released her seat belt and snuggled in his arms. She whispered to him, "Why can't every evening be just like this?"

"How do you mean?"

"Just cuddling up and feeling satisfied."

"Don't you get this feeling when we cuddle at home?"

"It doesn't seem quite the same. Maybe it's the freedom out here. All I know is, it feels wonderful."

After a long slow kiss, Carly moved away from Syd, carefully studying him as he turned the car back onto the road. She whispered to herself, "Such a shame. Such a shame."

Syd did not hear. The sun disappeared in a final burst of color.

A while later Syd announced, "About a half hour more, love."

Carly squeezed Syd's hand. "Oh! I'm so excited. This is going to be a great weekend."

"It already is, sweetie, and it'll get better and better."

"Oh! Yes, I know, mmm, mmm." Carly writhed, faking an orgasm.

"Stop it! I'll be driving off the road."

Carly sucked her finger and winked.

"You wicked little girl, I'll take you over my knee and spank you."

"Yes! Yes! Please do." Carly giggled again. The teasing continued until the lights of the resort appeared ahead.

"Oh! It looks so inviting. It's enchanting!" Carly exclaimed.

"Pictures don't do it justice, do they?" Syd mused.

"No, they don't. Smell that air, mmm. Oh! So clean and the stars. Where did they all come from?"

Syd did not reply as he parked at the entrance canopy while pulling the trunk release. A uniformed bellhop magically appeared and reached in for the luggage. "Just the two bags, sir?" The bellhop addressed Syd.

"Yes, thank you." Syd replied.

"Please take everything you need and leave the keys, sir. The attendant will park your vehicle. Thank you."

Carly gathered a few loose items from the car while Syd, who had already gone to the rear to close the trunk, waited. As Carly stepped to the sidewalk, she took a suspicious look around. The sight of a security camera stopped her cold.

"You go ahead Syd. I want to take in the view. I'll be right behind you after you check in."

"Oh! Okay! I won't be long."

Syd assumed Carly was just taking in the fresh night air. He turned and followed the bellhop through the lobby to the front desk. The desk clerk greeted him, "Good evening Sir, your name please?"

"Syd Barnes," Syd answered.

The clerk scanned his computer screen. "Ah! Yes right here. We have you booked in a nice corner room, number 312. May I have your credit card please?"

Syd handed his card to the clerk who in turn passed the security door card to Syd. "Please enjoy your stay. You may call the desk at any time of day or night for anything you may require."

"Thank you," Syd replied, as he turned to see Carly standing to one side of the lobby, unaware she was avoiding the security camera. He also hadn't noticed that, when they had entered the lobby, Carly had covered her face with her hands and quickly passed the exterior camera, only to spy another bubble housing in the center of the lobby ceiling. Keeping her hands on her face she quickly hurried to the side of the lobby to wait for Syd. She intentionally kept her back to the camera.

Syd walked over to Carly and, upon seeing her with her hand pressed to her face, asked, "Something wrong, love?"

"Just some dust. I'll be all right," Carly answered. Syd tried to help. "Let me see."

"No, no." Carly snapped.

"Oh! Sorry. I was just trying to help." Syd was starting to get used to Carly's sudden mood changes, however, he still stepped back in surprise.

Carly softened her tone a little. "I'm sorry. Let's go to our room." She followed Syd to the elevator, keeping her hand to her face until they were safely behind the closed door. As she lowered her hand, Syd stepped closer to look at her eyes.

"I don't see anything. Are you okay?" he asked.

"Yes, I am. It must have just been a tiny speck of dust, thank you." Before exposing her face, she had scanned the interior of the elevator, searching for signs of a security camera, and only lowered her hand when she was sure there was none. At the third floor, they left the elevator, but not before Carly partially covered her face while looking for more cameras. Not seeing any, she relaxed and followed Syd to room 312. Inside the room, their bags sat on the floor with a standard greeting note from the hotel wishing them a pleasant stay. Rushing to the window, Carly gushed.

"Look at the pool! Just look at that pool!"

Before Syd could look at anything, Carly had cart-wheeled onto the king sized bed.

"Come here, come here." She laughed.

Syd needed no more encouragement. He leaped onto the bed and landed beside his lovely Carly. They kissed and caressed for minutes before lying very still, gazing into each other's eyes.

Syd asked, "What would you like to do, love? Shall we clean up and go downstairs for a snack and some dancing?"
Carly wrinkled her nose and answered.

"We have all day tomorrow and Sunday. Why don't we order in and see what's on TV?"

Syd agreed. "Good idea. Let's look at the menu here."

From the room service menu, they decided on a mixed tray of appetizers and two bottles of champagne. Syd phoned in the order, then they snuggled and teased each other until, a half hour later, the food was delivered to their door. Carly found some romantic music on the bedside radio, and then she poured two wine glasses to the brim with the chilled confection. Raising their glasses and clinking them together, they settled in to eat, drink and enjoy the start of a wonderful weekend. As the first bottle was drained, and the second one started, the giggling and laughing grew louder.

Carly snickered. "Syd, I keep asking myself, what do I see in this guy, besides his big cock?"

Syd answered with a question, "You mean my pretty face doesn't count for anything?"

"Oh yes! The pretty face – yeah that's it – the pretty face."

Then it was Syd's turn. "I ask myself, what else is there other than those big tits?"

Carly stood up and pulled her jeans down. She bent over and asked, "What about this ass, mister?"

"Oh! Of course, that ass. Of course, of course."

Syd pulled Carly onto the floor, where the giggling and laughing soon turned to passion. They managed to make it into bed where, in their tipsy condition, they made slow, satisfying love before falling asleep in each other's arms.

Carly stirred first. It was a little after seven a.m. Without waking Syd, she slid from the bed and entered the bathroom. She took her time, brushed her teeth, washed her face, and combed her hair. Then she walked back into the bedroom and pulled on a pair of shorts just as Syd woke up.

"Oh! You're up, sweetie. Let's have a kiss." Carly walked to the bed and gave Syd a nice soft kiss.

"Come back in here." Syd grinned and patted the bed.

Carly pulled away. "I'll return soon. I want to look at the pool area in the morning sun."

"Okay, sweetie. I'll stay right here."

Carly finished dressing, completing her outfit with a large sun hat and dark glasses.

"Cool, oh! So cool," Syd remarked. Carly removed the glasses but kept them in her hand.

As she left the room she called, "See you soon, bye!"

"Okay, love. Hurry back," Syd called in answer, before the door closed.

Carly rode the elevator to the main floor, where she was glad to discover the exit to the pool and patio area did not require her to pass through the lobby. She scanned for security cameras on her way out to the pool, and realizing there didn't seem to be any, she decided to question a close by security officer. Approaching the officer, she kept her face hidden with her sun hat and dark glasses, and asked, "Sir, I wonder if you might help me?"

The officer smiled. "Sure, ma'am. What can I do for you?"

Carly cupped her face with one hand, feigning confidentiality. "Sir, I have some rather expensive jewelry, and I couldn't help noticing a lack of security cameras. For my peace of mind, could you tell me what security system is in place here, so I could sit near a secure area?"

"Ma'am, there are no cameras outside of the main lobby and entrance area. Management feels they are too intrusive to our guests. You will notice there is always a security person close by. We are not only trained in crime fighting but also in first aid and many other helpful ways to make our guests feel secure. I hope this is satisfactory, ma'am."

"Yes, much. Thank you."

Carly turned from the guard, quickly glanced around the pool and went back inside the building. She removed her glasses and hurried back to Syd, who was still in bed. Carly entered the room, closed the door and leaped on Syd. Soon her clothes were on the floor. A short while later, the happy lovers lay very still. Carly made a suggestion.

"Let's shower."

"Good idea, sweetie." Syd agreed.

Together, they sprung from the bed and entered the large, double shower. Then they lathered each other all over with frothy, sweet-smelling soap. "Nice soap!" Syd remarked.

"Yes, it sure is. Now you have the sweetest smelling balls." Carly giggled as she washed her hair with a sister shampoo to the soap. When the cleaning, kissing and giggling was all done, Syd stayed in the bathroom to brush his teeth and shave, and Carly sat on the bed drying her hair. When Syd emerged from the bathroom, Carly kissed him on the cheek.

"My turn, now. You look nice."

"Thank you, so do you," Syd answered.

"It gets better. Just wait." Carly skipped into the bathroom.

A short while later, she reentered the bedroom, her eyes dressed, lip gloss applied and her hair done up in a fancy ponytail. The only other makeup she ever used was moisturizing cream.

"Wow! You are a hot date." Syd gushed.

"Thank you. Aren't we a good-looking couple! What's the plan?"

"I think we should dress up a bit and go downstairs for breakfast. What do you think?"

"Good idea! I understand breakfast and lunch are served on the outside patio by the pool. I'm in!"

"Great! Let's get ready."

Shorts, shirts and sandals were quickly donned before they headed out to the patio. They chose a table and soon a waiter appeared with two menus. Carly noticed a security man not too far away as she selected a muffin, juice and coffee, while Syd went for the breakfast special, eggs, bacon, sausages, toast and coffee, no juice. They placed their order.

The food was quickly delivered, and at the sight of Syd's heaping plate, Carly remarked, "You're going to drown in the pool after eating all that. They'll never be able to pull you out."

Syd shrugged his shoulders. "I'll take my chances."

After the meal was eaten, Carly remarked on how much she enjoyed her choice.

"Oh! That muffin was so good. How about your feast?"

"Just great." Syd puffed out his stomach. "Oh! I'm so stuffed."

Carly had an idea. "Let's get our swim suits and lie by the pool."

Syd liked that suggestion. "I'm with you on that." Then he signaled the waiter.

The waiter walked over to the table, accepted the signed breakfast bill from Syd, thanked him and walked back to the food bar. Syd and Carly went back to their room, changed into swim suits and returned to the pool. Stretched out on lounge chairs, they relaxed, enjoying the pretty hills in the distance while trying to pick out images in the puffy summer clouds. As the hot sun beat down, the shimmering pool drew Carly's attention, "Let's swim," she called out. Without waiting for an answer, she removed her hat and glasses in one movement and gracefully dove into the soothing water. Powerful, smooth strokes took her the length of the pool several times as Syd watched, captivated by her graceful swimming style. She stopped by the side of the pool where Syd was now standing.

He leaned down to her. "I never would have guessed, never!"

"I can do anything. This body isn't only for looking at and fucking."

"Shh! People will hear you." Syd glanced around.

"That's their fucking problem. Fuck them. Come on in."

Syd slipped into the pool, powered to the far end, then back to Carly.

She was impressed. "Nice, very nice. Just a couple of water babies."

They swam to the deep end, embraced with a kiss and sank to the bottom. Then they very slowly rose to the surface. Refreshed from the swim, they returned to the lounges and warmed up in the sun. The morning passed as they alternately swam and warmed up until Carly grew restless.

"I want to do something else," she said.

"Like what, love?" Syd asked.

"How about a hike?"

"A hike?"

"Yes, a hike. I saw a brochure showing a short hike to a scenic little lake. Want to go?"

"Yes, sure. Let's go." Syd was elated that Carly would think of going on a hike with him. Picturing this scenic little lake in his mind, he was hoping he might finally start to learn more about Carly, a subject that was constantly buzzing in his head.

"You look happy." Carly remarked.

"I am. I was just thinking a hike with you would have been the farthest thing possible. This is such a meaningful surprise. I think we should do some talking as we hike. You know I don't know very much about you, and I'd really like to. Maybe this is a good time to bond. Is that okay with you?"

Carly turned serious and gripped Syd's shoulder. Syd braced himself. "Don't go there," Carly growled. "Let's just have some fun. Okay?"

"Sorry. Okay, let's just have some fun." Shook up, Syd studied Carly, wondering if she would ever warm up. He ached to know. Gathering up his towel, he tried to relax, even as his mind taunted him about Carly's secrets. "Time will tell, old boy, relax...relax." He forced pleasant images into his head. But no use. Thoughts of Carly prevailed as he struggled to push them aside.

"I'm sorry." Carly tried to console Syd. She saw the concern on his face as she kissed his cheek. "It's still too soon for me. Perhaps someday, but not now. Try to understand, it's still too soon. Will you try?"

"I will, love, but it's so difficult. We share our time and our bodies, but there could be so much more. I'll try."

"Thank you, sweetie." Carly went into her little girl act and danced away from Syd. "Let's have some fun. Let's have some fun."

"So right, love. Let's have some fun." Syd tried to join in but didn't quite get there. Carly didn't care, or did she? He wanted to know. But how?

As he led the way back to their room, Carly muttered to herself behind his back, "Someday, Syd? Yeah, right! When hell freezes over." The smirk on her face said it all, "Someday? Forget it! Fuck him and his big cock. Fuck him! I don't owe anybody anything."

A chill engulfed her as another feeling started to take over. A feeling a very foreign to her. She felt sorry for Syd. All the way back to the room, the debate in her head continued. "Why can't I love this man? Look at him, so strong, so humorous, and so smart. Just look at him. What's wrong with you, Carly?"

Then another very important matter surfaced: The Project, her life's dream. It was almost finished. She couldn't stop now. Carly cringed and wondered if she had bitten off too much. "No! It's got to be finished. Fuck Syd. Fuck him good. Then get on with it. I can't stop now. Oh! It's so close. So close!" She continued talking to herself. Syd had been watching Carly as they approached the room, afraid to interrupt. Now, as he unlocked the door, he decided he'd better try to find out what was troubling her.

"Where are you love? What's going on?"

Carly snapped back to earth. "Oh! Nothing, just the past and the future trying to screw up the present. Memories and dreams can be good or bad, can't they? We learn from our mistakes; or do we? Just a little debate in my head, nothing life threatening."

"But you look so serious. Can I help?"

"Thank you, but no. This is my little problem. I promise to work on it, then everything will be all right. Come here." She flashed her trademark smile and then smothered Syd with a soul-searching kiss. She pulled away, spun around and shouted "Look at this room. Look at you. Look at me. Look outside. The present is here. Let's play."

She danced around the room while Syd, too stunned to move, stood still. Not daring to pursue the puzzle further, he changed into shorts and walking shoes in silence, wondering if this riddle would ever be solved. Knowing the torture would continue, with no easy way out, he felt trapped, as he watched this beautiful woman finish dressing. Carly broke the silence.

"You look sporty," she remarked, as she admired Syd's hiking attire.

Syd nodded and returned the compliment. "Thank you, and so do you. Your turn to come here." Carly moved closer. Syd kissed her tenderly, than stepped back to look into her eyes. He wondered what lay beyond them. Would he ever know?

Carly sensed his confusion. "No! No! Don't go there," she scolded before smoothly changing the subject. "Let's pick up a snack from the restaurant. We can eat by the lake. Okay?"

Syd agreed with the thoughtful suggestion. "Another good idea, love. I'll call down for a take-out lunch." He asked what she would like from the restaurant and phoned in the order. A short while later, they went down to the restaurant, picked up the packed lunch, and headed out to the start of the lakeside trail. Syd did not relax until they had reached a treed area beyond the resort boundaries. The cool, fresh smelling trail offered him some hope that, in this environment, Carly would relax enough to open up and confide in him. He desperately wanted to know this woman who was sharing part of her life with him. Or was she really sharing? The same old questions still nagged him, but out here in the woods he experienced a pleasant calmness. Was Carly feeling the same? Not willing to stick his neck on the block again, he kept the conversation confined to nature and wildlife observations as they headed toward the lake. Pleasantries were exchanged with strangers along the way, both coming toward them and faster hikers passing them. On one steep uphill section, two extremely muscular female hikers passed them.

"Holy Christ, would you look at those women." Syd whispered. "If they're not careful, they'll have muscles in their shit."

"Oh Syd, wicked comment."

"Can't help myself, babe. I am a comedian at heart."

"Keep your day job."

"You don't appreciate good humor."

"That's just it, sweetie, I do." The hearty banter continued as they bounced down the trail and the pretty lake came into view. An invisible wall stopped them in their tracks.

"Oh Syd! So breathtaking! The pictures I remember don't look this good. Oh! So sweet! Oh, Syd."

Syd was just as impressed. "Yes, isn't it? So beautiful."

Would Carly be ready to talk about herself in the midst of such tranquility? Maybe when they found a quiet spot to eat, the time would be right, but Syd knew he had to approach the subject very carefully, or risk the wrath of Carly.

Pulling her by the hand, he picked up the pace.

"Come on, love. Let's get down to that heavenly body of water. Oh, doesn't it look inviting?"

"Yes, Daddy. I'm coming. You're pulling my arm off." Carly giggled.

"Sorry, love. Oh! I feel so free."

"You can feel free anytime you want to. I don't charge, you know." It was Carly's turn to joke.

"There are hidden costs, babe. Don't forget." Syd joked in turn.

"Those hidden costs. Yes, I did forget."

Before the hidden costs could be analyzed, they arrived at a small lookout above the lake. Now, nothing else seemed to matter except the view. Carly stood in front of Syd, his arms circled her waist, one hand tucked into the front of her shorts. They stood silently for minutes, mesmerized, breathing deeply. After encoding the scene in his mind, Syd nuzzled Carly's neck, his eyes closed. Carly pushed back into him, her eyes also closed, "Oh, Syd. Why can't every day be like this, so calm, so quiet, so…so…mind numbing. Let's take some of this home with us. Okay?" Carly turned to face Syd. They kissed. The kiss was long, deep and passionate. Tears fell. Atmosphere conquered all.

"Never mind taking this home, love, let's just stay here."

"I'm afraid the parks people would frown on that. Still it's a good thought, isn't it?"

Back on the trail to the lake, Syd hoped Carly was

experiencing the same feelings as he was, some kind of super closeness, almost a holy bonding.

His mind wandered.

'This has to be love. Nothing could feel this good.' Yet, mixed in with these emotions was a certain foreboding that all was not as it appeared. Would Carly ever be his completely, bringing with her all the emotions and feelings necessary for the joining of two souls? Would he find out today? He prayed.

"Earth to Syd. Earth to Syd."

"Hello…Carly. What?"

"You went somewhere. Just getting you back. That's all."

"Thanks. I'm still here. Just took a short detour."

"Anything I should know?"

"Maybe, but not right now. Let's find the trail around the lake."

Closer to the water, they located the start of the trail that would take them around the lake, back to this starting point. The trail turned right following the shoreline of the lake counter-clockwise. For most of the way it stayed close to the lake; however, in several areas, the path veered away from the water, to avoid steep drop-offs. Also, as well as those necessary bypasses, there were other trails leading away from the lake to scenic viewpoints. Syd and Carly explored every one as they circled the lake. At one point, approximately halfway around the lake, the trail turned sharply away from the water to pass by a large rock promontory. Syd and Carly studied the rock.

"Think you can climb up there?" Syd asked sarcastically.

"Think I can't?" Carly confidently answered.

"Let's do it!" Syd enthused. They picked a likely place to climb and then pushed and pulled each other until they reached the top, which was flat as a table.

Their efforts were rewarded with a stunning display of natural beauty.

"Pinch yourself." Carly said.

"What?"

"Pinch yourself. See if you're still here. I think we've crossed over, gone to our reward."

"Like…died?" Syd asked.

"Possibly!" Carly answered. "Nothing on earth could be this awe-inspiring. We must be in heaven. Did we have some kind of accident on the way here?"

"Not that I remember. Let me see if you're still alive." Syd pinched Carly's ass.

"Ow!" She jumped away.

"Nice to know, we're still here. This is still earth, so let's enjoy it!" Syd said, as he spread his arms.

Carly walked closer to the edge, looking for a place where they could enjoy the food they had brought with them.

"Fuck the view. I'm ready to eat," she announced.

"Same old Carly," Syd thought. Sitting on the edge of the rock, the happy couple enjoyed the food and the view before Carly spoke up.

"I'm sorry for that comment about the view, but I was hungry. What a foul mouth I have. Sorry!"

"You're forgiven, love. I know you won't change overnight; if ever."

"Miracles happen. Maybe even I can change. Wouldn't that be something?"

Syd did not answer, instead his attention turned back to the entrancing view spread out around them. To the right, traces of the path they had yet to follow could be seen along the shoreline, while to the left, glimpses of the path they had already walked appeared. In the far distance, the roof of the resort peeked out above the tree tops.

"Did we come all that way?" Carly asked.

"Interesting travels make short distances." Syd repeated an ancient saying.

"Don't they?" Carly whispered softly.

The view was forgotten after several long kisses. Syd decided this was the time. He hesitated slightly, then quietly asked, "Honey, can you tell me just a little bit about yourself? Maybe something from your past, or what you look for in the future?"

"Oh, sweetie, I'd love to tell you all about myself but please understand, I can't right now. I was a little girl once, like all other women were. Like many of them, I had good things and bad things happen to me. I also had dreams, like all other little girls have, and some of those dreams have been shattered over time. But I'm keeping one dream alive. That's what keeps me going."

"Tell me about it."

"I can't sweetie. It's top secret."

"Am I in there somewhere?"

"As a matter of fact..." Carly caught herself mid-sentence, "that's all I can say." She clammed up.

"Now I am curious," Syd said, hoping for more.

"You'll just have to stay that way." Carly held her ground.

Syd tried again. "Tell me about the bad things you remember from your childhood. They're obviously on your mind."

"Now THOSE are secrets. Please don't ask again." Carly grew impatient.

"But, honey, sometimes talking about something can make it seem better."

Carly exploded. "THE SUBJECT IS CLOSED!"

Syd jumped back. Carly, seeing the perturbed look on his face, pulled him close. She buried her head in his chest, unable to stop the wall of tears. Different tears than the ones shed only a short time ago. Syd stroked Carly's head as she shook uncontrollably. Syd wondered what nerve he had struck. His mind raced. After a time, that felt much longer than it actually was, Carly peeked up at Syd with a sheepish grin.

"You don't know how much I needed that."

"I can imagine, love."

"Be my friend. Be my friend," Carly pleaded.

"I am your friend. I am your best friend."

"Thank you. No more for now. Okay?"

"No more for now. I promise. Let's enjoy the rest of the day."

"Yes! Let's enjoy the day."

The climb down from the rock was more difficult than the ascent, taking their minds away from Carly's troubles. Negotiating the trail, with all its calming beauty, kept them away from the discussion, even as their thoughts still lingered there, although from two very different angles.

Syd suddenly realized that the light was fading. "We're losing our day. Better hurry," he exclaimed.

"Where has all the time gone?" Carly asked.

"Too much fun, love. That's where."

"It wasn't all fun."

"That's all part of life. Pain amplifies pleasure."

"You have an answer for everything. Don't you? That's what I like about you."

"That's all?"

"Oh no. There are other things." Carly grabbed Syd's crotch.

He pushed her hand away. "I told you before… I hate being a sex object."

Carly laughed, "Get used to it, because you are."

Syd did not see Carly making faces behind his back, nor did he hear her mutter, "And that's all you are."

Daylight was fading, and they suddenly realized that darkness seemed to fall much faster in the woods than in the city, and once it arrived, it was much darker.

"I'm glad you're here with me. This darkness scares me. Do you think the bears will get us?" Carly asked, trying to hide the fear in her voice.

"I'll fight them with my bare hands, love." Syd gestured wildly.

"My hero. Come on bears. Syd will show you who's boss. Over here bears, over here," Carly shouted.

"On second thought, maybe we should show those bears that we can out run them," Syd suggested.

Hand in hand, they raced around the lake, almost missing the turn back to the resort. It was Carly who noticed it, in the semi-darkness, correcting Syd when he insisted it was the wrong trail. She pointed out the lights in the distance once they had climbed away from the lake.

"See! Mr. Smarty."

"You're the smart one. You saved our lives."

"Just remember that," Carly grinned.

For the next twenty minutes, a fast walk was maintained in silence. Syd turned to Carly. "Almost there, love. How are you doing?"

"I'm getting a little tired, but not too tired for dancing."

"Dancing?"

"Yes, dancing. Remember?"

"How could I forget? Dancing. I'd love to," Syd feigned ecstasy.

"Oh, it won't be that bad. I'm tired too, but we won't stay out too late and anyway just think of me purring on your shoulder."

"Nice thought! Let's dance the night away." Syd danced down the trail. Carly danced behind him. Suddenly, Syd reached out and pulled Carly into his arms in a clumsy attempt to waltz along the trail, which was almost too dark to even walk on.

"No, no, we'll end up in the bushes. No...ha, ha! Oh! Ha. Ha. Careful!" Carly squealed as the two of them stumbled and tripped, blindly along. "I hope you can dance better than that to music."

"Much better. You'll see."

"I'll reserve my judgment."

A couple of minutes later the comical dance changed back to a brisk walk. Soon the lights from the resort made the going easier until they were out of the forest and onto the manicured lawn.

"Home, sweet home. Now for some dancing," Syd sang out.

"Some dancing lessons, maybe?" Carly kidded.

"You doubt me?" Syd asked.

"Not at all, you hunk." The joking continued until the door to their room closed behind them.

"Boy, am I pooped," Syd mumbled, as he flopped onto the bed, gesturing for Carly to follow.

"We can't. If we close our eyes, we'll never get dancing. Look at the time."

"Just for a few minutes?" Syd pleaded.

"No. You promised dancing, and dancing it will be. Now get into that shower."

"Yes, ma'am." Syd did as he was told. Carly surprised him when she entered the shower stall a couple of minutes later.

"Yielding to temptation, are you?" Syd laughed.

"No! Just getting clean and saving time," Carly answered, half joking. The hot water and soft aromatic soap started another round of sensuous play. But not for long.

Carly pushed Syd away.

"That's all for now," she said, with a grin on her face.

"What do you mean? I can't go dancing like this," Syd pointed to his erection.

"Maybe this will help," Carly offered. She stepped from the shower, reached back in, and turned the cold tap on full.

"Yeow! That's cold!" Syd leaped from the shower, almost knocking Carly off her feet.

"See, it's working already," Carly giggled.

Syd gave in. "You win. Let's go dancing."

"Thank you. We can play later." Carly kissed Syd on the cheek.

"It's going to be difficult, dancing while being all worked up." Syd griped.

"Oh! Just think of the anticipation, clinging to each other," Carly answered.

In their trendy evening clothes, they entered the hotel nightclub, with its large dance floor. The elegant room appeared to be about three quarters full with many of the couples dancing to the six-piece orchestra. The maitre d' showed them to a corner table where, once seated, a waiter took their order for wine.

Carly smiled at Syd.

"Think you can handle this?" she quipped.

"Come on and I'll show you." Syd pulled Carly to the dance floor where he showed her just what a smooth dancer he was. Carly did not realize that her smooth moves were helping him keep to her rhythm.

"My, you are graceful, love," Syd complimented.

"And you too. Had I known earlier, oh boy! Anyway, let's make up for lost time."

Dancing, sipping wine, talking and teasing took them well into early morning. In the small hours, the slow dances took on new meaning. Finally, during one very slow, romantic piece, Carly, clinging tightly to Syd, nuzzled his ear, "My man. My man. Take me to bed."

Syd felt bigger than life. "My beautiful girl. Of course."

The cumulation of the day's activities started to weigh heavily as they staggered back to their room. "Do you remember our room being this far away, love?" Syd asked.

"I think they moved it. That's what," Carly slurred, in her fuzzy condition.

"Yes, dear. You're absolutely right. They moved it. Well they can bloody well just move it right back," Syd bantered in an authorative voice, "We should complain to the management. The nerve of them, moving our room."

Then they both burst into giggles upon realizing they were standing in front of their room. "See they brought it back, thanks to me. They know who they're dealing with," Syd pontificated.

They entered the room and closed the door. After shedding some of their clothes, they stumbled into bed, where, after a feeble attempt to play, they fell fast asleep. In the morning, after making love, they fell asleep for two more hours. At eleven a.m., Carly playfully licked Syd's ear.

"Wake up, Doll. Look at the time." Then she rolled onto her back, arching into a luxurious, feline stretch. Turning back to Syd, one arm stroking his chest gently, she purred, "I'm so happy. My man, my man."

Syd melted. Life WAS good. He whispered softly, "Shall we shower?"

"Only if you promise to clean me all over," Carly giggled.

Syd nodded to that suggestion. "I promise! I promise! Let's go! Come on!" He leapt from the bed.

Soap, shampoo and kisses intermingled with hot water. Nothing was said. Nothing needed to be. As they dried off, Syd's inner glow paled as the same old doubtful thoughts penetrated his contentment. Would he be able to overcome Carly's defenses and find out what secret she is hiding? He must find out soon as he realized his future rested with this woman.

"Hello...come back, you're drifting." Carly broke his spell.

"Oh, I was, wasn't I? Sorry!"

"Not at all. Just a short trip? Did I interrupt?"

"Nothing important, love. Only a mental pinch to test all this happiness."

"I see," Carly scowled. "Don't go too deep, please. Just for me?"

Chastened again, Syd caught himself by pretending all was well. He faked cheerfulness. "Let's do lunch."

"You can do better than that; smarten up." Carly wasn't fooled.

"Sorry, love. The subject is closed, but I'm serious about lunch."

"That I can handle. Lunch it is."

Following a leisurely lunch on the outside patio, the swimming pool kept them occupied for the rest of the day and after that, a light snack before they packed their bags for the ride home. In the lobby, while Syd paid the bill, Carly again hid her face from the security cameras. This time Syd did not notice Carly's unusual activity. As they drove away from the resort grounds he attempted conversation.

"I hope you had as great a time as I did. We'll have to do it again."

"Uh. Yeah, again, soon." Carly's words trailed off as she lapsed into slumber, her seat tilted all the way back. Syd glanced over.

"You poor dear. You look so innocent sleeping there, but I know otherwise. Sleep on, my love. I shall deliver you home safely." Syd drove home in silence with the nagging questions keeping him awake, if not totally alert. The traffic close to town grew heavier, but not enough to keep Syd's mind off of Carly. Once home, she awoke long enough to stumble into the apartment, quickly prepare for bed and fall asleep. Syd, after taking his time cleaning up, climbed into bed next to her, where, knowing it was he and not Carly who would be getting up for work in the morning, still could not sleep. Who is this enticing creature beside him? He must find out, but how? The night eventually lulled him into semi-sleep, followed by a painful wakening. He kissed the sleeping beauty on her shoulder before leaving for work.

The weekend getaway did not supply Syd with any answers in his quest to understand Carly and her mysterious ways. As he navigated through the early morning traffic a conspicuous scowl creased his face where there should have been a happy smile.

Syd entered his office and Marty once again got the "Fuck Off" treatment. The wink from Syd told him it was in jest. He smiled and turned back to his desk, leaving Syd alone. Today, he would not get anything out of Syd. As he walked away, he mumbled to himself, "That boy had better stop partying or it will surely kill him. He looks so tired."

CHAPTER NINE

The next few weeks followed a more or less normal pattern. Sundays spent catching up on household chores or paperwork, such as bill paying. The occasional TV movie or in Syd's case a must-see game. Weeknight evenings had Syd either reading the paper or watching the TV news or sports; sometimes both at the same time. Carly was either studying or puttering around the house. Dinner was often on the table when Syd arrived home from work and he was starting to feel very comfortable, except for the nagging questions about Carly's past, which continually haunted him. With painful determination, he tried to avoid the subject.

As he read the newspaper, Syd would comment on articles he found interesting or amusing. Sometimes, he made things up, just to see if Carly was paying attention.

"Look, love! A man has just undergone an operation to have a donor hand attached to his arm after he lost his hand in an accident. Isn't that amazing?"

"Sure is! Science gallops on! What will we see next?"

"You know, I think they should attach a woman's hand to that fellow's arm."

Carly snapped to attention. "What the hell for?" she asked.

"For one thing, it would be more fun to masturbate." Syd laughed.

Carly shook her head. "Asshole! Just keep reading."

Syd laughed harder. A short time later he spotted another item, "Yes! Yes!"

Carly looked up, "Okay, now what?" She asked.

"They caught that child molester." Syd chimed.

"A lot of good that will do. He'll probably just get a slap on the wrist."

"Yes. Isn't that sad?" Syd agreed.

Carly expounded on a punishment she thought would be fitting. "They should give him the wire and fire treatment," she spit out.

"The what?" Syd asked.

"Wire and fire. First you take the guy to a small wooden building. Inside the building, you tie a piece of wire around his balls and attach the other end to a large bolt in the center of the room. Next, you spread dry hay all around the room, hand the guy a knife and set the hay on fire."

"Ouch! Carly! Kind of gives self-mutilation a whole new meaning, doesn't it?"

"Sure does! That'll fix the prick."

These exchanges were accompanied by little looks and gestures, followed by caresses and touching, which often led to good sex.

Thursday, Friday and Saturday evenings, Carly worked while Syd stayed home, rarely meeting with his friends at the Anchor. Slowly, he was settling into life where only he and Carly seemed to matter. He tried everything he could to gain her confidence enough to let him in on her innermost thoughts, but whenever he brought the subject of her past up, Carly, with her piercing stare, let him know, not yet.

Another thing that really bothered him was not having Carly's company away from the house. The same old excuse, "I'm not ready, please understand," kept his pestering to a minimum.

Syd tried. How he tried.

Into the eighth week, he arrived home from work and heard Carly singing an unfamiliar song.

"I'll have some fun

In the sun

In my garden

In my garden."

"What is that you're singing?" Syd asked. "I don't recognize it."

"I know you don't because you've never heard it before. It's my own song. I made it up."

"Interesting!"

"Syd. Sit down! I want to tell you something." Carly pointed to the couch.

Syd sat. Was Carly ready to open up? He crossed his fingers.

"I'm sitting. What's up?" he asked.

"I want to tell you about a secret place I go to sometimes when I want to be alone. I call it my garden."

"That is interesting. Where is it?"

"It's in the country, not too far from here. It's a refreshing and meaningful place for me. The air is so clear and it's like a whole other world. I am free, content and very happy when I am there."

"Sounds good. Do I get to see it?"

"Oh yes! I promise to take you there sometime. I promise."

"That's a deal, love. We have to go sometime. How about Sunday?"

"Not yet, but soon. Remember my muddy boots in the hall last week?"

"Yes."

"I lied to you. I didn't go the park. I went to my garden."

"I kind of got a feeling something wasn't quite right."

"I know, forgive me."

"There's nothing to forgive."

"I lied to you."

"Oh, that's just a little secret, no problem."

"Thank you."

During the next few weeks, Carly burst into song often, adding verses and changing verses as they came to her. One evening, as she sang, "In my garden, In my garden...."

Syd interrupted. "You're obsessed with that garden of yours, aren't you?"

"It's my safe place, sweetie. An important safe place just for me."

"When do I get to see it?" Syd asked.

"I'm still thinking that over. I want to enjoy it by myself a while longer. Maybe I shouldn't have told you about it." Carly's look said volumes. Syd knew the subject was closed. Not being able to spend time together in public was taking its toll and so another trip was planned to break up the monotony, but before that happened Syd brought up something interesting.

"I have a line on a new job, love."

"A new job? Tell me more."

"Another insurance company is searching for a few new managers. The word is they are looking for young, energetic employees to spur them into the future. And you know what? I think I qualify."

"Sounds like a great opportunity to me. Go for it!"

"Not so fast. I would have to relocate."

"Is this a problem?"

"The job is in Seattle."

"And that's a problem?"

"It is if I have to leave you."

"What makes you think I won't come with you?"

"You'd come to Seattle with me?"

"I've never been there before and from what I've heard, it's a lovely area, besides I can get work anywhere."

"Thank you. I'm so relieved. I think I'll throw my hat in the ring and take a run at it. Wish me luck."

Carly pulled Syd closer and kissed him softly. She whispered,

"Good luck, honey."

Her mind raced ahead. What perfect timing. So many things to think of, so much to do. "Get that job, Syd. Just get that job." She whispered to herself.

Syd noticed a change. "You seem delighted, love. What are you thinking?"

"Oh! Just the fact that sometimes circumstances and events seem to come along just when you need them."

Surprised at Carly's reactions to his announcement, he asked, "What do you mean? What's in this for you, besides a change of scenery?"

Carly tried to hide her glee. "Not a lot more than that. I really need a change and what better excuse than to support you in your upward mobility."

The words rang hollow to Syd, but considering the total mystery of Carly, he brushed it off. Maybe the west coast would bring them closer together, and Carly would feel free to let Syd explore her soul. He grasped at this possibility. Syd spent the next two days in his work cubicle preparing a resume, before he was satisfied with it. One evening, Carly assisted him in making a few significant changes. Syd agreed with the updates, then e-mailed the document to Northern Insurance, the aggressively expanding company. He crossed his fingers, and hoped for a positive reply. It was widely understood that the company was great to work for, so Syd figured, rightly, that many applications would be submitted. He waited patiently for a reply, which arrived more than three weeks later.

Good news. Syd had made the first cut. A few weeks later, a company representative arrived in town to conduct interviews of prospective candidates. Syd had marked his calendar with the date and time of his appointment with the recruiting officer ten days prior to the meeting, and he had used every spare minute leading up to that date to learn all he could about Northern Insurance's business, especially the company's goals. This research paid off handsomely for Syd during the interview. He left the company rep very impressed and the meeting was extended by a half hour while another nervous applicant fidgeted in the hallway outside the rented office. After this initial interview, events started to speed up between Syd and Northern Insurance. Two more high ranking Northern officials came to town specifically to meet with Syd. Each of them eagerly outlining the job opportunities available to employees at Northern, and the many benefits and perks.

One week following that interview, a junior vice president of Northern phoned Syd to tell him he was being considered for the position in Seattle, and that he was invited, at the company's expense, to travel to Seattle for a week of orientation and exposure to the area. When Syd told Carly, he was delighted to learn that she wanted to travel with him for this preview of life on the west coast, that would give them a good idea whether to make the move or not. He anticipated a big change in the relationship, imagining that all Carly needed was a change of scenery. He crossed his fingers.

Arrangements were made to leave for Seattle in two weeks time. Syd had enough time, banked from his job, to get away for a week. Carly had no trouble getting time off from her job; she simply told her boss to "fuck off" and was promptly fired. Syd laughed when he heard the details, but then got serious, asking Carly if she had not been presumptuous and whether she had enough funds put away to tide her over.

He was floored by her answer. "Something I didn't tell you, I get four thousand dollars a month for child support."

Syd gasped. "What? I don't understand. You've never had a baby."

"That's right. Isn't it strange?"

"I'm confused. Is this what you've been hiding all this time? Scared of getting caught?"

"Oh no! This is nothing."

"Nothing? Good God. What else is there?"

"Other things that don't concern you."

"So can you tell me about this child support?"

"Not really. It's just something I worked out."

"Where is the father in all this?"

"He is in a beautiful place and I'm sure he is very happy. Can we just drop this? Please."

"If you can't say anymore, I suppose so. It is kind of ironic that I spend all day chasing scammers, and here I am living with one."

"Don't make it sound so devious."

"But it is devious. Isn't it?"

"I don't think so. The father got what he wanted."

"Which is?"

"Lots of really good sex."

"And now he's paying."

"We all have to pay sometime."

"You scare me."

"I scare myself sometimes. Let's just drop it and have a nice evening."

"Okay, love, but you sure know how to keep things interesting."

Carly just snickered. Syd had trouble leaving the subject, 'What else is she hiding?' His torment showed.

Carly, secretly delighted in seeing him in agony, rubbed it in by humming to herself as she puttered around the apartment.

Northern supplied Syd with airline tickets, hotel reservations in downtown Seattle, as well as a credit account for meals and ground transportation expenses. But nothing prepared him for Carly.

One evening, she walked into the living room and asked for Syd's opinion, "Well?" She asked.

Syd jumped at the sight of her. "What the hell?" he stammered.

"Don't look so surprised. It's just a new look." Carly grinned.

"A new look? Is that all you call it? A new look? What

gives?"

"I just thought I needed a change to go along with the change of scenery. Know what I mean?"

While Syd was at work, a couple of days before their planned departure for Seattle, Carly had shortened her hair and lightened it by several shades, trimmed her finger nails, removed her jewelry, toned down her makeup and purchased some very plain clothes including fake eye glasses. This is how she greeted Syd on his arrival home that evening, almost giving him a heart attack.

"No. I don't know what you mean. Tell me," he demanded.

Carly looked him in the eye and answered.

"Look, stupid! We are going to Seattle to get you a very good job at Northern Insurance. We will be wined and dined by senior officers of that company."

"What has that got to do with your new look?"

"Are you completely dense? The last thing you need is for them to be distracted by some sex-pot in skin tight clothes with large tits. Now are you starting to get it?"

"Oh yeah! I guess that kind of makes sense. Sort of overdid it a bit, though. Don't you think?"

"Maybe just a little, but this can be our secret. Only you know what's really inside these clothes. Come here. Give me a smooch."

A few days later they flew to Seattle. Carly looked very plain while Syd looked a little confused. He had not bought into Carly's reasons for her changed appearance but knew better than to argue with her. The confusing mystery surrounding her deepened, but for now he would try to ignore the temptation to figure her out, as his thoughts focused on his own future. Carly and her ways would have to wait in line for his attention.

The approach to Sea-Tac airport was breathtaking.

Syd grasped Carly's hand.

"Do you feel what I feel?" Syd asked.

"What are YOU feeling?" Carly replied.

"I can't quite describe it. It's like...kind of like...this is where

I'm supposed to be."

"You mean like a good feeling?"

"Yes, that's it. A very good feeling. Like I'm making a good decision."

"You are making a good decision. We've gone through this a few times already, and now you're finally starting to realize that an interesting, fulfilling life requires you to take a large bite now and then to get the full benefit. I'm happy for you. Just go for it."

Syd stared into Carly's bright eyes and thought, 'What a lifesaver. What an attitude. Just walk through life, take a big bite, go for it, everything will work out. Some philosophy.' His mind raced ahead to a time when Carly would truly be a large part of his life. When he might finally understand her ways and their souls would intertwine.

"Where are you boy? You're drifting." Carly laughed.

Syd snapped awake, "Oh yeah! Just looking into the future, that's all. Thanks to you, it looks good."

"Don't get too far ahead. Your next assignment is to land that job. Understand?"

"Yes, ma'am! Understood."

The arrival terminal, luggage retrieval, taxi ride and hotel registration were boringly routine. For Syd, these events were blurred. The realization set in that his life was actually changing. The mental approach to the move had stirred up his emotions so much that, once in the hotel room, he flopped onto the bed feigning sexual pleasure.

"Yes! Yes! Yes!"

Carly jumped. "What's that all about?"

"I don't know, love. I'm just getting such a rush. Wow! Come over here."

Carly inched toward the bed. Syd pulled her down to him. "The excitement. Don't you feel it?"

"Excitement? We're in a mid-priced hotel in downtown Seattle. You haven't been getting out enough, have you?

Excitement, ha!"

Just as fast as the heady feeling had gripped Syd, it subsided when he suddenly understood something. While he felt his routine life was changing drastically, Carly was not a stranger to change. Why should she be excited? Carly embraced change. Change was foreign to Syd, and he was very grateful to have her by his side, helping him expand his horizons.

He tried to explain. "Sorry! I guess changing jobs and moving thousands of miles from home is routine for you. I'm kind of overwhelmed by it all."

"That's, okay. Settle down, relax. Everything is fine."

Carly pressed Syd's eyes shut and rubbed his temples. "Don't get me wrong. I'm enjoying myself immensely. We are going to have a great week, and you are going to get that job. So relax. That's it, relax." Carly snuggled into Syd. They dozed off.

Choosing to arrive in Seattle on a Friday, gave them the weekend to unwind and see some of the city. The evening snooze ended about nine p.m., when Carly poked Syd in the ribs, "Hey, mister! Want to go dancing?"

"What?" Syd was not fully awake.

"Just kidding! But I'll bet you're hungry."

"Safe bet, sweetie. What would you like to do?"

"Let's order some room service and watch TV. Is that okay?"

"Great idea. Let's see what's on the menu here."

They were in luck, the menu had a late evening selection and they were quickly able to choose. After phoning in the order, they propped themselves up in bed and began channel surfing. Groggy from travel and thinking of food kept their minds from absorbing most of the programs as they flashed on and off the screen. They settled on a noisy cop show until the food arrived. The gun fire and car chase hardly registered while they ate their food, still fully dressed, sitting up in bed. After the meal, each used the bathroom, undressed and returned to bed. Syd turned the TV off and they both got a good night's sleep.

In the morning, they woke up to a brilliant sunny day in Seattle. After soaking in the large double size tub, they left the hotel to find a quaint restaurant for breakfast, with plans to spend the rest of the day getting the feel for what may be their new home.

A nice little restaurant not far from the hotel looked inviting. Carly chose a table by the front window, giving them a view of the Saturday morning shoppers. Syd had picked up a tourist brochure from a hotel kiosk. After breakfast was ordered he shared the pages with Carly, looking for interesting things to do and see over the weekend.

He noticed that since leaving home, Carly seemed to be more outgoing, a little more fancy free. Maybe she really did need a change. He questioned why she still insisted wearing the fake glasses and plain clothes, when there were no company executives to impress. Carly's answer was that she wanted to feel natural in her new persona so that when the time came to meet the company representatives, she would disappear into the background, giving him all their attention. Syd did not find much substance in her answer, but knew it was pointless to pursue the matter. He would just have to be content and enjoy her company in her ugly clothes.

The breakfast was eaten in silence, and then they were on their way, hand in hand walking through downtown Seattle. Carly tilted her head back and sniffed the air.

"Oh! The air! So fresh! Isn't it crisp and clean?"

"That's what it is! The air. I couldn't figure out what was different. It's the air. Yes! You're right. It is wonderful!"

Carly gripped Syd's hand tighter and turned her head to meet his eyes. Syd grinned. "Nice glasses!"

Carly stuck her tongue out.

"Nice tongue!" Syd teased.

"Silly boy!" Carly laughed.

The mood was set. They were light-headed, light-hearted and free to play in this dynamic city until Syd's meetings on Monday. The setting was so enchanting that Syd almost forgot he was with the mysterious Carly, the girl with more questions than answers. The girl whose mind and thoughts he wished to explore as much as he had explored her body. The girl he felt so close to and yet so far away from. Even beautiful Seattle could not completely free him from the nagging, uneasy feelings that seemed to be constantly lurking subliminally in his mind. In this setting, with all its splendor, he was able to override the negative thoughts. He vowed to show Carly a great adventure, hoping it would lead to a future with stronger feelings and more openness on Carly's part.

"Hey! Hey! Hello!"

"What?"

"Hello! You're drifting again."

"Oh, Sorry! Just bouncing back and forth. So much happening, you know. I'll try not to let it happen again."

"You do that." Carly grinned. "By the way, where are we going?"

Syd had a plan, "If we head west on Pike St., we will come to the Pike Place Market area with its many interesting gift shops and eating places, and just past that is the waterfront with many other attractions waiting for us. How about it?"

"Why don't we just head north?" Carly asked.

"Okay. What's up there?"

"Not much. Just a couple of places I'd like to see."

"Like what?"

"Oh! Nordstrom, Bon Marche."

"What? Shopping?"

"Just kidding! But be warned. I am programmed. I like your idea. Let's go to the waterfront."

At Pike St., they turned toward the waterfront. Carly ignored Syd's shopping jokes as they passed Nordstrom. Then, with a joke of her own, she pretended to be pulled across the road by a powerful magnet. Syd dragged her to safety, saving her from the nasty shopping monster. The teasing continued to the end of Pike St., where the shops consumed a couple of hours before they headed over to Pier 57 and a ride on the carousel. The afternoon was taken up by browsing, sampling fudge and candy, and a stop on a warm bench to view the busy water traffic. Then it was on to Pier 56 for seafood. As they sat staring at the busy waterfront, from the cozy table that good fortune had steered them to, all their cares seemed to disappear.

Carly raised a glass of wine. "Life is good!"

Syd raised his glass. "I'm so glad you enjoyed your day!"

"An understatement, sweetie. I am overjoyed. All that enlivening artwork and the quaintness, and, look at that, even the sun doesn't want to leave."

Syd looked to the west. "Isn't that something? Just hanging there for us."

Syd had ordered a platter of seafood for two, containing samples of different offerings from the ocean. Very little was said while the food was enjoyed, then Carly suggested they start making their way back to the hotel.

"Shall we take a taxi?" Syd asked.

"No! You wimp. Let's walk. You can walk back. Can't you?"

"Of course. I was thinking of you."

"You just worry about yourself, and try to keep up." Carly laughed.

They walked up the steps to University St. and slowly back to the hotel. At the entrance to the lobby, Carly grabbed Syd by the shoulders.

"I'll admit I'm tired if you will." She confessed.

Syd agreed.

"Thank God! Of course, I'm tired. We have been walking and gawking all day and breathing in that sea air. Yes, I'm tired. But it's a good tired. Not exhausting. Just tired! I can't really explain it."

"I feel the same. Almost like I accomplished something. Where's that bed? Oh! I almost forgot. Remember that live show and dancing we planned?"

"Vaguely."

"Fuck it!"

"Good girl! Let's find that bed."

They took the elevator up to their floor and walked down the hall to their room, where it didn't take long for them to undress, cleanup and climb into bed. Propped up on pillows, they flicked through the TV channels.

Carly questioned, "If we find something to watch, do you think we will be able to stay awake?"

"I really don't know. What I do know, is that it will have to be damn good."

"That's right! Keep pushing that button. So far, I haven't seen anything even close to damn good."

"I suppose you'd like something on the Russian revolution or building the pyramids or maybe raising Mongolian goats."

"Yes! Yes! Do you think you can find something like that?" Carly played along with Syd's sarcastic suggestion.

"I was just joking."

"Ha! Ha! Got you. I'm not studying this week, so find a good movie."

They settled on an old classic movie but fell asleep before the end. Syd rolled over at 3 a.m. and turned off the TV. The room remained silent until 8:20 a.m. when Carly woke Syd by caressing his genitals. After making love, they lingered in the soaker tub to ease the aches from the previous day's walk and then left the hotel for another tour of the enchanting seaside city. At breakfast, in a different restaurant than the day before, armed with more brochures, they decided to take the Monorail to the Seattle Center. Carly mentioned several times that the Pacific Science Center was calling her. The way she said it, told Syd that the Science Center is probably where they would spend a large part of the day.

"The Science Center?" he asked.

"Yes. You don't sound enthusiastic."

"It's just that it's such a nice day, kind of a shame to spend it indoors."

"I know. I thought of that myself. How about just a couple of hours?" Carly pleaded.

Syd caved. "Sounds good. Let's do it."

Syd knew when to shut up. After eating a tasty breakfast, they rode the Monorail to the Seattle Center where they took the elevator to the observation deck of the Space Needle. Carly grasped Syd's hand as she gazed across the city.

"Oh! I never imagined. Get that job, Syd. I think I'll like it here."

Syd agreed. The panorama before them had a mesmerizing effect. "A great job in this energizing city, you by my side. What am I doing right, sweetie?"

"Everything, everything!"

The enchanting view, in all directions, kept them busy for more than an hour, as they absorbed the images of city, mountains, and water and the blending of these images as if they belonged to a living quilt. Carly kissed Syd before asking,

"Can I talk you into taking me to the Science Center mister?"

"Not a problem, love. Let's go."

One last look and they reluctantly descended to ground level.

Carly mused. "Funny! Feels like returning from a trip. Doesn't it?"

"Yeah! Sure does. Almost like a different dimension. I'd say."

"That's it, a different dimension. Way up high. Inspecting everything. Hey you down there, we're watching you," she laughed. Syd clasped her hand for the short stroll to the Science Center. Inside, Syd took a back seat to the exhibits, as he watched, in fascination, Carly's interest and knowledge of the presentations. He was impressed with her ability to carry on technical conversations with the attending staff members and more impressed when she offered up additional information and corrections without appearing overbearing. This was her world, learning. After about an hour of gadgets, heat, cold, wind, water, geology, biology, pictures, charts, graphs and various other hands-on and hands-off displays, Carly turned to Syd and pulled him into a quiet corner.

"I'm sorry! I didn't mean to ignore you. It's all so...interesting."

"Not at all, love. On the contrary, I'm practically speechless. I know you're smart, but this...You should be running this place."

"Not so fast. There are far more qualified people in charge here than I'll ever be. The attendants are mostly students; albeit very bright students. But I can't get over how much attention they are giving me. It's almost as though they know I'm smart."

"Don't get it, do you?" Syd asked.

"Don't get what?"

"Have you forgotten? Look in the mirror, Miss Librarian."

"Oh shit! Of course. How silly! Ha, Ha! That's a good one. I wonder how they'd treat me in my regular clothes."

"I'd say they would probably speak slower and use smaller words."

"Isn't that the truth? And stare."

This set them off on a giggling tangent. Minutes later, when they had settled down a bit, Carly said that she had noticed a change of attitude toward her from the general public. At first it concerned her until she realized it was her appearance.

"Funny how we gauge people. Isn't it?" she asked.

"How do you mean?" Syd answered with a question.

"Just that all our experiences program us to expect a certain behavior to be part of a particular look, and when we are confronted by an exception, we are confused."

"That makes sense. I think if you came in here in your skin tight pants and your boobs hanging out, you'd confuse them a bit, especially when you started telling them how a satellite orbits the globe or how soil is formed."

Now they giggled and laughed harder than before, causing other patrons to stare.

"Look! They're confused. See what you've started." Syd managed to say, in between chuckles.

The laughing continued until a little dignity set in.

Carly tried to get them back on track, "Can you put up with my brain for another half hour?"

"No problem. What do you have in mind?"

"I'd like to see some more space-related items. Is that okay?"

"I'd like to see them too. Let's go!"

Forty minutes later, after viewing several very interesting space exhibits, they stepped outside into the afternoon sunshine. Carly vowed to return sometime alone. Syd did not doubt her at all. He felt her hand tighten on his.

Carly appreciated Syd's patience. "Thank you for hanging in with me," she gushed.

"You don't have to thank me, love. I enjoyed every bit of it."

"I hope you're not just saying that."

"I really mean it. Now I wonder if there's an insurance museum around here."

"Asshole!"

"Hey! Hey!"

"Sorry! What should we do next?"

"I'm hungry! Aren't you?"

"Now that you mention it."

Not far from the Space Center, a cute bistro beckoned, where they enjoyed a quick snack before heading west to the waterfront, and a scenic streetcar ride along the harbor side. They transferred to a city bus and returned to their hotel by early evening. Syd purchased a newspaper in the lobby, indicating to Carly that he would be doing little else for the rest of the day, except for putting his feet up. Carly agreed with him. The room was a welcome sight for them and their tired feet. Before he plopped down to catch up on the news, Syd laid out his business suit for Monday morning's important meetings. A couple of hours later, the light was turned off and replenishing sleep carried them to morning.

"Good morning and good luck," Carly whispered, as she snuggled into Syd. Morning light, streaming through the window, had woken her before the hotel wakeup call.

"Thank you, love. I don't know how much luck I'll need. I'm feeling very confident right now."

"That's my guy!" Carly squealed.

Syd stretched and hopped out of bed, "Join me for breakfast?"

"Can we just order room service? I don't feel like getting dressed yet."

"Good idea. Would you put in my order please? Poached and bacon, thank you."

Carly phoned for room service, Syd entered the shower. A short time later, as she sat by the window overlooking the busy street, Carly remarked on Syd's appearance.

"You look so good! I would hire you myself."

"Thank you! You look great yourself."

"Like this?" Carly had brushed her teeth, splashed water on her face and put on the hotel robe.

"Yes, just like that. If I didn't have to go to work..."

They kissed just as the food arrived. Touching, giggling and eating: for them, the day was starting out great. Syd crossed his fingers to help keep the upbeat feelings going for the rest of the day. "Are you going to be all right by yourself today?" He asked.

"All right? All right? Are you kidding? All right? I'm going shopping. Of course, I'm going to be alright. Am I female? Is this a credit card? Wooee! Watch me go."

Syd corrected himself, "Silly me. Is Seattle going to be all right?"

"Oh! I think Seattle will be okay. But they may have to restock the shelves."

"No doubt! Anyway, I must be going. Have fun. See you later!"

"Good luck! See you tonight."

Syd kissed Carly lightly, then quickly left the hotel, hailed a taxi and was on his way to Northern Insurance for his first meeting with Ron Morrison, Regional Manager for the North Western States.

In the lobby of the Northern Insurance building, he straightened his tie and addressed the receptionist, "Hello, my name is Syd Barnes. I have an appointment with Mr. Morrison this morning."

"Mr. Barnes, I'll call up for you." The receptionist called up to Ron Morrison's secretary, then instructed Syd to take the elevator up to office number eleven twenty-two. Syd thanked the receptionist and took an elevator to office eleven twenty-two where the secretary asked him to take a seat for a few minutes. Ten minutes later a tall, thin, very elegantly dressed gentleman approached Syd.

"Mr. Barnes?" he asked.

"Yes!" Syd almost bounced out of his chair.

"I'm Ron Morrison. We finally get to meet. How was your trip?"

"Good…Great!"

"Glad to hear it. Sometimes business travel can be a pain. Welcome to Seattle."

"Thank you. I'm happy to be here."

"Good! Let's go into my office. I'd like to go over a few things with you and also lay out the rest of the week."

Ron Morrison steered Syd through his office to a corner lounge area complete with bar and fridge. He pushed a button on his phone. A female voice answered, "Hello, Marge here."

"Marge, would you bring some coffee in here please?"

"Anything you want."

"Anything?" Ron joked.

"Oh! Maybe not." Marge giggled, "Be right there."

"Thank you." Ron pushed the off button on the phone then pointed to three couches angled around a broad coffee table, "Plunk yourself down, Syd. Would you like some coffee? This place runs on coffee, I swear. Perhaps you'd like something else. Tea? Juice?"

"No, thank you. Coffee is fine," Syd answered.

Ron Morrison continued his introduction. "Marge will be here shortly. I don't know what I'd do without her. She's been here over twenty years, a few years longer than me. She's smart as a whip. If you want to know what's going on, ask Marge. She's my executive assistant, keeps the whole office humming along. A long time ago, I tried to stop her from making the coffee but she wouldn't hear of it. She says it gives her a little break from the pressures in the office and a chance to joke around with the staff. So you see we serve very expensive coffee here." He laughed out loud as he eased himself onto a couch opposite Syd.

"Now Syd, as far as your qualifications go, they're as good as we expected and then some. I see you've taken lots of outside courses. I am impressed with your marks but I'm puzzled by the fact you've stayed in your present job so long. Can you tell me why?"

"That's a difficult question to answer, Mr. Morrison."

"Call me Ron."

"Thank you, Ron. I really enjoy my job at Metro. I can get out of the office a lot and I get to work with law enforcement and the justice system. At times, it can get quite exciting. As far as advancement goes, very few positions come available at Metro, and when an attractive job does open up, management fills it with outside help."

"Like what I'm doing right now?"

"Oh! Yes, I guess it's just like this." Syd agreed.

Ron Morrison clarified his employee search. "It isn't as though we didn't try internally. We canvassed the whole company but only managed to fill a few spots. The truth is we need new blood, new ideas. Being in the fear business right now is frantic and we want to keep up by supplying the best service we can. That's why you're here. I hope you can help us achieve our goals."

"Thank you. I'd certainly like the opportunity."

Just then, Marge entered the room, pushing a rolling cart laden with steaming coffee, cream, cups and sugar. "Here's your coffee, Ron," she announced.

"Thank you, Marge." Ron got to his feet, Syd followed. "This is Syd Barnes, Marge. He's one of the candidates I'm meeting with."

Marge shook Syd's hand, and then took a step back, slowly studying him from feet to head. Licking her lips, she gave her opinion. "Yum! Keep this one," she laughed, then continued, "Sinclair called, said he had that settlement ready. I told him not to bother, we don't need it."

"WHAT! That's almost a half million dollars."

"Oh! Maybe I didn't tell him that. It'll be on your desk tomorrow morning."

"Get out of here." Ron pointed to the door.

Syd caught the joke. They all laughed, and Marge left as quickly as she had entered.

"That's Marge! Quite a girl, getting money out of Sinclair. Wow! That's something! Remind me to commend her. Here, help yourself to coffee."

Syd poured coffee for both of them. As they sipped, the conversation drifted around, covering different topics from sports personalities, office politics, west coast weather and back to Northern Insurance. All the while Ron was assessing Syd. Then, as noon approached, he told Syd the lunch arrangement, "We're meeting Jim Gordon, the major accounts general manager. He wants to meet you."

Syd glanced at his watch. "Holy cow! Where did the morning go?"

"Time goes by much faster in Seattle, Syd," Ron answered, as he gestured toward the door. A table was waiting in the small upscale restaurant across from the Northern building. The layout inside allowed for maximum privacy for the principal group of customers, business people. Jim Gordon was already seated when they arrived. He rose to greet them.

Ron introduced Syd to Jim, "Morning Jim, I'd like you to meet one of our prime candidates, Syd Barnes."

Jim shook Syd's hand. "Good morning, Syd. Please sit down."

"Morning Ron. How's Monday going for you?"

"It would be a little better if the weather wasn't so damn nice. I should be out fishing. Look at that sunshine out there."

"Yes, I know how you feel. Get out on the weekend?"

"Saturday morning. Picked up a nice spring salmon. It's in the freezer as we speak." Ron turned to Syd, "Done much fishing, Syd?"

"Not lately, Ron. When I was a kid I fished a few streams and lakes but never in the ocean. It sounds like something I should look forward to."

"You will probably enjoy it. There's nothing better tasting than a fresh salmon, stuffed with spices and lightly barbecued. It's to die for. In this area, some days you can fish, golf and ski on the same day. We're so lucky. Have I got your attention?"

"Count me in. Where do I sign?"

"At a boy! Jim how was your weekend?"

"Same old! Kids' ballgame, kids' soccer game. Great weekend but too short. There should be a law against sunshine on Mondays." Jim put his hands together in mock prayer and bowed toward Ron. "Don't get me wrong. I love coming to work, Ron."

Ron turned to Syd. "Let's ignore him. Here! Have a look at the menu."

Syd's eyebrows lifted when he saw the variety and quality of dishes presented, as he turned the pages. "It's only lunchtime," he thought.

Ron spoke up. "You look impressed. We call this the 'Closing Room.' So many deals are hammered out in here, we're thinking of offering the chef a percentage."

They made their food choices. Ron and Syd ordered wine and

Jim ordered a beer. The conversation remained on topics other than work except for a couple of items Jim offered up to Ron. When the food arrived the talk faded to praises for the chef. After the meal, Ron ordered a large pot of coffee and, almost as though a bell had been rung, steered them back to business. Syd noticed Jim heeding the leader and felt himself sitting a little straighter. Ron and Jim took turns explaining the local Northern territory, the various departments of Northern, some of the current problems they faced, their past successes and their goals for the future. The one constant theme was the emphasis on the strategic advantage Northern had over other insurance companies: Knowledge, enthusiasm and service supplied by the best employees in the business. Syd could feel the energy. Just before mid-afternoon, they went back across the street to Northern. Ron took the elevator back to his office, and Jim steered Syd to a magnificent curved staircase that led to a mezzanine floor housing the new accounts department. These stairs afforded easy access to potential clients. In Jim's office, a glassed-in corner, Syd paid attention as Jim produced charts and graphs showing market share of the various business segments related to Northern. He emphasized the potential for insurance growth within these specific segments, where Northern wants to advance in the most lucrative areas, and how they expect to achieve those goals. As he introduced each new piece of information, he asked Syd to provide insight from his perspective and experience. Syd was impressed with Jim's ability to define Northern's targets so clearly, and he in turn left no doubt as to his understanding of the insurance business and the world of commerce in general. Jim had some calls to make, so, very happy with the day's progress, told Syd to…"Go out in the sunshine, but be prepared for a busy day tomorrow. See you here at nine a.m. Thank you!"

Syd floated out to the street, and took a taxi back to the hotel, arriving a full hour before Carly. When she did get to the room, he helped a bellhop drag several large bags and boxes in from the hallway. The bellhop looked at Syd, shook his head and left. Carly kissed Syd.

"You can see I had a good day. How was yours?"

"Couldn't have gone better. Just fabulous. Let's see what you bought."

"Okay! Boy did I ever make some good deals today. I just happened to catch some great sales. Here, take a look." Carly started emptying the cartons and bags onto the bed, Syd sat at the small table by the window. Two pairs of pants, one pair of designer jeans, two silk blouses, a pair of boots, one sweater and a mix of sexy under garments spilled out of their containers.

"Wow! You'll never have to shop again, love."

"Are you kidding? I can't wait till tomorrow. Here, I'll model for you." As Carly undressed, she described her shopping experience.

"Remember the reaction I got from the staff at the Science Center?"

"Yes, I do."

"The same thing happened today. Slightly differently."

"How do you mean?"

"The sales clerks kept steering me to the plain clothes or the business suits. They couldn't understand why I was buying the fancy clothes. One poor girl asked me if I really wanted such a radical change. I had to keep myself from laughing. Then I really baffled them when I tried some of the outfits on. I kind of confused them a little. One good thing about looking like this, I was able to play the poor school teacher and got some better deals. Apparently, when you look like a million bucks, that's what they think you can afford. So even I can learn new tricks."

As she spoke, Carly had changed into one new pair of tight pants and a low-cut blouse. "How do you like me now?" She pranced over to Syd.

"Awesome, sweetie. Awesome. My girl is back."

"I may not wear them this week, but when we get back home I

certainly will." Carly modeled all the clothes for Syd, getting his full approval for each item and a well done for the good deals. Wearing the last of her purchases, a matching push-up bra and thong, she plunked herself down on Syd's knee and purred into his ear, "I need a hot bath. How about you?"

"I was thinking that myself." He smiled, ear to ear.

"Great!"

With Syd following her retreating rear, Carly skipped into the bathroom to fill the tub. After a refreshing soak, they made love then dressed to go to dinner. A short while later, they left the hotel and strolled hand in hand down the sidewalk. A cozy restaurant, not far from the hotel, had an appealing menu posted in the window. Syd was enticed by the selection. "Looks good to me. How about you?"

Carly patted her stomach. "I'm starved. Let's go!"

The head waiter showed them to a small table at the rear, and after they had placed their order, Carly asked Syd about his meetings that day. He told her about his confidence in his qualifications for the job and his enthusiasm for the attitude and plans at Northern and also, if the rest of the management were anything like Ron and Jim, it must be a terrific place to work. Carly congratulated Syd and kissed his cheek just as the food arrived. The talk turned to light banter as they ate, mostly about the distinctive weather and flavorsome meal. The hot soak, good sex, great food, Carly's shopping and Syd's meetings had taken their toll. By the end of the meal, both were ready for bed. They sauntered back to the hotel, where, before sleep overtook him, Syd phoned for a wakeup call. They slept soundly.

The phone woke Syd. He picked up the receiver.

"Six thirty, Mr. Barnes." A voice boomed out.

"Thank you," Syd answered, as he clumsily replaced the receiver. Carly didn't move; Syd gave her a playful shake. "Are you awake?" he asked.

"What time is it?" she answered with a question, not even

opening her eyes.

"Six thirty."

Still not opening her eyes, Carly replied, "SIX THIRTY! Are you crazy? Six thirty. What does it look like? I've never seen it. Six thirty…God!" She pulled a pillow over her head.

Syd laughed. "Oh! Sorry!" Then he showered and prepared himself for another interesting day at Northern Insurance. Before leaving the room, he kissed Carly on the cheek. "Bye, love! Have a good day!"

Carly rolled over. "I will. More shopping you know."

"Good girl! Go get 'em! See you later." He headed for his second day at Northern, arriving early for his appointment with Jim Gordon. Jim poured a cup of coffee for Syd, then briefed him about the day's activities. The morning would commence at nine thirty, with Syd meeting the accounts managers at the start of their weekly meeting. Then Syd would get a tour of the complete regional headquarters building. When they had finished their coffee, Jim led Syd to a large meeting room and introduced him to the accounts managers, who were already seated at a large table. Leaving the accounts managers to continue their meeting, Jim started the building tour by introducing Syd to most of the department managers who were available in the building. The layout, efficiency and dove-tailing between departments continued to impress Syd, as the tour moved from the ground floor reception area, to the executive suites and boardroom at the top of the building. The only dedicated office on the top floor was occupied by Arny Holt, North Pacific States Vice President, who was away on business. A cluster of offices adjacent to Mr. Holt's were shared by other company officers and executives when they were in town. At lunch time, Jim and Syd ate in the funky company cafeteria on the second floor. Syd remarked on the quality and selection of food, obviously prepared by a competent staff. One thing that he couldn't miss noticing, was the attitude of the other company employees enjoying lunch in the brightly lit room. It seemed to

Syd, happiness and enthusiasm were contagious in this building. He knew he would be at home here. After they had finished eating, Jim escorted Syd to Ron Morrison's office where Syd and Ron spent a couple of hours going over the duties and responsibilities associated with the position Syd was being groomed for, a territorial manager in the quickly expanding marketing and sales department. Very satisfied with Syd's knowledge and intelligent questions and answers, Ron offered Syd the job. Syd readily accepted. Papers were produced and signed, and after giving his enthusiastic congratulations, Ron invited Syd to join him for a quick tour of some outlying offices in the morning. Syd liked that idea and agreed to meet in Ron's office in the morning. Ron walked Syd to his office door, wished him a good evening and remarked that he looked forward to meeting Syd in the morning. Syd left the building in high spirits.

He arrived back at the hotel shortly after Carly.

"So! Where are all the parcels?" he asked.

"No parcels today," Carly answered.

"I'll call a doctor. You must be sick."

"No! Too busy to shop."

Syd moved toward a chair. "Let me sit down. I must hear this."

"Not much to hear, I'm afraid. I went back to the Science Center and then to a museum, and now here I am. How was your day?"

"I had a very good day, thank you! I got the job!"

"That's wonderful! Are you taking me out to dinner to celebrate?" Carly asked.

"Love to! Let's go."

They cleaned up, changed clothes and left the hotel in search of an interesting place to eat. A few blocks from the hotel, after they had surveyed and passed up several others, a nice restaurant enticed them inside. As they enjoyed a delicious meal the conversation alternated from Carly's knowledge filled day at the

Science Center and museum, to Syd's busy day signing papers and touring the company. The meal finished, a slow, hand in hand walk took them back to the hotel. Before going to bed, Syd sat at the small table reading the daily newspaper, Carly sat on the bed flicking through the TV channels. In the next hour, Syd brought several items to Carly's attention.

One in particular, "I don't believe it! Senator Levitz calling Senator Davies corrupt. That's absurd. Doesn't he know his own record?"

Carly perked up. "That is absurd. Talk about the pot calling the kettle black. Wow! A classic case of …. 'People who live in glass houses shouldn't throw stones.' Wouldn't you say?"

Syd couldn't resist. He answered, "If you ask me, I think people who live in glass houses, should fuck in the basement."

"Asshole! Time for bed. Right now!"

"Yes, ma'am."

Sleep took them to morning. Before he left the room, Syd told Carly they were invited to dinner that evening, with Jim and Ron and their wives. Carly said she looked forward to meeting them, after a day of shopping, of course.

Out on the street, Syd, once again, looked forward to a day at Northern Insurance as his mind continued to compare Northern with Metro. He couldn't pin down any one reason why Northern had a different feeling than Metro. It just did. The employees, management and the overall efficiency and enthusiasm seemed to consume him each time he was on the premises, just as now, when he walked through the front door on his way to meet Ron Morrison. In Ron's office, Syd sipped coffee while Ron finished a phone call. The call was completed in a couple of minutes, and Ron sat down across from Syd to go over the day's agenda. Ron had it planned to travel south to Tacoma for a visit with a couple of agents in that area and meet a major customer for lunch. After lunch, they would head north toward Everett to see another agent and visit a branch office, then back to the main building. Ron had reserved a company car and driver for the day, his preferred way to travel when he was with clients or coworkers. He led Syd to the waiting car in the company garage and indicated for Syd to enter by the left rear door while he got in the right rear door. Syd was surprised to see that the rear seat was divided by a work table, complete with wireless computer and telephone, which now separated him from Ron. The driver was instructed to drive to an address in Tacoma. As they traveled and talked, Ron fielded calls and took care of necessary business in a seamless style that impressed Syd.

No wasted time here, he thought. The morning went by quickly with a visit to two of Northern's agents again impressing Syd with the friendly, knowledgeable and cooperative service shown to customers and between staff members. Syd wondered if the whole west coast was as genuinely friendly as the people he had met at Northern.

Next, Syd and Ron met a special client, Harold Inness, at his favorite restaurant for lunch. Harold, a builder-developer for many years, had been a customer of Northern for almost as long as he had been in business. Today, with a few projects on the go, he and Ron would discuss his plans for the coming year. He liked to stay ahead of the curve. They met in the foyer of the restaurant, and were soon escorted to and seated at a secluded table in the rear of the restaurant. Food was ordered and after a short, three way ice-breaking conversation, Harold elaborated in great detail his plans for the rest of the year and into the next. Ron enjoyed any meeting with Harold. Over and above the insurance business he generated directly for Northern, he seldom missed the mark for future growth, providing the why, where and when with deadly accuracy. For Ron, the chance to distribute these gems throughout Northern helped keep the company on top. Syd sat entranced by Harold's quick mind. He was a man who could look at several rows of figures and instantly know the story they told. When the meal was over, Syd and Ron said their goodbyes to Harold and headed north through Seattle. Ron had not taken any notes during his conversation with Harold Inness, but now, in the car, he brought up the file for Harold's company on the computer and entered all the facts and figures from the lunch time meeting. He then proceeded to cross reference the information to other files that may be useful in the future.

Happy with the meeting, Ron expressed his admiration for Harold Inness, "He's a hard man to keep up with, Syd."

"I can see that. You must be glad he's on your side."

"I sure am. He's a treasured client and a great friend. An asset to the community."

North of Seattle, they spent a half hour with an agent of the company and forty-five minutes in a branch office before heading back into Seattle. Ron instructed the driver to stop at Syd's hotel. Syd and Ron exited the car and stood in the sunshine at the entrance to the hotel. Shaking Syd's hand, Ron commented on the day, "I hope you enjoyed the day as much as I did, Syd."

"Thank you. I did. I found it very informative and invigorating."

"Glad to hear it. Dinner's at seven at the Chalice. See you then."

"Thank you. We are looking forward to it. Seven it is."

Ron headed back to the office, Syd danced into the hotel, picking up a newspaper on his way to the room. Carly was lying on the bed, watching TV when Syd entered.

"So! How was Northern today?"

"Just great! Thank you. Quality, quality, quality everywhere and fun. I had a great day. How about you?"

"I had a fun day, sweetie. Went for a nice walk down to the pier, had a delicious lunch outside and walked back. Fabulous weather, isn't it?"

"Sure is. What happened to the shopping?"

"Sad to say, but I'm kind of shopped out, but don't worry, I'm sure it's only temporary. What time is dinner?"

"Seven o'clock. We have lots of time."

"Good! Get over here!"

Syd warmed to Carly's invitation, slowly shedding his clothes in a mock strip-tease as he inched toward the bed, while Carly stripped and tossed her garments to the floor. They made love before getting ready for the dinner date. When they had dressed, Syd was disappointed to see that Carly had made herself even less attractive than she had looked all week. He thought she would do the opposite for tonight's dinner; spruce up a little and use her good looks to charm Ron and Jim.

"Are you sure you want to go out to dinner looking like that, love?" he asked.

"Yes. Trust me. The wives will be reading me intensely. Any perceived threat to them may go against you, so let's keep it all business, if you don't mind."

"Okay, if you say so, but I can't wait to see the real Carly."

"You will when we get home tomorrow. I'll start wearing some of these new clothes, and get a sexy, new hairdo. Think you can wait?"

"One day? No problem!"

Carly kissed Syd lightly and they made their way down to the street where a waiting taxi took them to the Chalice. Ron and Jim, with their wives, had just arrived at the door, when Syd and Carly showed up. They entered the restaurant, introductions were made, and the head waiter escorted them to a large, round table in a far corner of the restaurant. Carly was right, the ladies, both elegantly dressed, tried hard to conceal their delight to outshine her. If this bothered Carly, it didn't show.

Wine and food was ordered and the men launched into sports talk, travel talk and a little business while the two wives wasted no time testing Carly, to determine if she would meet their standards socially or intellectually. Syd went into a juggling act, trying to indulge in intelligent conversation with Jim and Ron while listening to the grilling of Carly. A couple of times, he wanted to reach over and give her a shake when she pretended to know very little about a certain subject. He knew she was allowing the women to feel superior to her, but did she have to let them think she was stupid? He apologized a couple of times to Ron for lapses in the conversation, then decided to forget Carly and the women and give his full attention to Ron and Jim. He would talk to Carly later.

The meal was excellent. When it was finished, Ron took Syd aside and again congratulated him for joining Northern and that he looked forward to working with him. Goodbyes were exchanged, and Ron invited Syd to go home and start preparing for the move.

Syd thanked him and expressed his desire to become a valued employee at Northern Insurance.

He and Carly climbed into a taxi in front of the restaurant for a very quiet ride to the hotel, but once they were back in their room, he exploded.

"Did you really want those ladies to think you're so dense?" He spat out.

"I guess I did play the bimbo up a bit, didn't I? I couldn't help myself. They were trying so hard to upstage me. I enjoyed myself."

"You embarrassed me."

"I'm sorry. Over time they'll get to know me, but for now they'll probably just forget this little meeting and get on with their lives."

"I hope so."

"Can we forget it, please? You made a favorable impression and that's what counts. We'd better get some sleep. We have a plane to catch in the morning."

"You're right. Let's get some sleep. It's been a busy week. I'll be glad to get home."

They slept well. Early the next morning they flew out of Seattle, looking forward to returning soon to make it their new home.

CHAPTER TEN

The busy week and exhausting flight home finally caught up to Syd and Carly late Thursday evening, when they reached their front door. Luggage plugged the entrance hallway until noon Friday when Syd, after a good sleep, carted it into the bedroom for unpacking. The rest of Friday and all day Saturday and Sunday were spent sorting, packing, making lists and planning, especially for Syd. His mind was concentrated on his Monday morning resignation from Metro. Coworker consensus was that Syd would be there for life. Now, he wondered what the reaction would be to his leaving.

Monday morning, in the office, Marty hovered nearby waiting for a sign that Syd had noticed him. Figuring Marty had endured enough suspense, Syd finally looked up and smiled. Marty glided closer.

"Hi, stranger. I missed you," he chirped.

"That's nice. I didn't miss you," Syd sarcastically answered.

"Tell me about your trip. Anything juicy to report?"

"Nothing juicy, Marty. Sorry! However I did have a good time and you might say a life-changing event."

"Really? I have to hear this."

"Before the end of the day you probably will, but not from me. One thing I can tell you, I have a girlfriend."

"I knew it. These last few months you have confused me. Now it all makes sense. Congratulations!"

"Thank you. Now you can Fuck Off, Marty. I have work to do."

Marty knew there was much more to Syd's story, but he also knew it was time to retreat. Syd smiled at Marty's back as the distance between them grew, content to once again pre-occupy Marty's thoughts. Now he turned to a task that had been occupying his own thoughts: quitting his job.

Although he had already prepared several drafts of a letter of resignation, it still took him more than an hour to create a presentable document. He wasn't completely satisfied with it but it would have to do. He had never had to resign from employment before and found the process draining. A feeling of loss swept over him. What he had thought would be an easy task – giving the finger to Metro – was turning out to be very difficult. After re-reading the letter one last time, Syd folded it twice, placed it in an envelope and headed to his boss, Lorne Unger's office. Lorne, the claims department supervisor, already had Murray York, the head personnel officer, with him when Syd arrived.

"Good morning, Syd!"

"Good morning, Lorne, Murray!"

"Have a seat, Syd."

"Thanks, Lorne."

Syd handed the envelope to Lorne, and then sat at a small table opposite Murray York. Lorne Unger remained standing as he read Syd's letter. When he had finished, he looked directly at Syd.

"So the rumors are true then?" He surmised.

"Yes sir! I didn't think the secret would last."

"It wasn't much of a secret Syd. We knew Northern was fishing and your name appeared a couple of times in conversation, nothing specific. Beyond that all I can say is you have done some good work here and we'll miss you. Murray will go over your file with you to help clear your severance, and I'd like to work with you to clean up any loose ends on your accounts. What time frame did you have in mind?"

"I haven't given Northern a date Lorne, so I can finish my work here, thank you."

"How about two weeks, Syd?"

"That should be enough time."

"Good! One more thing, do you think you're making the right move?"

"Thanks for asking. I have given it lots of thought and not only the job but relocating. A lot of thought, Lorne. And I'm finally starting to feel more relaxed with my decision. I'm looking forward to a new direction and new experiences. I guess time will tell."

"Good luck, Syd!"

"Thank you!" Syd answered.

Lorne showed Syd to the door and after he had left, closed it, allowing a private conversation with Murray. They agreed with Syd's employment record, excellent work and very adaptable to difficult situations. Lorne mentioned he may have a little trouble finding a suitable replacement to handle the complex files that always landed on Syd's desk. His ample capabilities and knowledge were duly acknowledged as their meeting ended.

For the rest of the day, Syd stuck to his desk, finishing up any work he could and preparing on-going projects for someone else's hands. As he worked, he wondered why he had been so apprehensive about resigning. Before the meeting with Lorne, he had pictured himself being praised as a star employee and management begging him to stay, offering higher pay and other perks. When this didn't happen at the morning's meeting, he started to realize that maybe his ego was the cause of most of his concern, and that not only was he not expendable, but the company could get along quite nicely without him. Reluctantly accepting this fact, he vowed to finish up his work at Metro and leave on a good note. His mind now traveled to thoughts of how his fellow employees and friends would react as the news of his leaving Metro and moving to the west coast reached them. Leaving a tidy desk, he joyfully boarded the elevator at quitting time with a settled mind, too late for Marty, who could only watch the doors closing, to intercept. Syd snickered and waved as the gap narrowed. He wondered if there would be a Marty at Northern. Then he got the giggles, thanks to the aftermath of the day's and previous week's intensity.

Carly had a warm meal ready when he arrived home, hungry and happy. Seeing Carly back to her old self, makeup and form-fitting clothes, made him even happier. Carly saw his approving look and kissed him softly before guiding him to the table and serving up the food. They ate in silence before Carly asked about the reaction to his resignation.

"It went very smooth, love! I'm out of there! And, we're on our way."

"That's great. See, I told you it would go all right. Your fears were all unfounded."

"Yeah, I know. I don't understand why I was so concerned. Only one thing still bothers me."

"What's that?"

"They didn't seem to have any reaction to my leaving."

"What do you mean?"

"Just thank you, good job, clean up your work, good bye!"

"What did you expect?"

"I don't know. Possibly more regrets. How will we cope? Sort of thing."

"Silly boy! Nobody is indispensable. Don't you know that?"

"I do now."

"Good! Just remember you don't owe them anything, and they don't owe you anything. A day's pay for a day's work. You can only ask for a good, decent, interesting living. The rest is up to you, anything extra is gravy."

"You're so right. I'll try to keep that in mind."

"See that you do," Carly scolded in jest. Syd helped clean up the dinner dishes, and the talk turned to planning chores for the next few weeks. A rough flowchart was prepared with the known tasks listed, leaving lots of room for changes and updates. Notes were entered as briefly as possible with space for a cross-reference number. Any necessary detailed information was placed in a three ring binder, one page per note, in chronological order. Carly insisted they both list all bank accounts, memberships, driver's licenses, storage lockers, credit cards, safety deposit boxes and any other ties they may have. Syd asked why such urgency? Carly's answer was the need for a clean break allowing her to finally feel free to devote herself to him. A list was compiled with Carly's information in one column and Syd's in another, showing every detail they could think of, including all account numbers. Carly helped Syd in deciding which items from the to-do list could be attended to in the next few days. These items were entered and noted on the flowchart. Others were marked for the end of the month, to be taken care of as part of the physical move.

Carly's need for a complete severance started to grip Syd, spurring him on to comply with her well-organized program. If this was needed to gain her full confidence and intimacy, then he would willingly participate. He anticipated a blissful future while he worked.

With a large bite taken out of the planning, the mind-weary couple went to bed and slept soundly until morning. Carly stayed in bed as Syd readied himself for work. When he bent to kiss her goodbye, she reminded him to take the short list on the table containing things he could start on during the day, as time allowed.

"Oh! Almost forgot. I'll grab it on the way out. Have a good day. See you later!"

Syd left Carly's bedside, Carly called to his back. "I'm starting with my list this morning, and I should be out most of the day, but I'll see you for dinner. I'm so excited! We're on our way! See you later!"

Syd grabbed his list and scanned it from time to time as he drove across town to Metro. He parked, rode the elevator to his floor and entered his cubicle. Just as his ass touched his chair, Marty's head appeared over the top of the cubicle.

"Good Christ Marty! You scared me! Did you sleep here or something?"

"Sorry, Syd. No, I didn't sleep here. I just got here myself. You look happy. What's up?"

"I am happy. Very happy."

"I'm glad to hear that. Tell me more. I'm dying to know."

"I know you are. I'm not going to tell you, but you'll probably hear something today. Anyway, I have a busy day ahead, so I'll talk to you later."

"How about those Sharks?"

"Never mind the Sharks. I can't talk now. See you later."

Syd turned to his desk and Marty returned to his, more curious than ever. Pawing at his work, he was alert to any tidbit of news about Syd. It wouldn't be long before he heard something.

For most of the morning, Syd pored over several on-going accounts, completing a report on one and almost finishing a couple of others. Before lunch, he scanned his list, picked up his phone and closed a couple of club memberships.

His afternoon was another story. When the paperwork started to flow from the personnel department, the rumor mill went into full gear. Syd had anticipated a certain reaction to his leaving, but had not prepared for the explosive response that peppered his desk. All forms of messages and personal visits were overwhelming, including a speechless Marty, who was visibly shaken. After a couple of hours, without getting any work done, he stopped answering all incoming messages and waived all visitors away except Marty, who now was invited to sit across from Syd at his desk.

"Marty, how would you like to be my press secretary?" Syd joked.

"Are you going into politics, Syd?"

"No! No! You idiot. That's just a joke."

"Oh!"

Marty, too shook up to think straight, and unable to ask the questions that were hanging on his tongue, let Syd carry the conversation.

The overwhelming support and well-wishing farewells had taken away Syd's desire to continue on with his playful mind games at Marty's expense. He finally revealed some of his secrets. Marty beamed with importance, afraid to move.

Starting with his meeting Carly and their eventual getting together as a couple, and ending with the need he felt to try a new direction and location, Syd, without going into detail, sketched an outline of his life. It was enough to satisfy Marty. Swelling with smugness, as if this information was some sort of national secret, Marty could only nod as he struggled to his feet. Syd shook his hand and apologized for toying with him, thanked him for his friendship, told him to cheer for the Sharks and waved him back to his desk. The work and messages would have to wait until tomorrow. Syd had no energy left. He headed home early.

Carly had just started dinner when Syd breezed in.

"Honey, I'm home!" He mimicked Desi Arnaz.

"I'm in the kitchen." Carly did her best Lucy.

Syd entered the kitchen. Carly continued, "How was your day, busy boy?"

"Interesting, to say the least. I had to get out of there."

"Oh! What happened?"

"Nothing serious, just so many people contacting me. It was overwhelming. I'm not looking forward to tomorrow."

"Maybe things will peak sometime in the morning. Here! Sit down and eat. You'll feel better after you get some food inside."

Syd sat at the table and watched as Carly finished preparing the meal. And just as she had predicted, he felt a lot better after eating.

"Thanks, love. Once again you came through. What a girl!"

"This is nothing. I'm just getting started. You just wait. Super Woman is on her way."

"I feel so privileged. I can see the future now, and it looks so inviting."

"Looks good to me too. Here! Let me clean up."

Syd remained seated and quiet as Carly cleaned up the kitchen, then he remarked, "Looks like you've been busy. Where is all your nice stuff?"

"I found a good home for it."

"What do you mean a good home?"

"A friend of mine, who has always admired a lot of my keepsakes, has agreed to look after them."

"Forever?"

"More or less. If I ever want anything back, I only have to ask, but for now I know they're in a safe place and besides this is just another move to making a clean break. That's what you'd like, isn't it?"

"A fresh start is what we need, but I wasn't asking you to get rid of all your nice treasures."

"Don't worry about it. You can see I'm not upset. Now come and help me pack some books. Did you get into your list today?"

"I got a couple of things done, but after the flood of calls I didn't get to the bank. I'll try tomorrow."

"Oh tomorrow! I don't envy you one bit, but I'm sure you can handle it. Come on, let's get busy."

Syd opened a couple of cardboard boxes while Carly started to separate piles of books. With a sweeping hand gesture she explained the separate piles to Syd. "I'm getting rid of this pile here, and this pile I'm taking with me. There are some books I can't part with, ever. So don't ask me to."

"Yes, ma'am. I wouldn't dare."

"Smart man! Now start packing."

Syd knew that Carly was joking around but also realized that if she said a book was staying, it was staying. End of story. So, he packed and said nothing, his mind preoccupied with his own to-do list. The book shelves in Carly's study room were nearly empty when a mutual agreement was reached to stop for that evening. For about twenty minutes they reviewed the to-do lists and note book, adding and changing as they progressed. The flowchart was amended. When they were satisfied that no more changes could be thought of, Syd plunked himself down in his recliner with the daily newspaper, and Carly curled up on the couch flicking the TV channel changer. A short time later, Syd broke the silence.

"I see this Viagra pill is still selling like crazy. I should have bought shares."

"Sounds like a lot of men need the help. Tell me truthfully, did you ever have a problem?"

"Actually, no, but there was once."

"Oh?"

"It was after a night of drinking. I think I was going for thirds, and nothing happened."

"Couldn't get it up?"

"That's right. We tried, but it was like trying to put a marshmallow in a piggy bank, no go."

"Going for thirds, there's the piggy part," Carly chided.

"This reminds me of the fellow who complained about the erection cream he had purchased, telling the sales clerk it hadn't worked."

"Oh, oh! Here we go!" Carly grimaced.

"The clerk listened to his complaint and pointed to the fine print on the package. 'See here, it says: Must be applied by an eighteen year old female.'"

Carly giggled, "Oh shit! Whatever works? Isn't it time for bed, dear? All this erection talk has got my attention."

Syd raced for the bedroom. "Beat you there," he yelled.

Carly undressed in the doorway, teasing Syd with seductive moves. She gracefully pranced onto the bed and then it was blissful togetherness followed by deep sleep.

In the morning, Carly did not wake as Syd dressed for work. Letting her sleep, he left a note before leaving the house.

Good morning, sweetie. We didn't get to seconds or thirds but first was wonderful. Have a great day, see you tonight. Love, Syd. P.S. I have my list.

Just as he had envisioned, Syd's morning was frantic with messages coming at him. Ignoring his phone, he concentrated on his e-mail list, replying generically to most and to a select few he added more details. Before noon, he returned a couple of phone calls then left the office to do some banking. At the bank, he amalgamated some accounts, paid a couple of bills then went for lunch. In the afternoon, Syd ignored all messages and concentrated on his work until quitting time. On the way home, he managed to complete a couple of things on his list, keeping in mind that Carly would be on his ass until it was finished. When he finally walked in the door, he flopped down in his chair.

"Beer. I need beer," he pleaded.

Carly appeared with a can of beer. "Here you are. You poor man," she cooed.

"Thank you! Thank you! You saved my life. How can I repay you?"

"Cut it out, will you? I'm only trying to revive you so that you can give me some more help."

"Oh, I might have known there was a hook. Come here, I need a kiss."

Carly slid onto Syd's lap, angled her face to his and kissed him softly. Their tensions leached away to nothing.

She confided to him. "I don't have dinner ready, but you'll be glad to know, pizza's on its way. I hope that's okay?"

"It's more than okay, it's great. Oh, there's the door. You sure have good timing. How do you do it?"

"Just luck, and some practice. I'll get the door."

The pizza was eaten with a minimum of talk, and then Carly

put Syd back to work finishing the packing of her books. Looking around the study, he remarked, "You've been busy."

"You noticed. Yes, I cleaned out a couple of loads today. Things I don't need. Looks a little bare now, doesn't it?"

"Yeah! I can see the walls."

The chitchat continued as Carly assigned more chores to Syd: piling the boxes of books by the door, sorting and packing kitchen supplies and utensils for disposal, anything to ease the move when the time arrived. Finally, back to the flowchart and then to bed.

Before leaving the next morning, Syd kissed Carly softly and confided, "I had the most fantastic dream last night, I think you will find it very interesting."

"Tell me."

"Sorry. I don't have time. I'll tell you tonight. Have a good day. Bye!"

Syd left for work, Carly dozed awhile before starting her day.

Syd started his day by, once again, facing Marty's inquisitive presence, and to Marty's delight, instead of playing games, Syd kept him updated on the latest events. When the briefing was over, Syd dismissed him with a wave. Marty floated back to his desk.

The day went by closely mirroring the previous one for Syd. He managed to get a lot of work done for Metro and also shortened his to-do list by half, not as much as he had hoped, but still progress. Then it was time to head for home.

As he sat down to another of Carly's great dinners, he told her how well the day had gone. She told him of her accomplishments in her day, and then she asked, "How about that dream?"

"Oh. Yes! I must tell you. I have been reliving it off and on all day. What a blast!"

"Sounds like it."

"It's rather bizarre. Apparently, my doctor discovered that I somehow had developed a gene that gives me immunity from contracting HIV and AIDS, and further study revealed that I could pass on this immunity to females through sexual intercourse. So, naturally I went into business."

"Into business?"

"Yes, women lined up to pay me ten thousand dollars each to make love to them."

"Dream on!"

"Come on. I was just providing a medical service. How could I refuse?"

"Dr. Barnes, forgive me for bursting your bubble, but we have work to do."

"You're not impressed?"

"Not really. It is amusing, but I think it's more of a guy thing. Maybe tonight you can dream you have the ability to turn ugly girls into beauties just by screwing them. You could charge fifty thousand for that. Tell me, why it is that men always think their cock is so important? Don't you know it will probably get you into more trouble than it will get you out of?"

Taken aback, Syd stammered, "Gee, uh, sorry…it was just a dream."

"You're right, but I wouldn't try to get that one interpreted, if I were you. You might be diagnosed as having serious emotional problems." Carly cupped Syd's face in her hands, "Tell you what. Tonight dream about walking beside me on a west coast beach with the sun setting on the horizon."

"Too late. I have already had those dreams."

"You didn't tell me."

"Sorry. I didn't think they were interesting enough."

"Don't be silly. Girls want to hear those kinds of dreams and guess what?"

"What?"

"Your dreams are going to come true very shortly. So keep dreaming. Now let's get to work."

Carly kissed Syd tenderly, then pulled away and pointed toward the bedroom. "I'll clean up in here while you start on that closet. I'll help you when I'm finished."

She started clearing the dishes, while Syd slowly left his chair and walked to the bedroom.

Syd had agreed to help Carly sort through her spare closet full of seasonal clothes and other assorted articles. He started by distributing the items around the bedroom and living room in the categories he thought they should go. Carly soon joined him and together they assembled a pile for disposal and a larger pile to retain. When they had finished, the closet was marked on Carly's list as done. Before bedtime, the flowchart and note book were amended and updated. Syd promised to tackle some of his chores in the next couple of days.

Friday morning, Syd arrived early to work, eager to clean up some loose ends, which he did. Mid-afternoon, he slipped out of the office to tend to his personal list before going home.

Unable to convince Carly to accompany him to the Anchor in several attempts that week, he tried again as they each sipped a glass of wine.

"You go and have a good time. I'll be just fine here alone," Carly repeated several times in rebuttal to Syd's prodding. It was useless to try to change her mind. Once again, Syd headed to the bar alone to face his friends' curiosity about the invisible girlfriend.

Sitting with his friends, he was surprised at the number of well-wishers who continued to stop by his table all evening. Word of his job change and consequent upcoming move had spread. During the evening, a farewell party was planned for the following Friday. It was also suggested that maybe the elusive girlfriend would be introduced. Syd gave another lame excuse for her absence that evening and promised to do his best to get her to attend the upcoming party. On his way home, he wondered how he would accomplish that.

The weekend work started mid-morning Saturday, with Carly asking Syd to fetch his sporting goods and other items from his storage locker and close the account. When he returned, those belongings were laid out on the living room floor for sorting, some for disposal and some to keep. Carly would have dumped all of it, had it not been for Syd insisting that he was not parting with certain things and that was that. After the sorting was finished, Syd, at Carly's urging, carted the rejected articles to a goodwill outlet, bidding them a somber farewell. Saturday night they were early to bed after updating the paperwork. Sunday was spent sorting clothes, resulting in two very large piles, one his, one hers, designated to find new homes. Carly volunteered to take them to goodwill the next day while Syd was at work. Again, work was halted early, allowing for a leisurely meal with wine, a soak in the tub, lovemaking and sleep.

Monday morning, Marty peered over the side of Syd's cubicle, "Morning, Syd!"

"Good Morning, Marty! What can I do for you?"

"How was your weekend?"

"Busy. Work, work, work!"

"See those Sharks?"

"No, I didn't, cable's shut off."

"Oh! Too bad! Good game."

"Really? I'll just have to catch up after I move. Anyways, I have work to do. See you later."

Syd reached for his phone. Marty shuffled back to his desk.

The week passed by in a blur of activity. Syd cleaned up his Metro work, tended to his to-do list, responded to well-wishers and, in the evenings, paid heed to Carly's bidding.

Thursday night, the realization that tomorrow would be his last day at Metro caused Syd to toss and turn all night. The alarm had been deliberately turned off just so he could get up when he felt like it, which turned out to be well past his regular time.

Carly studied him. "Hi, sleepy," she murmured.

"You got that right. Good morning!"

"Your last day. Wow! You take your time now, and I'll make you a nice breakfast, and some strong coffee."

"Oh! That's so nice of you. Thank you!"

Carly washed, cleaned her teeth, pointed Syd to the shower, and then started to prepare breakfast. Syd was in no hurry. When he had finished cleaning up, Carly served up a great breakfast which they lingered over. After the meal, Carly walked Syd to the door. A soft kiss was shared before Syd turned to face his last day at Metro.

He arrived at his desk to find it and his whole work cubicle decorated with ribbons, flowers, cards, notes and banners proclaiming how much he would be missed and many wishes for good luck in his new endeavor. A small crowd gathered as he ceremoniously pored over the thoughtfully prepared greetings. He looked up to see a gold embossed card being thrust toward him. He took it in his hand and read.

PLEASE ATTEND:

TIME: 11:30 A.M. FRIDAY 19TH
PLACE: THE PELICAN BAR AND BISTRO
OCCASION: LUNCHEON IN HONOR OF
SYD BARNES

The lunch date was part of the office buzz all week. Syd had gotten wind of the occasion in spite of the office staff's attempts to keep it secret. He spread his arms as if to embrace those closest to him and emotionally expressed his feelings.

"Thank you! Thank you! This is all so nice! Wow! I need to sit down for a few minutes. You're all so kind. Thank you!"

His workmates had never seen Syd so moved and stuck for words, and a few barbs were aimed his way.

"Modesty is not your forte."

"Need a speech writer?"

"Is this our Syd?"

Straining to compose himself, Syd continued, "Thank you for the lunch invitation. I think I'll have more to say then. See you at the Pelican"

The crowd dispersed except for Marty. "If you want, I'll get some boxes for you to put this stuff in," he offered.

"Thank you, Marty. That would be very helpful."

Marty sprang into action. Syd sat staring at his decorated work space until Marty returned with several cardboard boxes. Marty then returned to his cubicle, leaving Syd to pack the personal items from his desk along with the cards and well-wishing notes. With everything stuffed into three boxes and loaded onto a hand cart, he wistfully said goodbye to his desk and turned toward the elevator. Realizing he was almost late for his own party, he hurried to his car, placed the boxes inside, locked the doors and ran down the street to the Pelican where a large entourage of work colleagues, young and old, awaited him. He entered to a standing chant, "Syd! Syd! Syd! Syd!"

The din did not die down until he had been escorted to a special table set on a low stage at one end of the room. Lorne Unger stood next to the table in front of a microphone. He quickly introduced Syd, and immediately had the special guests at that table start the buffet line-up at the far end of the room. Syd led the way, followed by Loretta, Lorne Unger, Murray York, several close friends from other departments, and a beaming Marty. After the group from the head table had returned to their seats, guests from each table, in turn, headed for the food, loaded up and returned to their seats until everyone was busy eating. When the meal was finished and staff had removed the dishes, Lorne addressed the crowd with a brief history of Syd's achievements at Metro, thanked him for his work and presented him with a large cut-glass serving bowl as a going away present. He then turned the microphone over to anyone who cared to add some Syd anecdotes to the party. While some of the guests took this opportunity to offer their well-wishes to Syd, others relished the chance to revisit forgotten stories from Syd's past. Then it was Syd's turn to reciprocate, and he did. Starting slowly, he regaled the room with shots at some of his colleagues who had spoken only a few minutes earlier and got in some digs at other employees who were not present. He ended by thanking all who had made his stay at Metro pleasant, promising to remember them fondly. Lorne closed the proceedings and everyone continued the giddy mood as they walked the few blocks back to Metro. In front of the building, Syd shook a few hands, thanked Lorne one more time and then sauntered slowly to his car. Normally, he couldn't wait to hurry away from the office, but this time – his last time – was different, compelling him to creep slowly into the traffic.

It was still mid-afternoon when he got home. Carly was not there. She arrived a short while later looking tired and untidy.

"Holy cow! Where have you been?" Syd asked as he looked her up and down.

"Oh! I just sneaked away to my garden," she answered.

"All day?"

"Yes, most of the day."

"Are you going to miss it, when we leave?

"Yes! I've been thinking about it and I will."

"Do you think you'll have time to show it to me before we go?"

"I've been thinking about that too and the answer is yes, maybe even next week. Come on, let's take a shower."

After they had cleaned up, Syd readied himself for the going away party at the Anchor. He would be going alone. All week he had cajoled and coerced Carly into changing her mind to accompany him, to no avail. He tried not to show his disappointment. Carly did notice.

"Don't pout. Just go and have a good time. I have lots to do here to keep me busy," she said.

Syd almost started the argument again, but Carly cut him off.

"No more. Dammit. Don't you listen?"

"All right! All right! I'm going alone, but I'll miss you."

"Miss me, shmiss me. Fuck you! Now get out of here."

Syd finished getting ready in silence, not in the mood to be going anywhere.

Carly winked at him, "Come on. Perk up. Go see your friends. Have some fun. I'll be waiting for you."

Before he left, Syd kissed Carly softly. "I'll see you later, love. Don't wait up for me."

"I wasn't planning to."

He closed the door with a thud. "Bitch!" he cursed and thought he heard something hitting the other side of the door. Whatever it was drowned out the word, "Bastard!"

Sitting in his car in the Anchor parking lot, Syd experienced several mood changes. The slow trip from home in heavy traffic allowed him too much time to think. Would Carly open up to him after the move to the west coast? Would he like his new job? Would his friends bug him tonight about meeting Carly? His spirits lifted when he caught a glimpse of the crowd through the bar window. This was his night. A loud cheer greeted him as he crossed the threshold.

"He's here!"

"Hooray for Syd!"

"Let's party!"

Judging by the e-mail and phone calls that flooded him all week, he had expected a good turnout, but nothing like this. Standing room only with very few faces he didn't recognize. It hadn't registered with him that there was one empty parking space left when he pulled into the lot. The one space that could be seen from inside. Someone pointed to his car outside and then he knew the space had been purposely saved in his honor. Syd's good friend Ed, who had traveled back to town just for this party, squeezed through the throng, handed Syd a beer and took his keys.

"You won't need these tonight. Come on. Let's party!"

Syd raised the glass and took a large drink. "Thanks Ed. Let's party!"

For the next few hours, Syd and his friends partied, taking them into the early morning. Cards and notes were thrust into

Syd's hands as he circulated through the room. More than a few enquiries were made as to the invisible girlfriend. Syd managed to side-step these without revealing that he wished Carly was with him to enjoy the great send-off. His mind flirted with the future even as the exuberance of the evening engulfed him. He pictured Carly dancing with him on a faraway beach, waves licking their feet as the moon looked on. The images came and went while the festive mood rolled on. As the guests filtered away leaving their well-wishes hanging in the air behind them, Syd knew where he wanted to be: snuggled up next to Carly. Ed offered up two options for Syd to choose from. He could walk to a nearby hotel where Ed was staying and sleep on the couch, or he could take a taxi home.

After some thought and wrangling, Syd took a taxi to the place where his thoughts had been throughout a large part of the night, home to Carly. At the door, he realized his keys were still with Ed. He hammered on the door. Hearing Syd's pounding, Carly ran and opened the door, stark naked.

"Hi, sailor," she joked. "Come on in."

Syd stumbled into the apartment. "Honey, I'm home," he tried to say, but it came out sounding more like "Hnnneee, I'mm hobve."

"Yes, you're safely hobve," Carly sarcastically answered as she closed the door. Pushing the staggering Hulk ahead of her, Carly inched them toward the bedroom where Syd fell face down on the bed and reached oblivion within minutes. Carly smiled at him, and then eased herself against his still clothed body, resting her face against the back of his neck. They slept well into the late morning.

Carly woke first, leaving Syd to sleep awhile longer. She slipped quietly from the bed, cleaned herself up and put on a pot of coffee. Returning to the bedroom with two cups of coffee, she chirped, "Good morning, party boy."

Syd eased his eyes open. "Oh! Thank you, love. You're a sweetie."

"I know. Can I get you some breakfast?"

"Just toast, if you don't mind? Thank you."

"Coming right up."

Carly bounded from the room, Syd leaned back, savoring the hot coffee. Carly soon returned with toast for both of them. While they ate, she kidded Syd about his looks, especially his red eyes. With the toast eaten and the first cup of coffee consumed, Syd headed for the shower, and then he joined Carly for a second cup of coffee in the kitchen. As he sipped, he phoned Ed to arrange a meeting at the Anchor to retrieve his car. Carly drove him to the parking lot and without stopping the car completely, bid him good day. Syd's feet just touched the pavement as she sped away. Ed, who had arrived a few minutes earlier, watched the action. He walked over to Syd.

"So that must be the shy girlfriend. What's her hurry?"

"Just following her pattern, Ed. Continuing to confuse me. I'm hoping to bring her out of that self-protecting shell of hers after we move. Wish me luck."

"Looks like you'll need it. How are you feeling this morning?"

"Pretty good, considering. Thanks for looking after me last night."

"No problem. You're welcome. From what I hear, you're going to be missed."

"And you know what? I'm going to miss the gang also. But I'm looking forward to a new direction and new experiences and perhaps even settling down. Only time will tell."

"I only caught a glimpse of your girlfriend, but from what I saw she looks very attractive. Good luck." They walked to Syd's car and Ed produced the confiscated keys. He then opened the trunk which was filled with cards, notes, gifts and flowers from the night before. Together they had a mini tailgate party, reading and re-reading all the cards and notes containing a host of memorable anecdotes. Neither one wanted to pull the pin to end the meeting as they reminisced and recounted stories from the past. Finally, with a big embrace, goodbyes were exchanged with Syd promising to call before he left town. Syd drove Ed back to his hotel, thanked him again and then retraced his route past the bar, where he blew a kiss good bye, then he continued a very leisurely drive home. When he entered the apartment, Carly launched into an apology.

"Sorry for that ejection at the pub. I wasn't trying to kill you."

"Yeah. What was that all about?"

"I don't know. I saw your friend there, and I thought you might drag me into an introduction. I guess I kind of panicked. Sorry."

"I'll never understand you." Syd shook his head.

"You probably never will. So don't try." Pretending to pout, she pleaded. "You're not mad at me, are you?"

"No. I'm not mad at you, just perplexed."

Carly looked into Syd's eyes, her hands encircling his neck. With just a touch of sarcasm, she hissed, "I'm such a bitch!"

Slightly stunned, Syd took several seconds to respond. "That's pretty strong. I don't think you're a bitch. You're just a little confusing. That's all."

"Okay, just a little confusing. If you're not mad at me, let's eat. Come and see what I made."

Just like that the topic was ended. Syd followed Carly in silence into the kitchen where the surprise waited, a scratch-made lasagna. With her patented stern voice she scolded, "If you think this is a guilt induced meal, you'll wear the fucking thing. Now sit down and eat."

Syd did as he was told without noticing that Carly was secretly enjoying pulling his chain. Breaking the nerve shattering silence near the end of the meal, she decided to end Syd's noticeable agony. She smiled, "Come on. Relax. I'm not that weird."

"I know. It's just that you can turn so fast. I don't like it. It's kind of scary."

"I'll admit it. I am quick tempered and hot-headed. I'll try to control myself. Changing the subject, if you don't mind, we are just going to relax this evening. You can read the paper. We can cuddle. Whatever you want, but you know what I think?"

"What?"

"You need some rest. You look tired."

"You're right. I am. If you don't mind I'd like to go to bed right now."

"Be my guest. I'll join you later."

A gentle kiss from Carly sent Syd straight to bed. Carly tidied the kitchen, then snuggled up beside him. In the morning, fresh and invigorated from a good sleep, they showered together and made love, then Syd leafed through the morning paper while Carly prepared a hearty breakfast. They ate in silence until Syd spoke up, "That was great, love. Thank you."

"You're quite welcome."

"What do you have planned for us today?" he asked.

"That's a good question. We have most items on the list done, don't we? Let's review everything and see if we can whittle it down some more, okay?"

"Sounds good to me, but isn't it a bit redundant? Look at this place, all these boxes. It's like living in a warehouse."

"You're right. We're pretty much caught up, but let's look anyway. I have to be sure."

Syd went along with Carly's overzealous pre-move planning. They did find a few things that had been listed for later in the week that could be started that day. Items such as phone calls to friends and preparing utility cut-off notices were tended to. Carly elected to scrap the to-do list and note books, which had become a nightmare of changes and amendments. She started a new, easy to follow done list alongside a short to-do list. This would take them up to the day they leave town which was in one week's time.

The day, evening meal and after dinner leisure time passed quickly and they went to bed anticipating the excitement of the few remaining days ahead of them. Monday morning, Carly finally cajoled Syd into combining his one remaining bank account with hers to create a joint account. Each would have full signing privileges. For the past two weeks they had argued the pros and cons of this arrangement with Syd not seeing any benefits and at the same time feeling a bit suspicious. Carly tried working every angle from sulking to threatening to pampering, until she finally got her way. Syd went to his bank to get the necessary papers. When he came back, all the forms were filled out and Carly wrote a check from her account for Syd to take back and deposit in their new account. They were, Carly said, "like a real couple." As Syd was leaving, she kissed him.

"I may be out when you get back, but I shouldn't be far behind you. And one more thing, I have a nice surprise for you later," she winked.

"A surprise? That sounds nice. Any hints?"

"I can't tell you. It's a surprise. See you later, bye!"

Syd left the house wondering what Carly had in store for him. Her expression and body language hadn't revealed any clues, not even a starting point. He was forced to wait until he got back home.

CHAPTER ELEVEN

After Syd left, Carly went to one of her favorite places, a used book store. Heading straight to the non-fiction section, she pored over any technical or academic book that caught her eye, and there were many. Two hours later, loaded down with a half dozen volumes she just had to have, Carly bade farewell to Nick, the proprietor and stepped awkwardly to the sidewalk. Among the books was one detailing the medical problems associated with space travel, a book on common garden insects and another studying soil composition and erosion. Rounding out the six was a book showing computer shortcuts, a dairy cow pedigree registry and an electrical grid manual. She thought that these books should satisfy her curiosity for a short while, but a couple might never be opened, destined to clutter the house as many others have. Before going home, she attended to one other chore. She rented a pickup truck, deliberately parking her car in a facility two blocks from the rental agency and walking the short distance to the lot. She drove the truck to her car, grabbed her new books and then stopped behind an appliance store where she loaded some cartons into the back of the truck and drove home, where she parked a few houses away from her door.

When she entered the house, Syd, who had arrived home a short time before, took one look at the books and freaked. "What are those?" he screamed.

"What do they look like? They're books." Carly sarcastically pointed out.

"We don't need any more books to move. Look around. Look at all these boxes. They're full of books. Don't you think you have enough?"

"Enough books? Don't be silly. There's no such thing. Besides what's a few more?"

"If you say so, but I don't agree."

"And I don't agree that there's never enough baseball."

"Oh! Guess we're even." Syd grinned.

"Just forget the books. Remember my surprise for you?"

"Yes, of course. What is it?"

Carly grabbed Syd's hand and pulled him toward the bedroom, "Come with me," she purred. Syd felt a tightening in his groin, anticipating the next few minutes of his life, having Carly satisfy his sexual urges.

"So what's the treat you have for me?"

"Patience, its coming."

"And I'll be coming too," Syd was thinking.

In the bedroom, Carly undressed Syd, then shed her own garments, scattering them on the floor. Pushing him onto the bed she teased and caressed him in all his favorite places then she deftly reached over to a sports bag by the bed, and picked out some items.

"What's all that stuff?" Syd asked.

"Just some bondage material, love."

"What? We don't have to get into bondage, do we?"

"We've tried everything else. Now I'd like to try a little bondage. A little more control, you might say."

"You already have full control, and you know it. If it makes you happy, just go ahead but no pain okay?"

"No pain, but be prepared, I'm going to drive you crazy. Now raise your arms over your head to each side of the bed." Carly tied a rope to each of Syd's wrists and then tied the ends of each rope to a corner of the headboard. She then did the same with each of Syd's ankles, leaving him spread out on the bed, unable to move much more than his head. "And now I tease you." She giggled.

She licked and tickled Syd's feet. Then slowly worked her way up, alternating from one leg to the other. As she did this, she used one hand to stimulate his genitals. Syd moaned in pleasure. Finally reaching his testicles, Carly licked and sucked Syd's genital area for a few minutes then turned her attention to his chest, licking and sucking his nipples, and after that, she worked her way down his chest and stomach back to his penis where she expertly brought him close to a climax, then she stopped.

"Untie me. I want to touch you, and I'm not comfortable," Syd pleaded.

"Just a little longer." Carly teased. "I love the control. It makes me feel so powerful." Carly then mounted Syd, easing into a slow up and down motion. Whenever Carly did this, Syd liked to cup her breasts lightly in his hands and sometimes stretch up to suck them, but now he could only watch them jiggle in front of his eyes. Carly quickened her pace, until she knew Syd wouldn't last much longer, and then she stopped.

"Don't stop now," he groaned.

"There's something else I have to do."

"You have to do it now?"

"Yes. You need a collar."

"A collar?"

"Yes. More control."

"Oh no! Just make it quick."

Carly reached over to the night table and pulled out a large plastic tie-wrap. In one motion, she encircled his neck, threaded one end of the tie-wrap into the locking grooves in the other end and pulled it snug on Syd's neck.

"Not too tight, those things are dangerous. Shouldn't you be using something a little less lethal?"

"I'll be careful with you. Don't worry."

With that she resumed the thrusting movements that had brought him to the brink a few minutes earlier.

Syd was pushing upwards with each of Carly's downward motions. They pumped in unison, each of them panting and moaning, ready to enjoy the climactic moment. Syd started to ejaculate. Feeling the warmth, Carly reached orgasm. As the love spasms waned, she grabbed the loose end of the tie-wrap on Syd's neck and pulled with all her strength. Syd's eyes bulged.

"Carly, Carly undo this thing." he tried to say, but only managed to spit and gag. Frantic, he tried to pull free of the bonds, laying the skin bare on his wrists.

Carly rolled off Syd and stood by the bed. "Don't thrash around like that, please just go quietly. Please," she whispered in a tiny little girl voice. Syd saw the ceiling start to disappear several times as he drifted into unconsciousness. His body jerked a couple of times and then was still.

Carly thought of a very sick joke. "Now you know how it feels to come and go at the same time, Syd."

Forcing the thought from her mind, she stared at Syd for several minutes, and then slowly sank to her knees until her chin rested on Syd's hand; tears glazed her eyes.

In a barely audible whisper, she talked to Syd, oblivious to the fact he had left her world.

"Syd you are finally going to see my beautiful garden. I know you will love it there. The air is so fresh and clear, and you won't be alone. I'll come to visit you now and then, and I'll sing my song just for you. You look so peaceful. No more worries. We'll be going to my garden in a little while, and then you'll see what I have been talking about."

Carly kissed Syd's hand and slowly rose to her feet, then she walked to the kitchen to pour a cup of coffee. Cradling the cup in both hands, she mentally planned the rest of the night in the fading light, and thought of the risky business ahead, praying nothing would go wrong. But she also knew that her garden had to be finished. Sitting, thinking and sipping, she started to hum her little song, quietly at first then bursting into full song,

"We're going to my love garden
We're going to my love garden
We'll forget all our cares
And we'll enjoy ourselves there
In my love garden."

Carly added and changed words, but the theme remained.

"My love garden
My love garden
My love garden
My love garden."

The singing gave her new energy. A half cup of coffee remained on the table as she left the kitchen to move the living room furniture. She pushed all of the furniture and boxes of packed household goods against the walls, enabling her to lay out the items needed for the night's work. Satisfied with her progress, she took a hot shower then dressed in a torn pair of jeans, a faded t-shirt and beat-up runners. Next, she gathered up various articles from different places in her suite: a shovel she had hidden away, a sports bag from her bedroom, body lotion from the bathroom and a change of clothes. She then made several trips to the pickup truck to retrieve the cartons, taking extra care with the large refrigerator container. She left one small box in the truck. In the living room, she piled all the boxes together except for the refrigerator container, which she placed in the center of the room. Next, she walked to the bedroom and cut Syd loose. After cutting the bonds, she dragged Syd's body to the container and stuffed it in. She then sealed it with several layers of industrial tape before adding some rope to be used as gripping aids for the difficult move from the living room to the truck.

Trying unsuccessfully to be quiet, she bounced the sinister box and its contents down the stairs to the alley. Then she retrieved the truck from its parking spot and parked next to the box. As she struggled to load the box into the truck, a passing gentleman, noticing her noble efforts, offered to help. Stepping next to Carly he gripped the rope handles.

"You'll hurt yourself, lady. Let me help you with that."

"Thank you very much," Carly grunted.

Together they loaded the box safely into the truck.

"Someone going away?" the stranger asked.

Carly grinned. "Yes! Yes! As a matter of fact there is."

"I thought so. Have a nice trip."

"Thank you! I'm sure we will, and thanks for the help."

"Not at all. My pleasure."

The stranger went on his way. Carly returned to the house where she placed the change of clothes, a towel, body lotion and a roll of industrial tape in the sports bag. She almost forgot to put a sharp knife and work gloves in the bag, but remembered just in time. Carrying the bag and shovel, she locked the house and headed for the truck, but as she got closer, she noticed a traffic cop standing with his foot resting on the front bumper. Her heart leaped into her throat as the guard approached her.

"This your truck, miss?"

"Yes, officer. Anything wrong?"

"There certainly is. Your truck is partially blocking the lane. We could have towed it away you know."

Carly recovered instantly. Sticking out her chest and flashing her best smile, she answered sweetly, "Oh! I'm sorry, officer. I didn't know. You see, I had to load some things, and I couldn't park close enough. I'm really sorry."

Catching a glimpse of those breasts and flashing eyes, the officer's demeanor quickly changed, "Oh! That's all right, miss. I just didn't want to see the truck get hit or anything. Now you just go and have a nice evening, okay?"

"Thank you, I will," Carly answered.

The officer's eyes didn't stray from Carly's chest, as she threw the shovel into the truck next to Syd, tossed the sports bag into the cab, bounced in next to it and drove away.

"Fucking jerk," she muttered. "Thank you, tits. You come in handy now and then." She shivered from the aftershock of the encounter and then got down to some serious driving. As a precaution, she didn't take the normal route to her garden until close to her destination, where she used familiar roads. When she reached the dirt road that left the highway, she stopped the truck, jumped out and listened for any other traffic. Satisfied there was no other vehicle nearby, she got back in the truck and headed up hill, away from the highway.

When she arrived at her garden, she drove the truck through the enclosing tree branches and stopped at a pile of brush. She shut off the engine and left the headlights shining on the brush. Then, after putting the work gloves on, she removed some of the branches to reveal freshly dug soil. She removed one glove and picked up a small amount of the soil with her bare hand. She squeezed the damp soil between her fingers and thought back to the day she discovered this secret place. It was secret in the fact that she was the only one in the whole world who knew what lay beneath the mess of brambles and what the future held in store for the small plot of land. After she had finished high school, she bought a car and began searching the country side not far from her home. At first, she didn't know exactly what she was looking for, but as her search intensified, she knew she would recognize the right place when she saw it. To her delight, not long after her search began, she chanced upon the perfect spot where she could complete a project she had dreamed of for years. Her dreams were vivid and compelling, repeating the same scene over and over until Carly couldn't resist the need to make them real.

As she felt the water content of the dirt in her hand, she thanked whatever source created the perfect growing conditions she had found. The place was halfway up a mountain for crying out loud. Wasn't damp growing soil supposed to be in the valley bottoms? Knowing a bit about geology, she assumed that some sort of underground spring was seeping above an impervious layer, keeping it just below the surface in this one small area. She thought it was perfect, just perfect! This explained the tangle of brambles, thick enough to keep all other vegetation from growing. Another plus for Carly was the ability of the brambles to keep anyone who happened by from seeing her preparations as they unfolded. The brambles covered an area approximately one quarter of an acre on a mild slope. Trees completely surrounded the plot, except for one car-sized opening just off the dirt access road. Hanging branches concealed the opening. When a vehicle, such as the rental truck Carly had today, pushed through the hanging branches, they closed in behind the vehicle, completely hiding it from view. Carly was very happy with this feature, although, judging by the overgrown access road, there was very little traffic…ever.

In her dreams, Carly conjured up a picture of beautiful flowers on a hillside, shimmering in bright sunlight. She envisioned sitting by the garden with her eyes closed, talking to the flowers and remembering good times they reminded her of. As work progressed, Carly realized she needed a name for her tranquil refuge, and taking a cue from the vision the flowers presented to her in dreams, decided to call it simply, the love garden. Everyone was looking for love. People always seemed to talk about it, so that was the name she decided on. Whenever she was there, she would remember good times and be re-energized to continue her quest to find her destiny. Time after time, opportunity to change her ways for the better presented itself only to be sabotaged by Carly's need to finish her project. A few very great men shared intimate and loving time with her, but the good times soon faded, and Carly felt the need to move on. Her garden took priority over everything else. She desperately tried to fight the need to complete her project, but whenever she came close to succeeding, the pull from her secret place overwhelmed her, and she succumbed to its spell.

Carly tossed the soil aside, wiped her hand and put her work glove back on. She removed more of the branches to reveal a long narrow excavation – Syd's grave. Using the knife, from the sports bag, she cut away the tape and ropes that were securing the box containing Syd. Then she dragged Syd to the grave, dumped him in and, using the soil piled next to the grave, covered him up, without any departing words whatsoever. Next, she placed the brush over the mound, threw the shovel aside and crushed the large cardboard box flat. It was now early morning. Daylight began to filter through the treetops on the eastern edge of the ridge, and soon the cool air would start to warm.

Carly stripped naked. Her clothes fell to the ground around her as she frantically tore at them. Then as the sun slowly ascended, she pranced around her garden, singing her song.

"My love garden
My love garden
Filled full of love
See my love garden
My love garden
From way up above."

Faster and faster, she cavorted past several brush covered mounds, chanting louder and louder.

"My love garden
My love garden
Filled full of love
See my love garden
My love garden
From way up above."

She stopped by a mound that was situated the farthest left in the clearing. It was shaped like an "L." She spoke to the mound, "Eddy you were the first guest in my garden. It's been a long time, hasn't it? You'll be happy to know I'm almost finished. Only two more, and then you will all get flowers. Won't that be nice? And Dan, next to Eddy all this time. Thanks for the check every month.

That trust fund sure comes in handy. You know with our looks, any child we conceived would have been perfect. Don't you think? I have a picture in my mind, Dan, and she's just perfect. So perfect! Too bad it didn't happen. I'm sad, and I'm sorry. It's been nice talking to you again. Next time, I'll stay a little longer. Bye for now!"

Carly then moved to the next mound, shaped like an "O."

"So, George, Peter, Mike, I would like to introduce you to our new guest, his name is Syd. He's much like you guys: all man. I think you'll like him. I'll tell you a little bit more about him next time. See you soon. Bye!"

She stepped to the third mound in the shape of a "V."

"Gary and Chris how are you? We have a new guest. His name is Syd, and he is such a great guy, just like you two, and you would never guess, one of his old friends is here. In fact, I'm going to talk to him right now. Take care! Oh! I almost forgot. My garden, our garden, will be finished soon, and you'll all get flowers. Soon. Soon! Very soon! YES!"

She yelled and turned to the vertical part of the final mound, which would end up looking like an "E."

"Sam! What a coincidence, your old friend Syd is right next to you. I think that is so cool. Such a small world. I almost passed out a couple of months ago when he showed me an article in the newspaper regarding your disappearance. The authorities had reached a dead end in their search for you and were asking for the public's assistance. One lead they were trying to follow up on was the rumor of a mysterious girlfriend. I still remember the rush I got when I read that line. And then when Syd told me you two had been friends since school, I lost it. I think I told him I had a touch of food poisoning. Anyway, I ran into the bathroom and locked the door. My puking was real noisy, so he believed my story. I have to talk to him now. I'll mention your name. Bye for now!"

Carly turned her head and looked at the top leg of the "E." The part with the fresh fill and twigs.

"Syd! I was just talking to your old friend Sam. You don't have to wonder any more about his whereabouts. He is here, next to you. And you guessed it, I'm that mysterious girlfriend everyone was looking for. I suppose this clears a few things up for you. I'm going to miss you, especially that big cock of yours. In a way, I'm sorry, but I do have to finish my garden. You do understand. Don't you? I knew you would. Just think, only two more and then I can remove these ugly sticks and plant all kinds of flowers on top of you boys. The word "Love" will shimmer in the sun. I'll hire an airplane and take photographs. Oh! It'll be so beautiful. Not long now, Syd. So close! My garden. So close!"

Carly resumed dancing and chanting, faster and faster until, out of breath and exhausted, she stopped by the truck, her beautiful, sweaty body glistening in the new light. She climbed onto the hood of the truck with the bottle of body lotion in her hand. Lying on her back, she spread the oil liberally all over her skin from head to toe, lavishing extra attention to her breasts and genital area, all the time singing her song. The song changed to a moan as her left hand squeezed and rubbed her nipples, and her right hand teased her vagina. Her body arched as the fingers in her vagina quickened their pace, creating warm waves of pleasure over her entire body. As she lost control, her breath stuck in her throat and her body pounded the hood of the truck. The thrashing grew harder and harder until, with an uncontrolled gasp, she shook violently and then lay still.

Shortly after, tears started, slowly at first, then they formed a steady stream, rolling down her beautiful high cheeks, along her ears and throat to the metal of the truck. She started to whimper. This turned into a little girl cry, and soon body-wrenching sobs pierced the still air. Bringing her knees up to her chin, she encircled both legs with her arms, and stayed this way, shaking and crying until, exhausted, she rolled onto her side and slept.

Later in the morning, crows roused her with their calls, causing her to sit up quickly and wince with pain from a throbbing headache. The pain intensified, as visions of the day's work ahead flashed through her mind. She climbed from the hood of the truck and placed the body oil in the sports bag, then, after drying off with the towel, she had one last thing to take care of before packing up to return home. Half running, half walking, she headed to a very old, weed-infested mound in the far left corner of the clearing. As she got closer to the mound, painful memories from her childhood emerged relentlessly. Her mood changed to hate. She could hear the breathing, smell the sweat, images she would never forget. She could also hear the lying words, "I love you!" As she reached the mound, a scary rage engulfed her. She screamed at the top of her lungs, "You bastard, you fucking bastard. I hate you! I hate you! I hate you! Rot in hell you, you bastard!" She then urinated on the mound, all the while continuing her uncontrollable tirade. As the hate subsided, she stumbled back to the truck. Shivers danced on her spine. She gathered up her clothes and sealed them in the small cardboard box in the back of the truck. Then she picked up the shovel and threw it into the truck on top of the crushed refrigerator carton. Satisfied that all items were secured and accounted for, she dressed in the clean clothes she had brought along, climbed into the truck and drove down to the highway, drained of all emotions.

Back in town, she used a dumpster behind a large building to discard all items including the sports bag. Then she washed the truck at a wash station, topped up the gas and returned the vehicle to the rental agency.

As she drove home in her car, thoughts of all the work ahead tormented her, but a quick flash of her garden nearing completion cheered her up. She parked and wearily climbed the steps to her door. A hot bath, two headache pills and a nap took her into the evening, then, waking slowly, she felt refreshed enough to start the hated job that had to be done. Gathering Syd's belongings in the living room, she systematically arranged them into separate piles: charity and disposal. Some clothing was cut into rags.

The next few days kept her busy distributing the items to recycling depots, charity agencies and garbage dumpsters.

A few days before the end of the month, she arranged to have all of her remaining belongings shipped to a large storage locker, which Syd had never been told about. It already contained many of the items that had been removed from the house in the previous weeks. Two large suitcases, some clothing and Carly's personal effects were all that remained in the house, along with cleaning supplies. With all of her goods safely stored in the storage locker, she scrubbed the empty house from top to bottom. Then she placed the house keys on the kitchen counter, loaded the suitcases and clothes into the car and drove away from this location for the last time. A while later, from a downtown public communications center, she sent a personal e-mail.

TO: Mr. Ron Morrison – Northern Insurance
SUBJECT: Job Placement – Syd Barnes
Dear Mr. Morrison,

Regrettably, due to some very personal difficulties, I am unable to accept the position at Northern Insurance that you so graciously offered me. The possibility of any future consideration is also not likely. I cannot receive a reply due to the fact that I am traveling in a very remote area. Thank you for all of your help.
Sincerely,
Syd Barnes

After sending the e-mail, she walked to a public phone and placed a call.

"Hello." A male voice answered.

"Hello, Jeff?" Carly asked.

"Yes, this is Jeff."

"Jeff. How are you? This is Carly."

"Carly?"

"Yes. Remember we met in the restaurant a few weeks ago,

and I said I'd call you?"

"Oh yes! I'd almost forgotten. How are you?"

"I'm fine, thank you! I'm terribly sorry, but I have to leave town for a while and won't be able to see you. However, I promise to call again. Take care of yourself. Bye." She ended the call abruptly.

Crossing her fingers and praying that everything would work out as she had planned, she drove to the main highway heading out of town. An hour later, the city grew smaller in her rear view mirror; the road ahead, obscured through falling tears, silently beckoned.

CHAPTER TWELVE

O nce again, Carly found herself on the familiar road to Sadie's house. The tranquil sanctuary was dancing in her head, luring her forward into its gentle fold. How she wished she were already there.

The monotonous freeway driving allowed her too much time to think. Subjects from long ago mingled with more recent happenings, creating an emotional roller coaster as Carly slowly approached her destination. When she reached the country road close to Sadie's soothing retreat, the beautiful scenery calmed her down, and her thoughts turned to Sadie and whether she would be welcome after again dropping in unannounced after a long absence. But picturing Sadie's understanding smile in her mind, she knew, just like after her last long absence, everything would be fine.

At last, she parked her car beside the ancient Chevy and the overwhelming garden, and the tears started. A few minutes later, after drying her eyes, she approached the pretty little house and gently knocked on the door. Sadie, who had been in the kitchen a few steps away, had not heard Carly's car pull up to the house and now wondered who her visitor could be. She walked down the hall and opened the door. The sight of Carly on her doorstep stole her breath away. Every molecule in her body tingled. Carly felt the same sensation. Sadie reached out to Carly's hands, pulled her into the house and closed the door.

"Dianne, Dianne!" she exclaimed. "Dianne! Oh! You look so good! Here, let me hold you."

She pulled Carly closer. Carly fell into her arms.

The embrace became more than a friendly hug; kisses, at first tender, turned to passion and old feelings re-surfaced. Nothing was said as Sadie led the way to the bedroom. Later Carly dozed, curled up in the arms that had held her so lovingly many times before. Sadie stirred first, "Dear girl, its supper time. I'll fix us something to eat. You stay here. I'll call you when it's ready."

Carly mumbled, "Okay" without waking. Sadie slipped from the bed, put on her robe and slippers, washed up and went into the kitchen. Soon, she returned to the bedroom to wake Carly by softly brushing her cheek and hair with her hand. "Wakey, wakey. I have a nice meal ready."

Carly stretched. Suddenly realizing where she was, she sat up. Sadie jumped back, "What is it, love? Have you been dreaming?"

"No. No. Just sleeping; really sleeping. What time is it?"

"Six thirty. Here's a spare robe you can use. Come on now. Wash and come out to the patio."

"Thank you. I'll be there in a minute."

Sadie went back to preparing the meal in the kitchen, joined a few minutes later by Carly.

"Anything I can help with?" Carly asked.

"Oh! Thank you. Here just take these things to the patio table and sit up. I'm almost finished."

Carly picked up a couple of food-laden dishes from Sadie's hands and carried them to the patio, but instead of sitting, she stood mesmerized by the beauty and tranquility of the garden. Sadie stepped up beside her.

"Come on. Let's eat before it gets cold. We'll still have a couple of hours to see the garden before it gets dark."

Carly smiled and sat, "This looks so good. Thank you."

"You're welcome. I must have known you were coming, the stew was simmering in the pot."

"I thought I smelled something when I arrived, but you know it would be a rare day when you weren't cooking or baking something wouldn't it?" Carly remarked.

"Yes, I suppose that is correct. Come on now, dig in."

The meal was enjoyed with little talk. Carly sat spellbound, taking in as many details of the landscaping as she could. Sadie was studying Carly just as intensely. To end the feast, each had a small slice of delicious homemade cheesecake. Right after desert was finished, Sadie jumped up and gestured. "I don't need any help, thank you. You just go and wander about. This will only take a few minutes."

While Sadie took charge of the dishes, Carly meandered along a narrow, grassy path lined each side by a profusion of flowering plants in no particular pattern. A short distance along the path she felt a warm hand encircling hers to which she responded with a little squeeze. Her free hand brought a pretty rose up to her face. In a whisper, she broke the silence, "It's just so, so beautiful. You're very lucky."

"Perhaps, but it feels much nicer now that you're here."

"Thank you. I'm glad you feel that way. I feel safe here. I can't really describe the feeling. Kind of like tranquil."

"It's no wonder, spending all that time in the city. Could drive anyone crazy. I don't know how you do it. I couldn't."

Carly turned to Sadie. "It's not so bad. It all depends on one's lifestyle. I have gotten myself into situations that have caused me some tension. That's all."

Sadie released her grip and placed both of her hands on Carly's shoulders. "And men," she scolded. "You've been seeing men again. Haven't you? When will you learn? They are the main cause of all your problems. They will only hurt you and break your heart, sending you back here, time after time, seeking solace. Can't you see the hurt you're giving yourself?"

Carly stared intently at the only person in the world who could confront her and get away with it. "Yes, you're right. I've been involved with a man again. But I wouldn't say he broke my heart. Just a few tense moments, nothing to worry about."

Sadie jumped in. "Nothing to worry about? I can feel the stress leaving you every time you come here and each time I see you get strong again only to get yourself in trouble again. It hurts me to see your pain. Why don't you come and stay here for good? You don't need all those problems."

This conversation, in one form or another, had occurred many times with the same result, nothing permanently resolved.

Carly ended it this time. "Please don't push me, Sadie. We can talk later when I'm feeling better. Okay?"

Sadie let out a deep sigh, "I'm sorry, dear. It's just that I don't like to see you hurt. You know how precious you are to me. Take your time. Stay as long as you want. Just remember, I'm here for you."

Carly softened. They kissed before strolling hand in hand through the garden back to the house, as the encompassing country darkness descended. In the house, Sadie filled the bathtub with hot water and scented oil, then she pulled Carly into the bathroom. "Here you are, my dear. You get in there and soak all your troubles away. I still have the dishes to do."

Carly stepped from the borrowed robe into the revitalizing liquid and allowed all meaningful thoughts to dissipate in the rising mist. Classical music drifted through the crack in the door, filtering out the clatter of dishes being scrubbed in the kitchen. Life was good right now in this house. Carly crossed her fingers, wishing with all her power to eventually find her place, her destiny. For the next few weeks, her place would be here in the flowers with Sadie, the fresh air, the silence, and healthy food. Maybe even longer, as long as it takes. She would know when her full strength returned and decision time came calling. In the meantime, relax, relax, relax, forget, forget, forget.

"You all right in there, dear?" Sadie's sweet voice interrupted Carly's drowsy wanderings.

"I'm fine, thank you. Can you get something for me?"

"What do you need dear?"

"I have no clothes or tooth brush."

"Oh! That's right. Still in the car aren't they? Where are your keys? I'll get your things for you."

"On the table. Thank you. Just bring the brown bag, please."

Carly was drying herself when the brown bag was slipped in the door.

"Thank you. I'll be out in a few minutes," she called.

"That's all right. There's no hurry. Just take your time. We have all night."

Carly did take her time, playing with her hair, oiling her skin, plucking here and there. Preened to satisfaction, she emerged from the bathroom, squeaky clean, dressed in a short, pink, silk nightie.

"You look lovely, dear," Sadie gushed. "Are you going straight to bed?"

"Yes. I think I will. I'm still tired."

"You just go right ahead. I have some things to do, and then I'll be right behind you. Night, night."

Carly blew a kiss to Sadie and disappeared into the bedroom. Soon, after an hour of sleep, she felt Sadie's gentle caresses. Waiting passions were ignited. The night was lost to the two dissimilar souls, each in her own state of confusion unable and unwilling to confront the reasons why their bodies must touch. Sadie knew she must have Diane in her life. The need to nurture and build a lasting bond overshadowed any notion of finding someone else, even as the long, discomfiting absences tore her apart. Carly had no such desires; she just helped herself to life as easy as stepping up to a buffet dinner. Take what you like, don't take what you don't like. Simple. And now, one of her times in need, she had to surrender to this caring, non-threatening person who had the ability to siphon her cares away.

The right or wrong of the situation didn't matter to Carly, as in all other aspects of her life; cravings had to be satisfied. The pattern, set years before, seemed unlikely to change, and for now, in Sadie's arms, the issue was shunted aside. Undeniable needs were being served.

Morning invaded the house as the new day demanded to be noticed. The piercing sun elbowed its way past leafy trees in its quest to light the tiny bedroom through the open window. Platoons of flowers, anchored in the soil below the sill, spewed their heavy perfume into the dancing breeze. Two pairs of eyes were teased into cognition. Two "good mornings" were traded. One hug was shared.

Carly placed a finger over her lips and whispered, "Listen! I can hear the brook."

Indeed, the creek that ran partway through the garden could be heard in among the bird songs.

"What a way to wake up! You're so lucky. You know, I almost forgot. How could I?"

"Well, dear, it has been a while, you know. Now maybe it will mean a little more to you." Sadie admonished. Carly got the hint.

"I'm sorry. I didn't mean to stay away so long; it just happened. If it will help any, I'm completely overwhelmed and very happy to be here."

"Thank you! Now, dear, you just stay here and listen to the birds. I'm going to fix us a nice breakfast."

"Thank you so much, Sadie. You're so sweet."

Carly propped herself up on her pillow and, with her eyes closed, tried to identify the birds by the calls they emitted. In the distance, beyond the fence, a lark, and from the tiny marsh, a red-wing blackbird's distinctive trill. Closer in, a sparrow, chickadees and a flicker noisily flashed by her mind's eye while some other bird sounds remained a mystery. Sadie's gentle voice startled her for an instant until the sight and aroma of a fresh cup of coffee added more enjoyment to the pleasant surroundings.

"Thank you, Sadie. Thank you."

"You're very welcome, dear. I hope you like this. It's one of my favorite blends." Sadie handed the cup to Carly and turned to leave. "I'll get my cup and join you, she called back from the doorway. With a full cup of coffee in hand, she returned and curled up comfortably on the foot of the bed. The sweet smells, cheerful chorus and rich coffee gave promise to the rest of the day. No sounds were made from inside the room until well after the cups were drained.

"It is pleasant. Isn't it?" Sadie said, in a soft, soothing voice. Then she sang out, "Time to get up now, breakfast on the patio."

Carly laughed as Sadie, an empty cup in each hand, danced with exaggerated animation back to the kitchen. It made her feel good to see Sadie this happy.

"I don't ever want to hurt you," she mumbled to herself and leaped from the bed.

Carly used the bathroom and appeared on the patio in the borrowed robe.

"I think we should dress for breakfast." She said with enthusiasm.

"That may be a good idea dear, but not too fancy. We want to be comfortable."

"Okay, not too fancy, just drop the robes."

"That's it, no robes, other clothing optional." Sadie got into the theme.

"Actually, you know, we could have a nude meal. Look at this place. No one can see us at all. How about it?" Carly asked and then dropped her robe.

"You silly...what?" Sadie started to protest as Carly gently undressed her.

"Now we can eat," Carly announced as she sat down at the table. Sadie, a little timid at first, sat down beside her. The scrambled eggs, sausages and sweet rolls seemed to taste better for some reason, as if being unclothed stimulated the senses to more awareness. Giggling like partying school girls, the happy couple finished eating, carried the dirty dishes into the kitchen, and cleaned up, still in the nude.

When everything was put away, Sadie asked, "What would you like to do today?"

Carly answered with a question, "Don't you have things you have to do?"

"No, dear. My days are quite free now. I work part time in the library, mostly just to keep busy, and I am involved with a group that does volunteer work. So you see, today is all for you."

After graduating college, Sadie had worked as a junior high school teacher. Shortly into her career, her father, a wealthy surgeon with several medical patents to his name, died and left a sizable will. By shrewdly investing her share, Sadie was able to semi-retire. A few years later, her beloved Aunt Norma offered this lovely little house and half acre at a bargain price. That was eight years ago when Sadie moved in and began to create the lush surroundings being enjoyed and appreciated at this moment. Carly had witnessed the progress almost from the beginning and while giving hints and advice from time to time, did not feel deserving of any credit for the results. This was Sadie's initiative and hers alone. Carly, and many others, marveled at the artistic energy flowing throughout the distinct sections. Changing moods and flora, and yet, cohesively united as a single living entity that could erase fears and prod the senses. Carly intended to remain in this Eden today, and without looking too far into the future, anticipated an unbroken string of days or weeks of rejuvenating leisure.

"I would like to help you in the garden today. Like we used to do. Is that okay?" Carly asked.

"I thought you'd say that. Of course, it's okay. That's all I want to do also, but I think we'd better get dressed." Sadie giggled.

Shorts, t-shirts, runners and no underwear were the chosen apparel for the day. Loose and free to match their feelings. After dressing, Carly walked out to the patio, sat at the table and savored another steaming cup of coffee. Facing skyward, she let out a yell, "Yes! Yes!"

"Goodness! Whatever do you have in your coffee?" Sadie asked.

"Nothing. Absolutely nothing. It's just the air, the birds. Everything! I'm so happy."

"And I'm happy for you, dear. You have cheered me right up."

"Oh! Have you not been feeling well?" Carly was genuinely concerned.

"I haven't been unhappy, more like melancholy. Lately, my thoughts have increasingly been on you. I really wondered if I would ever see you again."

A tear slipped down Carly's cheek. "Again, I'm sorry. Come here."

Sadie leaned over, and Carly kissed some of the pain away. Patting the chair next to her she coaxed. "Sit down, you're making me nervous. Come on, finish your coffee and let's just enjoy ourselves. Please."

Sadie stifled her emotions. "I'm sorry, dear. Forgive me. It's just…you're so much a part of me. And you're right, let's enjoy ourselves."

Carly changed the subject. "I like your patio set. It's beautiful. What happened to the old set?" she asked.

"That old cedar or pine, whatever it was, finally gave out. Lasted years, though, didn't it? Took me a long time to replace it. You know I didn't want plastic. I thought of metal, and then I found this. It's teak. I think from Indonesia. I bought everything you see here, as a set. The glider, two lounges, the table with six chairs and the barbecue stand. And I got a good deal."

Carly ran her hand over the table top, "It fits in beautifully. You did well and it's bulletproof."

Sadie's eyes widened. "Bulletproof? Heavens, I hope not."

Carly laughed. "That's just an expression. It's durable, sturdy, well made."

Sadie smiled. "Yes, you are so right. 'Bulletproof.' That's good. Very descriptive. I like that."

Carly held her hands out. "Here are two hands to help you. Give me something to do," she demanded.

"Coming right up," Sadie replied, as she walked toward a potting table at the far end of the patio. She returned and handed Carly a small pair of cutting tools and a plastic bucket.

"You can go around the patio here and snip off all the shriveled flower heads for me. Thank you. I'm going to trim back these vines."

The pleasant work began and continued through the morning until Carly, feeling pangs of hunger, called for a break. They washed their hands and, working efficiently and skillfully, whipped up a delicious lunch, again eaten on the patio, while they admired the morning's accomplishments. Carly commented, "You sure went at that vine. Didn't you? Agent Orange has nothing over you."

"Yes, I did." Sadie replied, "It's something I've been meaning to do for a while now. Sometimes I'm kind of hesitant to hack away at a healthy plant, but when I make up my mind, I fly at it. Looks better now. It was taking over the whole wall. Guess that's what I get for helping everything grow so well."

Carly chuckled, Sadie joined in.

They carried the dishes into the kitchen and left them on the counter to be cleaned later. Returning to the patio, Sadie complimented Carly's work.

"You did a great job. Thank you. Look at that pile of buds."

Carly spread her arms. "What do we do with all this?" she asked.

"Just wait here, and I'll show you." Sadie fetched a garden cart from the rear of the house. Everything goes in here," she declared, as she parked the cart beside the pile of buds and vines.

"Probably take two or three loads," Carly remarked.

"Yes. Looks like it," Sadie agreed.

With the cart topped up for the first trip, Carly asked, "Okay, now. Where to?"

"Over here," Sadie beckoned, and started down a brick path. Carly followed, pushing the laden cart. The meandering walkway took them through English flower gardens and ended at a clearing hidden from view by a hedge. At one end of the clearing sat a large, fiberglass contraption. Carly had not been shown this clearing the night before and now, as she faced the official looking object, she let out a squeal, "How nice! You finally replaced those plywood boxes."

"Yes, I did. They fell apart, same as the old garden furniture. Welcome to my new composter. It works well too."

"Great! I'll dump this stuff here and go back for another load," Carly said, as she tipped the cart. Then she wheeled it away toward the patio, leaving Sadie to load up the compost bin. When she returned, the bin was almost full and the first pile had disappeared.

"My, that was fast."

"Yes. Good thing I emptied this just last week. It will only take a little bit more, so we'll have to leave some on the ground here. Is there any more left on the patio?"

"No, I managed to get it all."

"I thought so. That's quite a load."

Carly dumped the second load. Sadie put some in the compost bin, added some soil and closed the lid, "There, that's done. Would you like to help me in the vegetable patch, dear?" she asked.

"Love to. That's why I'm here. let's go!" Carly cheerfully answered.

"Thank you. We'd better bring the cart."

Sadie led the way back along the path. They walked through the patio area toward the front of the property, close by the road. There, in the meticulously laid out vegetable garden, the work recommenced, harvesting what food was ready and weeding until dinnertime. The cart was loaded, half with harvested vegetables and half with weeds. Sadie then wheeled the cart back to the patio where she carefully unloaded the edible items. She left the weeds for Carly to deliver to the compost area. After that, the two carefree gardeners washed, cleaned the vegetables and prepared a warm, home-cooked meal. When the dinner was finished, the dishes were cleaned up, and the happy twosome relaxed in the living room to the sounds of soothing background music until bedtime.

This idyllic state extended through the next day and into the second week with little variation: gardening, housework, reading, TV, cuddling and loving. Two afternoons a week, Sadie worked at the local library, leaving Carly alone to relax by herself. One morning, the two went shopping in the nearby market to restock the pantry. Several times, Sadie tried to get Carly to open up her pent-up secrets, to no avail. Carly pleaded for more time. Sadie backed off.

At the end of two weeks, Carly woke early one morning in preparation for a planned trip to the city, some thirty miles down the highway, alone. Wanting to tag along, but sensing Carly's need to be alone, Sadie wished her a safe trip and watched as the car slipped away. Anxiety had gripped Carly the past few days, she didn't know exactly why, and Sadie had noticed. When she asked what was wrong, Carly had brushed her aside. This punished her thoughts now as she strained to see the vanishing car. Behind the wheel, Carly struggled to unravel the strange premonition, as the city beckoned to her with all the city sights and sounds. Finding her destination didn't take long, and soon she was parked at a small strip mall where a mail service outlet held her personal mail, which had been forwarded from her old address. A personable young clerk checked her ID, before he handed over a large armload of assorted mail. Carly had insisted on this as part of the contract for the service. She placed the envelopes on the car seat and drove to a quiet park where she sorted through the pile looking for anything out of the ordinary. A few bills, a small book she had ordered, advertising brochures, credit card statements, a bank account statement, and surprisingly a couple of checks, rebates from closed accounts, but nothing unexpected. Perhaps something more ominous waited at her next stop. Shivers danced on her spine as she steered across town to another strip mall and a different mail service. Approaching the clerk, she asked for any mail for Syd Barnes. There was. The clerk said he could only release it to Syd Barnes in person or Sally Kenyon.

"Are you Sally Kenyon?" he asked.

"Yes, I am," Carly answered, demurely.

"May I see some ID, please?"

Carly reached into a small compartment in the bottom of her purse and presented a couple of cards to the clerk. "Here you are."

The clerk looked at the cards and gave them back to Carly, then turned to a compartment on the wall behind him. He turned back and handed her Syd's mail, "Here's your mail. Just a couple. Have a nice day."

"Thank you. You too. Good bye."

Carly, gripping the ID cards and two envelopes, walked briskly back to her car. Before checking the mail, she made sure the two identification cards were safely stored in the undetectable slot in her purse. Relief pulsed over her when she saw that nothing troublesome had arrived, just a thank you note for Syd from a health club for past patronage and a small unpaid bill for cell phone service, which Carly would gladly pay. Now she faced another concern, had anything been missed? Over time she had pestered Syd to divulge details about his life, such as bank accounts, organizations, friends and relatives, which he readily proffered, hoping to gain her trust. At Syd's insistence, she offered up certain particulars concerning her own situation, although if Syd had bothered to check, he would have found most of it to be false. Now, just in case something had been overlooked, Syd's mail was being forwarded and intercepted, which in itself was risky, but necessary. Thankful that nothing worrisome had shown up, she decided to have lunch and check out some local shops that had struck her fancy some years before.

As she strolled to a small sandwich shop, she was delighted to see that more stores had opened in the last year. Eager to get started, she did not linger over lunch before plunging head first into some heavy duty shopping. Two hours later, happy with her purchases, she loaded the car but, instead of getting in, she placed a call at a nearby pay phone.

"Hello." A male voice answered.

"Jeff?" Carly asked.

"Yes. Jeff here."

"Jeff. It's Carly again."

"Oh yes. You called a couple of weeks ago. How are you?"

"I'm fine thanks, and I trust you're good too."

"Yes, I'm great. What is the purpose of your call?" Jeff asked.

"Nothing specific, Jeff. Just keeping in touch."

"That's nice. Can we meet for coffee?"

"I'm afraid not, Jeff. I'm calling from out of town."

"Okay, then. How about when you get back?"

"That's a great idea, but I don't really know when I'll get back."

"Are you working out of town?" Jeff asked.

"Not working, just taking care of some business. How's your work coming?" Carly inquired, knowing he was involved in a research project.

"Very good. I'm making some headway, but it keeps me busy. Thanks for asking."

"Maybe I can give you a break when I return."

"Sounds good. I'll hold you to it."

"It's a date. I'll keep in touch. Bye." Carly replaced the handset, jumped in her car and joined the evening commuters on the way out of town. Forty-five minutes later, she parked at the pretty little house. As she walked in the door, weighed down by packages, the delicious aroma of homemade soup and roast beef teased her nostrils. Sadie greeted her.

"Hello dear, come and sit up. Dinner's ready."

"I can tell. Smells good. I have to put these things in the bedroom. Be just a minute." She put the packages on the bed, washed her hands and skipped to the kitchen into Sadie's embrace.

Sadie asked, "Get everything done?"

"Oh, yes," Carly answered. "Picked up my mail and had time to do some shopping. All in all, a good day. How about you?"

"Oh, I kept busy. Look over there."

Carly followed Sadie's finger, "Pies! Yummy! That's what smells so good!"

"Yes! Now sit up and tell me about your shopping."

Between bites and expressions of praise for the delicious meal, Carly described her afternoon spent exploring the boutiques on Third Street, a trendy, upscale neighborhood. Sadie furrowed her brow. "How can you afford to shop there? I can't."

"I manage. I look for bargains and I can haggle, but sometimes there's something I just have to have. Come on I'll show you."

The pie would wait until later, as Carly grabbed Sadie's hand, eager to display her latest acquisitions. One by one, the packages were opened to reveal their treasured contents: a couple of tank tops, denim shorts, one pair of jeans, until one large bag remained. Carly handed it to Sadie.

"For me?" Sadie asked in surprise.

"Yes, for you. Go ahead, open it up."

Sadie gingerly opened the package, slowly revealing a beautiful burgundy trimmed, white terry bathrobe. Holding it in front of her, she gushed, "It's beautiful. Thank you! Thank you!"

Carly held the bag up to Sadie, "Here, there's something else."

Sadie reached in and pulled out a pair of fluffy slippers matching the bath robe. She squealed in delight, "They're beautiful! Thank you so much!"

"You're welcome! Go ahead put them on."

Sadie put the robe and slippers on and looked in the mirror,

"What's this here?" she asked, when she noticed some embroidery over her heart.

"That's your name, making it your personal robe."

Carly had purchased the robe at the start of her shopping spree, leaving it at the store to be embroidered with "Sadie" in gold script over a gold rose. Sadie was overcome. Carly embraced her, "Relax. It's just a robe. Enjoy it. Come on. Let's get rid of that old one."

The old threadbare robe and tattered slippers were tossed into the garbage. Then the happy couple sat down to enjoy some delicious cherry pie. Carly, dressed in her new shorts and tank top, and Sadie dressed in her new robe and slippers, were all smiles. That night, Sadie slept soundly in Carly's arms, safely confident that Carly really cared. The next morning she asked if Carly would like to accompany her to the local children's daycare center, where she volunteered. Carly, starting to tire of the home life, readily agreed. After breakfast they walked the few short blocks to the daycare center, located in the basement of the local church.

Carly, who had never had much experience with children, quickly took to the eager youngsters after being introduced by Irene, one of the two church ladies who ran the classes. The children, staring wide-eyed at the pretty lady with the beautiful smile, soon started to compete for her attention. As children often do, they began showing off their artwork and toys. Sadie, Irene and Sandra, Irene's business partner, couldn't compete with Carly, so they busied themselves organizing the various activities and intervening when some of the little ones became over exuberant. Intelligent and flexible, Carly had no trouble controlling the individual groups as they tended their artwork and projects. Her praise was genuine, but as they soon found out, when a scolding was served it was to be heeded, no back talk, no pouting. Toward the end of the afternoon, Carly directed the class to sit in a half circle on the floor. She read books to them, portraying the characters in the stories with voice changes and animated gestures, capturing the little audience's full attention. When it was time to leave at the end of the day, Carly listened to the tiny pleas asking for a return visit and promised to make an appearance at least once a week.

The walk home was silent after the initial praise for an outstanding job well done from Sadie.

"I suspected you would be good with children, but I never imagined. You're a natural," she gushed.

Carly only nodded, her twirling thoughts were just catching up with the day's activities. 'How open and honest these little children were with their unabashed acceptance of praise and attention. Why couldn't big people be more like that? Mind you, those were country children. Were they any different from city children?'

Questions stacked up like circling aircraft. 'Would she ever have children of her own? Did she even want children? What kind of father would she choose?' Before she could sort through and answer any of the persistent questions, her thoughts were interrupted by Sadie's soft voice, "We're home, dear. You look tired."

"I am. The energy level of those little kids. I'm drained."

"Yes, I know how you feel." Sadie agreed and then continued, "You'd think the energy would rub off, wouldn't you? But it doesn't seem to work like that."

"No, it doesn't, and I think that's so unfair." Carly allowed a nervous laugh to escape. She begged to forego helping with dinner, choosing to have a hot bath instead.

"With my blessing, dear." Sadie urged. "I'll have a nice meal ready for you when you're finished. Go ahead now and take your time."

After a lingering embrace, Carly ran herself a hot bath while Sadie prepared pasta. The soothing water eased her mind and body. She couldn't shake the closeness she felt to the little children she had enjoyed during the day. The unanswered questions in her head continued. When she finally appeared at the dinner table, Sadie noticed her melancholy mood and remained silent. At the end of the meal, Carly excused herself and padded off to bed, leaving Sadie to clean up. Working quickly and efficiently, Sadie made short work of the kitchen chores and slipped into bed next to a sobbing Carly. Her loving arms gently encircled the shivering flesh, holding the two of them together as one, through a fitful sleep until morning.

The rising sun improved Carly's mood. She thought of the familiar adage that things really do look better in the morning. Now she wondered, 'Why is that?' and started to laugh.

Sadie, having worried most of the night over what crisis Carly was enduring, felt better too. They kissed and intimate feelings swept them away, leaving all questions and discussions waiting until later. And it was later, almost noon in fact, when they left the bed and showered together that Sadie asked Carly what was bothering her.

"I don't really know. I keep seeing the happy faces of those children, and I start thinking of their future."

Sadie, who was softly lathering sweet-smelling soap on Carly's back, was puzzled by the reply, "I don't understand. What could their future mean to you?"

"Nothing, I suppose. It's just that right now they are like a new computer, ready to be programmed. The people in their lives and events they are witness to can influence and affect them deeply. I guess I'm worried that some evildoer might scar them for life, leading to who knows what down the road."

Sadie drew a deep breath. "You're trying to tell me something. Aren't you?"

"Maybe," was all Carly could answer. Sadie, clinging to any chance to explore Carly's anguish, tried once again to open the door to the answers she sought. "Remember the last time you were here, you started to tell me about your father and mother when you were a little girl?"

Carly stiffened. "Yes, I remember."

"Can you tell me now? I really need to know, dear." Sadie, in her sweetest voice, practically begged for something, anything. Her eyes asked for Carly's trust.

"I don't think I'm ready yet. You do understand. Don't you?" Carly whispered.

"But maybe you are, dear. I know you have something to tell me. I want to share everything with you. Can you do that for me? For us?"

Carly gently pushed Sadie away. "I don't know! I don't know!" she cried.

"Please! For us," Sadie implored.

"No! No! Not now. I can't. I'm not ready." Carly shivered.

"Please tell me." Sadie pleaded.

"NO! NO! I'M NOT READY." Carly screamed.

"Please don't ask me anymore. Please!" She slapped her head and started to cry.

Sadie grasped Carly's wrists. "I'm so sorry, dear. I didn't mean...I'm sorry! Please calm down. It's all right. Everything's all right."

Carly's explosive fit ended, but the crying continued. Sadie embraced her until the sobbing stopped. After a long and awkward silence, they dried themselves, got dressed and prepared lunch. The meal was eaten in silence. Carly was embarrassed. Sadie was awkwardly apologetic. Before the dishes were cleaned up, Carly rose from her chair, walked around to Sadie, dropped to her knees and buried her head in Sadie's lap. Holding back tears, she whispered, "I do want to tell you. I don't know where to begin, but I do want to tell you some things. Please be patient. I don't think I'm quite ready. Maybe in a while. I know you can help me, but not right now." Her little girl voice trailed off.

Feeling the burden of guilt ease, Sadie consoled her. "I know, dear. We will talk, but you're right, not now. I'll wait until you are ready. Oh! Look at that sunshine. Come on, let's enjoy the rest of the day. Life is so precious. Isn't it?"

The words, uttered so innocently, pierced Carly like a knife. Sadie, noticing the sudden tension and not understanding what exactly had caused it, wisely waited for Carly to calm down. Startled by Carly's change in appearance, she pointed her toward the patio door. "We can leave the dishes till later. Right now, I think you need some fresh air. You have to get your color back." As she pulled Carly outside, her mind skimmed over the many times the same conversation had been started and never finished, but now it felt more important to complete. She felt confident that it wouldn't be very long until Carly shared some happenings from her past that were troubling her. Events that were eating away at her that, if they were shared, could be erased and put to bed forever. It wouldn't be today, but Sadie knew it would be soon. It had to happen.

The rest of the day was spent in and around the garden and patio area, removing wilted flowers, planting cuttings and seedlings and harvesting edibles. Nothing more was mentioned concerning Carly's past, but there was a certain apprehension present as they each tried hard to be extra nice to the other. It was as if a milestone had been passed, and a new direction had to be chosen. A new route that would either strengthen their future together or severely constrict the relationship they were enjoying. As their hands did the garden work, their thoughts were far off in different directions. Two separate minds, facing the subject with their individual needs and questions, anticipating a breakthrough that would change their lives. Lucky for them the garden work didn't require their full attention. Carly had mentioned that she had a sort of garden, earlier in the day, and now as the afternoon work tapered off Sadie asked, "Who is looking after your garden while you are away?"

Carly, wishing she hadn't mentioned the subject, controlled herself, as her insides began to heave, "Nobody, really. It's not a real garden yet, more like in the planning stage, but I hope to finish it soon." As she spoke, her mind raced back to the clearing on the hill, and how she wanted to see her garden finished. The mental picture of her garden, conjured up in the tranquil surroundings of Sadie's house, triggered a conflict that had torn her on her last visit. But this time seemed different. Very, very different. For one thing, she had never gotten so involved with Sadie's activities before. She had always been happy to sit quietly in the garden while Sadie kept busy. This time, the visits to the library, grocery shopping and above all else, the beautiful little children, were so thoroughly enjoyable that she had almost forgotten this was not her home. Or was it? How long could she avoid making the decision to stay? The life-changing choice would not be ignored much longer. Her future and tender, loving Sadie's future were too important. As the struggle gripped her, Sadie interrupted her wandering thoughts.

"Planning stage? How far along are you?" she asked.

Carly tried to ease away from the touchy subject. "It's…it's kind of hard to explain. It's not a real garden, certainly not anything like yours. It is a very peaceful place in the country that holds some special memories for me. When I go there I recall many good times I have enjoyed over the years. In any case it's not important.

The far away look in Carly's eyes concerned Sadie. She wanted to hear more, but recognized the signs that told her the matter was closed for now. The day ended peacefully with a beautiful setting sun spreading soft light, muted by wispy shadows, over the evening meal being enthusiastically enjoyed by the hungry gardeners. Apprehension, hope and fear jostled for notice in each mind as the food disappeared in silence. Sadie wanted only one thing, Carly to stay, to be a part of her life while Carly, fighting her past and fearing her future, wished she could solve this dilemma as easily as she had with many other predicaments, just walk away. As disturbing emotions settled in, both of them waited for the day when some kind of resolution would be reached to this highly charged, nerve-racking problem. Until then, an undercurrent of urgency governed the actions of the confused couple as each exaggerated pleasantries toward the other.

The impasse hung in the air for the next week and a half. Each time Sadie attempted to open some kind of dialogue, Carly refused to continue the conversation, using one excuse or another to stall the inevitable. She planned another trip to the city. This would give them a break from each other and the mind-numbing tension.

A few days later, before driving to the city, Carly embraced Sadie and asked if she could get anything for her while she was away. Sadie answered, "No, just be safe and hurry home."

"Don't worry," Carly replied. "I'll see you tonight."

She hopped into her car and waved back to the sad figure in the driveway, as she accelerated away from the house. Arriving in the city, she picked up a few pieces of unimportant mail at the two mail outlets and then relaxed at a small coffee shop before spending some time browsing and shopping. Late in the afternoon, she placed a call from a payphone.

"Hello," a recognizable voice answered.

"Jeff?" Carly asked, although positive it was him.

"Yes, this is me. Is this Carly?"

"It is. How did you know?"

"Just a feeling, Carly. Kind of a guess. How are you and where are you?"

"I'm still away from home, and I'm doing well. Thank you. How are you?"

"I'm great. I really didn't think I'd be hearing from you again. Been a few weeks now. Hasn't it?"

"Yes, I guess it has, but I haven't forgotten you. I've been so busy and there are some things I must take care of before I see you. I can't elaborate now. I'm working on it. I hope you understand."

"Kind of. I don't know what I'm supposed to understand. Can you tell me anything?"

"It's all a bit personal, maybe even a little boring, so if you don't mind, I'd sooner not say. Is that okay?"

"I guess it'll have to be. Tell me what else is happening in your life."

"I can do that: just shopping, taking it easy and enjoying the sunshine. Nothing too strenuous."

"Sounds like you have an easy life."

"It does, doesn't it? I'm just taking a bit of a break, and I'm making the most of it. Sooner or later I'll have to return to reality, so until then…"

"You do what you have to do, Carly. Call me when you get back to town. We can get together then. Is that all right with you?"

"That sounds good. It's exactly what I had in mind. I'll keep in touch. Bye for now."

"Talk to you later, Carly."

Unable to erase the sound of Jeff's voice, Carly deliberately drove extra slowly away from the city, wishing she had not contacted him. What had compelled her to call, and why did she always try to find a reason to leave the solace of Sadie's tranquil haven?

With each passing mile, visions of the quiet retreat transformed into images of her own garden as a finished project. She had long visualized how her garden would appear when completed, but now after helping Sadie, the dazzling beauty of the conceptual picture grasped her attention.

She fought to justify the need to abandon her past and find a new, more meaningful direction. The bold profusion of color crowding her mind's eye, challenged all arguments. Perhaps if she revealed some of her darkest secrets to Sadie, the necessary strength and courage required to consummate a change would materialize. She would make that decision in the morning. Right now she had to get safely back before the sweat and shivering forced her off the road.

Sadie paced. To her, Carly was late. It wasn't really late but she worried just the same. The past few days had concerned her and now she questioned whether she had done enough to defuse the situation. All day, she had visited and revisited various conversations with Carly. Time had obliterated details and facts rendering the reminiscences almost meaningless.

There was still no car in Carly's parking space next to the ancient Chevy. Sadie decided a glance down the street may help. At the very least, a breath of evening air would offset the stifling stillness of the house.

She didn't see it at first, but then, as she neared the road, the sight made the hair on her neck stand up. The rear of Carly's car was protruding from a blackberry bush on the other side of the driveway. She rushed to the disturbing scene, but the prickly bush kept her from the door. She panicked at the sight of Carly slumped over the steering wheel.

She screamed out, "Dianne, Dianne. Are you all right? Dianne. Answer me! Please!"

Carly looked up through tear-filled eyes. "I'm okay. Yes, I'm okay. I must have missed the turn. Watch yourself. I'm going to back up."

Sadie stepped aside, relieved that Carly was all right. Carly dried her eyes, reversed out of the bush and parked properly. Sadie rushed over and pulled the door open. "Oh! Thank God. You're all right. I almost had a heart attack."

"I'm sorry. I guess I lost it for a minute."

"Lost it? Look at you. I don't know what you have been doing. But you're a mess. Come on, let me help you."

Sadie helped Carly from the car to the house. Once inside, all Carly wanted was a hot bath, some milk and then sleep. With Carly safely in bed, Sadie sat with her thoughts for a while, until deciding that the best thing to do was for her to try to get some sleep also. If any answers to her many questions were offered she wanted to be wide awake to digest them. Surprisingly, they both slept well.

In the morning, Sadie left the bed to get coffee and breakfast going. Carly, tracing the trail of the welcoming aroma, tiptoed meekly into the kitchen a few minutes later. No words were exchanged, other than good morning, until long after the meal was consumed on the patio and a second pot of coffee started. Sadie nervously broached the impending talk. "I don't want to pry, dear, but you must tell me what's been bothering you. Please let me help you." She implored through sad eyes and then continued. "Last night, I was scared to death."

Carly clamped her hands tightly on Sadie's, staring wide-eyed at the shaking figure next to her, who truly wanted to help her. She struggled to open the dialogue that had been denied for far too long.

"I'm sorry about last night. You didn't need to see me like that. Please forgive me."

"Oh! That's okay. I'm just so glad you're not hurt. The sight of your car gave me a start."

"I'm really sorry." Taking a deep breath, Carly pressed on. "I've been so unfair. You know so little about me, and I know your whole history. I don't know where to start, but I'll try to answer some of your questions."

Sadie cheered up and answered, "Thank you. I do know some of your past, but not very much. You told me once that you had a rotten childhood, but you didn't say why, and you also said something about your stepfather. You can start anywhere you like. Take your time. I'm here for you."

The anxiety eased as Carly released Sadie's hands and left the table. Pacing the patio, she searched for the right words to use; words that would divulge events from her past and personal information that no one else knew. The difficulty was where to begin. So many times and places confused the matter. Finally, she decided to start with Sadie's cue. "You remembered. I did tell you about my dreadful childhood, didn't I? This might seem strange, but I feel as though I remember my childhood being worse than it really was. Could that be?"

Sadie thought for a minute before answering, "Certainly, my dear. It's not that you recall it as being worse, the truth is probably closer to the fact that children deal with problems differently than adults. For one thing, they often wish bad things away or withdraw into some kind of fantasy land. If a child has suffered through some serious traumatic experience, he or she may suppress the disturbing thoughts until many years later. As an adult, they then begin to realize the magnitude of the situation. Sometimes, it's a very painful recollection. It's too bad that so many young people are unable to get the help they need until it's too late. I also think it's too bad that humans are not as successful as animals are when it comes to being parents. We do a great job of protecting children from physical danger, but fail to realize the potent time-bomb of the unprotected young mind. It's not good that you have had some bad times, but it's very good that you may finally be able to deal with them. Talking about your childhood and seeking help is the only way to slay your personal demons. Please let me help."

"I'll try. How is it that you know so much about children?"

"Have you forgotten? I trained as a psychologist and taught school for a few years. As a non-parent, I think I was able to view the kids from a different angle. I still remember some of them coming to me for help rather than asking their parents. I did my best to help most of them solve their problems, but there were a couple I still fret over from time to time. I pray that they turned out okay. Now back to your problems. If you let me in on what's been troubling you, I will do everything I can to help you resolve it once and for all. Take it slowly, and tell me what you can."

"You're right, I did forget you had some psychology training. There are so many thoughts buzzing around, but I'll do my best to tell you what you need to know. Thank you for being here for me."

Carly paced around the patio as she spoke. Sadie followed her fluid movements, clinging to every word.

"I'll start with some things you already know. My father died when I was four years old and I recall telling you that my mother remarried when I was almost six."

Sadie nodded in agreement.

"I never told you ...told...you..." Carly couldn't finish, convulsions and tears forced her to the ground. Sadie rushed to her side and held her tight.

"There, there, dear. Cry, cry, cry. Just keep crying." Sadie cried too. They lay locked together sobbing on the floor of the patio until there were no more tears left. Then Carly, regaining some inner strength, motioned for Sadie to return to her seat. She straightened herself, dried her eyes and continued where she had left off, speaking very softly, forcing Sadie to lean closer to catch every word.

"I hate that man! I hate that man!"

"Your stepfather?" Sadie asked.

"Yes, I hate him, I hate him!"

Sadie noticed Carly's furrowed brow and pulsating veins, then she looked down to see the clenched fists with beautiful finger nails digging into soft, fleshy palms. Impulsively, she reached out to hold them. "Stop. Stop right there." She interrupted before Carly's fear could derail her dialogue. "Close your eyes, take a deep breath. Take your time. We have all day. I'm not going anywhere."

Carly closed her eyes, paying heed to the soothing voice. Soon she was ready to continue. Without opening her eyes she began. "Sorry!" she squeaked.

"Nothing to be sorry about, dear. Now go slowly and relax. I'm right here for you."

"Okay! I don't know why my mother chose such an evil man when she remarried. She was so attractive, it doesn't make sense. I've tried to figure it out and all I can think of is that she felt some kind of guilt over my father's death and wanted to punish herself. Does that make sense?"

"That certainly is a possibility, dear. You say the man is evil. That's very strong language. Could you have misdirected your bitterness, over losing your father, to your mother's choice of substitute?"

Carly bristled, glared at Sadie, pulled her hands free, and screamed, "*I'm not making this up. The man was evil!*"

Sadie, shocked by the outburst, waited several minutes until Carly had composed herself before resuming her quest to learn more about her dear, troubled friend. Very gently, she pressed on, "I didn't say you are making things up. You were so young and losing your father at such a young age, who knows what effect that had on your mind. Now, if you can tell me, I would like to know why you think your stepfather is so evil."

"Was."

"Was? Are you saying he is no longer evil?"

"No. He disappeared when I was eighteen years old."

"And you're afraid you might run into him again."

"That would be impossible."

"Impossible? Is he locked up somewhere?"

"Not really. He's in a place where he can never hurt anyone again."

"You mean he's dead?"

Carly shivered and answered, "Let's just leave it at he will never hurt anyone ever again. Okay?"

Sadie wanted to hear more, but noticing the rising agitation in Carly's response, decided to take a break from the topic. "I'm sorry this is upsetting you so much. Let's take a walk in the garden. We need to feel the fresh air."

Carly agreed. She knew how much Sadie wanted to help her, and she really wanted to divulge the information from her past, but the pain of recounting the events was threatening to overpower her ability to tell. A walk in the garden would help clear her head. 'Bless Sadie,' she thought.

The fresh air and nose-tingling fragrances didn't ease the tense emotions by very much. The anguished couple purposely dawdled along the brick path. They were both very aware that eventually, when this interlude ended, the painful talk would resume. They strolled beyond the path, only stopping to smell the fragrant blossoms. A few minutes later, they reached the clearing with the compost bin, where they sat on a stone wall in the sun. The warming rays regenerated sagging spirits, offering some hope to the struggling pair before they slid from the perch and slowly retraced their steps back to the house. Upon reaching the patio, Carly plopped down on one of the teak chairs while Sadie went into the house to fetch a pitcher of water and a couple of glasses. When she returned to the table, they each finished one large glassful and part of another. Sadie, now sitting next to Carly, remarked, "How can a throat get so dry?"

"I was thinking that myself. Must be nerves, emotion, anticipation, I don't know. Thanks for the water."

"Oh, dear! You're very welcome. Do you feel a little better?"

"Yes, I do. Thank you! That little break did me good. I think I can continue our conversation. I'll try my best. I promise."

"Take your time. Take your time."

There was a long pause while Carly grappled with a stampede of words, times, dates and events. Sadie had the right to know her hidden past, but where was the limit? What should she reveal? What should remain her burden alone? Would she inadvertently blurt out some revealing details that could lead to more problems down the road? Steeling herself for Sadie's response, she erupted. "He raped me!" Stunned by her own words, she fell silent. Without showing any emotion to Carly's disclosure, Sadie waited for more. When she realized that Carly had surprised herself and had shut down in response to her own statement, she answered, "I know!"

Taken aback by this reply, Carly snapped. "You know? You know? How could you?"

"I'm sorry! I don't really know, but I suspected."

"Oh!"

"Yes! For quite some time now I have had pieces of the puzzle in place. Enough to convince me that such a terrible thing had happened to you."

"Why didn't you tell me?"

"I tried many times, but you weren't ready. It's not my place to just come right out with it. You see that might have added to any stigma you may be carrying. You had to find the right time and place to unburden yourself, such as you just did."

"Oh! I just said it. Didn't I? Do you think this is the right time?"

Carly looked for some kind of assurance. Sadie offered her soft words. "That is entirely up to you. At some point in time, you will have to share this with someone, and only you can tell when that will be. I can only try to help you."

Carly knew that Sadie was right. One thing was certain, she couldn't carry the load forever. She would have to tell someone. Who better than sweet Sadie? And would there be a better time? Gathering her thoughts, and determined to banish the poisonous recollections from her past, she decided that this is probably as good a time as any. She pressed on. "I was raped…many times. I was raped."

"Yes, dear. I know. It was painful." Sadie interrupted, "Can you tell me who, although I think I know?" Carly screamed, "MY STEPFATHER. THE BASTARD." She pounded the table. Sadie grabbed her wrists. "Yes! Yes! I know. Close your eyes. I know. Breathe deep. Close your eyes. Try to relax. I know. It must have been awful. I'm right here for you. Try to push all the pain into my hands. Just let the pain flow out of your fingers into mine. Let me absorb some of the pain."

Carly did as Sadie asked, forcing her fingers into Sadie's palms, her eyes tightly shut. The draining posture lasted until Carly's legs buckled, forcing her forward into Sadie's sheltering arms. Sadie knew the subject was closed for now, perhaps for a long time. The healing door was ready to be opened, and she pledged to do all in her power to help Carly reach beyond her self-imposed limits. Her training and intuition told her that some emotional baggage was keeping Carly from stepping past a fixed point. Was she afraid of failure? Was she deliberately stalling?

Satisfied that a very significant step had been taken, Sadie helped Carly to the couch, covered her with a blanket and went into the bathroom. She soaked a face cloth with warm water and returned to the couch to place it on Carly's feverish forehead. Soon the fragile, distressed beauty was sleeping peacefully.

The emotionally charged day had slipped by and Sadie, still churning from Carly's disturbing trials, knew she had to eat. In the kitchen, she quickly prepared a sandwich, and then carried it back to the couch. Tears stained her cheeks as she agonized over her troubled friend while nibbling at the now tasteless food. Should she wake Carly or let her sleep? Wishing and needing to cuddle up to Carly through a night she feared would be fretful, she made the tortuous decision to leave her in peace. After placing the half-eaten sandwich on the coffee table, she removed the face cloth from Carly's forehead and planted a kiss where it had been, then slowly shuffled to her large, lonely bed.

Sleep, usually her friend, betrayed her that night. Through the small hours of darkness, she tossed and turned, cried and agonized over Carly, searching for some key or avenue leading to a peaceful future. Sleep finally calmed her, but not for long. Before any morning light penetrated the little room, a moving figure startled her awake. She listened. Finally realizing it was Carly, she called, "Good morning!"

"Oh! Good morning. I'm sorry! I didn't mean to wake you."

"That's all right, dear. What time is it?"

"Five o'clock. Go back to sleep."

"Aren't you coming to bed?" Sadie asked.

"No. I'm kind of busy," Carly replied.

When her eyes adjusted to the dark, Sadie realized what Carly was doing, prompting her to bolt upright into a sitting position. "YOU'RE PACKING!" She cried. The sudden realization sent a cold shiver through her spine. Convulsions and tears followed. Carly rushed to her side.

"I'm sorry! I'm so sorry!" was all she could utter. "I'm so

sorry! I must..." Her voice trailed off as loud crying took over. They cried, locked together for many minutes. Finally, Sadie pushed Carly away, "Why, Diane? Why? Must I go through this again? When will it end? Can't you stay, get the help you need? Please." Her mind reeled while words cascaded in random chaos. Finally, when the initial shock abated, she sagged against her pillow, waiting for Carly's explanation. Carly offered no answer until the silence compelled her to begin.

"I must go. There are things I must do. Thank you for everything. I know how bad you're feeling, and I'm truly sorry. I'm still not sure if this is where I belong. So, to be fair to you and to myself, I think it's best for me to leave. I need some time for myself. I do hope you understand."

Sadie sadly nodded, unable to stop the steady flow of tears as she watched Carly pack her clothes. She knew, from past experience, that no words or actions could steer Carly from her chosen course. She had given up trying long ago and now resigned herself to a painful separation, like many times before.

Carly finished packing and loaded her car. Leaving her car to warm up, she returned to Sadie's bed. They embraced and cried tenderly. Carly apologized again. "I'm so, so sorry! Please forgive me."

"There's nothing to forgive, dear." Sadie answered and continued. "Nothing to forgive. You must do what you must do, and good luck to you. Just remember, you'll always have a place here. Now go! Please go!"

One last sad embrace, and Carly left the little house with its fragrant garden, backed her car out of the driveway with its ancient Chevy and headed back down the road that had brought her here. Feeling free and distressed at the same time, she hated to leave Sadie like this, but unsure of her true feelings, she felt that she must leave. With tears in her eyes, she followed the familiar road as thoughts of her unfinished garden danced in her head. The beautiful sight prodded her on.

Back at the little house, Sadie was suffering more pain than she could remember. She fumbled for the un-opened pill box in the rear of her medicine cabinet. Something told her Dianne was not coming back. Finding the container she had been hoarding for so long, she tore open the lid and scooped out a handful of little white pills.

CHAPTER THIRTEEN

C arly had only traveled a few miles when she looked at her wrist and realized she had left her watch and a few pieces of jewelry on Sadie's dresser. She pulled onto the shoulder of the road and waited for a break in the morning traffic, planning to turn around and retrieve the articles. The long line of cars gave her time to think of the emotional scene her return would cause. The situation was stressful enough as it stood, so why create more trouble? Besides, the items could be replaced and Sadie was welcome to keep them as mementos of their friendship. Happy with her decision not to return to Sadie's, she accelerated back onto the road. A few miles later, she turned onto the four lane highway leading home.

The uninteresting freeway driving gave her plenty of time to think. Once again, tears filled her eyes and stained her cheeks. Unable to quell the images of the past few weeks, she felt guilty for, once again, leaving Sadie to suffer immense pain. The WHY and WHAT questions started hammering her. Why does she behave the way she does? What can she do to stop? And Sadie was right, she needed help.

The captivating thoughts masked the miles as they slipped by beneath the humming tires, and soon familiar buildings and landmarks interrupted Carly's agony, turning her thoughts in another direction. She was home.

It was early evening and the traffic was heavy. Carly was thankful that most of the vehicles were leaving town. The incoming cars and trucks were tolerable. She had not arranged for a place to stay and all her furniture was in storage, but she had a plan. She parked by a pay phone and placed a call.

"Hello!" A man answered.

"Hello, Jeff?"

"Yes, this is Jeff."

"Jeff, how are you? It's Carly."

"Carly! My phone pal. I'm fine, thank you. How are you?"

"Great! Jeff. Have you eaten yet?"

"No. Why do you ask?"

"Can I treat you to dinner?"

"Are you cooking?"

"No, no. We can go to a restaurant. How about it?"

"This is so sudden. I don't know what to say."

"Just say yes or no. I'm hungry."

"Yes. Thank you. Where will I meet you?"

"Just give me your address, and I'll pick you up."

"Wow! Service. You're overwhelming me. Do you have a pen?"

"Yes, go ahead."

Carly wrote down Jeff's address, assured him she would be there within the hour and hung up the phone.

Forty-five minutes later, Carly found a parking spot close to Jeff's apartment. It was an upscale building in the downtown core. Carly rang Jeff's number on the intercom and he answered immediately. She entered the building and rode the elevator up to the twelfth floor where she saw Jeff standing in his open doorway. Pleasant greetings were exchanged, then Jeff asked, "Can I show you around?"

"Thank you," Carly answered. "I can see you have a very nice place, but maybe we can do that later. I have been driving, and I'm getting hungry."

"All right then, let's go." Jeff gestured toward the door. In the elevator, Carly remarked, "You look so yummy. I like your clothes."

Jeff flushed. Carly giggled. "You're embarrassed," she teased. "I'm sorry. I know you're shy, but you don't have to feel uncomfortable with me. I like you."

This remark only increased Jeff's discomfort. Carly, used to having men ogle and pursue her, found this painfully bashful good-looking man, very attractive. She squeezed his hand and changed the subject. "When we get to the restaurant, I'd like to hear all about your research work. It must be very interesting."

Jeff, not knowing how studied and knowledgeable Carly was, dismissed the suggestion as nothing more than an attempt to put him at ease. Still, if she wants to listen, he would gladly talk about his work, his life's passion, figuring that she would quickly grow bored and move onto something else. "You sure you want to hear about my work? It's pretty mundane," he asked.

"Trust me. I'm really interested," Carly answered.

The walk to the car was silent and once underway, Carly drove toward the highway that lead away from the city.

"I take it you have a destination in mind," Jeff enquired.

"I sure do. The Mountain Inn. That okay?"

"That's more than okay. A bit pricey, isn't it?" Jeff questioned, in surprise.

"My treat, Jeff. The food is great, and I like the atmosphere. Let's relax and have a good time. See where it takes us." Carly winked.

"I'm feeling more at ease already, Carly. Thank you."

Carly didn't answer. Very little was said for the next hour until the sight of the shimmering lights, outlining the Mountain Inn against the clear evening sky, evoked enthusiastic praise.

Carly broke the silence. "Always breathless. Isn't it?"

"Yes. It certainly is. I always find this view so enticing.

Thanks for the invitation," Jeff answered.

"You're very welcome. And thanks for the company." Carly smiled.

Silence returned for the last mile to the parking area.

The Mountain Inn had been in the same family for more than forty years. The son and daughter of the original builder had managed the business for the past six years, but their dad (known as "Dad" to all) still helped out on special occasions. Very little had changed over the years. Customers could always expect the same wonderful food and service, and the location was an adventure in itself.

Positioning and building the structure was considered folly by many and impossible by others, but "Dad" had a dream and made it come true. When he was young, he spent his summers at his uncle's farm across the valley. Each time he passed the well-known landmark, called "The Rock" his mind would take him on trips to the top. For years he wondered what it was really like way up there, until one day, during a summer break from college, he hired a helicopter to find out. Standing where the restaurant would eventually take shape, he looked out over the valley to the farms and hills in the distance and knew that his destiny and the spectacular promontory under his feet were somehow intertwined.

When they reached the parking lot, Carly parked a short distance from the elevator and stared straight up the cliff face to their destination. Jeff followed her gaze. After several minutes of silent staring, they exited the car and walked to the elevator loading platform.

The elevator descended to the parking level, the doors opened, and Carly and Jeff stepped inside. The slow skyward trip started. Carly and Jeff faced outward, bravely leaning on the brass rail. They absorbed details of the spectacular valley through the spotless glass sides of the tubular shaped conveyance. "Dad" deliberately had the elevator designed to travel slowly in order to allow his guests time to savor the changing scenery from bottom to top as successive waves of hills appeared during the climb. The slow ride was also an indication of the leisurely pace the patrons would enjoy throughout their pampered evening.

Carly had been here before. It was all new to Jeff. He thanked her again without diverting his eyes from the tranquil scenery.

Carly hushed him up, "Enough already! Just enjoy yourself. Please."

Her gruff admonishment shook Jeff, and she quickly changed her mock anger to compassion. She gently kissed his cheek. "I'm sorry. I didn't realize you are so sensitive. Please forgive me. You will won't you?" Carly expertly maneuvered the ball into Jeff's court, feigning the need for his forgiveness. Jeff took the bait.

"Of course, I forgive you, Carly. You startled me for a moment. You looked so angry."

Carly smiled. "And I'm sorry I alarmed you, Jeff. I guess I snapped a bit, didn't I? I'll try to think of your feelings. I'm sorry."

The brief exchange ended with a hug and smiles. It had helped Carly to reach one of her comfort plateaus and the need to have her wrath acknowledged and feared. She knew that Jeff's personality didn't deserve any of her harsh treatment, but old habits were hard to break. And besides, a little insurance was always good. She smiled to herself.

The elevator eased past the ground level of the restaurant building and gently stopped inside the elegant entrance area that protruded precariously from the top level. As the elevator door slid open, Carly and Jeff were met by the affable hostess who greeted them and offered several choices of window tables on either the west side or the east side of the large, elegant dining room. Carly chose a table on the west side with its vast sunset vista. The hostess seated them, placed two extensive wine lists and two very limited food menus on the table and returned to her post. Carly grasped Jeff's hands and stared out the window at the miles of endless scenery. Jeff studied Carly for a moment. He then followed her cue to drink in the intoxicating landscape, laid out as though it had been purposely placed there just for their pleasure. Even though Carly had seen it all before, the enchanting scenery always captivated her, but not as strongly as she felt tonight. She wondered if it was the time spent in Sadie's garden tending the plants, getting her hands dirty and listening to the soothing song birds that awakened some latent inner feelings. Or was it the presence of Jeff, a completely different man than any she had ever been involved with? The questions faded as the mesmerizing scene held her captive. She whispered softly while pointing to distant features glistening in the evening light. Jeff nodded in agreement. Carly turned to Jeff, giving his hands an extra squeeze.

"Makes you kind of horny, doesn't it?" she said with a wicked grin. Jeff's face reddened at the unexpected remark. Carly laughed. "I'm sorry! A little coarse?" She feigned embarrassment. "I have many sides, Jeff. I'll try to behave myself." She picked up a wine list and continued, "Let's find a good wine and enjoy ourselves, shall we?"

Her request sounded more like a command. Jeff complied, fumbling for his wine list, not sure what to say, so he stayed silent. He did not know one wine from another, so he placed the wine list back on the table. "Your treat, Carly, your choice."

"Thank you. I see a nice dry red from California that I like, if that's all right with you?" Carly didn't look up from the list.

Jeff answered, "Sounds good to me."

Carly got the attention of a waiter, ordered a bottle of the chosen wine and then leaned closer to Jeff. Staring intently into his eyes she purred, "I like you!"

Caught off guard, Jeff paused before answering, "Thank you, I'm very flattered, Carly, but I don't understand. You hardly know me. Our short phone conversations couldn't have revealed much about me. Shouldn't we wait awhile before expressing some feelings?"

Carly could see that Jeff was reading a little more into her statement than she had intended. Placing her hand in his, she attempted to explain what she had meant. She laughed. "No! No, I mean I like you as a person. Silly! I like your aura, your quietness, your intelligence. But that doesn't mean I don't find you attractive. You're very good-looking, and I can't believe you don't have someone hidden away somewhere. You're not gay are you?"

Then she started to giggle. Jeff turned red again, but Carly's infectious laugh quickly eased his discomfort, and he joined her in a good laugh. For the first time that evening, he relaxed. Carly sensed the change.

The wine arrived and, after a goofy toast to one another, Carly plunked her half-empty glass down and announced, "I do like you!" The giggling resumed where it had left off.

Happy tears obscured Carly's vision as she clumsily handed a menu to Jeff. Snorting and chuckling, she managed to convey the message that it was time for them to order some food. They made their choices and a waiter managed to interpret the order through the snickering, before turning away, unfazed by the joyous outbreak. He had seen it before and figured it must be the altitude.

When the hilarity subsided, Carly made another announcement. "Now we can talk."

She tried to act serious but another round of laughter took hold of them, and it was several more minutes before Jeff raised his hand.

"My turn. My turn."

Carly answered, "Okay. Go for it!"

"It appears we can't talk," he sputtered and tears rolled down both sets of cheeks as the belly laughs echoed throughout the restaurant. Several more toasts were proposed, and the laughter had diminished by the time the meal arrived. As they tucked into the sumptuous food the talk flowed easily. Each was impressed with the other's extensive knowledge. Little feeler questions were eased into the conversation, testing for informed answers. The subjects were far-ranging and the scope and depth kept expanding, until Carly called a halt, "Okay, okay! We're both smart. We can talk about all kinds of other things in greater detail later. Right now let's have a good time and talk about us."

Jeff looked puzzled. "Us?" he questioned.

"Yes, us, silly. Not us as "us," but us as in each other. Let's find out who we are. How about it?"

"Great idea, Carly. I know very little about you and I'm dying to learn more."

Carly answered apologetically, "I have been secretive, haven't I? Those mysterious phone calls must have piqued your curiosity. I'm sorry. I'll try to help you understand me. I feel very relaxed with you, but be warned I have some secrets that I may never be able to divulge."

The way Carly said that gave Jeff a cold shiver and his neck hair bristled. He was more intrigued by this beautiful woman with each passing minute and felt very special at being singled out to spend an evening with her. Leaning closer in anticipation, he was trapped in an unfamiliar spell from which he couldn't escape. Having no reason to doubt Carly's integrity, he urged her to begin. She smiled sweetly and started, without giving any thought to the possibility of telling the truth. She began to weave a tale she had related many times before, recalling threads from her early childhood fantasies. A little girl willing herself to visit and explore faraway places without ever leaving her confining home. Books and computers had allowed her to sample life in many diverse places all over the world. The story didn't change much from telling to telling. Carly was very comfortable with the final draft, relating times and places with the confidence of someone who had actually lived the experience. Here, in this beautiful setting, with Jeff absorbing her spellbinding words, she lost herself to her own imagination.

Nothing was said that was not believable or far-fetched in any way, just very romantic recollections of beautiful places and interesting people. Jeff listened intently. When Carly had finished the account of her travels, she leaned back and smiled. Then it was

Jeff's turn. He stared into Carly's eyes and hissed, "That's all bullshit."

Having her bluff called was a new experience for Carly, and she stiffened, stunned into silence. Regaining her voice, she angrily retorted, "What? You don't believe me?"

Jeff did not flinch. He quietly prodded, "Well?"

Carly searched for an easy way out. Her confidence eroded, she tried, "Most of it is true, Jeff. But you're right, I have embellished some facts."

Jeff's gaze did not change. He spoke slowly, "Carly, it's all bullshit, and one other thing: stop running."

Jeff's words stung. Carly's mind raced, wondering if and how he knew. She asked herself what she had gotten herself into. Jeff let Carly squirm for a few minutes before trying to ease her very obvious torment. In a soothing voice, he started very slowly. "Carly," he whispered. "Carly! Everything will be okay. Close your eyes." Carly followed Jeff's instructions. Her eyes closed. Surprised by the tension easing exercise, she forced a tiny smile, trying to signal Jeff that all was well, which she knew was also a lie. Forgetting the rule that it's sometimes better to keep quiet, she questioned Jeff.

"Do you know me?"

Jeff's reply was not what she expected, "No, I do not know anything about you Carly, except for the few times we talked over the telephone."

The way Jeff had so confidently refused to accept her stories, prompted Carly to believe he had somehow found out details from her past. His answer to her question confused her. She pressed him. "You must know something. Come on, tell me. What do you know?"

Jeff stuck to his story, "Honestly, I don't know anything about you, Carly."

Carly, still not convinced, continued, "But you didn't believe me. How do you know? What do you know? Why don't you believe me?"

Jeff tried again to reassure her. "It isn't as though I don't want to believe you, Carly. I do, but something told me you weren't being completely truthful about your exploits. I don't know how or why I sense when something isn't quite right, I just do. I don't think any less of you, but we can't be friends if we aren't truthful with each other. Now you can tell me everything or you can tell me nothing, whatever you are comfortable with."

The knowledge that Jeff really didn't know anything about her, erased some of the fear she was feeling, but she remained wary and chose her words carefully. Jeff's intuition had caught her off guard, and respectful of his intellectual capacity, she attempted some damage control.

"I'm sorry, Jeff. Why did I lie to you? Why do I lie to anybody? I don't know. Sometimes I go back to my childhood fantasy world and lock myself in. You are very wise to find me out. You get lots of points for that."

Carly racked her brain, knowing silence wasn't an option. She knew she had to speak up in order to establish a stronger understanding and friendship with Jeff. A long, silent pause caused her more confusion as words and thoughts crisscrossed her brain. She was tempted to reveal the truth about her childhood and early years. Only one person had ever been privy to these facts, and Carly had vowed that no other soul would learn of her past. This thought was quickly shunted aside. Gently caressing Jeff's hand, she quietly continued. "I haven't traveled to those exotic places, Jeff, and I haven't done any of those exciting things. They are all just made up. My fantasies. My big dream world. I'm sorry!"

"You don't have to be sorry, Carly. We all have dreams. Just think, all of those places are still waiting there for you. So, if you want to make some of your dreams come true, you can."

"You make it sound so easy. Just do it! I don't know. I must be scared to follow through. What do you think?"

"I'm no expert, Carly, but I suspect that a lot of people keep their hopes and dreams as just that, fantasy, out of the fear of disappointment or failure. In your case, I also detect a need to mask some other past unpleasant events. You are probably finding it more difficult to ignore those bad thoughts as time goes by. Is that what you are starting to feel?"

Startled by Jeff's clairvoyant reply, Carly's eyes glazed over. She drifted away. Jeff waited several long minutes then intervened. "Carly, Carly," he called softly. Then louder, "Carly!"

Carly jumped, "Oh! Oh, Jeff. You scared me."

"You scared ME. Are you all right?"

"I think so. I don't know what happened. Everything just went black. That's never ever occurred before. Wow!"

Jeff held a glass up, "Here! Have some water."

Carly eased the glass to her lips, "Thank you!"

She sipped slowly. Jeff resumed his soothing tone, "It appears you have taken your thoughts into very troubling territory... and we have had some good wine. You probably have matters and affairs that should be confronted, but not tonight. You need to regroup. Try to relax and relegate those troubling images for another day. Close your eyes, drift away and no bad thoughts. Hear the ocean, hear the wind, feel the sun. You are very warm and secure. You are relaxing in the sun."

Pretending to follow Jeff's instructions, Carly closed her eyes. But instead of allowing a sun-filled fantasy to absorb her, she frantically searched for an easy return to the carefree banter they had shared earlier in the evening. Her racing mind warned her not to bounce back too quickly, a sure indication of her bogus state. On the other hand, she did not want to drag the situation out any longer than necessary. In spite of all this turmoil, Jeff's suggestion slowly managed to take hold. A warm beach with a softly rhythmic surf appeared. At first, kind of fuzzy and distorted, then as dramatically as drapes being opened to reveal a sunny day, the image held Carly helplessly still.

Jeff squeezed Carly's hands and closed his eyes. "Where are

we?" he asked.

"We are on a beautiful beach," Carly softly replied.

Jeff continued, "Tell me what you see."

"I'm standing near the center point of a small bay, completely surrounded by gleaming white sand."

"Beautiful, Carly. What else do you see?"

"I see gulls soaring over the waves, calling and fighting each other over scraps of food."

"What do you hear?"

"I hear the waves lapping at the shore."

"That's the heartbeat of the ocean, Carly. Can you copy that sound?"

Carly copied the rhythm. "Shu u u – ah, shu u u – ah, shu u u – ah."

Jeff joined in. "Shu u u – ah, shu u u – ah, shu u u – ah." They lilted in unison. Jeff stopped to ask, "Do you see anything else, Carly?"

"Yes, I do. I see a tiny island just beyond the bay."

"Describe that island for me."

Carly studied the image for a few moments then outlined the island for Jeff. "It's not a large island. It's completely surrounded by a white sand beach with palm trees in the center. I wish I could live there. I would call it Freedom Island."

The name startled Jeff. He asked, "Why did you choose that name?"

"If I lived there I could forget all my troubling thoughts. I could forget the past and dance on the beach without anyone bothering me. I could swim in the ocean, breathe the clean air and be free. Free from all the evil."

Tears squeezed out from Carly's tightly closed eyes. Jeff gripped her hands firmly. Realizing that the attempt to calm Carly was about to backfire, he fought to retrieve the exercise.

"You will get to that island, Carly. You will be free. Free from evil and free from evil people. That island is waiting for you. First though, you must have faith. Faith in yourself and faith that others can help you. Keep that island in your mind, Carly. It's your future. Freedom Island'. You will get there. You will be free. Now push the island to the back of your mind, and let's enjoy the rest of the evening."

The short trip to the sunny beach slowly receded to the back of Carly's mind. Her eyelids fluttered as Jeff's features gingerly came into focus. She whimpered sheepishly, "Oh! Oh! That worked! It really worked. I'm...I'm amazed. I feel so much better. Thank you!"

Carly wasn't pretending now. She felt completely relaxed but suddenly very tired. Studying Jeff's face, she realized he was even more different than any other man she had been involved with. Smarter? Certainly. Quiet, shy, unassuming, yet deep down very confident. She had not counted on his intuition, which, as the depth of his perception flashed across her mind, caused her to tremble, but then, catching herself, she smiled. Running her tongue over her teeth, she teased. The change from pensive to playful surprised Jeff. He released her hands. "I thought we had lost you to some deep contemplation, but I see you're back." He spoke softly and quietly, as he read her reaction.

"Yes, my little island and your guiding voice took me away, but now I'm back," she lied. Hoping her flirtatious smile would cover any tell-tale signs of her inner turmoil, she vowed to follow her plan to completion. However, now she would have to stay on her toes and prepare for anything. She enjoyed a challenge, a little excitement, something to get her imagination aroused. Everyone had their weak point. She would find Jeff's, sooner or later. With new found confidence, she exclaimed, "You know what we need?"

"No." Jeff replied.

"C H O C O L A T E!" Carly loudly proclaimed.

Jeff looked puzzled. "Chocolate?" He asked.

"Yes, chocolate. Everyone feels good with chocolate."

Carly laughed.

Their waiter, who had been hovering nearby, wondering what was going on at that table, noticed Jeff's gesture and immediately responded. Stepping closer, he asked, "How may I help you, sir?"

"The lady would like some chocolate, please."

"Yes! Chocolate. Lots of chocolate," Carly giggled.

"Thank you, sir and madame. I shall get the dessert menu for you."

The menus were strategically placed a few feet away, allowing the waiter to quickly deliver two of them to the table. He handed one each to Carly and Jeff and then discretely stepped aside. The back page of the menu featured desserts, all beautifully illustrated. Carly scanned down the page, past the cakes, pies and ice cream, to the lower half of the page, reserved exclusively to chocolate, presented in many different dishes. Her finger rested at the bottom of the page, pointing to the last item, the one half pound sampler, a little bit of each of the preceding chocolate delights.

"That's the one!" she squealed, "Let's go for it."

Jeff saw where Carly was pointing and stared at the same spot on his menu. His eyebrow shot up. "Are you sure we can handle that?" he timidly asked.

"Are you kidding?" Carly replied, "It'll be fun, besides it's chocolate. If we don't eat it all, we can take the rest home. How about it?" She grasped Jeff's hands and flashed her most disarming smile.

Jeff, not a big chocolate fan, mocked Carly's enthusiasm. "Yeah! Let's go for it."

They both laughed. The waiter took the order from Jeff and turned toward the kitchen. Carly barely had time to comment on the fading light and the beautiful emerging stars, before he returned with the decadent platter, which he gently placed in the center of the table. "Please enjoy," he whispered and quickly departed.

Carly wasted no time, quickly scooping a large spoonful of dark mousse into her mouth, followed by a squeal of delight.

"Come on! Your turn now," she urged, not bothering to wait for Jeff's reply before plotting her next foray.

Jeff watched Carly's fork deftly move one attractive offering after another to her mouth before he gave in to the tempting feast. His choice, a white and dark chocolate marbleized pyramid, covered with a caramel sauce, visibly pleased him. "Good choice, Carly." Between nibbles she answered, "You just can't go wrong with chocolate." In all, there were a dozen mini creations. Carly had a little of each while Jeff sampled only three before quietly sitting back and watching Carly reduce the contents of the plate by half.

As she pushed the remaining scraps to the far end of the table with an exaggerated flourish, Jeff asked, "Happy now?"

Carly grinned. "Oh, yes! Yes, yes, yes! Thank you." She reached over and grasped Jeff's hands, "I've had a wonderful evening, thank you so much."

Perplexed, Jeff questioned, "This was your invitation. Shouldn't I be thanking you?"

Carly laughed. "I'm not thanking you for the food, silly. I'm thanking you for being you and for the gentle scolding I deserved. I'm feeling a little humbled, but at the same time I'm feeling good. Like my load is lighter. And so, thank you." She lied. Her plans were still in place, although now, impressed by Jeff's calculating intuitive mind, she would proceed very carefully.

Carly settled the bill, and then they rode the elevator to the darkened parking lot. Carly held a small container of precious chocolate tightly in her hand.

"You have a death grip on that bag, don't you?" Jeff joked.

"You bet! And don't try to mug me for it, mister." Carly pressed it to her chest.

"I wouldn't dare," Jeff replied, pretending to back away.

They walked to the car. Carly opened the passenger door for Jeff. "Please be seated, kind sir," she snickered.

"Thank you, pretty lady." Jeff played along.

Carly closed Jeff's door, circled the car and eased into the driver's seat. Before starting the engine, she contemplated surprising Jeff with a big kiss but decided to wait a while longer with a bigger shock. She guided the car slowly from the parking lot onto the highway leading to the city. There was little in the way of conversation, and it didn't seem very long before Carly was looking for a parking spot close to Jeff's apartment.

"You don't have to park, Carly. Just drop me off at the front door." Jeff motioned.

"No, love! I'm going to park. There's something I want to do," Carly answered.

Jeff, beginning to understand Carly, knew not to ask again. Carly found a spot, parked the car and they both stepped out into the fresh evening air. Jeff waited on the sidewalk for Carly to walk around the front of the car, but instead, she went to the rear of the car and opened the trunk. She reached in and pulled out a suitcase, closed the trunk, and skipped to Jeff's side. The look on his face was not unexpected. Before he could ask, Carly spoke up, "I'll explain when we get inside. Come on."

Bewildered, Jeff found himself being pulled toward the front door of his apartment building by Carly's free hand. He unlocked the main door, and they walked to the waiting elevator. Then they ascended to his floor in silence, walked to his door and entered. After Jeff locked the door behind them, Carly put her plan into action. She dropped the suitcase, threw her arms around Jeff's neck, and kissed him wildly. Then with one hand still holding him close, she used the other to unbutton his shirt. Jeff pulled away.

"What are you doing?"

"Kissing you, stupid!" Carly answered. "Come here!"

Jeff backed away. Feeling the rush of being very much in control, Carly kicked the action up a notch. While Jeff watched in awe, Carly danced around the room, slowly removing her clothes.

"Carly! Carly! What are you doing?" Jeff yelled.

"What does it look like? I'm getting ready for bed." Carly

laughed and continued dancing and removing her clothes until she was naked. Jeff was in shock. Carly walked over to where he was backed against the wall. "Ever see anything so beautiful?" She giggled. "You can touch, if you like. In fact, I would like you to touch."

Carly reached for Jeff's hand, but he pulled away.

"Carly, have you had too much to drink?" He questioned.

Carly laughed. "Not at all. Obviously, you haven't had enough." Her impish laugh filled the room.

"I don't understand. What are you doing?" Jeff stammered.

Carly moved away. "Oh! Yes. I guess I do owe you an explanation. Don't I?" she said, still giggling. "If you lead me to your bedroom, I'll tell you everything. I promise. Now come on. Loosen up a bit. Just for me. Please!" Carly pretended to pout.

Still in a bit of a daze, Jeff showed Carly to the bedroom. "Now, what do you want to tell me?" he asked.

"Not so fast, mister." Carly snapped. "We have to go to bed first."

"Can't you just tell me what's going on?" Jeff begged.

Carly glared. "Look stupid! We're in your bedroom. I have no clothes on. Are you completely dense?" she asked.

Now, very confused, Jeff tried again, for some reasoning, "I need to know why you're doing this, Carly. This is not normal behavior, you know."

Jeff's naïve words caused Carly to break out in a laughing fit. Eventually restraining herself long enough to reply, she spurted, "It's normal behavior for me," followed by more loud laughter.

As her laughing subsided, Carly, acknowledging Jeff's noticeable painful confusion, apologized. "I'm sorry. I guess I owe you some sort of explanation, don't I? I have to be nice and comfortable before I tell you. Is that okay?"

Jeff agreed, "If that's what you need, go ahead."

Carly wasted no time. Pulling back the covers on Jeff's bed, she jumped in, motioning for him to join her. Instead, he sat on the edge of the bed. Carly raised her voice. "No! No! Take your clothes off, and get in here. Now!"

Jeff nervously followed Carly's instructions, fumbling his buttons while his mind raced. His clothes removed, he gently eased into bed. Carly motioned for him to remain quiet and close his eyes before proceeding with her scheme, which she had conceived many weeks before.

Her expert teasing and playing couldn't be ignored; Jeff was hers, in her control. They made love. Gentle, slow, sensuous love. Then they slept, locked together in a tender embrace.

CHAPTER FOURTEEN

Early the next morning, Carly woke up in a playful mood, but when she turned to reach for Jeff, he wasn't there. She sat up, her eyes squinting in the morning light.

"Jeff, Jeff," she called. "Jeff, you here? Jeff."

"I'm in the kitchen," Jeff replied. "Just hang on a minute. I'll bring you some coffee."

Carly didn't answer. She made herself comfortable in anticipation of a delicious cup of coffee. Minutes later, Jeff entered the room and sat beside her. He extended a steaming cup to her waiting hands.

"Mmm, smells great," Carly exclaimed with a smile. "Thank you!"

"You're welcome. I'm glad you enjoy a good cup of coffee. That's one thing we can share."

Carly detected some kind of questioning tone in Jeff's voice.

"You don't think there's much else we can share?" she asked.

"It's not that, Carly. Just that everything's so sudden. I'm a little confused. I don't know you. I don't know what you want from me. I don't know what you see in me. Is your life just one fling after another? Will you quickly grow tired of me? And…"

Carly raised her hand to hush him, "Slow down," she urged. "Slow down, sweetheart. I'm right here with you. I'm not going anywhere, and one more thing…I like you a lot." She giggled and then stared directly into Jeff's eyes. "You are a very smart man, so listen very carefully to what I am saying. I'm not here with you just to get laid. I'm here because I want to be. If there are reasons for us to be together and enjoy each other, we will recognize the signs and your questions will be answered. If, on the other hand, there isn't any substantial reason for us to continue being together, and we part company, it won't be anyone's fault, and we will both be richer for knowing each other. Does that make sense?"

Jeff tried to digest Carly's reasoning and read between the lines at the same time. Slowly he formulated his reply. "Carly," he started. "Carly, you are making it sound like we are already together, like we have some sort of agreement. I'm sorry if I'm not on the same page. Shouldn't we take our time, get to know each other?"

Carly had no problem with the arrangement. It was no big deal to her, but seeing the confusion etched on Jeff's face, impelled her to attempt to ease his concerns. She placed her half-empty coffee cup on the night table and motioned for Jeff to place his there also. Then she pulled him into a warm embrace, cradling him as tenderly as she would a young baby. Rocking gently, her lips nuzzling Jeff's hair and ears, she tried to ease some of the tension out of him. After many minutes, she broke the silence, whispering into his ear, "Oh, sweetie, I didn't mean to unsettle you so much. In a way, I have been kind of planning something like this for a while, but please understand that I was also confused. Once I realized I had to see you, the rest was easy. Last night, the dinner, the wine, your handsome face, reinforced my decision without any regards to your needs. Somehow, I thought you would behave like most other men and relish the chance to be near me. I didn't realize that your reluctance to jump all over me is very attractive, and I might add a super turn-on. Here, feel how wet you make me."

Carly pushed Jeff's hand between her legs. "Make love to me," she urged, responding to Jeff's touch. He wanted to face some of his apprehensions and concerns that had been hounding him since he woke up earlier in the morning, but right now talking would have to wait as he eagerly fell under Carly's irresistible spell. Overpowered by the emotions surging through his body, he had to have her now, as much as she wanted him.

The lovemaking wasn't as soft and gentle as the night before, it was closer to the filling of an immediate need, a consuming, passionate form of communication between two people who had to bond without questioning why. It was working. The waves of pleasure were genuine, satisfying physical and emotional demands in their wake. The calming after-glow lulled the spent couple into a wonderful sleep. Later, when they awoke, Carly quietly murmured, "Thank you!"

Jeff was thinking that maybe he should say the same, but kept quiet. Carly stared at him. "You still need some kind of explanation, don't you?" she asked.

"Yes, I suppose I do," Jeff replied.

"Sorry, I can't help you there. We're together now. Can't we just leave it at that and see how we get along? We have nothing to lose."

Jeff sensed that Carly was not going to go any further with this talk and reluctantly agreed to let time work things out for them. He also knew that Carly was right to point out the fact that if they weren't meant to be together, they would part and nothing would be lost. His unfamiliarity with this kind of situation bothered him, but he was powerless to do much about it. Carly was in control. He contemplated calling his brother Tim, an entirely different personality, for advice. Tim, over the years, had many different girlfriends. Maybe he would have some answers. Tim lived a long way away and the two had not spoken in more than a year. They didn't have a lot in common, but for this kind of advice, Jeff figured it might be worth a try.

As these thoughts rolled around in Jeff's confused mind, he jumped at the sound of Carly's soft voice. "Hello! Jeff, hello! Still bothered, aren't you? Relax! Let's be friends. Let's enjoy ourselves, see where it takes us. Okay?" Carly's tone of voice changed to a grating harshness. Jeff got the message.

Carly settled back and flicked on the mid-morning TV news. Jeff left the bed and took a quick shower, then returned to the bedroom and started to put some clothes on. He turned to Carly. "Do you have any plans?" he asked.

Carly smirked, "I always have plans, but if you're asking about today and the next little while, no, I don't have anything scheduled. Oops! Sorry! I'm lying. Actually, I do have something in mind. Here, sit down." Carly patted the bed beside her. Jeff, half-dressed, sat, waiting to hear what Carly had in mind. Carly leaned closer. Jeff listened.

"Would it be okay if I stayed here for a while?" Carly asked. "You know there aren't many rentals available, and it would really help me out a lot. This place is so central and we could fuck every day."

Jeff winced. "Carly, please don't talk like that," he pleaded.

"Well, we could," Carly joked. "Anyway, do you think it would be okay? I won't be any bother to you." She put on her best puppy-dog face. There were a few minutes of quiet before Jeff answered, "This is a complete surprise, Carly. If it will help you out, I don't see any problems, and returning to our other conversation, it will be a fast forward way to get to know each other. It's probably time I had some company anyway, getting too independent may not be good for me."

Carly spoke up. "Let's look at it as a golden opportunity to share a slice of life together. It should do us both a lot of good. Thank you!"

"You're welcome, now if you don't mind I have to dress and look after some e-mail messages. Make yourself right at home."

As Jeff turned away to finish dressing, Carly stared at his back and fought the urge to stick out her tongue. Her world was moving in the right direction once again, but this time seemed a little different. Something soft and warm was stirring inside her, conflicting with the normal Carly-first attitude. Pushing the clashing thoughts to the back of her mind, she sprang from the bed and skipped to the shower. After her shower, she retrieved two large suitcases from her car and emptied the contents onto the bed. Methodically, she began to hang clothes at one end of Jeff's closet, which fortunately was less than half full. She placed other items in the two empty drawers in a large dresser. What luck, she thought, the poor boy doesn't have a lot of clothes.

By afternoon, she had finished storing her clothes and arranging her cosmetics in the bathroom. Then she pranced into Jeff's den, where he was working at his desk, and embraced him from behind. "How are you doing, sweetie?" she asked.

"I'm doing great. I heard you moving your things around. Do I still have room here?" he joked. His calm, subtle humor drew her attention. He was relaxing a bit, a good sign.

"Yes, you still have lots of room, but I see we have to take you shopping. There are so many nice clothes out there I would love to see you in. Think we can do that together?" Carly smiled her most disarming smile. Jeff put on a mock sneer as he answered, "Sounds interesting, but please don't change me too fast. I'm weak and vulnerable, my heart may not be able to take it."

Carly knew he was being facetious. Recalling the drubbing she had endured in the restaurant, she resisted her normal desire to control all situations by pretending to relent to his request. "I'm not going to push you into anything, just a few minor changes over time. A woman's job you know." Changing the subject, she addressed a more immediate concern. She was hungry.

"I'd like to prepare a nice meal for us. Do you have any food I can whip up?"

Jeff smiled at the thought. "That would be nice. Thank you! I think you'll find everything you need in the kitchen. Make yourself right at home." Then he added a little barb, "As if you haven't already. Let me know if you can't find anything and, by the way, if

226

you need help, I can cook."

Carly shook her head, "That won't be necessary, thank you. Just stay here and relax. I'll let you know if I need anything."

She kissed Jeff tenderly and murmured, "Mmm! Maybe there's something better to eat right here. Just kidding!"

She pulled away, laughed and skipped to the kitchen, where to her surprise, she found a well-stocked pantry and full refrigerator. Delighted to see all the ingredients and spices necessary for the preparation of a delicious pasta dish, she set to work. A half hour later, with her creation cooking in the oven, she glided back to Jeff in his den. A nostril pleasing aroma drifted in the air behind her.

Jeff pushed his office chair away from his desk and spun around to greet her, "If dinner tastes half as good as it smells, I may have to keep you here."

"Careful what you say, mister," Carly replied.

"You may never get rid of me. Can you hang on for another twenty minutes?"

"I'll try, Carly, but it's going to be tough. My nose is teasing me."

Carly kissed Jeff and returned to the kitchen to set a romantic table for two. She arranged the dishes with artistic flair, complete with two lit candles. A steaming bowl of pasta was placed between the candles and next to it, a bowl of light salad. An open bottle of wine sat strategically at one end of the table. Pleased by her efforts, Carly turned the lights down low and softly called to Jeff, "Dinner! Your wait is over."

Jeff, feigning starvation, stumbled down the hall. "Food...food," he gasped until he saw the inviting spread. Genuinely embarrassed by his uncharacteristic behavior, he straightened up. "Oh! Sorry, Carly. I didn't mean to make fun of you. Wow! What a spread!"

Carly melted as the real Jeff showed through, "You are such a sweetheart. You don't have to be sorry for being silly now and then. I know it was all in fun. Come on. We're going to eat and have some more fun. Come on now!"

Jeff obeyed Carly's beckoning. Once seated, he enthusiastically babbled on about how he was feeling so privileged and spoiled, until Carly hushed him up, urging him to eat up while the dish was still hot. They drank wine, joked and ate until satisfied, then Carly ushered Jeff from the room so that she could clean up. Jeff protested, wanting to help, but Carly was having none of it. Jeff retreated to his office while Carly cleaned the dishes and poured herself a nice hot bath.

She lounged in the bath for a long while, adding hot water from time to time, as necessary. She liked it hot. Emerging from the bath, she took her time drying and preening. Squeaky clean, powdered and oiled to perfection, she clutched the daily newspaper and eased into the comfy bed.

After finishing some business reports, Jeff left his office, entered the bedroom and noticed that Carly had fallen asleep reading the paper. Not wanting to wake her, he gently eased into bed and slowly drifted off listening to her rhythmic breathing. Sometime in the night, he was awakened and aroused by Carly's eager, loving advances.

The days stretched into weeks and soon into months while Carly looked after Jeff's needs. Jeff, still perplexed by the transformation in his life, started to relax. Carly, outwardly happy, was patiently waiting for the right moment when she would feel competent enough to implement some subtle changes. This would put a start to her plan. Unlike some of her past schemes, the challenge she faced was much more unnerving, but that made it more exciting.

What was making it much more difficult for her to concentrate, were the many pleasant thoughts that were pulling her in another direction. These emotions, though not entirely unknown to Carly, were a persistent reminder that something deep down inside was stirring. She wondered, was this love? Was something she had never given a second thought to finally going to capture her body and soul forever? Her unstructured days allowed for uninterrupted musings and anxiety, especially when Jeff was tending to his projects away from home. Those days, alone in the apartment, gave her too much time to think. When Jeff returned in the evening she fell into his arms, happy to push the conflicting thoughts aside. Nights were easy. Jeff belonged next to her. For some reason, when safely tucked into bed, she was able to blank out everything not required for cuddling, sleeping or making love.

If only her days were as happy and content as her nights. Forcing her mind to embrace her new life with Jeff through will power was not working. Was fate predetermined? She wondered.

The fact that Jeff was a kind, gentle, wonderful man added more turmoil to her struggling mind. Were he a tyrant or at least had faults she could not tolerate, she would justify a few evil musings. But no! He was faultless, so far. He must have some blemishes, something from his past. Carly almost wished it. Anything. She needed justification for the dark thoughts that showed up daily. Guilty pangs visited her sporadically throughout the day, adding to her confusion. Guilt was foreign to her. Reluctantly, she accepted the fact that more time was needed in her search for direction. Could she change her ways, settle down for good and become normal like other people? She had longed for someone like Jeff to come into her life, giving her the direction she needed. But even with this wonderful man beside her, the deep familiar pain festered.

Jeff's thoughts were so deeply entrenched in research he had no idea what Carly was going through. Carly, of course, couldn't let him in on her darkest secrets. What frustrated her most was her need to know more about Jeff without going too deeply into her own history. Other men had been more than willing to share practically any information she had asked for. Not Jeff. For her to feel relaxed and gain some tiny bit of direction, she needed information.

Family history, dates, times, places, all and any facts were absorbed by Carly and stored for future use as needed. Information was control and without it she felt vulnerable. This need had started when she was very young, and it would never change. She had managed to persuade Jeff, who liked to work at his desk all evening, to sit with her in the living room several nights a week to talk, read the newspaper or watch TV. The time together allowed an opportunity to learn more about each other. Most importantly, for Carly to find out as much as she could about Jeff. To her, the agonizing long wait for any tidbit of information was unnatural. Usually, she had a fairly complete composite within weeks, if not days. Jeff was different. He seemed to sense that, by sharing his background and personal secrets, he was surrendering his independence, even as he was starting to feel close to Carly.

So far, Carly had learned that Jeff's parents divorced when he was very young. He was raised by his mother who had remarried shortly after the divorce. His father, bitter from the divorce, did not participate in the family affairs in any way and eventually disappeared completely. Jeff, blaming his mother for the loss of his father, stopped communicating with her after he left home for university. He had mentioned a brother at one time, but he didn't want to talk about him except to say that they communicate once or twice a year, at most.

As for Jeff's work, he purposely chose to work alone by contracting his talents to several corporations. His thoroughness and high quality work gave him freedom to shun tight schedules. His specialty, testing different materials to find the optimum use for a client's specific needs, kept him very busy. Lately, environmental concerns were becoming more of an issue for manufacturers than they had been in earlier times. Some excellent material was being produced everyday but at what cost to the environment. The cost of complying with looming clean manufacturing laws had to be balanced with the need for certain material. This ruled out the use of some highly desirable choices. Environment protection organizations and agencies were not only looking at the impact made when products were put into service, but also down the road at the recycling costs; as the computer industry was quickly learning with short life span products containing hazardous components. Similar to the food sector that had to endure changes such as disclosure of ingredients, ethical treatment of farm animals and limited or prohibited use of herbicides and pesticides, the industrial sector would have to address this new way of doing business. Talented people such as Jeff were needed now as never before, and he loved it. Carly knew that his busy work was the reason that he wasn't involved with anyone. He was in love with his job, leaving him little time or desire to pursue other activities. But he had never met anyone like Carly, and whether he liked it or not that chance meeting was the start of huge changes in his life.

The consequences of that same chance meeting also applied to Carly. She had never met or been involved with anyone like Jeff before, and that was causing her to deal with an unfamiliar emotional conflict.

She toyed with the idea of getting a part-time job. Something to keep her mind occupied. Maybe she had too much free time to dwell on things. The quiet evenings with Jeff were very enjoyable. He was not a threat or an intruder, but more like a steady friend, unassuming, understanding and certainly very intelligent. So why wasn't she happy to just let the new found feelings whisk her away to a whole new life, giving and sharing with this wonderful man? There was no quick answer. Her childhood experiences and her unsettled life up to this time wouldn't allow an easy transition to a more conventional type of situation. Trust, or lack thereof to be more precise, had always played a part in her self-protection. This could prove to be the biggest obstacle of all if she were ever to have a solid, loving partnership. And of course, control was a by-product of not trusting. Would she, could she, even a tiny bit, be able to give up the need to be in control? She longed to find the happiness she had seen in other couples. The search for contentment had been just below the surface, and now with Jeff, the feeling surged forward. Was it strong enough to overcome the years of conscious and sub-conscious self-preservation? In order to give her mind a break from the nagging doubts, she had taken ownership of one end of Jeff's office. After he had moved some of his things she crammed many books and computer equipment into the limited space.

She had never shared her private work place with anyone and wondered if the arrangement would work out. Her concerns were unfounded when it was discovered how well she and Jeff worked together, like a well-oiled machine. Jeff, amazed by Carly's knowledge and research ability, soon had her helping with some of his work. Carly's approach to problems, different from Jeff's, allowed them to discuss solutions from each other's perspective. Jeff's work, impeccable as it was, gained a little more depth. As for Carly, learning and storing knowledge was therapy. Her inquisitive mind relished these challenges. Jeff's research, materials and how to get the most advantageous use for a given material, often involved the recently re-tweaked Von Neumann formula: the organization and amalgamation of the formulating crystals within a given material. He was not interested in the use any material would be put to. What the product was used for, was somebody else's problem. One would think that when working on a contract to find a suitable material for a specified use, he would want to know what that use was. In Jeff's thinking, this would divert his mind too much toward the end use. That was the job of the engineers and designers of the contracting party. They knew the requirements of the material. Give the specs to Jeff, and he would meet them or tell you why your request was not feasible. The ability of humans, ever since the earliest known tools, to take naturally occurring substances and manipulate them in so many different ways fascinated him. He contracted the services of several laboratories to test his calculations and theories. By directing the experiments and modifications of known formulas, he was very successful in meeting the needs of his clients. His biggest problem was lack of time. Experimenting and lab work was time consuming but necessary. Even when calculations and theoretical results were obvious, they had to be empirically proven. Jeff wouldn't have it any other way, for his peace of mind and for his client's.

It was this exclusive work that Carly found herself so completely suited for. It wasn't long before she could produce files and search for data almost instantly at Jeff's request. Her tech skills and natural ability to analyze and organize saved Jeff a great deal of time. This allowed him to concentrate more on problem solving and calculating. When Jeff was away or otherwise occupied, Carly kept busy with her own quest for knowledge, including adding more books to her collection. The limited space in Jeff's apartment prevented her from emptying her storage locker. It was still jammed tight with her books, spare computer, clothes, furniture, jewelry and other personal items.

Carly made one major change to Jeff's daily routine. She asked him to refrain from any work after dinner except for items considered urgent. She explained to Jeff the need to slow down. The pace he was accustomed to was not sustainable and one day he would pay dearly if he didn't learn to relax. It took a while but Carly eventually convinced Jeff to enjoy a couple of hours each evening talking or reading.

The quiet evenings seemed to refresh both of them, especially Jeff. Before Carly's help, Jeff had worked almost every night. Now he had time to relax and had a little balance in his life. Carly frequently used this downtime to test Jeff with her far-out sense of humor. Not that Jeff didn't have a sense of humor, but he was much more intellectual and dry, requiring knowledge and thought. To his surprise, Carly always caught on to his science-based jokes. Not so for Jeff with Carly's ribald musings, which were often below his thought range. Still, he enjoyed a good laugh when he allowed himself to digest the context and point of a given joke, but he couldn't shake the uncomfortable feeling he had of participating at that level. That only encouraged Carly to push his buttons even more.

One evening, while they sat in the living room, each with a section of the newspaper, Carly broke the silence. "There's an international health conference being held in Japan, the theme being the rise of sexually transmitted diseases, especially AIDS. Oh! And look here. My, my, it's being held in a city named...are you ready?"

Jeff, sensing what was coming, nodded.

"The city is named, Fuck You, Okay."

Jeff looked up. "A city called fuck you?" he asked.

"No! No, it's named 'Fuck you okay!' The okay is part of the name."

Jeff slowly repeated the name.'Fuck you okay.' You're putting me on. Let me see that."

Carly handed the section of paper to Jeff. "Here, look! See for yourself."

Jeff glanced at the article and groaned. "That's Fukuoka," he corrected her, and then started to laugh when he realized he'd been caught asleep at the switch.

Carly, now rolling around on the floor in uncontrolled laughing spasms, stopped long enough to pull Jeff down to the floor with her. "Come here!" she chortled, but she couldn't stop laughing long enough to say anything else. Jeff, unable to resist, joined in with body-shuddering hoots. Whenever the giggling seemed to be slowing, one or the other would utter, "Fuck You Okay?" leading to another side-splitting round of mirth. They repeated the phrase over and over, using every dialect and accent they could think of until they could laugh no longer. Only faint chuckles escaped their tear-stained faces as the happy couple limped off to bed.

In bed, Carly attempted to continue the theme with the names of two other cities, Phuket and Bangkok, but the laughing mood had passed, and it was quickly replaced by deep feelings of desire. Fiery, nourishing lovemaking prepared the spent couple for a satisfying sleep until morning.

During another relaxing evening, an interesting article caught Carly's attention. When she attempted to read it to Jeff, he groaned and teased, "Okay out with it. Come on!"

Carly smiled, "This one's real funny. Listen! Due to the ever decreasing number of smokers and the increase in jurisdictions where smoking is banned, a pastime enjoyed by males while using public urinals is coming to an end: chasing a cigarette butt around the bottom of a urinal while using the fixture in the manner it was meant to be used. Not wishing to see millions of men deprived of this skill-testing exercise, a young man has come up with a substitute game: chase the ball and score. A small stainless steel ball is free to be propelled through a maze, by a stream of urine, to one of several scoring points. The higher the score, the more, shall we say, stamina is required. After the ball has entered a scoring area, it automatically returns to the starting point. To date no name has been decided on, but we're betting there won't be a shortage of suggestions. And also, could team urinating be far off?" Carly leaned back. "Men have all the fun," she proclaimed. "And furthermore, Mr. Smarty pants, I suppose you know what they are talking about?"

Jeff answered quietly, "Guilty!"

Carly nodded in agreement. "I haven't heard much about the urinal games men play, perhaps you could enlighten me a little. Please!" She pretended to pout. Jeff involuntarily sucked in some air. Starting slowly, he reached for words, "I...I really didn't think I would ever be asked to explain such a thing, but I'll do my best to fill you in, pardon the pun. Quite often, when a man walks up to a urinal, he sees several cigarette butts lying in the bottom. Seeing as he's peeing there anyway, it's only natural that he notices the butts moving when they are hit.

Carly leaned forward. "Really! How fascinating." A slight

smirk on Carly's face gave her away. Jeff's tone changed. "You're toying with me. Stop it." He went quiet.

Carly laughed, "I'm sorry. I'm pulling your chain a little, but I am interested. Is there any more you can tell me?"

Jeff laughed, "I suppose so, since I've already started. Listen carefully. When a man pisses directly on a soggy butt it explodes, leaving only the filter. He can see how many times he can get the filter to circle the bowl, or see if he can force it through one of the drain holes in the bottom of the urinal. There is not much more I can tell you. I hope you are not too disappointed."

Carly ignored him. After a few seconds of silence, she spoke up. "I can see where all the males could go into withdrawal at losing all that fun. Maybe we should think up a name for the exciting new game. How about 'piss ball.' The catch phrase could be: 'Have a pee move the pea.'"

Carly laughed. Jeff remained silent. She looked at him and stopped laughing. "Not into this, are you?" she asked.

"Not as much as you are," he answered and added. "But I do find the article very amusing. It's amazing where a person can find inspiration. I wonder if that young man stepped up for a piss, only to be disappointed when he didn't find anything to chase around."

Carly interrupted him with a joke. "One man's urinal is another man's toy," she laughed.

Jeff continued. "If you don't mind, I think I'll abstain from the naming games, but you seem to be having fun so be my guest. And I think a good place for that would be in bed. Do you agree?"

Carly nodded, and they raced to the bedroom.

Over the next few months, as Carly continued to add more books and personal items to the small apartment, it became apparent that something had to change such as finding a larger living space. She had broached the subject a couple of times but each time Jeff had argued against any type of move. He liked the location and was comfortable in his own space. Lately, however, he felt a little cramped and Carly was making more points with her reasoning. With Jeff's blessing, she started looking for a larger place for them to relocate to. It wasn't long before she had a short list of potential homes for them to check out. Jeff rejected more than half of them outright, citing location, rent payments, floor layout or other details not to his liking. Finally, with the remaining list in hand, they decided to do a brief drive-by inspection. After the drive-by, which reduced the list further, only three places remained.

Carly made arrangements to inspect the interior of the three remaining choices. Returning to their apartment, after the Saturday afternoon spent viewing these units, Carly knew they would be moving into the second one. To her, it was perfect. Jeff agreed. The spacious, one year old, two story townhouse with a finished basement had everything Carly was looking for and at a fair rent. She knew they would be moving to this home because while Jeff was looking at the garage, she slipped a large deposit check to the rental agent. Now, she figured, it was only fair for Jeff to find out where his next home was.

Carly pushed Jeff onto the couch in the living room and bounced into his lap. "We're moving! We're moving!"

Jeff, surprised at Carly's song, questioned her, "What do you mean...moving? Don't we have to make some arrangements? Like agree on a place, pay some rent? And I have to give my notice."

Carly interrupted. "I'm way ahead of you. Remember that nice place, the second one with the private patio?

Jeff nodded.

"It's ours."

"Ours?" Jeff questioned.

"Yes ours. Look! Here's the receipt."

Jeff reeled back, "You are independent, aren't you? What if I don't want the place? Don't I get any say here? Maybe you should move there by yourself."

Not expecting Jeff to be so upset, Carly attempted to pacify him. "In the car you agreed the place was perfect, besides I saw your face when we were there. You liked it."

Jeff quietly answered, "Yes, you are right. I do like it."

Carly looked him in the eye. "So! What's the problem?"

Jeff reached for words, "There's no…there's no real problem. It's just that you took complete control. This whole moving business is all your idea, and I guess I'm feeling a little left out."

Carly had foreseen this whole conversation. It was rolling out as she had planned, giving her a bit more control. She loved it. Her pout softened. Pushing Jeff back, she nestled into his shoulder. "I'm sorry!" she murmured. "I was only trying to help. Are you mad at me?"

Jeff took the bait. "Oh no! Not at all, sweetheart. Not at all. You are right. I do like the place, the floor plan, location, everything. Yes! We will like it there. I'm sorry I questioned your judgment. Forgive me."

Carly smiled and gloated inside. "I don't have to forgive you, love. You didn't do anything wrong. I'm just so used to being in control and forged ahead without your involvement. I know you like the place and I didn't think you would mind, but on reflection, it is a type of life change, and I should not have secured the lease without your okay. But having said all that, you must know, when I walked through that front door, I fell in love. I was home." A tender kiss eased Jeff's tense feelings. Carly continued. "A few minutes ago you suggested that maybe I should move there by myself."

Jeff winced. "That was just a reflex. I didn't mean it. It just slipped out." He was back-pedaling.

Carly loved it. "Oh really? Just think. If I moved out, who would give you such good blow jobs?" Dropping to her knees, she unzipped Jeff's pants.

Moving to a new home was more unfamiliar to Jeff than it was to Carly. He had been living in his apartment for several years, and before that he had changed homes only twice since finishing university. He didn't get attached emotionally to his dwelling but it was mostly a place for him to work out of. Once he settled in, with his work station arranged for efficient use, that was it. He stayed. Carly needed a lot more in her home. Many times over the years she was convinced she had found just the right residence, only to become bored and restless after a few months, leading to further searching. She had never surmised that it may not be a physical home she was looking for, but rather something intangible, like a personal requirement not yet recognized. After all those years, was she still fooling herself thinking that a charming, inviting, comfortable place would settle her down? Of course, none of her thoughts were going anywhere near this territory. She was feeling as she had many, many times before, a type of euphoria. An enlightened feeling suggesting that by settling into this new environment, decorating it just so, she would find the answer to her restlessness. These buoyant longings acted as a fuel source to her energy reserves. The physical labor and detailed requirements of the move would barely be noticed. Let the adventure begin.

Carly volunteered to be the chief coordinator for all the necessary work involved in the move to the new home. This left Jeff free to continue work on several important projects he had to complete. When he complained that the move came at an inappropriate time, Carly asked him when a better time would be. He, of course, didn't have an answer.

The preparations began in Carly's capable hands. Several lists were compiled and prioritized by category such as utilities, mail address change, packing supplies, mover appointments, discard items and a miscellaneous list. Moving to a new home was not new to Carly, but moving with someone else and all his belongings was completely new. She jumped at the chance to pack Jeff's private papers. Perhaps a few tidbits of useful information would be chanced upon, and stored away for future use. This golden opportunity was not to be missed and sorting through files and papers, unnoticed by Jeff, took Carly much longer than necessary. She was not disappointed when more than a few facts caught her eye, and a couple were very intriguing. After the move, she would pursue them further.

Jeff, impressed by Carly's seemingly endless energy, asked a few times if he could help. Each time, he was politely told that his help was not necessary, and that if it was needed he would be called upon. Finally, he asked once too often and was told, not very politely, to butt out and leave the work to Carly until such time as he was needed – end of story. He got the message.

The apartment became crowded with empty boxes and piles of sorted belongings, which slowly became rows of neatly stacked boxes ready to be moved to the new house. Moving day arrived and everything was loaded by the movers. The last items were Jeff's computer and work files, ready to be set up as quickly as possible in their new location.

At the new home Carly supervised the placing of the furniture by the movers. Several large pieces were placed in different arrangements that normally would have tried their patience, but with Carly flashing her eyes and leaning over them in a tight, low-cut sweater, they didn't seem to mind. In fact, they appeared to enjoy it. Had they only known, Carly was toying with them, she knew exactly where every piece was going before it was unloaded and wanted to have a little fun at their expense. Jeff was trying to stay out of the way, not wishing to second guess Carly. Several times, she asked for his opinion to make it look legitimate, and like the movers, he didn't catch on either. When the contents of the truck were finally placed in the house, Carly exaggerated her gratitude to the movers causing their chests to puff out proudly for the service they had just performed. She held the door for them and they floated effortlessly to their truck without noticing her middle finger saluting their departure.

Jeff set up his computer and after he had determined that it was working properly, Carly stopped him from going any further. She had him help in making up the bed, and then she wanted to play.

The new home worked out much better than either of them had expected. The bonus for Carly was her own office work space. She soon had it crammed full of books, files and computer equipment, after purchasing several shelf units and a large work station.

Jeff was once again able to spread his work out freely, without Carly trying to rearrange it for her space needs. There was still an area next to Jeff's chair for Carly to use when her help was needed. Toward the end of their time cramped together in Jeff's apartment office, stress levels were beginning to rise. The new separate spaces eliminated a potential problem. The change was noticed but not mentioned. With more room available, Carly happily hit the book stores, gathering more reference books for future use or as with many of her previous purchases, never to be opened again. But she had to have them and that was that.

Another area giving Carly relaxation and pleasure was the outside patio, with its shrubs and potted plants. It had not been neglected by the former tenants, but lacked imagination. Carly, recalling Sadie's rich and vivid landscape, recognized the problem areas. With her normal determined self-discipline she set about turning the space into a lush, peaceful retreat. Within weeks, the results of her effort surpassed even her own expectations. Jeff, having seen the transformation from start to finish could only shake his head and proclaim his sincere appreciation and astonishment at the results. The praise lifted Carly with an unfamiliar feeling of self-esteem. She had never taken compliments seriously, believing there had to be some sort of unrelated motive involved. Jeff's genuine congratulations pierced her armor, leaving her with a nice warm feeling. She retreated to her work room to analyze the pleasant glow, wanting to know if she was losing her need to control. Was the new sensation a sign of weakness? She could not remember a time when she had enjoyed praise for something she had accomplished. Usually, she found a way to sabotage kind words. This time there was no phony excuse, no brush-off, no attempt to mitigate or belittle, only a good happy feeling that she had done something well, had enjoyed doing it and was now savoring a pleasant warmth from Jeff's congratulations. Wow, it felt good! She waited for some negative thoughts to burst the bubble, but not one surfaced. Smiling inside, she whispered, "Jeff, you are a special man. Bless you."

Life became much easier with the extra space, especially for Jeff. He felt energized, so much so, that many evenings Carly had to interrupt his work by begging him to join her in the living room for a little relaxing time. While she plied the newspapers, he managed to sneak in work-related papers from time to time, insisting the reading was necessary to meet a deadline. Carly knew this was not always the case, but let it slide as long as Jeff didn't get too immersed. When he appeared to be involved visibly, she would encourage him to relax and often break the silence with some news item or interesting column. Jeff had no choice but to listen. One particular story caught his full attention, not for the content, but for Carly's reaction. She blurted out, "Oh! Fuck, not again. Will they never learn?"

Jeff dropped his book and questioned, "What? What's up?"

Carly filled him in. "It's these drug raids and shootings, all so unnecessary; a total waste of time and money."

Jeff studied Carly. When she offered up no more information, he asked, "What waste of time and money, love? Don't we have to control drug trafficking?"

"Not the way we are doing it," Carly blurted, visibly upset.

Jeff motioned for her to slow down. Speaking quietly, he asked for the full story. "Carly, I'd like to hear what you have to say. What are we doing wrong? And don't get so upset. You worry me sometimes."

"I'm sorry!" Carly whispered. "But the failure to control street drugs should have been addressed by now. Why can't anyone acknowledge that? Surely we are not going to wait until it's too late. And the solution is so simple. Someone has to wake up."

Jeff leaned forward.

"There's a simple solution? I'm listening."

For several years, Carly had been concerned with the way the so-called war on drugs was being waged. After reading many articles and books on the subject outlining the problems and possible solutions, she had formed her own simple (radical to many others) idea on how to control and defeat the drug traffickers. With all this information and analysis in her head, the words came easy to her. She started. "The drug problem is huge, sweetie, bigger than most of us can comprehend. Do you know why?"

Jeff stared at Carly. "Tell me."

"Okay, I will. It all comes down to money and profit. Money represents power, prestige, control, respect, freedom, toys. The list is endless. Leaders, politicians and business people all know this, so should we be surprised that when a highly sought-after, cheap to produce product is available, certain members of society jump at the chance to supply it? No! Of course not. The rewards are too tempting."

Jeff interrupted. "I think a lot of people know why drug dealers exist and the harm that the drugs cause to society and also the fact that fighting the dealers is constant and frustrating. I'm curious to see what you would do differently."

Carly smiled. "First off, the term in business is market share. If you have 60 percent of a given market, your competitors have 40 percent. Your goal is to increase your market share by many different means such as lower prices, product differential, target advertising or some other way. The same approach can be used to defeat the drug dealers."

Jeff was now very curious. "How do we do that?"

Carly exclaimed, "Simple! We, the people, take the customer."

Jeff looked puzzled. "What do you mean by that?"

Carly screamed, "Stupid! We become the supplier. One

hundred percent market share. No competition."

Jeff lost it. "You mean the authorities become drug pushers?"

Frustrated, Carly elaborated. "Not pushers. Suppliers, stupid! Suppliers. There's a difference, a big difference."

"You'll have to explain. It sounds rather interesting."

Carly continued. "Contrary to all business goals, we want the market to shrink. We continue to have one hundred percent market share, but the goal is to eliminate demand for the product."

Smugly, Jeff spoke up. "So, supplying drugs to addicts solves the drug problem. Brilliant! Wish I'd thought of that. 'Here! Over here! Come and get your drugs.' The government could use the money. Brilliant, Carly."

"Asshole! Don't make fun. The government won't charge for the drugs. The doses will be free. You didn't listen to me when I said the market will shrink...dry up. No more. The end, over."

"How can you do that when you are supplying the product?" Jeff asked.

"I'll answer that. Go back to where I started. You may remember me saying that the drug trade is huge. The solution to this problem is just as huge at the beginning, tapering off in a few years even ending up tiny, in as little as ten years. The policing saving alone, after the first year, would probably cover the cost of the new program."

Jeff needed details. He asked again, "Do you have a plan to go with this scheme? I hope you do."

Carly brightened. "I do! The solution must start with dedication at the top, the very top. I'm calling for leadership, unwavering leadership. North America would be called a free drug zone with the goal of turning that around to drug free. Every city in North America would be required to maintain a treatment center where, at the beginning, registered drug users would get their drug of choice administered by medical personnel. The centers would also have to supply wholesome meals and private rooms for addicts to sleep when needed. All other social services needed for addicts would be coordinated through the centers. Services such as counseling, job training, education and of course the ultimate help for every addict, eliminating the need for drugs. Self-esteem has to be returned to each drug user, and the key to this is to gain their trust. If this radical program was implemented properly, thousands of citizens would have the opportunity to shake the use of drugs and return to become useful members of society."

Jeff spoke up. "What's to stop addicts from simply continuing to use drugs supplied free by government?"

Carly quickly answered, "Nothing! Absolutely nothing! Except many would soon realize that any help they may need to eliminate their drug use or reduce their desire for drugs is readily available. As I just said, trust is key. We can't fool these people. They will be getting real drugs and real help. Something they have never had before. It's common knowledge that many addicts really want to go clean but lack the help needed to achieve that goal. With the necessary resources concentrated in the centers, the help would be supplied. I believe that many addicts would use the services to help them get off drugs, but even if most don't completely stop using drugs, the law of attrition ensures that the number of drug users drops steadily until the problem is almost eliminated. Another thing to keep in mind is that there will be no new addicts joining the registration ranks, simply because there will be no drugs available on the streets. Who in their right mind would risk importing an illegal product for which there are no customers? The penalties for importing could even be increased. After all, you would now be competing against the government, and they don't like competition. The cost to produce the product is pennies. Controlling the use makes sense. Why can't anyone see this? Right now, all we are doing is increasing the retail price and playing into the hands of the dealers. At the same time, addicts have to turn to crime in order to pay for the product that we have driven the price up on. How absurd!"

Carly collapsed. Jeff cradled her gently, then carried her to bed where she sobbed in his arms for most of the night.

The next morning, Jeff had to leave early to attend a couple of business meetings while Carly stayed in bed until noon and then took a hot bubble bath. Whenever she talked about one of her many pet subjects, the emotional toll drained her. Often it took more than a day to recover. Today, would be a slow day for Carly. The biggest problem was her perception that most people in charge of these problem subjects were so incompetent. Were many of the highly paid executives and staff just working the system and prolonging their employment? She assumed that they were. Some of the other problem areas that frequently occupied her mind were poverty, housing, women's' rights, politics, religion and a host of others.

For many of these social ills, Carly had figured out solutions. What she found most disturbing was seeing the same problems being hashed over and over in the news and media without anyone finding answers as she did. As the day wore on Carly managed to push her drug war tirade into the background and concentrate on housework.

When Jeff returned from work in the late afternoon, Carly had dinner ready and the table set, complete with candles. Warm and bubbly, she gave Jeff a long kiss. Jeff remarked on the reception, "Good job! How did you know? I've gone through a few strenuous meetings today. You're a sweetheart!"

Carly flashed her smile, "My pleasure. I need a pick up too. Let's eat!"

Good food and wine were enjoyed with light joking and laughter. Serious talk and world problems were avoided, especially the drug war.

The days, weeks and months passed quickly for the busy couple. To Carly's surprise, their one year anniversary together was approaching. She had never spent so much time with any man, and now realizing how quickly the last few months had passed, felt a sense of accomplishment. However, some old doubts and insecure feelings had surfaced alongside this revelation. To divert her mind from these nagging thoughts, she decided to head downtown to shop and tend to some personal business and banking.

Early the next morning, after Jeff had left the house for work, she drove downtown and parked in an underground parkade in the center of the business district. After shopping for some needed items of clothing, she returned to her car and locked the items in the trunk. Then she walked a short distance to a very high building to visit her banker in his office near the top floor. After a brief meeting, during which her banker reviewed her portfolio and offered his opinions and help with her investments, she walked to the elevator. While waiting for the elevator to arrive, she glanced out the hallway window and froze at the sight of the sun shining on the distant hills. The sudden draining of blood from her head caused her to lean on the wall for support. Mixed thoughts and emotions pushed and shoved inside her head. For a long time, she had been very self-disciplined at avoiding any place or topic that may bring her past into focus and now the quick glimpse of the familiar hills, with the secrets and memories they held, overpowered her attempts to ignore the topic any longer. With tears in her eyes, she made her way down to the parking floor. Back in her car, she cried and pounded the steering wheel, as a tangle of unpleasant memories re-asserted themselves. From past experience, she knew this day would arrive. Painful images flashed in and out of focus. Amidst all the unpleasant thoughts, one thing was clear: she would very soon have to make an important decision. The idea scared her, but she knew there was no escape.

Somehow she drove home. Jeff arrived shortly after. Concerned at her appearance, he asked what was wrong. Carly shrugged it off to a bad day of shopping and a splitting headache, but Jeff knew better. He didn't pursue it; instead, he nervously read the newspaper while Carly took a hot bath and went to bed. When Jeff finally slid in beside her, he noticed the heavy tears, unlike any he had seen her shed before.

Feeling helpless, he hoped there would be some kind of rational explanation in the morning. He shuddered as he realized there was a lot more to Carly than he may ever know.

CHAPTER FIFTEEN

C arly tossed and turned all night. Her past, present and future alternately materialized in a jumble of obscure images, eliminating any chance of sleep. Jeff shared Carly's pain. The thought of several important meetings he had to attend in the morning compelled him to try to sleep but to no avail. As the day emerged, he dreaded leaving Carly in obvious agony. As much as he wanted to, he knew any attempt to help would have to wait until Carly was ready. Very little of the showering, shaving and dressing registered with him, due to the disturbing thoughts of Carly and how or if he could help. When he left the house, he knew it would be a long day.

Carly sensed Jeff's departure but painful thoughts kept her from giving more than a fleeting acknowledgment. An hour later, she shuffled to the bathroom. The mirror told the whole story – what a mess! Red eyes, puffy lips. Carly looked and jumped back. "Shit, what's happening?" she wondered. "Pull yourself together girl. Settle down!"

A hot shower followed by a liberal application of body cream helped erase some of the physical aches. Nothing however, could lessen the painful thoughts that had been constantly hounding her since the day in the bank when she had allowed her eyes to focus on the very scene she had been avoiding for so long. She knew from her past experience there would be pain. Nothing could have warned her that the hurt throbbing through her body, from the top of her head to the bottom of her feet, would be so intense. Her mind went into overdrive. She wondered if there was room in her head for questions. Room for answers? Were there answers? She knew the questions. Was the pain caused by guilt? Is that why people face up to their indiscretions? Would it get worse? Could it be ignored? She clung to one question. Could anyone help? Years compressed into minutes interfering with her ability to focus or reason.

In spite of all this confusion crashing around in her head, she managed to dress and pour a cup of coffee from the half-full coffee maker in the kitchen. Sitting with both hands tightly squeezing the coffee cup, she knew, as so often she had known in the past, that it was decision time. Dreaded but necessary. Necessary in the sense that, for Carly, after a period of stability, a feeling of unease caused her to review where she had been and where she was going. Decision time always meant a change in direction, new places, new people, and new experiences. Her beloved garden always featured prominently. What she couldn't understand was why now? Wasn't she in the most enviable position a girl could ever imagine? A good-looking, intelligent man, a comfortable home, spending money, satisfying sex. Still, the unsettling thoughts returned, pushing aside any other activities Carly had planned. Struggling to understand the stream of confusing images was proving to be very painful and tiring. As the morning turned to afternoon, one scene repeated over and over, increasing in frequency.

Carly could feel the pull. The picture finally pushed all else aside, causing her to concentrate on the one place she had desperately tried to avoid. Yielding to the lure, she recognized a calmness she had succumbed to before, and she knew. She had to go. The struggle was over. She would go. What would happen when she got there didn't matter. She had to go. And then the words came to her.

"My love garden
My love garden
I'm going to my love garden
I'm going to my love garden."

It had been a long time since she last sang her tune, but the words quickly returned and new ones were added as she laughed out loud and pranced around the house.

"I have to see my love garden
My love garden
My beautiful love garden
My beautiful love garden
La la la la love garden
La la la la love garden
The flowers will grow
Into a beautiful show
In my love garden
In my love gar…
Oh!"

"That's an interesting song. I see you're in a much better mood."

Carly had not noticed Jeff standing in the doorway. She flushed and quickly recovered. "It is a nice song, isn't it? I always feel better when I sing it." She changed the subject. "I'm sorry. I don't have anything prepared for supper. I'll get right on it."

Jeff held up his hand to hush her. "I have a better idea." he said. "Let's just go out somewhere for a quick bite. I've had a very busy day. I need a break. Is that all right with you?"

Carly was caught a little off guard. Jeff never did anything on the spur of the moment. He wasn't ridiculously meticulous, but liked to have some idea of a day's or week's activities. His work required volumes of plans and time-frames, which carried over to his private life. Suppressing a smirk, Carly couldn't resist a dig at Jeff's expense. "Just like that you expect me to get dressed up and traipse out to some place for a quick bite as you put it. You sure your day calendar won't be compromised?" She stared directly into Jeff's eyes, as he awkwardly tried to figure out what just happened. He stammered, "I...I'm sorry! I thought that maybe you'd like to go out to eat."

Carly couldn't contain the ruse any longer. Her glare changed to a wide grin. "Of course, you big silly, I'd love to. Just give me a minute, and I'll be ready." She skipped to the bedroom, leaving Jeff standing alone, shaking his head slowly from side to side. As she re-emerged, she coaxed. "Come on, let's go!" Nothing was said from the time they left the house until they had driven a couple of blocks.

Jeff started the conversation. "Do you have any preferences this evening?" he asked.

Carly hesitated for a few seconds before answering. "Now that you mention it, I do. How about Italian? You know that little place by the park?"

Jeff nodded. "Good idea. We haven't been there for a while, have we? That's just perfect."

He changed the subject. "Could you sing some more of your song for me? I'm trying to remember if I've heard it before."

Carly struggled to stay calm. It seemed that Jeff was intruding into thoughts that she wished could be erased from her mind. Masking her inner turmoil, she answered, "I doubt if you have ever heard it before. I think I picked it up in some little place a long time ago, and, if you don't mind, I just like to sing it when I am all alone and need a little pick up. Sorry!"

Jeff knew that was the end of that conversation. Many people find certain music can change their moods, and if this song makes Carly feel better, let her sing it. He quickly pushed it from his mind as he parked close to the quaint Italian restaurant.

Inside the restaurant, which was less than half full, they were escorted by the owner's daughter to a quiet corner. They quickly placed their food and wine order. Then Carly reached out for Jeff's hand. She spoke softly, "You've had a bad day. Try to relax. If you'd like, you can tell me or keep it to yourself. It's your choice. If it would help, I don't mind hearing what you've gone through today. Okay?"

Jeff gave his hand to Carly and let out a sigh, "You don't have to know the details, just work stuff, you know, but I will tell you that I didn't want to leave you this morning in the condition you were in. It bothered me all day. Maybe I should be listening to your problems. Anything I can help you with?"

Carly pulled away. "No! No, it's kind of personal; something I have to work on by myself. I hope you understand. Thank you for asking. I appreciate your offer, but I have to settle this by myself. If I need your help, I know you will be there."

Jeff knew there was more, but he also knew he wouldn't learn anymore at this time and he would have to wait. The food and wine arrived, taking some of the edge off of the conversation. Part way through the meal, Jeff mentioned a couple of items that he had to deal with in a meeting earlier in the day. Carly listened intently. After a little thought, she added some comments and suggestions from her point of view. The conversation carried through to the end of the meal, with Jeff parading other concerns from the day's business before Carly and listening to her thoughtful perceptions and understanding. Before they left the table, Jeff felt a whole lot better, when he realized that most of his problem extended from the mood he was in when he left the house in the morning. One remark that Carly had made during the dinner was that it sounded to her as though there were too many type "A"s at the meetings. Jeff thought about that and agreed. The meetings he had attended today were different than most of his meetings where he dealt with doers like engineers, technicians and such to discuss and solve problems and tackle projects. Today's meetings were comprised of mostly top executives, leaders who designated others to fulfill their ideas and needs. Jeff could see what Carly had detected, too many leaders in the room, if not checked by each other, often leads to one-upmanship and sidetracks the meeting. Fortunately for Jeff, these meetings with higher-ups didn't happen too often, and he vowed to avoid as many of them as he could in the future. He wondered why he was invited to some of the meetings anyway, when, as happened today, after being questioned by some executive, his answers were misunderstood, or worse, totally ignored. He was happy fulfilling his contracts and working with the doers, and that was how it would stay. He thanked Carly for her clarifying input.

She smiled, "You don't have to thank me, sweetie, I told you I might be able to help you. The problems are mostly people' problems. Relax, you're doing just fine."

Jeff felt a little better regarding his troublesome day but continued his deep concern over Carly's bad night. He was unable to hide his feeling and thoughts from her.

She sensed what he was going through, but her own mind was again caught up in the same turmoil she had endured last night, and so she was not going to be any help to him. He could suffer or ignore her, but there were things she had to do in the coming days. How she wished it would be different just for once, but having come this far in her thoughts, she knew what was coming. There was no room for poor Jeff. She was in the grip of a powerful vortex, as she had been many times before. Did she have the will to fight this time? To somehow escape? In between the punishing thoughts, she uttered a little vow to try. If there was a way out, she would find it, but in the meantime…Jeff startled her.

"I've paid the bill, we can go now."

Carly jumped. "Oh! Sorry, you lost me there, didn't you?"

Jeff thought for a moment and answered, "I know you're going through something, and I wish I could help. But I also know how you feel about that, so just be reassured that if you need me, you only have to ask. I'm willing to leave it at that. Okay with you?"

Carly tried to smile. "Thank you. That's appreciated. I have some things to sort out, but if I need your help I will gladly seek it.

I look forward to the day we can work together through everything. Here's hoping."

Carly crossed her fingers. Tears dribbled down her cheeks. She whispered, "Take me home."

That night, Carly managed to sleep a little better than the night before. As she drifted off, she decided on a plan, which helped her relax. The conflicting thoughts and doubts were still present but not strong enough to change her mind. She knew tomorrow would be a very busy day, sleep or no sleep.

In the morning, Jeff left Carly asleep as he showered in preparation for a full day at a client's office. He dressed, fixed himself a cup of coffee and sat down at his computer to glance at any new messages. He turned his head at the sound of bare feet behind him. "Oh, you're up." He smiled.

Carly returned the smile. "Yes," she answered. "Can't sleep anymore. I'll get myself a coffee. Be right back."

Jeff watched her leave. He wondered what was going on with her. He turned back to the computer. Carly returned, a full cup of coffee clenched in her hands. She sat down.

"Anything new or interesting in there?" she asked, not really caring one way or the other. Jeff looked up.

"No! Just the same old: meetings, reports, questions, answers. Nothing exciting. Work stuff, you know."

Carly wrinkled her nose and Jeff laughed. He failed to mention one item that caught his attention: an e-mail from his brother, whom he had not heard from in more than a year. He now wanted to talk. The two had drifted apart years ago and rarely communicated. Jeff was happy to hear from Tim, but he would wait to learn the reason for the contact before telling Carly. His brother could be very troublesome at times, and just to be safe, he would not introduce Carly and Tim, or even hint at one's existence to the other, until he felt very comfortable to do so. He was having enough stress with Carly's latest mood swing and didn't need any more. He would get back to his brother later to find out what he wanted. He stood up and turned to Carly who remained seated. She wasted no time. Dropping to the floor, she unzipped his pants and had him aroused. He closed his eyes, and a few minutes later shuddered to orgasm. Carly continued to caress him.

He looked down. "Oh! You always surprise me. That was so nice."

Carly looked up and giggled. "Nice surprise? I'm glad you liked it. I'm just a little cocksucker." She laughed out loud.

"Carly!" Jeff scolded.

Carly laughed louder, falling back on the floor while pointing to the door, "You'd better straighten up for work. Wouldn't want to be late now, would you? What would you use for an excuse? If you had to report to someone, I could write you a note. 'Dear sir, Jeff was late for work this morning because I was giving him a blow job.'" She rolled on the floor, consumed by fits of giggles. Jeff shook his head and went to the bathroom to clean up.

When he returned, Carly was still on the floor. She jumped to her feet. "Feel better, mister?" She grinned.

"Yes, I do," Jeff replied. "And I noticed you seem to be feeling much better. Am I wrong?"

Carly grimaced. "Partly. I still have things to work out, but I'm trying. I'm trying. Don't worry yourself about my troubles. They're mine, and I'll deal with them. And like you said before, if I need your help, I just have to ask."

Carly went silent. Jeff knew not to say anymore. He turned to the hallway. Carly followed. At the entrance, they kissed gently. After Jeff left, Carly closed the door, stuck her tongue out and raised her middle finger. Now it was time to put her plan into action. No second thoughts. No hesitation. She started to hum. Then the familiar words, quietly at first, then, gradually louder and louder.

"My love garden, my love garden
My beautiful love garden.
I have to go.

And put on a show.

In my love garden.

My love garden."

Carly danced, sang and rolled on the floor. She had no doubts, no questions, no guilt. It was time for action. Her plan had to proceed. She had to go. Maybe the sight of her garden after such a long time would help to get rid of her conflicting emotions and mood swings. It was a long shot, but in her desperate situation, she was willing to grasp anything, no matter how unlikely the idea was.

As she sang and danced, she prepared for a busy day. Nothing could be left to chance. A phone call to the truck rental agency. A look in her purse for false ID and false credit card. The bogus cards along with a false driver's license were placed in the main pocket of her purse. Her proper cards were placed in the secret pocket where the phony cards had been. Then she donned jeans, t-shirt and hiking boots. Before leaving the house, she placed a wig and dark glasses in a plastic bag, a disguise to be applied away from any neighbors' eyes. Nothing was overlooked. Close to the truck rental agency, she parked in a pay by the day covered parking lot and changed her looks to resemble her fake photo ID. Then she walked the short distance to the truck rental office, picked up a waiting truck and headed away from the city. Driving through the city traffic kept her occupied enough to keep her mind from focusing on any stressful matters, but once she was out on the open highway, disturbing thoughts bubbled to the surface like an overflowing cauldron. The painful images, many of which she thought had been dealt with, nagged unrelentingly at her decision making process. The biggest problem was whether she was making the right choice. Why couldn't she just settle into her new life? Be satisfied? Be happy? Why? Her palms dampened in spite of the beautiful weather and resplendent scenery. Suddenly, familiar landmarks forced her to ease up on the gas pedal. She was so close.

As she scanned the hills, looking for any changes or ominous signs, she realized nothing had changed. Could she be missing something? She searched for anything that would help her to change her mind, anything. Surely the force that was pushing her to revisit her past could be persuaded to reconsider the mission and send her back to happily enjoy her new, comfortable life. But no! Nothing could cause her to change direction, erase old happenings or events from her mind once and for all time. She was suddenly jolted awake by the scene ahead. The turn off from the highway was a short distance away. Her heart beat faster as she slowed the truck.

She came to the dirt road and glanced up and down the highway, looking for other traffic. There were no other vehicles in sight, so she turned off the highway. She was turning away from everything she thought would make her happy to face previous hurt, open old wounds and search for answers. Would this be the last time she would travel this road? Could she finally close this chapter? Or was she returning to a place that would keep her enslaved forever?

As she bumped along the trail, she noticed signs that told her one or more vehicles had been there recently. This concerned her but perhaps it was nothing to worry about. Still, she would be extra cautious. Halfway from the highway to her garden, she rounded a curve and froze. There, just ahead, were several police cars in a clearing by the road. As she slowed, a couple of policemen approached her truck. Neither one was smiling. Carly rolled down her window.

"Where are you going, miss?" one officer barked.

Carly tried to think of a believable answer. What would someone be doing up here? Looking for their horse? Perhaps a lost dog? She tried to answer, "Uh, uh, actually, I don't really have a destination." Then it came to her. She flashed her best smile. "I came up here to enjoy the nice weather and go for a long walk. It helps me calm down from the hectic city life. Should I not be here?" she asked. The gruff officer answered. "I'm sorry! We can't allow anyone past this spot in order for us to conduct an investigation. You don't look like someone who would be involved in this type of crime."

Carly's fingernails dug into the steering wheel. She forced out a question. "Some kind of crime?"

Shaking from head to toe now, Carly was happy to see that the officer had stepped a few feet from the truck and was not paying attention to her. He turned toward her and spoke over his shoulder, "Property crime, miss. Stolen vehicle. See, down that gully?"

Carly leaned over to the passenger side and looked down the embankment. Near the bottom, barely visible were the wheels of an overturned vehicle. She was flooded with relief at the sight of this scene. The officer turned back to the truck. He volunteered more information. "We have reason to believe this vehicle was used in a number of armed robberies. It was reported stolen last week. Our helicopter spotted it here this morning. We are conducting a search of the area in case there is any discarded evidence, but more than likely there won't be any. Still, you never know. We won't take long. It's not like we're looking for murder victims or anything like that. Probably be finished tonight. I'm sorry, but you'll have to turn around and find another place to go for a walk. I'll help you, drive right over here."

The officer guided Carly's jerky efforts to turn the truck around, shaking his head at women drivers. He hadn't noticed Carly's violent physical reaction when he had mentioned murder victims. The jolt was still affecting her motor skills. Finally pointing downhill, she waved to the officer and slowly left the policemen to do their job, her mind focused on this latest development.

"Wow! Of all the days to pick, I come here today." She laughed. A tenuous, nervous laugh, but a laugh nonetheless. Questions popped into her head. Was this a warning? Some kind of sign? She suddenly stopped the truck. Using the rearview mirror, she backed up to the spot where the police officer was still standing. Straining to conceal her nervousness, she leaned out the window to ask the officer a question, "Sir, I'm a little curious. When you say you are conducting a search, how far do you have to look? Like do you intend to cover this whole mountain?" The policeman studied Carly for a moment before answering. Carly's gleaming smile disarmed any mistrust he may have had. He answered her question, "Oh no! Not in this situation, just a couple of hundred feet around the scene. That's all! Sometimes we bring in a dog to help. Speeds things up. Never know what they will find. Amazing sometimes. They can smell things for miles. One of our best tools. We asked for one this morning, but none was available. Too bad, this would have been a great place for a little exercise and training." He leaned closer, an emboldened smile glued to his face. "That answer your question, miss?"

Carly pulled back, startled by the officer's clumsy come on. She wasn't prepared for the officer's quick change of character, but he is a man, and she is Carly, so no problem. Smiling very sweetly, she answered, "Yes, it does." Thinking the officer may wonder why she asked, she continued. "The reason I asked is because I will be coming back here for a long walk, and I'll keep my eyes open for anything suspicious. Maybe I'll find something that could help you. Is that okay?" The officer puffed up and smiled even more, "Of course. Of course! The public is always welcome to help us. Thank you! Here is my card. Call if you find something. Have a safe trip back. Bye for now."

The officer almost ripped the pocket from his shirt as he grabbed one of his cards and shoved it at Carly. She took the card, winked and left him standing in a cloud of dust when she accelerated away. Before reaching the highway, she steered with one hand while she stuffed the cop's card down the front of her jeans with the other hand. "Here, take a good sniff, asshole. That's as close as you'll ever get," she muttered.

At the highway, she eased into the light traffic. After a few miles she reached into her pants, pulled the damp card from her crotch and tossed it out the window.

The easy highway driving freed her mind to search for answers and directions after the disturbing encounter. She shuddered when she recalled the officer mentioning that a search dog was not available that day. "Thank God," she thought. "No saying what a dog may have unearthed if let loose on that mountain." In a way, she found the chance meeting a little exciting. A rush for sure. That's something she didn't realize she had been missing. Was she being challenged? Images of her garden couldn't be ignored. She made a decision. Tomorrow. Tomorrow, she had to complete her visit and there was no better time than first thing tomorrow. She started to sing.

"My love garden! My love garden!

I'm going to see my love garden

I'm going to see my love garden

My love garden! My love garden!"

Softly at first, then, as old emotions gripped her, louder and louder.

"My love garden! My love garden!

Yes! I'm going to my love garden

I haven't forgotten my love garden

I'll think of you tonight

You're such a lovely sight

My love garden! My love garden!"

Tears and words flowed all the way back to the city. She returned the truck to the rental agency and reserved it for the morning. Then she walked to her car and changed back to "Carly". She drove home, arriving in time to prepare a nice dinner. Jeff arrived home while the meal was still being prepared. When he saw Carly, he instinctively knew something was bothering her. He didn't know whether to ask or keep quiet until she was ready to divulge any information. He played it safe. He kept quiet. Carly forced a smile and kissed him on the cheek.

"Have a nice day?" she asked.

Jeff thought she was acting phony, but played along not wishing to disturb a hornet's nest. "Not too bad, same old you know, meetings and business. And you?"

"Nothing special, a little running around, catching up on errands. That's all. Dinner is almost ready. I hope you're hungry."

Jeff detected a little bit of bullshit. He was starting to read Carly better as time passed. The thought of a tasty dinner helped him push any attempt to chase after Carly's plight aside.

"Yes, now that you mention it, I am very hungry. I'll put my case away. Call me when it's time to eat." He carried his briefcase down the hall to his office. Staring at his back, Carly stuck out her tongue. She knew he was onto her, but thought what the hell, that was his problem. She continued with the dinner preparation. A short time later, the table set and the food cooked, she called, "Dinner! Come and get it."

Jeff left the computer messages he was viewing and sauntered into the kitchen, "Mmm! Looks and smells great. Thank you!"

"You're welcome! Sit up and eat. I'm hungry too," Carly answered.

The meal was eaten in silence except for the occasional remark on how good it tasted. They were both really hungry, Carly after her interesting day and Jeff from a very intense round of meetings and problem solving. After the meal, Jeff went back to his office to finish up some paperwork while Carly cleaned up the dinner dishes and took a long hot bath. Later, when they went to bed, there was no goodnight kiss. Neither one was able to sleep very well. Carly was focused on tomorrow's activities, and Jeff was concerned with Carly's distant behavior. In the morning, Carly pretended to sleep until she heard the door close behind Jeff. He left to attend a business meeting. Jeff suspected Carly was not sleeping but he was in no mood to address any problem that was obviously interfering with their happy life.

Shortly after Jeff had gone, Carly wearily struggled from the bed. Visions and thoughts of her garden quickly lifted her spirits, and she sang out loud while drinking a strong cup of coffee. Everything she had done yesterday to prepare for a visit to her garden was repeated in the same exact detail. She locked the door behind her and headed for her car, still singing softly.

After picking up the rental truck and maneuvering through the morning traffic, she welcomed the open highway. Yesterday's surprising event was now causing her some concern. Yesterday, although being apprehensive, she was still able to sing her song and plan the visit to her garden. Today, she was asking herself whether she should be doing this and whether yesterday's run-in with the police was an omen. Unable to shake the very uneasy feeling and stubborn enough not to turn back, she replayed yesterday's activity over and over until the turnoff beckoned, as it had numerous times before. She slowed, checked the traffic and turned off the highway. Unlike all the other times, something didn't feel right.

Flashes of her many previous visits pulsed through her mind, interspersed with yesterday's shocking surprise. A pounding head, dry throat and difficult breathing forced her to stop. She started to cry. With the engine stopped, loud sobs echoed from the open window, disturbing the quiet country air. For how long she didn't know, but she felt a little better when the tears would no longer flow. But not good enough to continue. She had to rest. A large sun-drenched rock caught her attention. Stretched out on the rock, with her eyes closed and her face in the sun, she allowed the soothing bird songs to ease her pain. To regain the courage she had lost to doubtful thoughts, she practiced a meditation exercise, requiring nothing but pleasing thoughts. It worked! Her eyes fluttered open. She sniffed the clean air. No time to waste. She jumped into the truck. Moving forward once again, she burst into song.

"I'm going to my love garden
My love garden
My love garden

I'm going to my love garden
It's the nicest garden
A garden could be
I'll fix it up nice
So the whole world will see
My love garden
My love garden."

Yesterday's interruption to her mission was forgotten, as the truck bounced along under the control of the obsessed driver. A cloud of dust and bouncing pebbles followed. And then she was there. Her heart skipped. She parked the truck and ran into the opening beyond the tree cover.

"Boys! Boys, I'm back! I'm so sorry! So sorry! I didn't mean to stay away so long. Please forgive me. I'm so selfish. And I've been a little unfaithful. But maybe I can make it up to you."

She sprinted around the perimeter of the garden mounds apologizing and promising to make amends for her perceived wrongs. Slowing down, she approached the first mound, the "L," as she had during each previous visit. New vegetation tangled with the dry brush Carly had used to cover the mounds, making her passage difficult. Finally, after pushing her way through the weeds, she reached the first mound. Her heart pounded deep inside her heaving chest as she tearfully began, "Eddy! Oh Eddy! I'm so, so sorry. I don't know what to say, except sorry for taking so long and Dan, same thing, sorry, sorry, sorry!"

Carly moved her head from side to side as she plowed on to the "O."

"George, George. Oh! Peter and Mike. You must have thought I had forgotten you. Sorry, sorry! No! I didn't forget you. Please believe me. I've been busy and time passed. Please forgive me. Mike, oh Mike! I still laugh when I think of our afterlife conversation. Remember you said if you ever came back to another life you would like to be six inches taller and three inches longer. Funny, funny! I transposed the numbers three inches taller and six inches longer gets my attention. Now that's a picture! Oh! So funny!"

Carly paused, snickering to herself before moving over to the "V" mound.

"Gary and Chris, Gary and Chris. How are you? And I apologize to you boys also. I'm sorry for being away so long. Please forgive me. And rest assured, you are still in my thoughts. You might say I took a long breather, but I'm back. I'm back! Not long now. Only two more. My garden will be finished. You'll be so happy."

A couple of steps through the tangle of weeds and she faced the final, unfinished mound. Barely audible, she whispered, "Sam, Syd. Don't tell the others, but you two are my favorites, just between us. I'm sorry if I took so long getting back to you. It's a long story. I may tell you some time. But I'm back and now that I've seen you all, I feel much better."

Carly's movements from when she exited the truck until reaching the final mound, took her through several emotional steps. She went from a very agitated, heart-pounding excitement to a satisfying, serene feeling. She was now very relaxed and focused.

Climbing uphill, she headed toward a small knoll that overlooked the clearing. Clamoring to the top of the small hill, she turned and addressed the tangle of twigs and mounds below. "Boys! Boys? Men! Yes! Men! My men! Again, I apologize. How could I leave you for so long? I don't know. I'm sorry! I have to confess. I was pulled in a different direction. A bit of a change, to put it mildly. And I think I have been a little unfaithful. I was unfair to all of you and my garden, your garden, our garden. I won't go into details but I'm going to tell you that I tried to put you way back in my mind, out of sight. I tried a new type of life, a different, settled down existence. Something I have longed for as long as I can remember. A loving, quiet life I have seen so many others enjoy. And I was so sure I had found it, until a short time ago. Lately, you have all been on my mind. I had to come and see you. And now I know our garden has to be finished. It will be finished."

Tears poured down Carly's face. Her body shook uncontrollably. "It will be finished!" she sobbed.

"I promise, our garden will be finished." Somehow, adding "our" instead of "my" in her address gave a hint of legitimacy by involving her "boys", as though they had been waiting for it to be finished. Carly thanked them for their patience and stumbled back down to the area just above the mounds. Instead of going around and back down to the truck she skirted along the ridge above the mounds to the very old mound in the upper far corner of the clearing. Her contrite anguish turned to rage as she drew closer. Reaching the mound, she exploded.

"You bastard! You bastard! You fucking bastard!" she shouted as she jumped up and down and kicked at the mound. "You fucking bastard. I hate you. It's a good thing you're not a part of my garden. See this line here? My garden ends here. Right here."

Carly carved a rough line through the soil and weeds with her foot, just below the mound, separating it from her garden. "You bastard!"

After venting her anger at the mound, she lowered her jeans and pissed on it. Then she staggered back to the truck. Drained of all emotion, she needed to get home to a nice hot bath. That's all she concentrated on throughout the erratic drive back to the city. Shortly into the drive she felt a throbbing headache develop and then the inevitable tears, followed by a very welcome development. Disturbing thoughts ceased. Her mind was free except for the vision of a relaxing soak in steaming hot water.

CHAPTER SIXTEEN

C arly hurried back to the city. She returned the rental truck and walked quickly to her car, where she changed her appearance back to Carly. Wasting no time, she drove straight home. Once inside, she stripped off her clothes while the bathtub was filling. Before the tub was full, she opened a bottle of wine and placed it next to the tub along with a tall wine glass. As she eased into the hot water, she knew she would stay there as long as it took for her to gain control over the jumble of disorganized thoughts and pounding headache. A decision had been made and once her mind was set, she wouldn't waver in her efforts to reach the intended goal. The hot water and wine worked in soothing unison as she assumed her favorite planning mode. Re-awakened power surged through her body as each exciting idea energized the next. Nothing had to be written down. Carly had mental organizing down to an art form. Each plan had a beginning, a middle and an end. A goal was decided on and the many steps necessary to reach that goal were mapped out mentally. Each step was laid out at first, and revisited as necessary to flesh out the details. Over time, when certain items could not be overlooked, Carly wrote coded notes as reminders. She was back in control, powerful control, feeling good, until a gentle voice startled her out of the enveloping trance.

"Hello! Bathing beauty," Jeff called.

"Oh! Shit! Can't you knock?" Carly growled. "You scared the crap out of me."

"Sorry, I didn't mean to scare you. I thought you would have heard me come in," Jeff apologetically mumbled.

"I didn't and you startled me. You'll have to get your own dinner, 'cause I'm not getting out of here. Close the door. I'll talk to you later," Carly spit out.

Jeff gently closed the door and backed away, knowing Carly's mood swings were not worth pursuing or worrying about. If she wanted him to know what was bothering her, she would tell him, if she didn't want him to know, she would never tell him. He was starting not to care either way, with other things occupying his thoughts, especially work contracts. If Carly needed his help, he would be there if she asked, but he wouldn't go out of his way, as he remembered the times when he had been admonished for trying to help her without her permission. He quickly dismissed her moodiness while fixing a sandwich for dinner. After eating, he went to his office computer and stayed there all evening. Carly, engrossed in her thoughts, stayed in the bathtub another two hours, replenishing the hot water as it cooled. She didn't give a second thought to her treatment of Jeff. Nice was over. Or was it? Scanning back over her plan, she realized that some semblance of a harmonious household was needed in order for the plan to work. When she finally emerged from the bathroom, she sauntered into Jeff's office, where he was still hard at work, and softly kissed him on the neck.

"Sorry! I think I'm kind of tired. Maybe I'll feel better in the morning. Night, night!"

Carly made her way into bed. A short time later, Jeff followed. Neither of them got much sleep. Carly cried softly, and Jeff, once again, continued to wonder what her problem was. He hadn't believed her story of being tired, and try as he might, he couldn't dismiss it as one of Carly's mood swings, in order to get some sleep.

In the morning, in spite of her red eyes and lack of sleep, Carly reverted to her bouncy, lovable self. Jeff stared at her with a surprised look on his face.

Carly remarked. "Yes, I know. Me again! What a chameleon, huh! I'm getting up. What about you?" Jeff closed his eyes. "I'm staying here for a while. Please close the door."

"Okay! I will. Stay here as long as you want. I'll be quiet." Carly closed the door behind her and went to the kitchen where, instead of making coffee, she had a glass of milk. After downing the milk, she went to the couch in the living room and lay down. Sleep overcame her until mid-afternoon. She awoke, went to the bedroom, roused Jeff from his sleep and they made love.

For the next few weeks, Carly tried hard to act normal but Jeff could see that something was not quite right. This was, in part, intentional and part of the plan. Carly dropped a few hints, trying to give Jeff a message that she was a little restless and was becoming bored. Finally, they confronted the situation with a long sit down chat. Carly initiated the talk. "Sweetie, I must apologize for my behavior. I'm sorry. I must confuse you so much! We have to talk."

Jeff, relieved that he may finally be getting answers to some of Carly's mysterious ways, sat facing her in anticipation. He spoke quietly, "Thank you. Yes, you're right. I have been confused lately." Then he added, "Even more than usual."

They both laughed. Carly resumed the conversation. "Sweetie, that's because I have been a little more uncomfortable lately. I think maybe I need some kind of change, something different. I don't know. See! I'm confused too."

Jeff nodded, and asked, "Change? Tell me what's bothering you. I'm listening."

Carly was at the top of her game, sliding effortlessly into the beginning of a well thought out series of steps, leading to her objective. Confidently, she continued the charade. "I'm going to jog your memory a little. Remember a couple of months ago, I brought up the idea of moving to a warmer climate?"

Jeff nodded. "Yes, I remember."

"Good! Because that has been on my mind lately. I think we'd both be better off if we relocated. What do you think?"

Jeff answered with a question, "You mean just up and move?"

Carly, warming up, answered. "Yes! If you put it that way. But no, not just up and move. It would have to be done properly and methodically. It is possible, isn't it?" Carly, in full scheme mode, put on her best puppy-dog face. "Isn't it?" she repeated.

Jeff stammered, "I...I...suppose so. I never thought about it. You didn't bring it up again."

"You're right. I didn't. I was scared to." She lied. Jeff bought it. He tried to sooth her. "You don't have to be afraid. You know we can talk about almost anything. And in answer to your question, I don't think it would be impossible. Also this may surprise you, but a change might do me some good as well. Have you given thought to any details? How or where we get started?"

Again, Carly lied. "No. I haven't, but if you like, I can draw up a rough plan to see if there would be any problems. Is that okay?"

Jeff smiled. "Yes! Your organizing ability is legendary, just let me know how I can help, and I'll get right on it."

Carly returned Jeff's smile. "Thank you. I don't need much help to start with, but one thing I will need to know is how a move away from this area will affect your work? It won't do us much good if you can't change your work location. Can you see any problems there?"

Jeff slowly moved his head from side to side. "Coincidently, no. I'm approaching completion on a couple of contracts and haven't really thought about what will be next. My customers are up to speed in regards to my work load, and unless there is some urgent work that must be done, they let me tend to the work I'm involved with. I'm blessed with the freedom to not have to plan ahead for work. The work comes to me. I feel so lucky. When you're ready for more details, I'll lay it all out for you and give you a timeline. I'm sure you have a lot of other things to look after to start with. Besides, where do you think we will be moving to?"

Carly hesitated before giving a plausible answer. She really didn't have a destination, but for Jeff's benefit she patched together a reply. "To be honest, I don't have any particular place in mind, but I will say I'm leaning toward a much warmer climate. In fairness to you, ' she continued the lie, "your work is most important. Any place where you can't find lucrative work is, of course, out of the question." She grinned and continued. "I'm so glad you're with me on this. There's going to be some changes made around here. Brace yourself and watch me go. I'm starting right away. Bye, bye!"

She skipped away from Jeff, straight to her work station. Jeff knew the talk was over. He sighed and went to his computer to catch up on work that had been missed during the day. He decided to send a short note to Tim, mostly out of courtesy, to let him know that his message had been received. He didn't say much except to let Tim know that he was in good health and his work was going well. He definitely didn't mention Carly, and he also didn't ask why Tim had contacted him. If Tim had an important reason for his message, he would send another one. After Jeff pushed the send button, he dismissed the communication from his mind and turned to work related items. While he was busy, Carly had started to organize lists, much as she had for the move to this home. After several lists were well under way, she took a break and explored several Internet sites looking for possible cities to relocate to. In her earlier musings about moving, she was only browsing. Now, in a more serious vein, she realized that there was a lot more to consider for a faraway move than just the climate. She prepared to research all possibilities. Her forte. Charts were prepared with cities laid out by attributes and down sides. Too many bad signs and a potential city was circled red. There were so many variables to think about such as economic opportunity, transportation, home prices, entertainment, culture, politics and a host of others. She soon realized the choice would not be easy, but as usual she was up to the challenge. Change was in the air. When she had tired from all the information and images on her screen, she pushed her chair away from the desk and called, "Bed time!"

Jeff appeared in the doorway. "You're right, it is, isn't it? And now that you mention it, I'm tired!" Carly nodded in agreement. Jeff peeked over Carly's shoulder and asked, "How are all the lists going?"

Carly wrinkled her nose and responded, "The organizing is going very well, but I think we are going to have a different problem."

Jeff asked her to explain.

"Oh! I didn't mean to alarm you," she offered, noticing the serious look on Jeff's face, "It's just that I have been searching and analyzing a whole bunch of cities. The more information I get, the more confused I am. I can see that we will really have to put our heads together on this one. I didn't realize there are so many nice places out there. We had better be careful. Don't want to get this wrong. Do we?"

Jeff sucked in a large breath before answering. "This surprises me. Here, I thought you had a specific location all picked out, just ready for us. But you are right on with the need to be vigilant. Might I suggest you prepare some kind of comparison chart. When you need me, we'll sit down and hash it all out. One good thing, we are not in a hurry. In fact, I think it will be fun. Come on, let's put it away for now and go to bed."

Carly smiled, thanked Jeff and turned the computer off. Jeff left the room for bed. Carly sat for a few minutes, her mind going over the short conversation. One thing she didn't agree with Jeff was his remark that there was no need to hurry. She muttered, "Maybe for you there's no rush, but I have things to do and so little time." She felt a sense of urgency but pushed it aside realizing that her plan couldn't be rushed. Nothing could be missed.

The delay would be painful but she knew for a successful outcome, diligence was to be maintained at all cost. She went to bed. Jeff was already asleep.

Carly and Jeff left the bed at the same time the next morning. Jeff expressed surprise that Carly had gotten up so early. She reminded him that she was on a mission and would stick to it until all the necessary details required for a smooth, successful move were taken care of. Jeff nodded in acknowledgment. He wished her good luck when he left for work. She thanked him, but when he turned his back, she stuck out her tongue and then set right to work. Sitting at her computer, she reviewed her lists one by one, making notes, changes and additions or deletions as the day wore on. In the early afternoon, she stopped and decided that some physical activity was needed to offset the fatiguing desk work. Starting with her clothes, she made several piles: keep on hand, go to storage, get rid of and miscellaneous. Hours later, when Jeff came home, she stopped long enough to help prepare dinner and eat. After eating, she showed Jeff her progress and offered to help him do the same with his clothes. He really didn't want to, at this early date, but knew he couldn't refuse Carly. She pulled him gently to his closet, and soon his wardrobe was arranged in separate piles next to Carly's. He tried to protest, but Carly wasn't about to listen.

At bedtime, she thanked him for his helpful effort and assured him that tomorrow night he wouldn't have to do any manual work, but she would like to sit down with him to get some idea when and how he could wind down his work contracts. Jeff agreed to help with that information.

In bed, Carly fell fast asleep, drained by the physical and emotional exertion. Jeff, feeling pushed against his will, forced himself to sleep, aware that this was just the beginning.

In the morning, Carly didn't get up with Jeff. Instead, she slept another hour after he left the house. When she did get up, she went straight to her computer, where she gathered information until early afternoon. After that, she started comparing and analyzing everything she could find on prospective places she would be happy to move to. It seemed to her to be no use. The more data she studied, the more confused and uncertain she became. She closed the file, deciding to look another day.

Jeff arrived home, and after dinner, sat with Carly to fill her in on details about his contract completion dates. Carly started the conversation by telling him what she had accomplished during the day.

"I managed to consolidate a couple of my lists and condense a couple of others. Also, I checked off a number of items, so everything looks really good. What I would like from you now is some idea or time line for your completion dates. I would like to enter it on my flowchart so my other chores can be coordinated to coincide with your final days of work."

Jeff hesitated. Carly questioned him before he started, "You look puzzled. Don't you want to give me that information, or don't you know when you will finish your projects?"

She waited as he chose his words. He did not want to ruffle Carly's feathers, "It's not that...it's just ...you make it seem so...so urgent. Like we have to be out of here by a certain date or something. Perhaps you can tell me what the rush is. I seem to be missing something."

Carly had not expected any opposition from Jeff. She went into damage control, "I'm sorry! I guess my springing this move business on you is a little shocking. Please forgive me. You do know me well enough to know that when I decide on something, I want it right now. I'll try to slow down. Let's just take the evening off, and you can feed me any work related information when you feel more comfortable. Is that okay?'

Jeff nodded. "Yes, it is. Thank you! I promise to get you the dates you require, but you should know, this whole idea is so new to me. Please let me ease into it slowly."

Carly smiled, a forced smile, but a smile just the same. "Of course. How selfish of me." She lied. Then she attempted to ease Jeff's apprehension. "You're right! It's all so new to you. I'll tell you what. I'll try to make it as much fun as I can. Some kind of adventure. Yes, that's it, an adventure. I can see you're concerned, so let's stop right now and relax. No more talk tonight. Okay?"

Jeff stared at Carly. He had a feeling that nothing had been resolved, especially a few questions he wanted to ask. He also wanted to get to the bottom of her obsessive need to rush, but didn't have the nerve to continue the discussion. The rest of the evening was spent reading and scanning the TV.

The next three or four weeks followed in a similar pattern. Carly methodically organized and completed tasks required for the move. Jeff helped when needed and supplied Carly with information as she asked for it. The pace was painfully slow for Carly, given this aching need to complete the plan spinning in her head. So far, everything looked good except for having difficulty fighting the need for urgency. She kept telling herself to relax so she wouldn't miss anything. She double checked and triple checked all the important items that couldn't be missed. She continually wracked her brain searching for anything important she may have overlooked. She stopped searching for a place to move when she realized it wasn't really necessary. In Jeff's eyes she was still looking. All the personal information she had gleaned, either directly or surreptitiously from Jeff, was safely filed away, ready to be put to use at the right time. On a Friday night, Jeff gave her the date she had been waiting for, his final day at work. As he walked in the door, he announced, "Only two more weeks. That make you happy? Only two more weeks."

Carly brightened. "Yes, that is good news. Aren't you excited?"

Jeff thought for a minute. "Yes! Yes, I am. I'm starting to get very excited."

Carly jumped right in. "I knew you'd come around. Now we can have so much fun exploring new places."

Jeff replied with a question. "Speaking of new places, how is your search for our new home coming?"

Carly formed a fake frown. "Oh! I meant to tell you, I've kind of changed our plans."

Jeff stepped back. "Changed our plans? What do you mean by that?"

Carly pulled him into the living room and sat him down on the couch. She remained standing while relating her well-rehearsed story, "As you know, I've been having a hell of a time trying to decide where we should relocate to, so I came up with a great idea. I think you'll like it."

Jeff didn't dare interrupt. Carly continued, "You have some savings, I have some savings, and we both have lots of time, so why don't we take a few months off and see lots of new places?"

Jeff nodded, "Interesting. Go on. Tell me more."

Carly started again, "I thought maybe we could get a motor home and visit all those interesting places I have been reading about. You know, stay a while in each one...kind of get the flavor. Wouldn't that be fun? We both know you do need a break. You've been working for years. Is this a silly idea?"

Carly had dropped to her knees. Her eyes pleading for Jeff's approval of the plan.

Jeff sucked in a deep breath. "Wow! I'm just starting to get used to the idea of making a move and now this. I need to digest this a bit, but off the top of my head, it could work. One thing it will do for us is eliminate or at the least reduce our chances of making a mistake and moving to an unacceptable location. In answer to your last question: No, it isn't a silly idea, and as usual, you manage to surprise me with your imagination. Yes! I think it would work just fine. I suppose you have our itinerary all worked out?" he added in jest.

Carly snickered, "No I don't, but I have looked into some prices. It's nothing we can't handle. Come on, let's eat."

Carly jumped up and pulled Jeff from the couch. They

embraced, kissed then hand in hand, walked into the kitchen to prepare a quick meal. As they worked, Carly giggled, danced and hummed to herself. Not so much because Jeff was on board with her scheme but because she had pulled it off so smoothly. Everything was falling into place. Yes! Her plan was going as she had visualized. It was all she could do to stop herself from singing her song out loud. Now was not the time. Not in front of Jeff. She didn't want any more of his questions about her garden. In fact, she hoped he had forgotten all about it. She would wait until she was alone to sing out loud and dance around the house in anticipation of seeing her finished garden.

The next week and a half went by very quickly. Jeff kept busy cleaning up his final projects and Carly plugged away at all the details for the coming move. On the Wednesday of his final week of work, he came home to find Carly busy at her computer, as she was most evenings. He walked up behind her chair and cheerfully announced, "Only two more days and I'm free. All because of you, I feel a kind of relief, like being unshackled from my work. Not that I didn't enjoy my work, but I always felt some kind of obligation to constantly turn in excellent results. You are so right, I do need a break. Thank you so much."

Carly checked a guilty flash as she turned to see Jeff's smiling face. She whispered, "Please don't thank me. I don't think it's appropriate right now. All I need is your cooperation and help in the next few weeks. There is still lots to do you know." She forced a smile then added, "Let's eat! I'm hungry."

Something in her tone didn't seem right, but as he had done many times before, Jeff chose to overlook whatever was bothering Carly. He sighed and agreed with Carly's prodding. "Yes! Let's eat. I'm hungry too now that you mention it."

During the preparation and consuming of the meal, the talk was controlled by Carly. She reviewed some of her to-do lists and the outstanding items that Jeff was to complete and asked if he had managed to get any done that day? Jeff surprised her by telling her that he had indeed completed a couple of tasks that Carly had been pushing him to finish. She was pleased. He was only tidying up loose ends at work, and sending good bye greetings to old colleagues, so he had time to look after some chores that Carly had asked him to complete. He mentioned that a couple of corporations had organized a lunch for him on his last day, which was a Friday. He wanted her to attend. Carly refused his invitation, claiming not to be interested in lunch with a boring bunch of business people. She apologized for not being present for his send-off. She then added that it didn't matter if she were present anyway, because he wasn't leaving her. Jeff knew her excuse was feeble, what with her intelligence and ability to fit into any situation, but he also knew the subject was closed. After they agreed that the preparations for the move were progressing on time and going well, they spent the rest of the evening relaxing and reading the newspaper.

In the morning, Jeff went to work while Carly stayed in bed. At work, Jeff had just started to answer his messages when he got a call on his cell phone. Expecting another well-wisher call, he leaned back and answered, "Hello!"

"Hi Jeff!" Jeff knew the voice immediately.

"Tim! Tim you old bugger. Nice to hear from you. How are you doing?"

"I am doing quite well, which may surprise you. Thanks for asking. I assume you are doing well, as usual."

Jeff, not used to his brother being so pleasant, hesitated before answering, "I'm doing very well, thank you." Jeff assumed his brother wanted something from him or needed his help. He asked, "You're being too nice, Tim. What do you want?"

Tim laughed. "Surprise! I don't want anything."

"Come on. You must want something. Let's have it. What do you want?"

Tim laughed louder. "I'm sorry! I can't help you. I really don't need anything."

Jeff continued questioning, "Then why the call? Please fill me in."

Tim stopped laughing, "Okay! You're not going to believe me, but I just thought I should get in touch with you. I'm coming up your way. I thought it would be nice if we could re-connect. Does that sound good to you?"

Jeff, still skeptical, answered, "I suppose so, but I must warn you, don't lay anything on me. If you have anything to say, say it now. You know how much trouble you've caused me in the past. I don't need any more shit from you, so if that's what you have on your mind you can just forget it. Okay?"

Tim, aware of all the pain he had caused his brother over the years, had conveniently pushed it to the back of his mind. Now, he realized that Jeff had not been able to do the same. He tried to make amends. "Jeff, I guess I'm guilty on all charges. I did pull some stunts. Didn't I? I'm sorry! I do think we should meet. I know you don't trust my promises, but I'll be on my best behavior. Do I get another chance?"

Jeff snapped back. "I don't know, Tim. I don't know. You fucked me around so many times. I really don't trust you. Besides, it's kind of a bad time right now, I'm in the middle of moving. My house is a mess. I don't think it's a good idea right now."

Tim backed off, "Moving, huh? That's always fun. What I really should have told you is that my trip is a business trip. I hope you are sitting down because here's a surprise for you: I have a steady job. Almost two years now, and I'm doing very well. So you see, I don't want anything from you. Seeing as I'm going to be in the area anyway, I think we should get together. If you agree, I'd really like to see you. I'll leave it up to you."

Jeff didn't know what to say. "I'm happy to hear you have a good job. I hope you can stick to it. Good for you. Now, about us meeting up, let me sit on it for a while. Give me a call before you travel this way. I'll have an answer for you then. I wish you well. Take care!"

Tim thanked him for listening and said goodbye.

Jeff smacked the phone down, thinking, "That no-good

brother of mine. What's he up to now?"

Had he been pressed for time, he would have cut the conversation much shorter. The day slowly dragged by as bitter memories of long ago pranks and pain caused by Tim reappeared in random order. A few phone calls and e-mails from old friends helped him through to quitting time. Messed up on the inside and visibly disheveled on the outside, Jeff rushed straight home. As he walked in the front door, Carly jumped back and gasped, "Whatever happened to you? You're a mess."

Jeff didn't answer. Carly asked again, "Well! Tough day? Come on, you can tell me."

Jeff finally spoke up, "Nothing much. Nothing much. Just some work problems. They'll take care of themselves. I think everything is finally catching up with me, you know my final day is tomorrow and also my farewell lunch. I think I have to sit down and unwind a bit. Is that okay?"

Now it was Carly's turn to wonder whether Jeff was telling the truth. She didn't like that at all. She wanted to confront him right there, but managed to control the urge. Maybe later she could cajole whatever was bothering him out into the open. Right now, she agreed with him. He needed to sit down and rest. She gestured to the couch in the living room.

"Of course love, of course. Rest up all you need to. I will look after dinner and anything else you want. Sit down, get comfortable, put any nasty thoughts aside. If there is anything bothering you that you would like to talk about, I'm a good listener and problem solver." Carly couldn't resist one last try for information. Jeff shook his head. He wasn't going to mention Tim to Carly. Tim was his problem and he crossed his fingers, hoping there wouldn't be a follow-up call, but feared there would be.

The next day was the day all his contracts officially closed. Jeff went in to the office late. He had already cleaned out most of his belongings from the small mini-office that served as a hub for his business in the center of the city. The co-op office space served several small business tenants that didn't require their own office staff. Office services were provided on a pay for time or pay for service basis. This allowed Jeff to keep his time reserved for job-related work. He relied on the competent staff in the secretary pool for all of the routine bureaucratic paperwork his daily business required. That morning he packed up a few final items from his desk and placed them in his car. As lunch time approached, one of the secretaries gave a signal and all work in the office complex stopped. The entire work force and other office tenants surrounded Jeff in his now barren looking office space. He was very surprised, but recovered quickly to hear their heartfelt goodbyes. Gloria, the officer manager, presented Jeff with a large card signed by everyone present and many others who had passed through the office in the last few weeks. She had an expressive speech prepared, but didn't need to refer to it as her genuine words hushed the giddy crowd. Her talk covered the years Jeff had been a tenant in the office and how he had become a part of the family. She conveyed how much he would be missed and wished him luck in his future endeavors. When she had finished the small crowd cheered, and then it was Jeff's turn to reply. He had not expected a send-off like this. He tried to find the appropriate words to describe his feelings but the audience didn't need to hear his words. They could tell he was genuinely touched. He thanked the staff for making his work over the years easier and said that he would miss them very much. He also promised to keep in touch and would visit whenever he was in the area. After he offered one last thank you, the group slowly dispersed, leaving a few who wanted to give Jeff their personal goodbyes. After they had all gone back to their desks, he tucked the large card under his arm, said goodbye to Gloria and left the office.

Jeff walked slowly to his car, mixed emotions surging through his body. After what seemed like a very long drive, he walked into the house and collapsed on the couch. Carly could see he had experienced a very emotional day. She tried to comfort him.

"Feeling a little queasy?" she asked. "Is it all a little too much for you?"

Jeff nodded and gripped Carly's hand. She continued with softly soothing words, "Everything's going to be fine, love. Relax! Everything's going to be just fine. I know! It's a big change for you, but just think...you're free. Free to do anything you want. Free to see what comes next. Close your eyes. Lean your head back. Relax! Relax! That's it! Relax! Let it all out! Everything is going to be great. You'll see."

Carly pulled away, still talking softly, "I have a nice bottle of wine, and I'd be honored if you shared it with me. Okay?"

Jeff nodded, not opening his eyes. Carly slowly lifted herself up and padded to the kitchen. She soon returned with a tall crystal glass full of wine in each hand. "Here, baby! Look what I have for you."

Jeff opened his eyes. "Oh! Thank you! You're so sweet."

He took a glass from Carly's outstretched hand. She raised her glass offering a toast, "Here's to the future, whatever it brings."

The glasses clinked together and the toast was consummated. Jeff managed a smile.

He replied softly, "Yes! To the future! You are definitely correct. To the future!"

Carly remarked on his noticeable change, "That's better! Such an attractive smile. I know, it's all so new to you. Being out of work must feel so different. But as I said a few minutes ago, you're free to be and do whatever you want. Let's make the most of it and have fun. Is it a deal?"

Jeff nodded his head slowly. Still smiling, he answered in a whisper, "It's a deal. We can't go back now, can we? I'll get over it. I promise. But it is a strange feeling for me. I can't quite figure it out. It's sort of like a loss and a liberation tied together. Very confusing. I suppose, I have to lean toward the liberation side. Don't you think?"

Carly quickly answered, "Of course, silly. You have always

been free. You just didn't know it. Now you are even more free than you have ever been in your life. So here's to the future."

Another toast was proposed, and Jeff felt his emotional load lighten.

Carly changed the subject. "Friday night and guess what?"

Jeff bit. "What?"

Carly grinned. "I am not going to ask you to do anything. We are both free to do what we want. Putter, read, TV, anything. I know you're tired and drained. So that's it for today. Think you can handle that?" Jeff looked relieved. His answer jumped from his lips, "Oh, yes! I thought you would have me running around tonight. Thank you! I think I'll read the paper. And you?"

Carly grabbed Jeff's hand. "Don't worry about me. I have a few things to do. I won't disturb you, and later I'll fix a nice snack. So just relax and read that paper."

Carly motioned for Jeff to stay seated. He picked up the main section of the newspaper as Carly turned toward her nearly empty office to check off some items from her lists. She managed to kill two hours of time, packing some remaining books and stationery that were now redundant since Jeff had finished his work. Happy with her progress, she decided to prepare the snack she had promised. As she walked by Jeff, who was still reading, she asked, "Ready for that snack now?"

He smiled. "Yes, I am, thank you. After that great lunch, I didn't think I'd be hungry again this soon, but I am. Need some help?"

Carly shook her head. "No, thank you. You keep reading. I'll call you when it's ready. Won't be long."

In the kitchen, Carly, with her natural efficiency, whipped up a tasty snack and poured some more white wine. She called out, "All ready, love! Come and get it."

Jeff appeared wide-eyed in the doorway. He let out a long breath. "I'm still amazed. You always manage to impress me. It's all so inviting. And so fast. I don't know how you do it but, don't stop. Promise?"

Carly frowned and stuck out her tongue. "Just enjoy the snack. I don't need any praise, thank you."

Jeff knew it was time to shut up and eat. He wondered if he'd ever figure Carly out, but for now he would ignore the mood change as he had done many, many times before. He sat down, anticipating the tasty food laid out in front of him. Just as quickly as she had frowned, Carly burst into a radiant smile. No explanation, nothing.

She shouted as she raised her glass, "Here's to freedom."

Jeff raised his glass to Carly's. He did not speak. Carly prolonged the toast. "Yes! Freedom, freedom. We're free, free, free. To do anything we like."

Carly noticed Jeff's skeptical look. "Not sure, are you? I know, it's still new to you, but it won't take long. You'll feel free. It'll be good for you. A whole new life. A whole new world. Freedom, you'll love it and I'll help. Come on now, smile. That's it, smile."

Jeff managed a faint smile. They toasted Carly's freedom spiel and dug into the inviting meal.

Partway through the feast, Carly revealed the plans she had for both of them on the weekend. Saturday morning would be spent reviewing their agenda for their final few weeks remaining in the home, and any errands that needed to be done would be taken care of in the afternoon. Any packing and loose ends that could be finished would be done in the evening. Sunday would be spent in the same way, except Sunday evening would be a time to rest.

Jeff answered sarcastically upon hearing details of Carly's scheme, "Will I get bathroom and coffee breaks during the day, or do I have to negotiate those items?"

Carly started to explode, but caught herself when she realized she had been had by Jeff's wit. What she failed to notice was that Jeff was using his humor to make a point or was she intentionally disregarding it? In any case, he hoped she caught a little of his drift.

He continued, still inserting a bit of dry humor, "I see you have the weekend mapped out nicely. That'll save me from having to think. You're doing a great job. Thank you."

Carly glared at him. "Stop it right now," she screamed. "I'm only trying to get ahead of the game so we don't have a whole lot of running around to do when it's time to leave. Is that okay?"

Jeff, standing up to Carly more than usual, smirked. "Yes, that is okay. In fact, it's really okay. It's okay with me if it's okay with you. Is that okay?"

For once Carly was a little subdued. She sat back and stared at Jeff and then started laughing. Refilling the now empty wine glasses, she proposed another toast. "Here's to everything's okay. It's okay with me and it's okay with you. Everything's okay. Cheers!"

When they had eaten their fill and finished the wine, the dirty dishes were stacked on the kitchen counter to be taken care of in the morning. Carly waved Jeff from loading the dishwasher. "Come on! Let's get into that bed."

Jeff backed away from the counter and followed Carly into the bedroom. Bathroom duties were attended to, then once in bed, they both slept soundly until morning. Jeff, free from work for the first time he could remember, woke up very refreshed, ready to greet the work Carly had set out for him. Carly awoke feeling the same way. She peeked out the window, "Oh! What a nice day! We are going to have a great weekend. Even if we are working, we'll have fun. Know what I'm going to do? I'm going to put the coffee on, then I'm going to have a bath, then I'm going to make us a tasty breakfast. I'm not going to ask you if it's okay because I'm telling you that it's okay."

Jeff smiled, "If you say it's okay, then it's okay."

Carly laughed, kissed Jeff and then ran into the kitchen. She prepared the coffee and after bouncing into the bathroom, ran a hot bath. Scented bubbles were added to the filling tub and once it was full, Carly slipped into the soothing hot water. Jeff, still relaxing in bed, was seduced by the aroma of fresh coffee. Yielding to the inviting fragrance, he left the bed, brushed his teeth and padded into the kitchen where the fresh brew was ready and waiting.

He called to Carly, "Coffee's ready. Want me to bring you a cup?"

Carly sang a happy response, "Oh! Yes, sweetie. I'd love one. Thank you!"

Jeff filled two cups to the brim and carried them to the comfortable, bathing Carly. "Here's that coffee I promised."

"Oh! You're a sweetheart. Thank you!" Carly whispered as she reached for the cup.

"You're welcome!" Jeff answered and continued, "But you're forgetting, you prepared it."

Carly frowned. "Yes, I did, didn't I? Anyway, you brought it to me, and that's all that counts. Cheers!"

Jeff perched on the side of the tub. Carly closed her eyes and took a long sip from her cup. Jeff followed her lead, "Mmm! Good!"

Carly murmured, "So, so good! I feel wonderful: hot bath, tasty coffee. There's only one thing left to help me start my day."

"What would that be?" Jeff asked.

Carly smirked wickedly. "Sex! Some really great sex. Doesn't that sound great? Sex, sex, sex," she sang.

Jeff smiled. "I should have guessed. You're in a fun mood, rested, bathed, caffeinated. How could I miss it? You have my full attention."

Carly pulled Jeff down to her waiting lips. The long, tender kiss stirred anxious emotions. Gently releasing Jeff, she gracefully eased her silky body from the foamy water. Grabbing a towel, she pulled Jeff to his feet. "Come on! Let's go back to bed."

Jeff, his libido fast catching up to Carly's, willingly allowed himself to submit to her coaxing, as she led the way to the bedroom. Hopping into bed, still wet with soapy bathwater, she aggressively initiated the lovemaking. After their sensual and generous liaison, the glowing couple dozed for the rest of the morning. At noon, Carly stirred. "Oh, my goodness! I'm going to say it again, what a nice day! Remember that breakfast I was going to make? It's now going to be brunch. I'm out of here. I'll call you when it's ready."

Carly sprang from the bed, quickly dressed and pranced to the kitchen. She had almost forgotten the mess from the previous evening but undismayed, due to her happy start to the day, quickly had everything cleaned up and the meal underway. Just as Carly was about to call him, Jeff sauntered in.

"Smells good!" he exclaimed.

"Yes. Doesn't it?" Carly answered. She continued, "Good timing! I was about to call you. Now go ahead sit up. It's all ready."

Jeff sat down at the table. Carly served up two large portions including muffins and fresh coffee. She then sat down and without any chitchat the meal was enjoyed. While the last sips of coffee were being savored, Carly reviewed the day's activities, getting Jeff's opinion as she proceeded. There wasn't anything pressing, but because it was now afternoon, they would both be on the go for the rest of the day. Carly dressed and left the house to attend to her list of errands. Jeff tidied the kitchen and then he too proceeded to deal with items on his errand list. He vowed to himself to complete as much as he could that day as he drove away from the house.

When he returned, late in the afternoon, he found Carly already home, busy preparing supper. As he entered the kitchen, he kissed her on the cheek and asked, "Have a nice day?"

"I sure did and how about you?"

"Very, very good! Got a whole bunch done. A whole bunch, and I'm feeling a lot better about everything."

Carly looked up from her meal preparations. "I knew you would. I have a nice dinner ready for us. Come on. Let's eat and enjoy ourselves."

Jeff sat down at the set table. Carly served up the sumptuous food, poured two glasses of wine and sat across from Jeff. Raising her glass, she proposed, "Here's to smooth sailing and clear skies ahead or...whatever!"

Jeff raised his glass. "Or whatever!"

They laughed, touched glasses, sipped and then dug into the tempting spread. After the meal, Carly ushered Jeff into the living room to relax. She cleaned up the kitchen ignoring his offers to help.

Finished in the kitchen, Carly joined Jeff in the living room for a while before the tired couple made their way to bed for a long sound sleep until morning. Carly woke early, leaving Jeff peacefully sleeping. She freshened up, went to the kitchen and started breakfast. When the sausage and eggs were almost ready, she called for Jeff to come and get it.

The pleasing aroma of breakfast cooking and fresh coffee had already enticed Jeff from the bed, and he instantly appeared in the doorway.

"Good morning," he warbled.

Carly tried to copy his sing-song greeting. "Good morning," she replied. Gesturing to the table, she urged. "Look what I have for you. Come on! Sit up!"

Jeff eagerly complied, plopping himself on his favorite chair. Carly expertly served up the dishes and coffee and copying Jeff's exaggerated movements, plopped down across the table from him.

He grinned, "I guess I did overdo the entrance a bit, didn't I?"

Carly laughed, "Oh! That's all right. You're in a good mood. That's great. Eat up now. Enjoy it like it's your last meal."

As the food and coffee quickly disappeared, Jeff asked, "Is there anything pressing today, or do we just stick to our lists?"

Carly thought for a minute then replied, "I don't think there is anything urgent today. I have some things to attend to that have to wait until business hours during the week. So today, let's continue to whittle away at the lists. There's still a couple of weeks left, so we can pace ourselves accordingly. It's nice to have some breathing room, and thank you for being such a sweetheart. I know you were feeling a little pressure, what with the life change and all. I appreciate your help. Very much."

Jeff, still trying to fit into his new slowed-down lifestyle simply replied, "You're welcome!"

He then stood up, clutched Carly by the shoulder blades and steered her down the hall to her office work station. "Go! Do your work. I'll clean up." Releasing his grip, he kissed the back of her neck and turned back to the kitchen.

Carly, watched him go. She wanted to give him the finger but instead a tear rolled down her cheek. The tender feelings did not last long, and she was soon tackling her chores.

Jeff cleaned up the kitchen. He then sat at his computer for about an hour checking messages and tidying up files. There was nothing he needed to do away from home, so he kept busy with packing and turfing items that were not required at the moment. Carly kept at her computer for most of the morning after which she grabbed a couple of her lists and informed Jeff he'd be having lunch alone. She left the house to take care of a few of the tasks listed. She managed to finish a number of things that had been bothering her and returned home in the late afternoon.

She entered and walked up behind Jeff, who was now back at his computer.

"Hungry?" she asked.

"Now that you ask, yes. And hello! How are you?" he sarcastically replied.

Carly stepped back. "I guess I owe you some kind of explanation for being so aloof earlier. Sorry! I don't have any reason. I just wanted to be quiet and do my own thing. I'm feeling much better now, and I'm ready to cook a nice meal. I don't need any help, and I'll call you when it's ready."

She turned and bounded from the room. Jeff watched her disappear, shaking his head from side to side before turning back to his computer screen. A short time later, tempting aromas wafted from the kitchen, but Jeff fought the urge to investigate the source until Carly called. A half hour later she did.

"Already, hungry man. Come and get it."

Jeff was hungry. Hearing the harkening words, he quickly covered the distance from his office to the kitchen. The tantalizing smells did not lie, the feast set before him looked every bit as pleasing as his nose had implied. Before he could say anything, Carly spoke up. "Just a little something I whipped up. Come on. Sit up. Enjoy!"

All Jeff could answer was, "Thank you! I will."

Carly had just whipped up a beautiful meal of pork chops baked in a classic sauce she had discovered complete with all the trimmings and, of course, a bottle of wine. They each loaded their plates, and Carly poured the wine.

Jeff proposed a toast. "To another great meal prepared by an amazing cook. Yes! Let's enjoy!"

The glasses clinked together, and the toast was consummated. Then the food was, true to the toast, enjoyed. Toward the end of the meal, Carly exchanged notes with Jeff on the day's activity and accomplishments. Then she laid out the next day's agenda, short and sweet.

"I will be up early tomorrow and out the door. I have a very busy day ahead of me, and I want to get a head start. I know you have a few things to do, so we'll have to meet up later in the day. Right now, I'm going to take a hot bath and relax while you clean up the kitchen like a good boy."

Without waiting for any response from Jeff, she fled the room to run a hot bath, leaving him to once again contemplate what had just happened.

Carly immersed herself in the hot water. Instead of experiencing a relaxing session, she pondered and stressed over the next day's activities. The bath only slightly eased her turmoil. She soon gave up trying to relax and turned her attention to a full run-through of tomorrow's events. All the details were reviewed in chronological order. After deciding that nothing had been missed or should be changed, she left the bath, dried herself and climbed into bed.

Jeff, meanwhile, tried to release Carly from his thoughts while he did a thorough job of cleaning the kitchen. As he worked, fleeting glimpses of Carly's many facets intruded on his concentration. He wished he could somehow help her deal with her disturbing problems, but lately, other thoughts were challenging these concerns. He was reflecting on his life with Carly and what may be in store for him in the future. The more he pondered the subject, the easier it was becoming for him to consider a break from Carly. He was not in love with her. He liked her immensely for her intelligence and fun-loving style. The sex was good, of course, but having to deal with her mood swings and her penchant for assuming control, even at times when it was only to make a point, was wearing on him. He prepared for a chance to air his thoughts, waiting for the right moment. He would tread lightly because with Carly, anything was possible. Nevertheless, whatever her reaction, he would have to confront her with his concerns. No matter how hard he tried, he couldn't convince himself that it would be easy. He knew it had to be done. He had never had to do anything like this, so the grinding thoughts were agony. To do nothing was out of the question. He needed a change. Satisfied with the spotless kitchen, he made his way to bed. Pushing his jumbling thoughts aside, he tried to sleep. Adding to his puzzlement was the fact that Carly was peacefully dozing beside him. He finally dropped off into a fitful sleep.

When he woke Carly was gone. Jeff stayed in bed immersed in thought for a while, then left the bed to prepare some strong coffee.

CHAPTER SEVENTEEN

C arly left the house early, drove to a familiar parking garage and changed her appearance and her ID. She then walked to the truck rental agency and picked up a waiting truck. After that, she drove to her storage unit and gathered up a shovel, pick and work gloves. She climbed back into the truck, checked that everything she needed was there, and then headed out to the familiar highway. Before reaching the city limits, she started to hum softly. Upon reaching the highway the words spilled out.

"My love garden, my love garden

I'll be there soon, my love garden

I'm on my way, be there today

My love garden, my love garden"

Verses came, verses went, some worked, some didn't. It really didn't matter to Carly as she sang and drove. Trying to remember old verses and make up new ones while still concentrating on the upcoming chores was difficult, so she just sang whatever popped into her head. Then suddenly, there it was, the dirt road leading from the highway to her garden. Her heart raced as she slowed. She carefully checked for other traffic and left the highway.

* * * *

Jeff sipped hot coffee, waiting for the toast to pop up in the toaster. He was happy Carly wasn't there. He needed a full day to himself to help him slowly adjust to not heading out to work. The toast popped up. Jeff retrieved and buttered the two slices and ate them. The phone rang.

He walked over to the phone and answered, "Hello!"

"Hi, Jeff. Tim here. How are you?"

Jeff's mood changed instantly, "Okay! And you?"

Tim continued, "You don't sound okay. Anything to do with me?"

Jeff jumped right on the question, "You've got that right. What can I do for you?"

Tim tried to soften him, "You don't have to do anything for me. I'd like to meet up with you. Think you can handle that?"

Jeff answered hesitantly, "I don't know. Since we last spoke, I've been too busy to think about corresponding with you. What do you have in mind?"

Tim made his pitch, "I'm in town at the Continental. I'd like to treat you to lunch. Nothing heavy. What do you say?"

Jeff let out a breath, "Oh! This is a surprise! I'm not doing anything, so I guess I can handle it. Thank you. Just one thing, don't fuck me around. If there's something you want, tell me now. I don't need any shit. Got that?"

The assertive tone impressed Tim. He replied, "Wow! You have balls. Good on you. Look! I promise no shit. Just a nice lunch on me. I'll even let you rant on about the past piss-off I've been. I'd really like to see you for old time's sake. Can you do that?"

Jeff relented, "Yes! I think I can. Where will we meet?"

Tim, already in the downtown district, thought of a nice restaurant, "How about the French Quarter at noon. Sound good?"

Jeff agreed, "That's very good. See you at noon."

Tim finished off, "Great. See you then. Bye!"

Jeff slowly replaced the receiver thinking that at least he now had part of his day taken care of. He wondered what that prick wanted but knew he'd find out soon enough. He went to his computer until it was time to meet up with Tim.

* * * *

Carly slowly inched up the dirt road, keeping a sharp eye out for any changes to the surrounding area. Nothing seemed out of the ordinary as she neared her destination: her garden. The closer she got, the more excited she felt. Her blood was pumping and her brow was sweating. The delirious rush was back, stirring up familiar emotions. Her throat was now too dry to continue singing, but after easing the truck into the bush next to her garden, she found her voice. As she jumped from the truck, she yelled, "Yes! Yes, boys, I'm back, and I have some great news." Then she ran into the clearing and continued, "I am going to finish our garden. I'm starting today, and very soon you will have some company. I think you'll like him. Isn't that good?"

She paid a visit to each mound, starting at the "L" and ending at the unfinished "E" talking non-stop all the way. Then she ran to the truck, changed into some work clothes, grabbed the pick and shovel and ran back to the "E." Dropping the tools, she pulled the sticks and brush from the mound. With the pick, she drew an outline of the center leg of the "E", then started chopping at the soil inside the outline. Alternating between the pick and shovel, she soon had a neat trench started. About every half hour, she stopped to sip from a water bottle she had brought with her. Those were the only breaks she took until, about four hours later, she pushed the tools aside and admired her efforts. Very happy with the finished product, she started to dance and sing her song, "My love garden, My love garden..."

* * * *

Jeff shut off his computer in preparation for his lunch meeting with his brother. The work, what little he could get done, was not hampered by thoughts of Carly but by intruding flashbacks of Tim. Over the years, Jeff had pushed any thoughts of Tim away back in his mind, but now with the new contact, familiar lost scenes pushed all else aside. He didn't really want to see Tim, but he had promised, and Tim did seem genuinely changed. He vowed to himself to remain in control during the meeting, as he guided his car through the late morning traffic. After parking nearby, he nervously approached the restaurant, then slowly pulled the large, intricate door open. When he stepped inside, the receptionist flushed and stammered, "You're...over there." She pointed to a table and tried to continue, "But you're here. No, you're over there?"

Jeff knew Tim was already seated. He reassured the receptionist, "Yes! I'm here and there." He grinned. "My twin brother."

The receptionist, still flushed, led Jeff to the table where Tim was seated. As he passed other tables, all heads turned. No two people, anywhere on earth, looked more alike than Jeff and Tim. The resemblance was scary. Their hair, teeth, height, weight, walk, mannerisms, speech patterns, all matched perfectly.

The only thing different about them was their personality. Jeff was the thinker, quiet, methodical, hard working. Tim, the rowdy one, flamboyant, outgoing, a party guy. Because of their identical looks, Tim often had Jeff take blame for his misdeeds as a youngster. Things got so bad in school, such as Jeff being coerced into writing exams for Tim, that eventually they were forced to attend separate schools. Jeff went on to gain a university degree, while Tim only completed high school. Not that Jeff was any smarter than Tim, both were about equal intellectually. It was Tim's spirited personality that led him astray. In many ways, it had seemed that Tim was smarter than Jeff when it came to wit and cunning, especially with his ability to slide effortlessly into Jeff's personality. He had often used Jeff as an unwitting foil in his schemes and Jeff, remembering his suffering, was still bitter. Now, after many years, he wondered what would happen today.

As he approached Tim's table, garbled images of long forgotten events flooded his mind, causing him to stumble in an awkward greeting, "He...e...ello," was all he could utter.

Tim looked up, "Still the suave man about town, I see."

Jeff flushed, then released his pent-up emotions, "Look, I told you, no shit. Do I make myself clear?"

Dropping into the chair across from Tim, he leaned forward, still venting his frustrations, "If you have something decent to say, then get on with it. If you can't be nice, then I'm out of here. Understand?" He stared straight into Tim's eyes.

Tim squirmed. "Wow! You look like Jeff. But you don't sound like Jeff. I'm impressed."

He stuck out his hand. Jeff didn't move. A few moments of silence, then Tim tried some damage control, "Okay! You've changed. That's good. I've changed a little bit too. I've learned to listen. So if we can get this train started, I'd like to find out how my brother is doing. Tell me, what have you been up to? You're looking good, so I'm assuming that everything's going all right."

Jeff guardedly started to reply to his devious brother's request, "I can do that, but first let's look at these menus. I'm going to take you up on the offer of a nice lunch."

Tim agreed, "Yes, let's eat. The menu is wide open to you. Don't be shy. Have whatever you like. All on me. I know that sounds a little bit strange, but life is strange. Isn't it?"

Jeff didn't reply. Tim caught a waitress's eye, and ordered a bottle of wine. A few minutes later, the bottle arrived, and a steak dinner special was ordered by each of the brothers as a wide-eyed waitress stared in wonder. When she left to place the order, Jeff whispered, "I forgot what a curiosity we are together. I guess that's one thing that'll never change."

Tim nodded, as he raised his wine glass. He toasted, "Here's to you, Bro...for all the times I mistreated you."

Jeff, not completely buying this line, added, "To you brother, who may finally be taking some responsibility."

Tim winced, and they sipped the wine. The atmosphere warmed a little. The food arrived, and as the two hungry men dug in, Jeff related his story starting from when they had last been together. It was when Jeff had begun university, Tim wanted to enroll in a nearby college and asked Jeff to sit in on his exams. In high school, Tim had badgered Jeff to write some of his tests, at times arousing suspicion regarding the high marks. Jeff had always resented his brother for taking advantage of him in this way. He refused to help Tim with his college exams and the two had a violent argument, leading to them going their separate ways. Tim never did enroll in college. They had talked over the telephone a couple of times over the years, but that was the extent of their contact. Now as Tim listened intently, Jeff began to tell his story, starting with his university studies. He filled Tim in with the details of his chosen field, engineering, and the high marks he achieved leading to his degree. He followed up his schooling experiences with the employment record he had accomplished, and why he had chosen to freelance his talents for freedom and self-satisfaction. Tim's ears perked up when Jeff inadvertently let slip his living arrangement with Carly. Intrigued, he wanted to know more. Putting it in the back of his mind, he thought he would try to learn more later in the conversation. Jeff finished the story with his current situation and leaned back.

Tim smiled, "Congratulations! You've done well. My story isn't as high tech as yours. Would you like to hear it?"

Jeff nodded, "Yes, I would. Very much. Thank you for listening to me. I'm surprised."

Tim laughed, "No problem! Listening is one of the things, perhaps the most important thing, I have learned in my new profession. I'll start right where you did."

Tim went back to the split, when Jeff started university, touching on the many schemes and near-scams he had been involved in, until a couple of years ago, when he took some specialized courses and put his natural selling talents to work. He joined a national hardware company, advancing rapidly, and recently was promoted to a territory sales manager. This was the reason for his local visit. Jeff congratulated him for finally straightening out.

Tim laughed and then surprised Jeff by asking, "You mentioned a girl a few minutes ago. What's her name? What's that all about?"

Jeff, sorry he had let it slip out in the conversation, answered, "Carly is her name."

Tim continued, "Carly. Nice name. Girlfriend?"

Jeff sighed, "One might say that. I don't know. I just don't know."

Tim studied Jeff who was now very silent. He tried to find out more, "You look confused. Can I help?"

Jeff laughed, "When I hear you say that, I know I'm in trouble, but maybe I should unload. I have to discuss it with someone. It might as well be you."

Tim leaned forward, anxious to learn all the details about Jeff's time with Carly. Jeff didn't disappoint. He went back to when he first met Carly and then told the detailed story of living with her up to the present time when she asked him to quit his job and relocate. He finished talking and slumped back in his chair.

Tim, puzzled by his brother's demeanor, asked, "So, what's the problem? You don't look happy."

"I'm not," Jeff answered.

Tim had to find out why. He asked, "Think I can help?"

Jeff looked up, "Maybe," he answered, meekly. "Maybe."

Tim let Jeff gather his thoughts, hoping to hear some juicy gossip. Jeff, glad to be airing some of his deep, private thoughts, started, "Carly is a beautiful girl. A very beautiful girl. Tall, sexy, all woman. Very smart and street wise. You would like her."

As Jeff described his sex life, Tim leaned forward, a knowing grin etched on his features.

"You lucky bastard," he thought.

Following the tantalizing sex stories, Jeff changed his tone, "She has something in her past that she is trying to deal with. I don't know if she'll ever get over it without some kind of help, and she won't talk about it, whatever it is. This really bothers me along with another thing, her mood swings, vicious, vicious mood swings, scary mood swings. So, I don't really know where I'm going. I think I have to extricate myself from the scene. I really do, the more I think about it, but how?"

Tim quizzed him, "So you're not in love?"

Jeff quickly shot back, "No! I'm not. Definitely not."

Tim jumped in, "Then there's no problem. Just tell her to fuck off. I've done it many times. It works."

Jeff shook his head, "I don't think I can do that. It might aggravate what she is already going through. I don't want to be responsible for anything that might happen to her, and I'm also afraid of her explosive nature. I seriously wonder what she might do."

Tim offered his help, "I think you're taking this too personally. It's not your problem. From what you say, she's a bit of a tough cookie. She'll be okay. Just look after yourself."

Jeff countered, "Most people have some weakness. I know Carly does, but I haven't been able to get inside her shell. I really would like to help her find her way and be really happy. I just haven't been able to. I've been trying and trying, but so far...no luck. So maybe you can help. What do you think?"

Tim stuck to his theme, "Just walk out. Leave. Get out of there. For your own well-being. Get out." Then he flashed an evil grin and continued, "You don't suppose... Yes! I think I have it. The old switcheroo. That might work."

Jeff lurched backward in his seat, "What?"

Tim babbled on, "The old swicheroo. Remember? Back in school. That was so much fun. We may be able to pull it off again and get you out of this jam. What do you think?"

This sudden reminiscence of an old high school prank jolted Jeff. He stammered, "We can't do that. What are you thinking? It'll never work."

Then, as his mind raced through the possibilities, he suddenly changed gears, realizing that this might be a way out of his problem. He smiled, "On the other hand, you just might have something. I do need help."

Back in high school, the brothers had switched dates and a few times, even girlfriends, simply because they could. Some of the girls never did find out. Tim was suggesting that they use this maneuver as a way to help Jeff split from Carly. After paying the bill, he suggested a stroll to a nearby park to work out details of his devious plan. When they walked through the restaurant to leave, all eyes followed them, just like when Jeff had entered and approached Tim's table. Out on the street, all the way to the park, it was the same: people staring, wide-eyed. In the little park, they found a secluded picnic table and settled in to hash out their scheme.

* * * *

Realizing it was still early afternoon, Carly, in a wave of excitement, and so close to finishing her garden knew she couldn't stop working, with so little left to do. She had piled the material from her morning's work on top of the vertical and top legs of the mound, leaving the space for the lower leg ready to excavate. She had not planned it, but in her new found enthusiasm, she was pleased to see the empty space ready to be dug up. Feverishly, she began to hack away at the final piece needed to complete her masterpiece.

* * * *

The short walk to the park had allowed Tim to concoct a plan that might work. He outlined his thinking to Jeff while sitting at the picnic table, "I think I have it," he said.

Fearing some far-out story, Jeff interrupted. "Okay, out with it."

Tim dove right in, "The timing is perfect. Perfect! I have a hotel room, and you don't have to report to work. Perfect. We could start tonight."

Jeff's eyebrows shot up, "Tonight? How?"

"Easy," Tim replied. "I go to your house tonight, and you stay at the hotel."

Jeff let out a breath. "Wow! You don't waste any time do you? Same old Tim. I suppose the sooner the better, and now that you mention it, the timing does look good. Let's detail it out, see if there's a down side."

Elated that Jeff was open to his idea, Tim pulled a note pad from his pocket and started jotting down elements of the strategy needed for the scheme to succeed. With Jeff's help, a list was started with items to be considered. Tim handed a blank sheet of paper to Jeff, asking him to sketch out his house floor plan and list everything he could think of regarding his personal life, in order for him to "become" Jeff for a night. He gave Jeff another sheet of paper to tally details of Carly he should be aware of. As the lists and sketches became unruly on the small sheets of paper, Tim suggested going back to the hotel, where he had a good supply of paper and pens in his briefcase. At the hotel, Tim went in the main door, and a few minutes later Jeff entered a side entrance, in order not to attract attention. Tim let Jeff into his room on the sixth floor where, at a small round table, they spent two hours plotting and scheming for Tim to do Jeff's dirty work; break up with Carly. The plan was for Tim to go to Jeff's house, wearing Jeff's clothes and using his car, start an argument with Carly and escalate the fight to a point where he could terminate the relationship. The most difficult part was giving Tim enough personal information for him to plausibly pass as Jeff. As the information flowed, Tim entered coded notes in his phone for reference, if needed. Late in the afternoon, he changed clothes with Jeff, exchanged ID, took Jeff's car keys and headed out to a home and lady he had never seen before. What he had not told Jeff was that he planned to get laid before starting any argument with Carly.

* * * *

After finishing the excavation of the lower leg of the "E," Carly filled it back in loosely and covered it with brush. It would not be utilized anytime soon, but she wanted it to be ready when it was needed. She placed her tools and work gloves in the truck and visited her "boys" one more time, promising them a new guest very soon. Then she ran to the mound in the far corner of her garden, pissed on it, ran back to the truck and started the weary drive home.

Back in the city, she stopped beside a public phone. Pulling a small piece of paper from her pocket, she walked to the phone, glanced at the paper and placed a call.

A man answered, "Hello."

"Hello. Is this Larry?"

"Yes, this is Larry. May I ask who is calling?"

"This is Carly calling."

"Carly? Carly? Do I know you?"

"I'm sorry, Larry. Let me refresh your memory. Remember a couple of weeks ago, we talked in a little book store? We had quite a chat."

"Yes. Yes. I remember. You're the pretty girl with the brain, looking at science books. Carly, How are you?"

"I'm very good, Larry. Thank you and yourself?"

"I'm very well, thanks. It's very nice to hear from you. How is your reading going?"

"Oh, Larry, I really haven't had a lot of time for reading. I've been so busy."

"Busy? Some kind of work you have to get done?"

"You might say that. It's a project I have been working on for some time, and I'm almost finished. So, I'm very busy cleaning up some final details."

"You say a project. Can you let me in on it?"

"Sure. It involves a bit of gardening. Have you ever done any gardening?"

"No, not much, but I'm sure I can learn. Can you teach me?"

"I can do better than that. I can make you a partner where you can get right down to earth and make things happen. Sound good?"

"Yes, I would love that. When do I start?"

"I'm sorry to say, not for a couple of weeks. I have some personal things to take care of, and then I'll call you. I must go now, so you take care. Bye."

"Bye, Carly. I'll wait for your call."

Carly clicked the phone down and burst out laughing. Toying with Larry had erased some of the tension she had built up in her garden. She got back in the truck, drove to her storage unit, loaded a refrigerator carton, tape and a box cutter into the truck and then drove toward home. Parking two blocks down the street, she walked the rest of the way, stepped inside, stripped naked and poured a welcoming bath.

CHAPTER EIGHTEEN

Carly eased into the warm water. A million details danced in her head, demanding she not get too comfortable. It was going to be a very busy night.

Tim steered Jeff's car into the empty space next to where Carly's car was normally parked. Jeff had briefed him on the possibility that Carly may still be away from home, and if that was the case, he was to let himself in and make himself comfortable. He did. He entered the home and wandered down the hall, not expecting Carly to be home. He turned into the bathroom and startled her.

"Oh! I'm sorry, I didn't know you were home," he stammered.

Stunned by Carly's beauty, he started to back out of the room, almost forgetting he was "Jeff." Then he caught himself, and in his best "Jeff" tone, greeted Carly.

"Hi, I'm home. How are you?"

Carly answered, "I'm fine. You noticed...no car. It broke down and is in the garage." She had her story prepared for Jeff, "I took a taxi home. No problem. How are you?"

"I'm fine. I'm fine," Tim answered, without taking his eyes from the beauty in the tub. Carly motioned to him, "Don't just stand there. Come over here and sit down." She patted the side of the tub.

Tim, in one fluid motion, glided to the edge of the tub and plunked himself down. Carly pulled him into a warm embrace. Tim was in heaven. He kissed her deeply.

"Wow!" Carly exclaimed. "You're ready, and guess what? So am I. Come on, let's go to bed."

All Tim could think about was "that lucky bastard, that lucky bastard" as he followed the dripping Carly to the bedroom. Still high from her gardening, she prolonged the sexual activities as long as she could, leading to an explosive finish for both of them. After a short rest, she left the bed, went down the hall to the bathroom and added more hot water to the tub. She returned to the bedroom and told Tim to go soak in the tub while she fixed him a nice drink that she would bring to him.

Then she turned toward the kitchen, her beautiful shape watched by Tim. He walked to the bathroom and quickly slid into the tub, anticipating more pleasure. Maybe he could postpone the breakup with Carly for a while, maybe a long while. Carly prepared a vodka cocktail for Tim. Before stirring the glass, she added the contents of a small jar she had taken from her purse. She returned to the bathroom and handed the glass to Tim.

"Here's a nice drink for you. Drink up! Enjoy yourself." She said, as she handed the glass to Tim.

Tim thanked her and took a large gulp.

Carly watched, "That's it, all the way down, good boy," she thought, before getting into the bath. "You seem to be so much more playful tonight," she remarked. "Your new found freedom kicking in?" She didn't wait for an answer, instead she performed oral sex on Tim, keeping him fully aroused.

"Drink up, we can play some more."

Tim drained the drink. Carly continued teasing until, a few minutes later, Tim complained.

"I'm not feeling very well. I'm kind of dizzy. Let me sit up. Here! Help me."

Carly helped Tim to sit up, stroked his hair and waited for

time to do its work. It wasn't long before he slumped back in the tub again, unable to support himself. He tried to talk, "I...I...sick...diz...zy...diz...sick...sit...si...up...up."

Carly watched. Tears stained her face. "It's okay, love. It's okay. Remember when I told you that I would soon take you to my garden? Guess what? We will be going there very shortly. You will love it, and you will meet some old friends of mine."

Carly lifted one of Tim's arms. She released it and watched as it splashed back down to his side. He tried to lift it. It felt like lead. Carly straddled Tim, facing his legs, and slowly lowered herself. All Tim saw was her well-rounded ass getting closer and then her velvety flesh pushing his head into the water. Unable to move, he felt the warm water engulf him, and then nothing. Carly cried. She leaned forward, staying there, shuddering and crying until the water started to cool.

When she did stir, she recovered quickly. She left the tub, dried herself and dressed in work jeans and a t-shirt. Then she returned to the truck, which was parked down the street, and moved it close to the house where she unloaded the refrigerator box and some small items. Next, came the exhausting task of dragging Tim from the tub to the living room and placing him in the box. Thoughts of her garden supplied her with the strength to keep going. After Tim was secure in the box, she managed to drag the box out to and into the truck. Then she packed a change of clothes, made sure her disguise kit and fake ID were in place, and checked that all other needed tools were accounted for. With everything in order, she locked the door and climbed into the truck, prepared for a long emotional night. She reached the highway and began to sing.

"My love garden
My love garden
I neglected you before
But I won't anymore
Please forgive me

My love garden."

Carly sang until the turn off to the mountain road came into view. She checked for traffic and shortly after, the truck was bumping along the dirt road. She turned her head and apologized to Tim for the rough ride. At her garden, she eased the truck through the bush into the clearing and stopped. She shut off the engine and listened. There was not a sound.

"Good! Everything is going so well," she thought. She grabbed a small flashlight from her bag, clicked it on and raced into the clearing.

"Boys! Boys! Men! How are you? I told you I wouldn't be long, didn't I? Our garden is almost finished. Oh! I'm so excited. A-a-and I have a new guest, Jeff, a great guy. You will like him. I'll talk to you in a while. I have work to do. Our garden must be finished."

She raced back to the truck, opened the tail gate and pushed the refrigerator box out of the truck and onto the ground with a thud.

"Sorry," she grunted. A box cutter was used to slice the carton open from one end to the other. Then came the hardest part, moving Tim up a slight grade to the "E." With great effort, this was finally accomplished, and Tim was laid to rest in the middle arm of the "E." Carly then filled in the excavation and covered the mound with brush, all the time humming and singing her song. With the physical work completed, she spoke softly to her newest "guest."

"Jeff, I'm going to miss you. But you are now a part of something special. A very beautiful place. It will soon to be finished and then I will plant flowers. They will glow in the sunlight and you will love it here. I am going to visit your new friends, and I will call out their names so you can meet them. Listen carefully! I'll come back to you in a little while."

Carly picked up her flashlight and made her way to the first mound.

"Eddy! Dan!" she called out. "Meet Jeff, he's your new friend. Please make him welcome. He's not quite like some of you, but he is a great guy, and he was very good to me."

She made her way from mound to mound, talking and introducing Jeff to his new friends. Back at the "E", after finishing her visit to the "O" and "V," she spoke softly to Sam and Syd.

"Sam, Syd, you two are close to a very good friend of mine. I don't think it will be long until I come back to see you again. Jeff, these two guys are smart and funny, you are in good company. I must go now, but I won't forget you. Bye!"

Carly sauntered back to the truck and climbed in. Swallowing a pain killer she had taken from her purse, she leaned her head back and soon the energy-sapping events lulled her into a sound sleep. The pain killer prevented her from waking with a headache, but when she did wake, it was well past daybreak.

"Holy shit!" she squealed. Then she leaped from the truck and ran past the mounds.

"Morning, boys. Can't stop. Gotta see the asshole up the hill. See you later."

Reaching the mound at the far corner of the clearing, she pulled down her jeans, pissed on the mound, and pulled them back up. "You bastard! You fucking bastard!" she screamed.

As she passed the mounds on her way back to the truck, she called out, "Hi, boys! Bye, boys!"

At the truck, she loaded everything into the rear box and carefully checked that all was secure and accounted for. Then she hopped into the cab and started down the dirt track. Words came to her as she drove toward home.

"My love garden
My love garden
You are almost finished
Your beauty won't be diminished
My love garden
My love garden."

She sang all the way back to the city. Not wishing to visit her storage unit, she drove to the parking lot where her car sat, placed her tools in the trunk and jumped back into the truck. Inside the truck, she changed her clothes and appearance and then drove away from the parking lot to look for an unlocked dumpster. She found one in an alley and disposed of her work clothes and refrigerator carton. She next drove the truck through a car wash, topped up the gas tank and returned the truck to the rental agency. After settling the bill, she walked the short distance to her car. In the car, she changed her appearance back to Carly. The drive from the parking lot to her home became a chore, as fatigue drained her of all feeling. A hot bath and sleep would get her through the rest of the day.

Jeff paced the hotel room. "What's that bugger up to? He was supposed to come back late last night or at the latest, early this morning," he mumbled to himself.

In the evening, unable to wait any longer, he decided to drive by the house in Tim's car. Why? He didn't know. He just had to go by and check. When he scanned the area, he saw that both his car and Carly's were parked in their places, as he had expected. "Shit! That prick has done it to me again. I should have seen this coming. Probably partying away. Showing Carly that Jeff can be a fun guy. Just get the job done, Tim. Just get the job done," he babbled, as he passed the house.

Back at the hotel, Jeff paced some more and came up with a plan. If Tim didn't return by tomorrow morning, he would go to the house and confront the two of them. Carly would probably fly into a rage and throw him out, along with Tim. A little messy, but at least his goal would be achieved. He showered and went to bed and quickly fell fast asleep. He awoke early in the morning and helped himself to some of Tim's clean clothes. A small breakfast was next, in the hotel lobby restaurant, where he bought a newspaper. He then returned to the room to wait for any word from Tim. Shuffling through the newspaper and glancing at the clock every few minutes grew boring, forcing him to call it quits by eleven thirty. Steeling himself for any possibility, he left the hotel for a confrontation with Carly and Tim. On the drive over to the house, he recalled how uncaring his brother could be and kicked himself for going along with the hare-brained scheme. It was too late now, as he mentally prepared himself for the worst. He parked close to the house and noticed the two cars still in their spaces. Hesitating, after closing the car door behind him, he squared his shoulders and strode briskly to the door. Trying to decide whether to knock or let himself in, he decided to use his spare key, in the hopes a surprise entrance may give him some kind of edge. As he entered the house, he noticed several piles of clothes and more boxes. Carly had been busy. Had he not been preoccupied with Tim, he may have noticed that the items piled neatly against the wall were from his wardrobe. He stopped and listened. There was no noise except for the gentle clicking of Carly's keyboard. He walked up behind her.

"Hi," he whispered.

Carly froze. Glancing over her shoulder, she let out a spine tingling scream and flung herself into a stack of books in the corner of the room. She cowered against the wall, shivering, her hair standing on end, her face wildly contorted. She tried to talk, still screaming, "YOU. YOU. AAAEEE YOU!"

Jeff stepped closer, not understanding, and he too started to shake. Carly put up her hands, warning Jeff not to come any closer. "NO! NO! NO!" she screamed. They remained still for minutes, Carly, not believing her eyes, and Jeff trying to make sense of Carly's terrifying appearance. Carly, her beautiful skin now pure white, finally stifled her shrieks. She slumped to the floor, a sobbing, shaking, pitiful mess. Jeff, his mind racing, wondered if her perpetual problem had finally caught up to her. He wondered what could trigger such a climactic reaction. He glanced at the computer for some sort of clue. Nothing there except a few unidentifiable notes. He ventured a question, softly, "Where's my brother?"

No reaction. He waited, then a little louder, "Where's my brother?"

Carly scrunched up her face. Still no answer.

Desperate for information, Jeff tried again. "My brother. My twin brother. He was here. Where is he?"

Carly tried to comprehend. She mumbled, "T-W-I-N? T-W-I-N? TWIN? No! No!"

She collapsed, sobbing and shuddering violently enough to send several books flying. Jeff waited patiently, not daring to get any closer. Carly stirred, continuing to mumble, "No! No! My garden ruined. A stranger in my garden. No! No!" She sobbed for minutes, as Jeff helplessly watched.

When Carly had slowed her crying, Jeff asked again, "My brother came here. I know. It was a little joke. Where is he?"

Carly tried to grasp the words, "Joke? Joke? Twin? Brother?" She slurred her mumblings, "Joke? Joke?"

Jeff tried to clarify, "Not really a joke. That was a poor choice of words. It was just something we worked out. My brother came over here, pretending to be me. To help me. It was mostly his idea."

Carly strained to understand, "Brother…help…twin?" she whispered.

Jeff stepped back, giving Carly time to piece his words together. Many minutes passed before she could start to overcome the shock of seeing Jeff. Her shaking didn't abate, as she tried constructing sentences. She continued to whisper, "You sent? You sent? Brother? You sent brother? You sent...sent your brother?"

Jeff answered, "Yes. Yes, I did. To help me."

Carly, still whispering and shaking, asked again, "Help? Help? You sent...sent brother to help?"

Jeff answered again, "Yes, that's correct. He came here to help me. That's correct. Where is he now?"

Carly didn't answer his question, still trying to figure out the reason for Tim's visit to the house. She raised her voice slightly above her earlier whisperings, "You sent your brother here to help you. You sent him to help. You sent your brother here. You sent your brother here to fuck me." She glared at Jeff. The meanest look he had ever seen. "You sent your brother here to fuck me," She screamed, "YOU SENT YOUR BROTHER HERE TO FUCK ME. YOU BASTARD! YOU BASTARD! WHAT WERE YOU THINKING?"

Jeff tried to calm the volatile situation, "No! No! That wasn't what we had planned. He was supposed to help me break up with you."

Carly questioned, still glaring at Jeff. "Break up with me? Break up with me?"

"Yes. I had been thinking that we may be better off going our separate ways. I don't love you, Carly, but I was too cowardly to tell you. So, Tim offered to do my dirty work. I'm so sorry he took advantage of you. That prick. Wait till I catch up to him."

Carly concentrated on one thing. "Break up. Break up," she said. "Break up? I think you've achieved that. We are no longer a couple. So sad! So sad! There is something you must know. I owe you an explanation. A very long explanation. I had better start right away, while I'm in the mood and still can. I need some coffee. Would you make us some strong coffee, please?"

Jeff watched as Carly struggled to her feet and shuffled to her computer. She stared at the screen. Jeff backed away toward the kitchen. He prepared a pot of coffee while Carly started typing. After a couple of sentences, she went into the bathroom and swallowed a couple of pills. Returning to her keyboard, she started over.

My dearest Jeff,

These past two days have changed things so drastically; they have changed me...us. I can now tell my story to someone...you. There is so much to tell. I will start away back. Way back to my childhood.

Tears splashed on the keyboard as Carly outlined bitter memories of traumatic events from her days as a young girl. Hurtful happenings that she had been unable to erase from her thoughts to this day, causing her to lead a double life. She described a dream of creating a garden where she could keep her good thoughts and memories. A garden in the country, covered with beautiful flowers where she could sing and dance and relive many, many good times. Getting into her story got easier as details jumped from her fingers to the computer screen. Jeff brought a cup of coffee into the room and placed it next to Carly. Not wanting to disturb her concentration, he left her quietly. He went into the living room to read the newspaper, ready to respond to any needs she may ask for. About every ten minutes, Carly went into the bathroom and took another couple of pills, then returned quickly to her work. She told in detail, how she had discovered the location for her garden and how she had started by locking her terrible memories away in the far corner. She disclosed all the names of her guests in her garden starting with the first, the bad memory, all the way to unlucky Tim.

I'm sorry, Jeff. Poor Tim. Today, when I realized what had happened, I thought a stranger in my garden might spoil it, but Tim is so much like you, I think it will be all right. I am now asking of you, the biggest favor you will ever be asked in your life.

Carly wrote instructions for what she wanted Jeff to do for her and drew a sketch of her garden and a map leading from the city to the clearing on the mountainside. She finished the long story with "regrets and love. Not bothering to check for errors or typos, she printed a copy and sealed it in a large envelope, then she called to Jeff, "Can you come in here? I'm finished."

Jeff, growing impatient after waiting almost two hours, hustled into the room upon hearing the summons.

Carly handed him the envelope. "This is for you. It's my story. I hope it clears a few things up for you. Sorry I took so long. You'll see I'm asking a very, very big favor of you. I've given you some instructions. Can you make me a promise to try and do this for me? Please," Carly pleaded.

Jeff answered with a question, "Have I ever let you down?"

"No, you haven't. Still this time I'm asking. Can you promise?"

"I don't know without seeing what you want from me. That's so difficult."

Carly begged, "Please. Can you promise to try?"

Jeff relented, "For you. Yes. I promise to try my best to follow your instructions."

"Thank you," Carly whispered. She squeezed past Jeff and headed to the kitchen. From the kitchen, she called back, "I'm going to take a bath. Please read that after I'm finished."

She picked up an open bottle of wine and a large wine glass, then headed back down the hall to the bathroom. Closing the bathroom door behind her, she filled the tub with hot water and the wine glass with cool wine. When the tub had filled, she turned off the water and undressed. Before getting in, she picked up the half-empty pill container, said a prayer, and gulped down the remaining pills. In one drowsy motion, she picked up the wine glass and splashed into the steaming water. Closing her eyes, she sipped from the glass as visions of a hillside filled with shimmering flowers danced in her head. The word LOVE outlined in glorious color helped to ease her final journey. The wine glass fell from her hand. She slipped away.

Jeff, used to Carly's long baths, waited almost an hour, before realizing something may be amiss. He ran to the bathroom and threw the door open. Too late. He knew. She was gone. He reached for her hand.

"I'm so sorry. So, so sorry. What have you been going through? What led to this? I'm so, so sorry." Jeff dropped to the floor and stroked Carly's hand. Crying and talking, he tried desperately to make sense of his current predicament and Carly's demise. He knew he wouldn't do anything else until after he had read Carly's story. While waiting for Carly to finish her bath, he had fingered and fidgeted with the envelope, holding it close to his chest, realizing it held answers he craved. It was time. He crossed Carly's arms over her chest, left her in the cooling water and with a changed gait, due to his newly acquired burden, shuffled to the living room. He picked up the envelope, slumped into his chair and tore it open. His hands shook as he prepared to gain some insight into Carly's problems. Devouring every word, he nodded knowingly as the words describing the actions of the person responsible for her torment seared into his brain. The one she described as "The Monster." Tears streaked his cheek and shirt. Still more tears as he read a short anecdote describing Carly's time spent with each of her "guests." As he got further into the riveting story, he broke down, fearing what was coming. He forced himself to read on to the final guest...Tim. He read the short sentence and Carly's apology several times, shuddering violently with the realization that Carly had meant for him to occupy Tim's resting place. The story leading up to Tim engrossed his mind. After reading about Tim, he was too overwhelmed to continue. He took a break and paced the room, shaken to the core. Was this for real? Had he missed something? The sight of Carly in the bathtub gave substance to the story. Yes! Real! All too real. Wearily, he picked up the last page to find out what Carly was asking him to do. He squirmed as he absorbed her request. "Shit," he moaned. "Shit! Shit! Shit!" Reading further, he agonized, "Carly, I don't know, but I did promise, didn't I?" He spoke out loud, "But you know I think you're right. It may be the cleanest way to tie this all up, and I am in pretty deep already. Just for you, I think I can help. God knows someone has to. Yes, I think I can do it."

As he spoke, he walked toward the bathroom, projecting his voice so the words would reach Carly's unhearing ears. He returned to the living room, sat down and pored over the letter one more time, then he made a decision. Leaping from the chair, he called, "Carly, I can do it. Your wishes will be done. I can do it."

He called out loud, in hopes the ringing statement would spur him on to tackle the unsavory task. It was early evening, and mentally prepared, he decided to start immediately. The first thing he did was to fetch Carly's snugly robe and lay it out on the couch. Then he gently carried Carly to the living room and placed her on the robe. With the robe secured tightly around her, she had a look of comfortable dignity. Next, referring to Carly's notes, he gathered up her gardening shovel, a flashlight and a pair of work gloves. After placing the items in his car, he went back to the living room to collect the most precious cargo he would ever have to transport. Kneeling by the couch, he took her cold hand in his. He spoke softly, "My dear, sweet Carly, quoting from your letter, I'm finally going to see your garden. Not quite as you had planned...can't say that I mind that. Your pain has been alleviated, gone, finished. You are free from all of your distressing thoughts. You didn't deserve to end up this way, and it's so sad you didn't receive the help you required a long time ago. But it's too late for that now and too late for all of the innocent souls who suffered because of something that happened a long time ago. You've put your trust in me to keep these secrets to myself. It will be difficult, but I promise you...your dark, troubling past will remain hidden. I promise."

In silence, he carried Carly to his car and placed her soft cocoon in a fetal position on the rear seat. He returned to the house, picked up the letter and map and locked the front door in a trance. Sliding into the front seat of the car, he tried to envision what would greet him in Carly's garden. That was all he could think of as he drove away from the cozy little home. Just before reaching the highway, he stopped at the side of the road to get directions from Carly's map. She had drawn in several landmarks and included distances, making it easier for him to find the turn off in the fading light. With the day's events vying for attention in competition with the unknown, which lay in wait just ahead, he found it difficult to concentrate on the highway, until the odometer told him he was very close to the dirt road. There was very little other traffic. He slowed to a crawl, scanning the side of the highway until the dirt road appeared in his headlights. Warily, he turned and started up the bumpy trail, mentally ticking off the bends and turns Carly had sketched. Her directions were easy to follow, and very quickly he found himself facing a bushy shield that Carly emphasized he must plow the vehicle through to find the clearing with her garden. He pushed into the bush until the car was out the other side, and the foliage had closed behind it. There in the light from the headlights, was the garden. Had he looked at this scene with its covering of weeds and branches, and not known its contents, he would not have noticed anything unusual. As the realization of what he was staring at sunk in, he started to tremble.

He had never felt so disembodied in his life. He was floating in space, observing something nobody on earth had seen, save for one other person, Carly. His senses abandoned him, leaving him groping about in some sort of vacuum. He sucked in mouthful after mouthful of air, thinking that he would lose consciousness if he didn't. Eventually, some feeling returned, and he was able to read Carly's sketch directing him to the "E." He shut off the engine, grabbed the flashlight and opened the car door. Long weeds startled him as he stepped into their territory. He turned on the flashlight and fought his way through the mess until, in the beam, he could pick out the "E" mound. His heart pounded. Three large paces took him to the side of the "E" where he tore at the covering sticks and dropped to his knees beside the middle leg. Minutes passed as he composed himself, then he talked softly to his brother.

"Tim, Tim. I would never have bet you would ever give up your life for mine, but that's exactly what happened. How ironic is that? I'm supposed to be in there, not you. I'm not happy for you, but I am kind of glad for me. I always thought I would get revenge for all the shit you put me through, but I never thought it would turn out like this. I'm sorry! You talked yourself into this one and, unfortunately, you paid a very high price. One consolation, Tim, you are going to be resting next to the one woman who could have given you a good run for your money. I think you two would have made a unique couple. It would have been very interesting. It's my turn now, Tim. I'm going to wrap up your affairs. I'm going to quit your job and take your severance pay, and I'm going to sell your car. Most of your possessions will go to needy people who can use them. I will close your bank accounts, and then you will vanish into thin air. So rest in peace next to Carly. Good bye."

Jeff went back to the car to fetch the shovel and work gloves, then returned to the "E" to dig out the soft soil on the bottom segment, which had been loosened by Carly. He pushed aside a couple of branches and went to work. The loose dirt presented no problems for Jeff. Although he was not used to this kind of work, he worked hard, and soon he had Carly's final resting place ready, exactly as she had prepared it for somebody else. He removed his gloves and laid them next to the shovel. Then he returned to the car, picked Carly up and carried her back to the E, where he very gently lowered her into the ground. Kneeling by her side, he watched her for minutes, as his tears splashed in the dry dirt.

An emotional goodbye passed over his dry lips, "Carly. Dear, dear Carly. Your torment is over. You can rest. Very few people could have known the pain you have been carrying, but for a long time, I have suspected something was seriously amiss. I am not upset over the plans you had for me. You were under the control of a force too powerful to overcome, the poisoned mind of a young child, festering into explosive consequences. I'm so sorry! I'm going to finish the packing you so meticulously started and dispose of all your books and clothes. Everything will be going to good homes, to needy people. I apologize for not being able to complete all of your request. I am not going to come back here to clean up and plant flowers. It's too much of a risk for me and, also it would attract too much attention. Imagine what would happen if your garden was found out. The fuss, investigation and outcry would be massive, and you would be disturbed. I think it is better for this whole ugly mess to stay as is, tranquil and hidden from view. Much as I think I should relate your story to the proper authorities, I am going to keep it a secret. Your type of problems are not completely unknown. There are probably documented cases somewhere, so I don't think behavior science will make any earth-shattering gains by studying you, Carly. I am going to move on in a completely different direction. I'm going to travel to distant places, where my knowledge and skills can be put to use helping poor and uneducated people learn to better their lives. This is something I have been thinking about for some time. And now, all of this unnecessary suffering has given a boost to my vision, where I could be of great help to large numbers of inhabitants living in impoverished regions. As a side benefit, it may be the only way to stop the reality of you and your garden from destroying me. There's one more thing. I just realized...I love you."

Jeff cried, a well needed, deep down, purging cry. Then quiet. He reached down, to pull the robe over Carly's peaceful features before picking up the work gloves and shovel. In a daze, he sprinkled the cool soil in a running pattern up and down until the "E" mound was completed. He covered the exposed two segments of the mound with twigs and weeds, and then took the shovel, gloves, flashlight and letter back to the car. After dumping everything in the car, except the flashlight, he had to complete one last chore Carly had asked of him. Following the beam of light from the flashlight, he forced his way through the bush to the old mound in the far corner of the clearing. Standing beside the mound he unzipped his pants and pissed. Angry words fractured the still air, "You fucking monster. I read about you. You'll never know the carnage you reaped. Carly mentioned that you suffered. The way I see it, you deserved whatever she dished out and more. The fears you instilled in the young child never left her, the scars were too deep, and now she's gone. She started life blessed with so many positive attributes, all to be brutally snatched away by you. YOU FUCKING MONSTER."

Jeff spit on the mound, turned and ran back to the car. He jumped inside, gunned the engine and backed out of the bush. Shifting to drive, he started down the hill. Halfway down, a tune he had heard a couple of times, pushed past his disturbing thoughts. He started to hum. Then, in his own words, he began to sing.

"The love garden
The love garden
Preyed upon by a monster
Who turned her mind to hate
No one could know the anguish
That drove her to create
The love garden
The love garden."

ABOUT THE AUTHOR

David Blackburn lives in Kelowna, British Columbia, Western Canada. He is retired. Hayley, his only daughter, and Ava, his Granddaughter, live close by. His interests and pastimes are many and varied. Sports provide fun, fresh air and exercise. They include: Snow skiing, water skiing, scuba diving, personal water craft, power boating and sailing. Other interests include; renovating a large house, photography, pets, traveling, politics, news, weather, reading and writing.

The Love Garden is the first full length novel to spring from his pen. Other work includes short stories and business reports.

www.ingramcontent.com/pod-product-compliance
Lightning Source LLC
Chambersburg PA
CBHW061933170626
46813CB00006B/2382